Frog Kissing for Beginners

Frog Kissing for Beginners

Hanna Clarin

*Bibliografische Information der Deutschen Nationalbibliothek:
Die Deutsche Nationalbibliothek verzeichnet diese Publikation
in der Deutschen Nationalbibliografie; detaillierte bibliografische Daten sind im Internet über http://dnb.dnb.de abrufbar.*

*German version: Fröscheküssen für Anfänger
© 2014 and 2019, Hanna Clarin*

English version: © 2019 Hanna Clarin

Translation support: Geoff Collins (Thank you so much!)

Cover: Niels and Mathieu Labove

For more information: www.hanna-clarin.jimdo.com

Herstellung und Verlag: BoD – Books on Demand, Norderstedt

ISBN: 9783743114944

The fact that a frog you kiss

Doesn't turn into a prince

Doesn't mean

That you're not a princess

Klara

For what felt like the 375th time, I was sitting in a church that was dressed up for the occasion, just like me and the strangers around me were, and I smiled. Smiled. Smiled.

'Konrad Paul Dobberin, do you take this woman to be your lawful wedded wife, to live together according to God's ordinance in the Holy Estate of Matrimony? Will you love her, comfort her, honour and keep her in sickness and in health; and, forsaking all others, keep you only unto her as long as you both shall live?'

Konrad turned around. His eyes wandered from face to face, looking for the one face his heart was yearning for: Mine. His look dived into my eyes and delved into my heart. The united beat of our churning hearts took our breath away. He wrested his hand from hers, left his previous life behind, flying on the wings of his suddenly burning love, straight to his destiny. He came rushing towards me, fell on his knees. 'Johanna, when I just saw you, I knew: You are the woman I have always been searching for. The woman with whom I want to share my life and my dreams and never grow old. The woman of my dreams and of my life. Johanna, will you marry me?'

My eyes filled with tears. This was somewhat unexpected. I did not really know him. And he was just about to marry my best friend. Really, I could not... On the other hand...

'I do.'

Konrad's response hit me right in the face and beat the silly daydream out of my head. He was still standing in front of the altar to marry Klara, he was still holding her hand, he was still smiling at her. Of course he was.

And I realized that I had just watched too many romantic comedies.

'Klara Miller, do you take this man to be your lawful wedded husband, to live together according to God's ordinance in the Holy Estate of Matrimony? Will you love him, comfort him, honour and keep him in sickness and in health; and, forsaking all others, keep you only unto him as long as you both shall live?'

'I do.'

Klara's smile was beaming at her Konrad, her family, her friends, the day – her life. She was a beautiful bride: tall, slim, in a classic dress – white, of course – that underlined her impeccable figure, with pink flowers in her blonde hair, matching her bouquet, to which she had been clinging as if her life had depended on it and which she, now that the question of questions had been answered in the positive, held in an almost relaxed manner. Had it not been Klara, I would have fallen easy prey to jealousy.

The late summer sun sent its light through the stained glass windows and bathed the faces of the happy couple in a soft, warm glow.

Klara had planned all the details of this day, ever since our schooldays, so that it felt like I had known the bridegroom for ages, even though Klara had only introduced us earlier in the day. Well, in a way, he was an old acquaintance, after all: Klara and I had spent hours on the phone, discussing this charming, friendly, humorous, educated and, on top of it all, attractive, in summary perfect doctor.

Him, who had been living next door to Klara briefly before moving to the other end of Berlin. 'But not because of a woman or anything like that. Not that this would be any of my business, of course. Or matter to me. But, anyway, well, at the moment, he is single.' – 'Yes, of course, Klara, whatever you say.'

Him, whose departure naturally was completely unrelated to the fact that Klara had also moved close to him, shortly thereafter.

Him, who – Coincidence, thou moody master of fate! – by mere chance had crossed Klara's path at the local riding club. 'What? You did not know that I have started to take riding lessons? Jo, I always wanted to do that. Didn't I tell you?' – Yeah, right.

Him, whom she had invited to the opera when a friend had unfortunately and unexpectedly become ill and could not join her. – Had she ever told me that friend's name, by the way?

Him, with whom it had clicked 'so unexpectedly – for both of us'. – As previously indicated: Yeah, right.

Him – the man she was just marrying.

The Konrad whom she loved so much that she was now overcoming one of her greatest fears. Even during music class in school, Klara had been confined to the triangle while the others were singing, due to her stage-fright-induced lack of talent. But now she turned around to the congregation: 'Dear friends, dear family. You know how much I dislike singing. In particular in public. But now, I have found the person with whom I am not afraid of anything or anyone any more. And this is why I now want to sing our song for him. Konrad, do you recall? It was playing when you brought me home after the opera, after our first, kind-of-date. And it expresses exactly what I feel with you. What I feel for you. This will not be an artistic highlight, but, Konrad, with you, I am more than I can be. With you, I am strong – and I can even sing.'

So, Klara sang 'You Raise Me Up' in front of her family, in front of her friends, but mostly for her Konrad.

With every wrong note and every Kleenex that made its way out of a handbag or pocket, my heart felt happier. And with every word, it felt sadder. I was happy for Klara. Of course, I was happy for Klara. And for Konrad. For both. Sincerely. From the bottom of my heart. But while I enjoyed being happy with and for those dear to me, I would equally have enjoyed being happy for myself, for a change. Egoistic? Of course. But it became harder and harder to suppress this feeling of 'What about me?', here and now. Weddings are always a milestone. Naturally for the newlyweds. But the solemnly-happy 'I do' of the protagonists also calls us onlookers to take stock of our own state of mind and state of heart. To ask ourselves where we stand in life and in love, why things are the way they are and what we really want.

I was 39. And had never really been in love. When I was attracted to a man, he inevitably mentioned his girlfriend / fiancée / wife or, if not that, his boyfriend / fiancé / husband. Or he was about to emigrate abroad or to a monastery or – no, not even I had met an astronaut about to leave on a mission to Mars. Yet.

Years ago, life had seemed clear: high school, college, university, PhD, job. And somewhere along the way, fate would automatically guide me to the one it had chosen for me. We would get married, or not, have children, or not, have a house, or not. In any event, we would enjoy life, solve all the problems of mankind in long and deep discussions or just fool around. We would go to the theatre, the movies, museums or dancing, hang out on the sofa, have friends over for dinner, laugh, hike, bike, travel, cook, sing – we would just do everything that is more fun when doing it with the right someone rather than by yourself. But then, without me noticing, one year after another had come and gone, and I had stayed alone. Around me, everyone was getting married and having children, but I stayed alone. When the I-love-you virus had hit the office, some years ago, I had been the only one who had not opened the infected email. Someone loving me? That seemed fishy. Well, coming from my boss (who had obviously not seen anything fishy in the world's loving him), such a confession would have shocked rather than tickled me, admittedly.

My friends tried to reassure me by telling me about couples that had met at a – yes, at this point in time, it was undeniably an 'advanced' age. However, the coincidences became more and more coincidental ('You! Won't! Believe! This! So, she arrives at the top of the mountain, and there is no one around, apart from this one guy sitting there, leaning against the summit cross. They look at each other, and – boom!'). At some point, I would really no longer believe it. And I would still be alone. Soon, it would no longer be my friends but their children inviting me to their weddings. 'Oh, please invite Aunt Johanna. She would be so happy to come. And maybe, you could find someone you can seat her next to.' Nice try.

The music tore me away from my musing. The married couple was walking down the aisle. The choir was singing. Mendelssohn-Bartholdy. 'For He shall give His angels charge over thee, that they shall protect thee in all the ways thou goest, that their hands shall uphold and guide thee, lest thou dash thy foot against a stone.'

Sigh. What a wonderful thought. Konrad would be this angel for Klara, just like she would be for him. This was the life and the love that Klara had dreamt of. And me, too. I sank into my inner cloud of kitsch and self-pity.

Upon recovering from myself, I joined the congregation's procession out into the sunlight – and there, again, everything was perfect: The sun was shining, the bells were ringing. Klara was still stunningly beautiful (of course). Konrad was still attractive (of course). Granted – who cares about the looks of the groom at a wedding, anyway? As long as he puts on his suit and tie properly and with the front at the front and the back at the back, and manages to keep it clean, he meets all the key requirements. It was probably no coincidence that the basic word was 'bride' and the 'bridegroom' a deviation. Usually, the male form is the basis – heir and heiress, mister and mistress, governor and governess ... no, that was not right. Anyway: Adam first, then Eve, I guess. Only for the wedding, things were different. It must have been Eve's idea. Apparently, there was a message hidden somewhere. But I did not really have time to dig for it.

I postponed the thinking and started taking photos of Klara and Konrad at the reception line, engulfed in a parade of smiles, embraces and good wishes.

Of course, Klara had a professional photographer, but she had asked me to take snapshots of the guests. Apparently, the photographer was also fine with this distribution of tasks, so that he only tried to push me away when I got too close to the married couple, sneering 'This is my angle!' While this was certainly not a friendly gesture among almost-colleagues, I understood that he had to make a living, after all.

I liked taking pictures at weddings, and given that I never participated in the main action, I had a wealth of practice. At weddings, everyone at least subjectively looks good, everyone smiles – unless they cry. But even the crying at weddings tends to be of the photogenic type. And behind the camera, I also did not have to worry about any photographers proudly presenting the atrocities they had been able to ban for eternity, claiming that the photo of me chewing too big a bite of my sandwich was one of their best works so far. Digital photography certainly constituted technical progress – but socially, it had taken us a big step back. While the legal scholars were still disputing how to protect privacy in the digital age, the bearers of this right frantically pilloried each other socially or at least aesthetically online. And they called this 'social'. Just to make sure that the great-grandchildren, too, would see great-grandma enjoying her first drunken stupor. And while cautious people installed timers to pretend they were at home during their absence, they also spread the word on all available channels that they were on vacation, for two weeks, at the movies or just now at a wedding in Potsdam. Well, I did not have to understand everything that happened around me. Obviously, I was too old for that. Or too complicated. Or too simple.

I have to admit though, that when Sinéad and Bernd stepped forward, I was a tiny little bit tempted to just shoot whatever passed by my lens. I had met the two of them in the morning – briefly, but long enough.

'Hi, I am Bernd. And this is my wife SinHead.'

Obviously, he loved his Sinéad so much that he felt she deserved her very own version of her beautiful name.

'Nice to…'

'I have known Konrad for years. I manage his insurances. Great guy. Here is my card. You never know, do you? Are you also a doctor?'

'Thank you, that is…'

'Actually, this is the second wedding for us, this week. And my SinHead looks stag-ge-ring, again. She easily gets one up on any bride.'

Sinéad took a deep breath to interrupt him, but he continued, 'Darling, you do not have to be so modest. Don't you agree that she looks just stag-ge-ring, Mrs ...? What was your name, again?'

'My na...'

'Well, anyway, I told her this morning 'Darling,' I said, I mean, 'You just look stag-ge-ring. You are just the hottest ever.' Well, that's just a fact, she just looks stag-ge-ring. Don't you agree that she looks stag-ge-ring?'

I hoped that Sinéad would punch him and send him stag-ge-ring, preferably right into a one-day-coma.

Naturally, Sinéad could look or be as hot as she wanted to for a proper assessment, I lacked both true expertise and investigative interest. But the mere question was completely misplaced. I would not begrudge her the fact that Bernd viewed creation as completed through his wife. But here and today, no Sinéad could be as gorgeous and beautiful as Klara, the radiant bride. Period.

And now, this stag-ge-ring couple approached Klara. Bernd was baring his teeth, his Sinéad was wearing a hat. Dark blue velvet. With a wide brim and a peacock's feather. And a huge bird dropping. Placed in the middle like a medal, well visible and still very fresh. I tipped Bernd on the shoulder and hinted at the portable bird loo. His complexion assimilated the bird poo's colour. He grabbed his Sinéad's arm and skeltered towards the parking lot. 'I told you not to wait under the tree with all the birds. Obviously, this had to happen, but, no, Madam has to sit in the shade, in direct shooting line. Shooting line? Shitting line! Because of Madam's delicate skin. Too stupid to sit. You know that I promised my boss to lend her the hat, tomorrow. And how are we going to get the shit off? That's velvet! Velvet! But don't count on me, you can do that yourself, Madam. You are just too stupid.'

Now, I almost pitied his Sinéad. On the other side, she

had picked him among several billion men on this planet. Probably, he was the price you had to pay for being the pride of creation.

The newlyweds handshook, hugged and kissed through the parade one after the other, and I, too, got in line. Konrad first. He smiled. Inquiring. No, he could not have noticed my little escapism in church. Could he? Probably, he just didn't remember who I was. I put my hand forward. 'I am Johanna, Klara's friend from school. Hey, look after her. Klara is a very special person. Make her happy!' He ignored my hand, hugged me and placed a big kiss on my cheek. His beard was tickling. 'Of course! Johanna! Klara has told me so much about you. Sorry that I did not recognize you, at first. So many new people. No worries, I know how lucky I am to have Klara.' He pulled her towards him, they looked at each other and their looks merged. Can looks merge? It did not matter. At weddings, I tended to fall easy prey to kitsch. Again, I allowed myself to.

I whispered into Klara's ear. 'I am so happy for you. Be happy.'

She hugged me. 'I am. And next time, we dance on your wedding, Jo.'

That was too much. Now, I had to cry.

Desi

In a flower-bedecked limousine, the newlyweds and the photographer left for the obligatory photo session, and the crowd took a break.

Fortunately, Bernd and his Sinéad had made it just in time to congratulate the happy couple; Bernd storming and his hatless Sinéad looking to the ground. Now, I really pitied Bernd's Sinéad.

I approached her. 'That was really bad luck, with the bird. On the dark hat at that... Try vinegar and lemon. Or soap water. I saw a drugstore near the post office. And you look staggering, even without the hat.'

Bernd's Sinéad smiled. 'Thank you, that is sweet of you. You know, it is just because Bernd had promised his boss he'd lend her the hat. It is really important for his career.'

'That's unfortunate, of course, but such is life. Sometimes, shit just happ...' Too late, I had almost said it. Stupid me! Fortunately, Bernd's Sinéad's basset gaze told me that she had missed the unintended irony.

Still, I preferred to relocate temporarily. 'I think I should take some more photos. Klara has asked me to. After all, she will marry just once. And the crowd is disappearing, anyway. See you later!'

Returning to the church door, I found the unmated aunts who belong to any wedding and who were just exchanging the latest news.

'What, you haven't heard about that? Yes, all of a sudden. Heart attack and whoops. She's so lucky – or rather was. Of course, not so nice for the children. But it was a beautiful ceremony. Very dignified and tasteful. The pastor was really marvellous.'

'Was that the same one that Trudy had? I want him to speak at my funeral, too. I really like him.'

'Oh no, Ruth! Hancock is about to retire. So, I really hope that you stay with us a bit longer than that. And, by the way, if you like him that much, then you should make sure to get his attention before your death and not thereafter. One hears he is a widower.'

They were giggling like debutantes awaiting their first

ball – and I had my shot. Three gaudy aunts. All a matter of perspective and patience. In life and in photography. By the way, another word with a female root: Widow.

I pushed the lingering guests around back and forth and relentlessly thrust my camera into their faces until they had to laugh. Real laughter. I did not like photo smiles, it made people look the same, on all photos, just never like themselves.

Finally, on my last round, a familiar face. Desi, actually Lady Adalberta Desideria Georgina Kestrell, a former colleague from the time when Klara and I – and Desi, of course – had worked for the same law firm in Berlin. Gosh, five years had passed already, since those days.

'Johanna? Johanna, is that you? I almost did not recognize you. Did you lose weight? You look marvellous.'

'Hello, Desideria!' Of course, I would never call her Desi, certainly not into her face. 'How are you? Yes, I did. Is that so obvious?'

'Yes, absolutely. It is very becoming, indeed.'

'Well, it was really about time. Too much work, all the fast food, no sports, no sleep, no vacation. But who am I talking to?'

Truth being told, Desi had always demonstrated her noblesse by gracefully allowing the lower ranks to take the bigger chunks of the work. But that was water under a bridge that I no longer wanted to cross, anyway.

'Johanna, now I can say it: You really did work too much. In any event: Congratulations. You look very well.'

'That is sweet of you. Thank you. Well, you always look great, so can't tell you anything new, in this regard. So, how is everyone at the office doing? Who is even still there from the old troops?'

The question was justified. We had seen many come and succumb to work intoxication, to the exaltation derived from the awareness of their own indispensability, and to their hope for a thriving career. I, too, had proudly received my first work mobile phone, in the fulfilling awareness that I had just been granted the seal of importance. Shortly thereafter, I sometimes wished to neither be nor seem important. My first thought in the morning and my last at night belonged to the mailbox, just like so many thoughts in between. Life was shaped by permanent availability, all-nighters, cancelled holidays and an all-encompassing *Amour Fou* with our mobile phones. Until the highly qualified work drudge realized that, taking into account hundreds of hours of unpaid overtime, it actually made less money than its cleaning lady. The plodder left the hamster's wheel to be replaced by talented, hungry new blood. And the wheel continued to spin.

Oh, how right I was. 'I believe you would know hardly anyone any more. Some of the old secretaries are still around, but there, too, a lot has changed. Of the lawyers, only Schlump and I have stayed. And *REX*, of course.'

REX, in full *R*ichard *E*rnest *X*avier, was the managing partner of the law firm. Generally travelling and with each cell of his body fully aware of his preeminent importance for the history of mankind. When he, as an exception, happened to be at the office, his sheer presence disseminated stress and unproductive hectic. One could physically sense his presence in the whole building, down to the main entrance hall – even though his office was on the 18th floor. REX, who fired and hired his assistant Susan on an hourly basis. And then opened 'her' I-love-you email. Who claimed that one had to make a secretary cry at least once a month so that she would be at one's beck and call. And at least in the beginning, one had to keep her at work until midnight, every day, so that she knew who was wearing the breeches. Well, I had just asked my secretary whether she would stay late if necessary. She had said yes, and that had settled the issue to my full satisfaction. I was wondering why personality disorders like those REX displayed so abundantly obviously pushed your career. That had also been one of the reasons for me to leave the law firm. I did not want to become like that.

'We also have some new colleagues, though. One of them is a countess. Very likeable. It is markedly pleasant to be in a position to have an exchange with someone of noble descent.'

Hallelujah! 'Someone of noble descent.' I decided that I did not have to comment on this quirk of our baroness.

'Is REX talking to Schlump, again?' During my years at the firm, the two had only communicated in writing or via their assistants. Rumour had it that the root cause was a disagreement over the formatting of the Christmas card. Apparently, the epicentre of the crisis was the life-and-death decision whether the text should be centred ('That's elegant!' 'That's what everyone does!') or left-aligned ('That looks like a business letter.' 'That's right. Because we are a business.'). Like cranky three-year-olds. It was not known to me whether any cards had been sent that or any subsequent year, at all.

'Absolutely, they talk to each other, now. But they no longer talk to the colleagues in Paris. And you? What do you do, these days?'

'I am still with Blau-Weiss Insurance in Zurich. Legal department. I'm in charge of whatever comes my way from a billion dollar US class action to a customer complaint because the sun does not shine. And all in English, German or French. When I start work in the morning, I never know what I will have done by the end of the day. I enjoy that. And this time, I am really lucky with my boss. Brilliant lawyer, still always friendly, takes his time, listens, discusses, lets me finish my sentence, responds to email, says thank you. Can you imagine that from REX? Simply a constructive working relationship. I had almost forgotten what that was.'

Desi sighed. 'Yes, with REX, things are not that easy. Last week, he fired Susan. Again. And this time, she really left, for good.'

'What? Susan has left? Susan? But she is married to the firm.' I could not believe it.

'Yes. This time, she just had enough. She had come to the office in the afternoon after her varicose vein operation, because REX was around. But REX was his usual inconsiderate self. She was not as fast as usual, so he yelled at her, asking who had shit into her brain and whether he was surrounded by cripples and idiots. Excuse my language, I am quoting. He said that once she was at the office, she had to work. Susan calmly responded that if she had wanted to work with spoiled three-year-old brats, she would have become a kindergarten teacher. And then she left.'

Desi seemed to be asking herself the painful question why she was not leaving herself.

I changed subject. 'Say, what else is going on in your life besides work?'

Desi shook her head. 'I am still single. Where should I meet someone, anyway? At the office? In my car? In my apartment? At my parents' place? And, naturally, the choice is even more limited when you are aristocratic.'

I could not let her nobility-isms go by twice. 'Well, that should really not be a limiting factor. In case of doubt, such a title only means that some ancestor was better at robbing, murdering, machinating and pillaging than the average. Just like in Australia, where the really old families all derive from criminals. You should really look for something better than such a degenerated noble bod.'

Actually, this was not really nice of me. But I trusted in the superior self-control of the Lady and was not disappointed.

Indeed, after her instant of shock paralysis had passed, she responded. 'And, what about you? Have you found someone?'

Touché! 'No, I am also still single. At our age, almost everyone is married. At least the good ones. Plus in Switzerland, it is more difficult to meet people, anyway.'

'More difficult than in Germany?'

'Yes, I would say so. The Swiss make their real friends in kindergarten or at the latest at school. Well, at the very, very latest at university or the military. Of course, it is great if you happen to be one of those old friends, but otherwise it is difficult. Besides, they hardly ever invite more than one friend or a couple at a time. Granted, it is a compliment that they really want to spend the evening just with you, but it simply means that you will never meet someone through mutual friends.'

'And if you invite them?'

'Oh, I do that - trust me. But I know my guests, so by inviting them I will not meet anyone new. Everyone enjoys my parties and loves to come, but they hardly ever invite me in return. And if they do, it is a huge party every ten years with all the couples they know. Plus me.'

'What has become of the parties where we would stand in the kitchen with a glass of wine, discuss everything between heaven and earth and just meet new people?'

'I am afraid those are still taking place, but without us. At our age almost everyone is in a relationship. And for the few who are not, there is often a good reason.'

Desi laughed. 'Do you also have these discussions with your friends when they go through their mental address books searching for eligible candidates? For you are such a wonderful woman, no, such a marvellous person that it simply cannot be that you do not find a partner? And then they go through their friends, one by one, and whenever one suggests someone, the other one provides a striking argument why that candidate does not belong by your side but in psychiatric care.'

'Oh yes, I know those, too. Johanna's all season sale. 'Darling, you know, Johanna is interested in arts. What about Anthony?' 'Darling, you can't be serious. Anthony does colouring by numbers. That's not very artistic. And he does not have time, anyway. Because he does colouring by numbers 24/7.' Or 'Darling, what about Malcolm?' 'Are you serious? Malcolm? I don't know. He is still living with his mom. And, by the way, Johanna, what do you think about Sadomaso?' They seriously expected a response. True. This has really happened, I am not joking.'

Desi had to laugh. 'Recently, friends recommended a potential partner who was, as they called it, 'a bit lala on the upper deck'. They assured me that he would never argue with me. I would basically be able to continue my life as if he did not exist. Or as if I had a dog.' She hesitated but eventually burst into laughter. 'But he was aristocratic. Ancient nobility. A prince.'

I could not leave this ball lying in my court. 'Definitely a further argument for marriage outside nobility. Reduced lala risk.'

We both had to laugh. Unfortunately, though, the two of us were listed items in this all season sale, as well. Maybe, friends of ours were talking to their male single friend, right now. 'JimPeterPaulTomBill, you are such a wonderful man, no, such a marvellous person that it simply cannot be that you do not find a partner.' 'Darling, what about Johanna?' 'Darling, you can't be serious. Johanna is…'

Whatever followed, no one would ever tell me. Even though I would have liked to know why I was not considered – how had Desi put it? – 'eligible'.

Desi bid me farewell to change dresses. 'After all, you cannot celebrate two occasions in the same dress.'

Actually, just that was exactly my plan. And given that my closet was in Zurich, about 470 miles away, this gruesome fate was now inevitable. I deemed it survivable, though. Given that no living soul took notice of the groom, there should also be enough room under the radar for me. After all, it was not about me but about the bride – well, and a little bit about the groom. And my name was not Sinéad and I was not the property of any Bernd. Accordingly, I did not have to look stag-ge-ring.

Of course, I knew that this attitude was not helpful in the search for a partner. I just happened to be too in-vain. Or was it un-vain? Was there even a word for the opposite of vain? Or was that such a rare condition that it lacked an adjective? How had my father said? 'Child, you have to do more for your looks. Men are much better lookers than thinkers.' Of course, he was right. Intelligent women had to look twice as stunning. Or pretend to be a little less intelligent than they were. But I had not come to that point. Yet. Furthermore, I was convinced that the most optically-oriented man, too, would at some point realize that even a female head that wore make-up and a proper hairdo, yes, even a head wearing a hat actually tended to accommodate a brain. Well, unless that man's name was Bernd, maybe. But he was clearly a class of his own.

Anyway, it was too late for a new dress, and if today was to be the day of days on which Mr Oneandonly was to step into my life, then he would have to actuate his brain and not his hormone level.

SinHead

While the guests whose parents had apparently read them the relevant chapters from Debrett's as a bedtime story were gearing up appropriately for the second occasion, and while the married couple was having its love eternalized in bits and bytes and maybe even on kodachrome, I set off to Kartzow Castle. Ever since a school trip far too many years ago, this had been the place where Klara and I would marry a couple of twins or at least brothers in an overwhelming festival of love. We had spent hours imagining our big day. And today, Klara was celebrating there, in real life. Konrad was a single child. Of course.

When I arrived at the Castle after a good walk (smart choice not to wear high heels), I found the usual situation at weddings: Couples, hit by Amor's wildly and abundantly disseminated ricochets, engulfed by the reignited love they had almost lost under heaps of diapers and annuity payments, who would much rather have been alone.

Given that there was no designated singles table, I joined one of the seemingly less smitten couples.

Her: 'Nice location.' Silence.

Him: 'Yes, really nice location.' Silence.

Her: 'The ceremony was also nice.' Silence.

Me: 'Hi, my name is Johanna. I am a friend of Klara's, from school.' Silence.

Him: 'Yes. Really nice ceremony.'

Ah, yes, that was an answer, too. And quite an accomplishment on my side to be the fifth wheel – on a bike. I got myself lost – which was not too hard.

Unfortunately, my other attempts at making contact were equally successful. I switched to my photographer-me, and the miracle happened: Take a picture, and the world will smile at you! That never failed. And it further clarified the situation. 'Closer together, please – and please embrace each other!' People who were looking at each other and at me in alienation, forcing themselves to approach each other by the inch were (hopefully) not joined in matrimony as long as they both shall live. However, the first impression had not fooled me: Couples wherever I looked. Click.

While re-endlessed love was still floating through the garden in waves, showers and shocks, Bernd sprinted past me to the gate, dragging his Sinéad along. She was wearing a perfect (and, in particular, clean) evening gown. She looked stag-ge-ring. Seriously. Of course, I would not have worn a dress cut so low in the back, given the temperatures. Plus you never knew who had been sitting in the chair which Sinéad's sexily exposed back would lean against naked-back-to-backrest, tonight. But that was her decision, not mine. Obviously, I was too in-vain, indeed.

The source of the commotion that quickly took hold of the whole congregation? The married couple's limousine had arrived. Konrad got off and rushed to help his wife – 'that their hands shall uphold and guide thee, lest thou dash thy foot against a stone'. And Klara needed the help, because the vision in white that she was wearing did not leave her much room to breathe or move, despite her slender physique. Whatever, Klara was beaming.

The official photographer had cleared the arena after his private audience, but his services were no longer required, anyway. At least half the attendees pulled out their mobile phones and flashed Klara's path through the early dusk. I was happy for her that she had this Hollywood entrance. Did I mention? Klara was beaming.

Konrad led Klara to a red velvet chair, no, throne. He stood next to her and placed his hand on her shoulder. Klara held his hand as he read. 'Dear family, dear friends, dear colleagues! Most importantly: Dear Klara. As you know, I am not really a man of words. Anyway, words can never describe how happy I am to have you, Klara, here by my side today, as my wife. Accordingly, I will make it short: This is the happiest day in my life, and I thank each and every one of you that you share it with us – especially as some of you have travelled from afar to witness this unexpected event. Yes, unexpected. In the past 20 years, my mates from university have used every appropriate and inappropriate opportunity – in particular the inappropriate ones – to prophesy to me and the world that a queer old stick like me would stay single. And that this was a blessing for womankind. Well, guys, you did not expect this, did you! In particular, I want to thank our former landlady, Ms Beanston, who certainly had no clue that Amor was sitting on Klara's shoulder when she moved into the apartment next to mine. Fortunately, this little guy remained adamant when I moved away, shortly thereafter, and he also pushed Klara all over Berlin, straight to me. Some men apparently do not only need a broad hint but rather a broad hit on the head. And so, I ask you all to raise the glass with me to Amor, to the luck of the old sticks, to my gorgeous, intelligent, fun and simply perfect wife and to an evening on which we want to celebrate all of that. Klara, you are the best that ever happened to me, you are the wind beneath my wings. I love you.'

The crowd uttered a collective sigh, glasses were clinking, Kleenex use soared, and the evening had begun. Klara was beaming. What else? And shivering. The wedding gown was a dream, or rather a soupçon of a dream – and simply not warm enough for a late summer cocktail reception in the garden. I wrapped her into my coat, and after a short protest ('Jo, I look ridiculous!' 'You look warm and like a bride who will wake up without pneumonia, tomorrow, and go on her honeymoon, on Monday.' 'Yes, but what about you?' 'I am not going on a honeymoon, on Monday. Don't be so difficult, Klara!'), Klara spent the rest of the garden reception with wedding dress and coat. One has to suffer for beauty. If you don't want to suffer, be beautiful on the inside. Well, today, Klara was the most beautiful woman in the world, anyway.

'That's what I call a caring friend,' a deep voice behind me said. I turned around. Tall, massive, grey hair, glasses, around sixty, a glass of champagne in his hand, his mouth first dominated by a smirk, then by a pipe. No, I did not know this guy.

'I cannot allow her to go on her honeymoon all-sick. That would be a gross violation of my fiduciary duties, after all.'

He laughed. 'Oh, you are a lawyer? And what is the legal basis of your fiduciary duties? Well, if you are the bride's mother, then I have to pay you a major compliment, Ma'am.'

I had to laugh, as well. 'Johanna. Johanna Lenné. I am a school friend of Klara's, that's also a sufficient basis. And a lawyer. I assume that's also true for you – the lawyer part, I mean.'

'Kinsey. Dr Mark Kinsey, a friend of the Dobberin family. And, yes, I plead guilty on that count: I am a lawyer.'

How embarrassing for a lawyer to introduce himself with his PhD. I would never have done that. That was not me. But his voice: A bass like a bed of clouds – to sink into. Unfortunately, every sexy bass word came with a very unsexy emission of smoke.

'Well, nice to meet you, Dr Mark Kinsey: Cheese, please!' Click. 'Maybe a picture with your wife?' An old single reflex, I could not help it.

'No, I am not...'

'Okay, then, I will see you later.' I was not really that interested in his status, after all.

I joined Desi who was smalltalking with Bernd and his Sinéad. Sinéad turned around. 'Thank you, again, for the idea with the lemon juice and the vinegar. I managed to get it clean. Thank God.' 'No worries.'

A waiter offered finger food: spring rolls with curry sauce. When Sinéad reached for one, Bernd slapped her on the fingers. 'No, you better stop that. One such disaster per day is totally enough. I am insurance manager and not Mr Muscle. I will not let you make a fool of me twice in one day. And in any event, you are getting too fat, anyway. Come, SinHead, let's go in and look for our table.'

Having said that, he swung around – and stumbled into the next waiter, serving meatballs. With cocktail sauce. It never ceased to amaze me how comprehensively liquids disbursed in or on any given space. And cocktail sauce was no exception. Bernd's suit would bring a challenge to any dry cleaner's day. Too bad that Bernd was insurance agent and not Mr Muscle, as he had so rightfully pointed out. Too... what is worse than 'too bad'? 'Too worse'? Anyway, even worse that he was perfectly capable of making a fool of himself without any assistance, paving his way through the crowds towards the parking lot, ripping out with predominantly X-rated comments. I thought I saw a grin flashing on Sinéad's face before she dutifully followed Bernd. For better, for worse and for Bernd.

Both were a little late for dinner, Bernd wearing his

church suit. At least, I was no longer the only unchanged guest.

Desi and I lingered around for a little while, let the finger food come and go and exchanged our scant information on the guests when Desi suddenly straightened. The Baroness had winded. 'Is this not Dr Kinsey?'

'Yup.'

'Dr Kinsey, the general counsel of the Maienwald group? What brings a man like him here?'

'He says he's a friend of Konrad's family.'

'What? You have spoken to him?'

'Kind of. So?'

'I reckon you are not aware of the importance of the situation. Dr Kinsey is our most important client, only REX himself is attending to him. Do you not remember? For years, I have been hoping to meet him.'

From the dark and through the mist of a complete lack of interest, the memory of long nights I spent writing memos for the Maienwald group crept up into my brain.

'Plus he is not married. Could you please introduce me, Johanna?'

'Desideria, I have also only just met him. Not even met him. We have exchanged three words, maybe five. And why do I have to introduce you? You are old enough to do that without me.'

Desi's eyes begged. Of course, a Lady had to be introduced. Only plebs like me would introduce themselves. Or introduce Ladies who were chicken. 'Alright, let's go, then.'

'Mr Kinsey, may I introduce you to Lady Desideria von Kestrell? Lady Kestrell – Mr Kinsey.'

'What a pleasant surprise. Two such charming young ladies. I am delighted. But that's just the way it is. Wherever Dr Kinsey is, you will also find the beautiful young ladies. Enchanté!'

What a bootlicker! Of course, he had to bring on the PhD. How embarrassing.

Desi was even worse, however. She giggled. 'Dr Kinsey, the pleasure is all mine. I have heard so much about you.'

Good grief! The only thing missing were the hand kiss and the violins. Ah, yes, pink light and a boys' choir, maybe. I pulled my camera and manoeuvred them close to each other. With this, I considered my introduction job done. Click and go.

Off to check the seating order. Another vexatious issue at weddings. If you were lucky, you ended up at a table with other singles who, however, became younger and younger the older you got. Sometimes, I felt like the governess at the children's table. Or you were the uneven addendum to a table of couples flying on the wings of love back to their own wedding or silently holding the hand of the love of their life for a magical evening of love and devotion. How nice for them.

And today? I was placed – oops? – at the table of the married couple. Probably the only time in my life.

Luckily, Klara came by. 'I hope you don't mind. You know, my dad doesn't have anyone, now that my mom is dead, so I thought you could sit next to him. He knows you.'

'Sure, Klara. Happy to do that. I like your dad.'

I had not noticed any, to quote Desi, eligible bachelors, anyway. Talking about Desi: She sat next to the Doctor. Congrats, Klara, you do know your friends. Maybe, something would come of that.

Mr Miller

Klara had asked me to photograph all guests with a plush frog I had given her years ago – for practising, so that she would be ready when the right one would step into her life. This idea was so typical for Klara, and she had pulled it through: The wedding was frog themed. On the tables stood bowls with water lilies, surrounded by frogs made of clay, wood, china and everything one can make frogs of. One for each guest as a takeaway.

So, Froggy and I were lurking near the door, jumping at everyone who entered and coercing them to kiss my plushy companion. Fortunately, no one could keep a straight face in such ambush. Not even the Doctor, who, however, insisted on not being alone on the photo. Since when was his courtship my problem? Fortunately, Desi was lingering around, so I shoved her into the picture. Still, he was pouting, claiming that this was not what he had meant. Who cared? Click and basta la pasta. Some people were just high maintenance.

Anyway, when completing this task, I had casually found out that Messrs Miller and Kinsey were the only bachelors on the menu – aside from the cuddly students and early thirties drooling over the equally cuddly half models. Cute! Single ladies my age were abounding, though. As usual.

Mr Miller – more grey and less tall than in my recollection – stood up, 'Good evening. May I introduce myself? My name is Horst Miller. I am Klara's father.' He had obviously dug out his formal side and polished it carefully.

'Good evening, Mr Miller. It's me, Johanna. Klara and I went to school together, don't you remember?'

Mr Miller dropped the formalities. 'Boy, Johanna! Wow, you have grown. Lemme look at you. You're a real lady. I really didn't recognize you. Who would've thought that?'

'Well, at almost 40 years, one should be fully grown. But I promise that I won't grow any taller, now. I haven't seen you in ages. How are you, Mr Miller? Have you made it through the day alright? Wasn't this a beautiful wedding? Klara is such a bride-sy bride.'

Mr Miller beamed Klara's smile at me. 'Yes, isn't she beautiful? My little princess. It's like she sat on my lap just yesterday. And now, she's a married woman. If only my wife could see that!'

I took his hand and we sat silently for a bit.

When all guests had found their place, the bridegroom wished everyone an enjoyable evening, once more, and the salad was served. Mr Miller looked at the many knives and forks near his plate and wavered. I whispered, 'From the outside to the inside, Mr Miller. Just use what I use and you will be fine.' We understood each other.

After the salad, the best man's speech was prepared well and served snippily, with the right level of humour, some appropriately embarrassing anecdotes about Konrad and due admiration for Klara. He had definitely done this before and enjoyed his gig.

We raised our glasses, and after the toast, the happy couple and everyone else sat down, but Mr Miller remained standing and ticked his glass with his knife to attract attention.

Klara hissed at him. 'Not now, dad!'

'But, Klara, I wanna say something, too!'

'Yes, Papa, you can, but not now.'

If looks could kill!

Mr Miller, however, was immune to input. 'My daughter doesn't want her old father to speak, but this just needs to be said, and it needs to be said, now.'

Klara looked at me beseechingly. I pulled Mr Miller's sleeve as inconspicuously as possible, but he was stronger and absolutely determined. 'Well, dear Klara, dear Konrad – or may I now say: My dear children! Today, I am the proudest father in the whole world. Klara, you make me very, very happy. Konrad is the man I wished you would find, because I know that you love each other and that he will make you happy. And this is what a father wants. More than anything else.'

He looked around. I do not know whether it was Klara's daggering looks or the festive atmosphere; anyway, he apparently felt that he had to finish what he had started.

'Klara, we often clashed with each other, because we are both such pig heads, but I hope that you know how much I love you. And that I have always been proud of you, even though you often made my heart stop a beat or two. I was worried when you had to climb every tree or as an itsy bitsy little worm wanted to jump from the ten-metre-board, standing up there so small that I could hardly see you. But you did dive. Or when you got your motorcycle licence at 18, bought an old machine and drove down to Greece. That's my Klara. Gets her motorbike licence, buys a motorbike, immediately and rides to Greece, the next day. I was so worried. I mean, such a pretty young girl all alone with the Greek.'

Klara hissed. 'Daddy, not now.'

In vain. Mr Miller had gathered way. 'But I was always proud of you. And I am today. And of Konrad, too. You both make such a perfect couple, and this is what I was so hoping you would find. Your mom would also be so terribly, terribly proud of you. Oh, Klara, I miss your mother so much. I know that you miss her, too, especially today. But somehow, she is with us, anyway. Through you, Klara. She was a wonderful woman, and when I look at you, I see her at our wedding. She was the most beautiful bride one could imagine. Just like you are today.'

Klara had given up and looked at her father with weary emotion and swelling tears in her eyes.

'By now, I am an old man, and so I deserve the right to give you both some advice. Never go to bed before resolving any dispute. Always resolve it. Your mother always insisted on that, no matter how much that bugged me. And she was right. Then, you can get through everything. Together. Then, you will be together until death shall part you. Like your mom and me. Oh, Klara, I so wished she was here.'

By now, everyone had pulled out their handkerchiefs, again. A chorus of snuffles filled the room, and Klara sat amidst a funeral party, on the happiest day of her life. Fortunately, her old man pulled himself together. 'And you must not only tell each other that you love each other, you have to show it. Every day. How did old Willie say? 'Suit the action to the word, and all of that.' So, let us toast to my wonderful daughter Klara and to my new son-in-law, Konrad. And, while we are at it, also to good old Shakespeare. Welcome to the family, Konrad.'

Konrad and Klara embraced Mr Miller and the soup was served.

Klara burst into laughter. 'Oh, no, I don't believe it. Soup! We are having soup! I had completely forgotten about that.'

She obviously read the questions in our eyes, so she explained, 'I thought we were already waiting for the rack of venison. And my inner eye saw it burning to coal, tricky as it is. This is why I wanted you to wait a little, Dad. Oh, Daddy, that was so sweet of you, but I could hardly listen, because all I could think of was that stupid venison. Daddy, I love you so much.'

I was at ease and checked the photos from the last minutes. Klara looked like Snow White's stepmother in cursing mode, with red flashy eyes and her lips tight. Marvellous, no photoshopping on those.

Konrad passed by behind me and looked over my shoulder. 'Excellent, you have to keep those.'

Klara was not paying attention, and I used the opportunity to inquire about a question that had been lingering on my mind, for a while, 'Say, Konrad, the fact that Josh Groban was, by pure coincidence, playing when you drove her home. Could it possibly be that this was not purely coincidental?'

Konrad grinned. 'Guilty! But you must promise not to give me away to Klara. Well, Klara believes that we met, again, by mere coincidence. But, you know, I had fallen in love with her on the spot when I had first laid eyes on her. I had just not dared telling her. Until it was too late and I had to move away. When she suddenly showed up in the riding club, I swore to myself that I would not miss out on this amazing woman, a second time. This is why we 'coincidentally' constantly crossed each other's path until I had melted her. And the thing with Josh Groban, that was easy. She had played the CD up and down and at quite a volume. But, please, promise not to tell her anything. She believes it was a hint of fate.'

I had goose bumps. These two were really made for each other. 'Never. Promised.'

After dinner, a band played – waltz. Klara, the gorgeous bride, danced with her father who passed her on to her husband – and then asked me. After a teeny bit of a shock, I enjoyed the seconds on the almost deserted dance floor. And fortunately, I knew more or less how to waltz. An inexplicably small piece of this was also my bridal dance.

The band changed to the music that Klara and I had danced to at the disco, ages ago, and I had to solve the all-too-common question: What now? Quickly, a handful of couples (including Bernd and his Sinéad) graced the dance floor and levitated from side to side in perfect harmony, acquired in years of living and dancing together. Gingers and Bernds, all of them. Beautiful. Frustrating. Frustratingly beautiful. Even Mr Miller had found his Cinderella and graced the dance floor with aunt Ruth, who seemed to have forgotten all about the good-looking Mr Hancock and her funeral. Just like on every wedding, I decided to take dancing lessons. Knowing that, as always, the plan would fail for lack of a partner. Single men were a rare species in dancing classes, including those for singles. About as common as parrots in deep sea diving. And that even though dancing classes would have been the ideal place to meet women.

I had given it some thought, and come to the conclusion that it was easy for men to find a partner. All they had to do was enter the unmanned zones where women tended to hunt for men: dancing classes, cooking classes, study trips or generally anything cultural. Comparable bastions of manhood were football stadiums, Harley clubs or male choral societies. Or the virtual world. It seemed that male and female pastimes were pretty incompatible. Difficult.

After the semi-pros, it was now time for the 'normal' couples to enter the floor. Wait one more song, then … Bingo! Now, the boppy women with unboppy partners gave up their reserve and danced with each other. As always. Sometimes, I wondered how mankind had survived the good old times when couples met on elaborate balls, dancing dances so complicated that only specifically trained professional dancers would engage in them, these days. The average modern man seemed challenged to just avoid growing roots into the dance floor.

I approached Desi, who was standing near the dance floor, 'Doesn't Mr Kinsey want to dance?'

'No, Dr Kinsey has knee issues.'

'Well, at his age … Shall we?'

Desi wanted to, and we danced until a gong sounded.

'We now ask all single ladies to the dance floor. The bride will throw the bouquet.'

It sounded like we were summoned to fatigue duty. Still, about twenty more or less single women gathered, including Desi and myself. I stayed in the background, expecting that Klara would aim at the one who was about to marry next, anyway. There was always a cousin or a friend already planning her own wedding, and any bride would aim at her. This was what always happened and how it had to be done. Given that I was about as far away from a wedding as a pot whale from toe dance, I considered myself safe. Unfortunately, though, Klara did not know what she was supposed to do. Or her throwing skills were even worse than her singing skills. In any event, the bridal bouquet came flying straight at me. Completely taken by surprise, my reflexes took control. After years of playing volleyball, 'reflex' in this context meant that I skilfully pitched the round something flying at me back to the sender. Lucky enough, Klara had not played volleyball, so she caught the flowers instead of dashing them back.

After a short second of shock, Klara laughed, 'Well, it

seems like fate is not really sure about this.' She threw it, a second time, and the bouquet landed in Desi's open arms. Our world was back to normal. More or less.

I approached Klara to apologize. 'Klara, I am terribly sorry. I just hadn't expected that you would throw in my direction.'

Such bagatelles of life could not reach Klara on Cloud Nine. 'That's fine. Look, Desi is all happy. So, you have done a good deed.'

Indeed, Desi was holding the flowers to her chest, took a smell at them and smiled.

I absconded from the dance floor, passing the Doctor – whose comment was about the last thing that I needed.

'Very impressive technique, young lady! Kudos! Can I hire you if I should ever expect people to throw rotten eggs at me?' He obviously felt very cool. No one needed this guy, really. I ignored him.

Desi was waiting for me at the bar – the bouquet in a champagne bucket. 'Johanna, you must not take this to heart. Some people may not even have noticed. I also dropped a bridal bouquet, once. You know, I was never good at ball games. But the main thing is that I caught it today. So, even if you did not catch it, there is still hope for you, as well. Maybe at my wedding. What do you think about Dr Kinsey, by the way?' An almost imperceptible smile escaped a corner of her mouth before it had even arrived.

Oh, no! 'Well, given that he already thinks that he is just the greatest, I don't have to join into this choir. And apart from that, he is not even noble.' Had I just said that?

'No, no, you are right. But he really is extremely charming and so cultivated. He plays the piano and he studied in Russia, when Brezhnev was still in power. And he is interested in so many things.'

'Exactly – Brezhnev. Not Putin, not Andropov, not Gorbachev, Chern ... whatever this guy's name was. Brezhnev! He must have been dead for at least, well at the very least ... how should I know how long he has been dead for!'

Desi nodded just briefly.

I waged the constructive counter proposal. 'Desideria, I can't believe that we are standing at a wedding all by ourselves and discuss old men. Say, have you tried the Internet? There must be dating sites for the nobility. You-and-your-prince-dotcom.'

Desi barely concealed her disgust. 'No. Seriously – no. One meets at weddings. Or funerals. Family festivities in the broadest sense. But not online. Not the real nobles, anyway. And I do not tend to believe in that, anyway.'

'Well, I would not have such a negative attitude. My neighbours met on the Internet. At first, they chatted. And after a while, they realized that they both lived in Zurich, in the same borough, in the same street – and, even better, in the same building. Imagine that! That's crazy, isn't it? For years, they had just greeted each other when meeting in the stairway, but not more. And now, they live together and I live in his former apartment. You see, it can work.'

'Well, the fact that it appears to have resulted in success, once, does not necessarily allow any general conclusions.'

'No, no, that's not just once. Do you remember my brother, Christian? He lived near San Francisco and was looking for a wife. Probably the only man there who was looking for a woman, which obviously did not make it any easier. And his now-wife had moved to New York with her baby after a nasty divorce and was completely fed up with men. But, well, she is a journalist and had to write an article about dating online. To do so, she had to date online. And to make sure that nothing would come of it, she responded to only one ad of someone who lived in her hometown, near her parents, near San Francisco. As far away as possible. Exactly – my brother. Well, and when she visited her parents, one thing led to another and to the next, and now they are happily married. Their daughters are six and twelve, now.'

'But if it is so easy, why are you still single?'

Yes, why was that? Good question.

'Well, I don't know. Maybe, I am a coward and don't dare to present me on such a platform. What if no one likes me? I am not blonde and tall and thin. And then the platforms with psychological testing. I might be someone I don't even like. Or I just don't like the man who is my perfect match.'

'Exactly, so we are of the same opinion. How can a computer choose your partner? How many couples do you know who, objectively speaking, represent diametrical opposites, but which do work as couples? A computer would never have calculated that.'

'Well, but there are also couples who would never have met without the computer.' However, I could not completely discard Desi's argument, 'But you are right, it is strange to imagine that love can be defined and wrapped mathematically. You get a hit list, and they say that the first one on the list is the best person that can be found for you. It all seems so objective.'

'Exactly. If someone or something tells you that someone is your perfect match, you look at that someone. And the other side does the same, and if you are only his number 25, tough luck. I just do not believe that a program can determine who is the right partner for me. I consider myself more complex than that. And if you cannot sell yourself, you have lost. But, naturally, this is also true in real life.'

'Exactly. All I say is, please protect me from what I want. If Brad Pitt wakes up next to you, unshaven and sulky, he may not be Mr Wonderful, either. Maybe you would be far better off with Tom Smith next door. Even though, so far, I have also not met a Tom Smith. He is probably sitting at his computer, has pizza delivered twice a day and has grown physical ties with his sofa.'

Desi uttered a sigh. 'Yes, unfortunately. And the biological clock is ticking. I wish I were a man.'

'Yes, men definitely have the long end of the stick. Nothing runs out for them, except maybe the scales. But that doesn't matter, because they also deem themselves the perfect partner for any top model, even with a paunch. Meanwhile, we start counting every oat flake at the latest when we are thirty.'

Desi sighed louder. 'It is what it is. Women get old, men develop striking features. And the good ones are in steady relationships, anyway.'

'Exactly. Men are like toilets: Occupied, shitty or just for men. But somewhere, there must be others, too, we just have to look harder or closer or both. What about this: We meet again, right here, a year from now. The one who has a partner by then gets the hen night from the other.'

Desi's reaction was all Lady – maybe this notion was not completely unwarranted. 'No, I would not bet on such an important issue. And I will not have a hen night, either. We can meet, again, but without a bet.'

So, Desi automatically assumed that she would win. Naturally, this was inacceptable. For me, the bet was on, 'Okay, so we will meet in a year, here in Kartzow Castle. I will make a reservation, right away.'

It was late, or rather it was early. I bid good night to Desi, Konrad and Klara, convinced the waiter to take a reservation for a table for two – yes, exactly, for a year from today –, and went to bed. Maybe, my Mr Right would reveal in my dreams where he was hiding. Wasn't the dream you dreamt in the first night in a new bed bound to become true? Somehow, a hotel bed was also a new bed. I should travel more.

Unfortunately, the dream order system did not quite work as I had hoped. Instead of meeting my Prince Charming, I found myself on a meadow, kissing the cold and wet lips of frog upon frog until I had salty lips. Were there salt-water frogs? No, I did not think so. So, this was a dream. And I should be allowed to wish for something. Please, please, send me my Prince Charming! Eureka! There, on the horizon, a white knight in glistening armour appeared! I hurried towards him, across the meadow, which turned more into morass with every step. My fairy-like, levitating steps transformed into a hardly elegant battle for every inch. Fortunately, the knight also came closer – but it became harder and harder to recognize him, because a cloud of smoke around him grew more and more dense. It was – Kinsey. I turned around and waded back to my frogs. It was not possible to kiss this man enough to transform him into a Prince. Every high-sea frog stood a better chance. What, there were no high-sea frogs? Exactly!

Tina

Klara, Konrad and the other non-local guests were already having breakfast. Desi and most Berliners had obviously left after the party. Too bad, I would have liked to tell her about my dream, given that she seemed to like

Kinsey. For whatever reason.

I approached Klara and Konrad, 'Good morning, you two. So, how did you sleep as a fully official couple with blessing from above?'

'Not much different. Apart from the fact that the night was much too short and that I have quite a hangover,' Klara was still Klara. Comforting.

'Klara, I will send you the photos, next week, if that's fine.'

'Great. Thank you so much for doing that. I hope you still had some fun. Say, did I get that right that you were talking to Dr Kinsey?'

'Well, I would not really call that talking; we were exchanging a few words. But I think Desi has thrown an eye on him. Even though he is not a noble.'

Klara grinned. 'No kidding! Thanks for telling me. I will have to do some investigating, then. Darling, could you please remind me that I need to call Kinsey? And Desi.' She turned back to me, 'And, no one for you?'

'Well, the choice was not really overwhelming, as long as I want to abstain from molesting children. But never mind. Desi and I will tackle this systematically, now. After all, you cannot dance at other people's weddings, forever.'

'What was that? Gimme all the gruesome details. You know I need that. By the way, I have read that one should just go out on the balcony and inform the universe what one desires, and the stars will attend to the rest.' She whispered, 'Obviously, I could not do that, with Konrad living next door to me.'

'And I do not even have a balcony, so that won't work for me, either.'

Klara laughed. 'In the end, we both are incurable non-romantics.'

'Well, actually, now that I am thinking about it, I think it might work, after all. I have even tried it.'

'What? Really? Tell me all about it!'

'Well, it was not THAT exciting. You know that I like biking. In the summer, I was biking along the Aare river and heard a very rhythmic gasping approaching from behind. So, I wished for myself and more or less to the universe for this to be a really likeable guy, for biking and for a good conversation. And whatever.'

'And whatever? Johanna Lenné! And you have not told me anything about this? Shame on you!'

'I just said, it was not THAT exciting. Well, anyway, he came closer and closer, and when he was almost by my side, he asked whether he could join me. A man. Likeable.' I ticked off the imaginary check boxes of my wish list in the air. 'For biking. For a good conversation. But not for whatever. We spent half an hour biking next to each other peacefully and he told me about himself, his son – and his grandson who had finished university and was just in his foundation year at the clinic. Obviously, I should have included an age limit in my wish.'

Klara had to laugh, 'Well, Jo, so this is what happens when once in your life, your prayers are answered. You find the Frog Prince, and it is not Prince Charles but Prince Philip. Another chapter in the book of things that only happen to Jo.'

She had a point, there. It was true that the stories of my encounters with men usually ended in a punch line and not in bed.

'We really have to work on that, Jo. I have to think about a possible match. And apart from that: Go out, keep your eyes open, but stay who you are, remain true to yourself! No man is worth that.'

Yes, I knew all of that. Yes, it was absolutely logical.

No, it did not help me, at all. Maybe, this thing about every Jack having his Jill was just a rumour and there was no Jack for me. Or he was dyslexic and could not see that he was with a Jane. Or he was running around Timbuktu shouting 'Jill, where are you?' all day. Or he was more into a Bill and did not even see that he should be after a Jill. Or maybe, something was wrong with me and I was a Gill, so that there was no Jack for me, after all. Well, I would not be able to solve this, here and now.

Mr Miller came to join us. I changed subject. After all, there was enough to talk about, at a wedding.

After helping Klara and Konrad loading their presents into the car, I went off to see my friends Tina and Lars.

Those two were an ideal couple. Most couples consisted of a great one and a lucky one. 'X is so lucky to have found Y. He/she is great.' Being the generally accepted lucky one probably did wonders for the overall happiness in life, but hearing it too often was likely not too good for the ego. Tina and Lars, however, were both both: lucky and great.

We had met on a study trip in Egypt – one couple (not Tina and Lars), two single men, fifteen single women. All in all, a rather typical combination for a group trip. Unfortunately, Egypt had proven to be an extraordinarily nerve-wrecking destination for women. The hawkers constantly thrust their merchandise into our hands and then approached any man to negotiate the price for us women. A mystery of the orient: Why do the hawkers not realize that Westerners just want to look around and not be harassed, constantly? That the offer to be exchanged for one, ten, fifty or one hundred camels is not really funny the first five times, but definitely absolutely unfunny after the fiftieth such offer? And that, in case of doubt, we rather take flight than being pulled into a tiny store full of Anubis and Nefertiti statues to negotiate insane prices for things we do not need down to half insane prices for things we still did not need? And did they not know that Berliners could see the original Nefertiti, any day they wanted to at the *Neues Museum*, right around the corner. As a result, a harem of women requiring protection from the hawkers had gathered around Lars, including Tina, Kate and myself. And the chemistry had started to do its magic between Lars and Kate. But back at home, when everyday life lashed out at their love, it faded away almost as fast as their suntan, proportionately with the distance between them and their lives.

However, Tina's thus far unrequited affection for Lars had not faded. She kept on the ball, and when we sporadically chatted on the phone, she would tell me about meetings, then about small trips, then about her vacation with Lars – and sent me a wedding announcement, years later. Tina was at least as great as Lars, and both were lucky. I was happy for them.

I admired women with a pronounced animal spirit. Unfortunately, no such huntworthy showpiece had yet crossed my firing line.

We met in *Tiergarten*, and Tina had obvious news – she was expecting. The child would be born, in late December. I was happy for them. And for their child whose choice of parents had already proven that it was about to inherit their lucky touch.

Of course, this quickly led to a discussion of my situation. Alone in Zurich.

Tina's advice was about as profound as the balcony prayer, 'You will see that it will hit you when you least expect it. 'Boom', and you will know that this is your Mr Right. Don't worry about it. Just let it happen, and it will happen. I was not looking, either, when we were in Egypt.'

I had been given this advice, so many times. Too many times. 'Well, I know you cannot force it, but you do have to create opportunities. I am quite sure that the man of my dreams will not swing from house to house on a liana, casually and coincidentally landing on the sofa next to me. And just like everywhere else, only Jehovah's Witnesses ring on the door in Switzerland. Besides, I am 39 years old, and of those, I have not been searching actively and not expecting 'it' to happen, for at least 35 years. And you see where I stand. Why should this change if I don't change it?'

'All I'm saying is that you shouldn't force it. See, it was the same for Lars and me. We met and hit it off. I did, that is. It took Lars a bit longer to get there, that's true.'

'Yes, but how long can that bit longer take? Let's assume for the sake of argument, purely hypothetically, that there was a colleague whom I was very interested in. Intelligent, smart, sporty, good looking, great sense of humour, interested in anything and everything, and a laugh that sends shivers down my spine.'

'Good. And what would the name of your hypothetical wonder man be? Just to give the theory a name.'

'Well, hypothetically, its name or rather his name would be Urs, and he would be Swiss. Anyway, every once in a while, I suggest that we go out for dinner, and we do. I invite him with my friends, and he comes and I see that he is enjoying himself. And then, he leaves when everybody else does. I get tickets for the movies on the lake, we wait for the movie to start while the sun is setting, we share a blanket when it's getting cold, and he does not pull away when I put my hand on his...'

Tina interrupted. 'Urs, the bear. That sounds great.

Where is the problem?'

'The problem is that the initiative always has to come from me, and he does not carry it any further. If I don't contact him, I don't hear from him. For months. He only allows things to happen, his hand does not wander, he…'

'And this has been going on for how long?'

'Three years.'

'Have you ever asked him whether he is interested?'

'He knows that I am interested. I have really shown him.'

'Well, Jo, I know that in principle, you are an intelligent person. But still, I'm telling you: You can show him a thousand times, that does not mean that he has even a remote idea that you are interested. Men don't marry. They get married. But they have to believe that they were the huntsmen. Has he ever said anything about partnership?'

'Yes. He says that he treasures his freedom. This is why he appreciates our friendship so much. It is all so wonderfully uncomplicated.'

'Well, then let the bear play in his forest. I am sure he likes you, and it is convenient for him that you organize his spare time. And hardly anything tickles a man's ego as nicely as an attractive, intelligent woman like you running after him. But even Lars showed a reaction, at some point. A three-year performance of *Me, the lonely wolf* or rather *Me, the lonely bear* won't get you anywhere. And if he misses you, after all, he will show up.'

Where she was right, she was right.

'Jo, we will check whom we know, and then we will organise something.'

I knew this would not happen, due to lack of resources, and I changed topic.

After a long walk, Tina drove me to the home where

my uncle lived or, as it was officially called, to the retirement residence. This difference in wording actually did make a difference, as it was really a very well kept and well-run home. On the other hand, it made no difference, as you get cabin fever regardless of whether it is Uncle Tom's or the Rockefellers' cabin that you cannot leave.

As always, my visit at Uncle Walter's evoked mixed feelings. He visibly drifted off into dementia, more and more. This time, at least he recognized me. But of course, I was by far less interesting than the piece of cake I had brought. Eating it cost him so much strength that he fell asleep, immediately and happily. As always. There was not much left of the uncle who had thrown me up into the air as a child, who had played gee-gees with me for hours, who had taught me how to do the perfect header, who had had a long and intricate, but in the end usually funny story for every situation. Just a small, sunk down bundle of man. It was good and yet it hurt to be with him.

I would end my life in a home, as well, presumably. Hopefully, I would have visitors, every now and then. However, my nieces would hardly fly in from the U.S. to see me eat cake. A clear downside of globalization: families were spread. I pushed away the clouds. I felt too young for that.

Walhalla

Obviously, some higher power felt that I had just been with too many nice people and decided that it was time to send someone more challenging my way, straight to Berlin Tegel Airport. Said someone was a real woman: Blonde, with the curves of a Rubens angel, the voice of two Wagner tenors and the combined fighting spirit of all Valkyries. Plus a good portion of chutzpa. She paved her way through the waiting line, her mother on her coat-tails, jangling. 'We have to check in. My mother is handicapped. Let me through! Don't you hear me? Don't stand in my way like a tree. We have to get through.'

Hearing was not the problem, though. Her audience just did not believe their ears. The mother, a fragile elderly lady with a crutch, desperately searched for a hole in the ground and, when her search proved in vain, resorted to apologetic smiling. Obviously, something had gone astray in the upbringing of her little sunshine. And mommy was just realizing that, as well. A little late, though.

No one appeared inclined to engage in a physical argument, so that the unlikely pair quickly progressed to the counter, but not to the fulfilment of its wishes. Grace to her Wagner genes, we all shared the questionable joy of following the conversation. 'I will not squeeze into such a small middle seat. And my mother has to sit in an aisle seat, with her leg and all. So, either we sit in a row with two seats or you leave the seat between us free. That's my preferred option, anyway.'

I pitied the lady at the counter. 'Ma'am, as I mentioned, all rows with two seats are taken, and the flight is full. So, I cannot leave a seat free.'

'I couldn't care less, darling. Is this what you call customer service? Move someone!'

'Ma'am, I am not your darling. Of course, you can ask someone on the plane if they want to switch with you, but those passengers have paid extra to get those seats. For your next flight, I would recommend that you either book business class or two economy seats, if you need more space.'

'So, now, you are telling me that I am fat? That takes

the biscuit. No, that really takes a whole cake! I want to speak with your superior, immediately.'

My, the flight took an hour. She should even survive that if she had to stand. Or maybe in the cargo area, preferably next to a skunk with dysfunctional glands? I liked the thought of this Valhalla (the epitome of all Valkyries) arguing a sick skunk.

The superior came, took away our little lump of sweetness and accompanied the two to security control.

There, the involuntary entertainment program continued. 'What? No, this is a vintage whiskey. I will definitely take it with me on the plane. ... And who will pay me if I leave that here, now? It has cost more than 200 Euros. ... Good, so you will get me my suitcase, here and now. But if the bottle breaks, you will pay for the damage.'

Unfortunately, life was mischievous, today. When the suitcase arrived, the next clamour arose. 'So, first you take the bottles, and now the corn parer? I always have it in my hand luggage. Yes, of course, I need it. I don't believe this. Who do you think you are, young man? ... Good, I will leave it here and pick it up on the way back. ... No, I will not pack it into the suitcase. ... That's none of your business. It is still my decision what I pack where.'

A corneal file? In the land luggage? Because you need it, underway? Thank you so much for this beautiful image. And kudos to the security control. Where is Wotan when you need him to discipline a Valkyrie with bad manners? Bad analogy, Wotan himself was not a shining example of good manners. Probably, our darling took after him.

When passing the control point, I saw the Corpus Disputandi: An iron file with a six inch blade. Double yuck! I refused to get the message that was to be drawn from the fact that she was executing her bodily hygiene with metal working tools.

The avenger of the irritated really seemed to have a bad day, so that she was already engaged in the next dispute when I arrived in the waiting area. This time, she insisted that her mother (who was sitting in a quiet corner and probably wondering whether her adorable little sweetheart had been switched after birth and in what kind of a family her real daughter had grown up) had to sit in a chair directly next to the gate. It had to be the chair that a man with his leg in plaster was brazenly occupying. He would not budge. What a chuff! Valhalla trudged off. Presumably, she was calling upon some gods of vengeance for help, doing a rain dance or crafting voodoo dolls.

By now, I had reached the stage of relaxed amusement and, with this mind-set, followed the last act: An announcement. 'Ladies and gentlemen, may we ask for your attention, please? Unfortunately, the plane for flight LX467 to Zurich is too heavy. We therefore have to leave the two heaviest suitcases, here and will take them on the next flight leaving tomorrow morning. We kindly ask passengers Malischke and Gramlich to the counter.'

Yep. Valhalla and her mother headed towards the counter. They were not amused. Every now and then, weight issues were a good thing.

On the plane (no, no one had offered their two-seat-row to the messenger of Wotan's wild wrath), I laid out my plan of action. Every week, I would grant the universe at least one opportunity to meet its delivery obligation and to wash the amazing stranger (?) upon the shores of my life.

So, where could Mr Right be hiding, why was he hiding and, most importantly, how could I find him?

I made a list:

1. Work
2. Coincidence

3. Friends
4. Hobbies: Singing, biking, travel (single trip?)
5. Speed dating
6. Online dating / Websites
7. Newspaper

And, how did I view my chances?

Work. Of course, it is a common theme that major companies are, truth being told, nothing but a huge wedding market. Unfortunately, apart from Urs, the one-way-street, I did not really see anything or anyone at first glance.

But even upon further inspection, the situation remained bleak. My American lawyer colleagues were not only far away but also fully occupied with being and, even more so, being perceived as being important. My Swiss colleagues were married or in steady relationships, and blessed with children. The only single was Mr Werthuber. After four years, we were still on a cosy last name basis. I had even invited him for lunch, once, hoping for hidden trouvailles – in vain. Granted, I had learned a lot. About tanks. Mr Werthuber was on the board of a tank club and wallowed for an hour in the dazzling array of these shapely and practical vehicles. If I got it right, the conclusion was that everyone should have one of those, at home.

Indeed, this was a rare but appropriate hobby in Switzerland with its militia system. Up to a certain age, the men regularly throw into gear. In case of an emergency, the idea is that they fetch the army rifle from their closet and gloriously defeat the enemy. Preferably, war should not break out when everyone was at the office or out hiking, though. Oh, and not during lunch break.

Once, I had asked a Swiss colleague whether it was not

somewhat dangerous, after all, if such a large part of the population had a gun at hand right in their homes. The response was a classic, 'No, no, that is not dangerous. The ammunition is sealed, you know. You must not open it.'

In front of my inner eye, a Swiss Rambo rose – let's call him Hansruedi. He was wearing a camouflage suit, heavy boots and a red-and-white bandana with an Enzian pattern. He ran to his closet in the bedroom, pulled out the gun and yelled. 'I kill you all. Everyone. I'll stiff you all.' His right hand reached out for the ammunition, but pulled back as if he had touched a hot plate. 'Shit, they are sealed.' After which he stored away the rifle and buried in his pillow to cry. Or went to the barn to milk the cows. Or to the investment bank to trade. Whatever one does when one cannot get to the ammunition to go on a private war.

Anyway. In summary, there was an acute lack of worthy objects of desire at my workplace. I really did not feel any urge to pursue matters with Mr Werthuber.

So, let us continue.

Coincidence. Obviously, coincidence could also hit hard. Preferably out of nowhere. My goddaughter had met her fiancé at the disco. Twice. The only times that they had ever been to the disco. That had been a sign. Even though I still could not fathom how they had managed to communicate at all in the mind banging noise. Posing the question made me painfully aware that I was too old for this. Once, I had been to an 'Over30 disco', but to be honest, the ubiquitous and strained demonstration of the fact that these particular over thirties were all feelin' good, I mean, really good, I mean, excellent, cool and young, had depressed me. At our age, one should not feel stressed to stress how one feels.

Friends of mine had met strolling across the Hamburg Fish Market when he was visiting from abroad and she was doing her daily shopping. They had fallen in love in a flash, still going strong after 20 years.

Another friend of mine had met his wife when she asked him for directions in the street. Well, this one was no longer an option, in the age of the GPS; no one was searching or asking for the way, any more. At least not in the verbal sense.

My favorite coincidental story was that of my neighbour, a German in Switzerland. After the War, her parents had sent her over to live with relatives, mainly to get some decent food. The uncle was a baker. When she got off the train, a fellow traveler helped her with her suitcase, and she asked him for the way to her relatives (again, the question for directions). It turned out that he was her uncle's apprentice. And so, the first Swiss she ever met became her future husband.

I mused about who had been 'my' first Swiss. Yes, it must have been the hotel porter at the first hotel where I stayed. He had come to my room to change the light bulb. After which he pointed at my (single) bed. 'You travel alone?' I had to agree. 'You are alone, I am alone. Why don't we sleep with each other?' I gracefully declined this generous offer but still faced a small, sweaty 60+ man with unambiguous intentions in my room. When I steered him towards the door, he pulled the Swiss all-purpose weapon. 'I will bring chocolate, too.' Thanks a lot for that. Switzerland seemed to be a low price island, in this regard (contrary to all other regards). While I did manage to manoeuver him out of the room, I did not really feel well. When I reported the incident to the director, the next day, he apologized and asked for my understanding. The poor man's wife had just tried to commit suicide. He had probably been searching for comfort. Thanks a lot for that, too. Things that only happen to Jo.

Analyzing the situation in due sobriety, I had to conclude that (a) luck was apparently not on my side, (b) coincidences could not be created in a systematic manner, and (c) I could not constantly linger around on markets or in deserted streets or hop on and off trains. Apparently, my luck was a bit slow and needed more time than I had patience to hang around anywhere. And we had already discussed the 'It happens when you least expect it' allegation.

Friends. Most of my friends were married or otherwise in a relationship. Obviously, I was really the last leftover. Not really motivating.

And friends of friends? Johanna's all season sale? I had stopped hoping for that, as my friends were clearly running low on male stock.

On the other hand, it had worked out for my friend Stella. For years, she had kissed frogs, hoping for them to transform simply into good men (indeed, no one is actually searching for a prince, these days, apart from Kate Middleton), but finding that the frogs just continued croaking. Every now and then, she had found someone who would, actually, make for a good partner – but not for her. Stella and her friends had then organized a 'lid- the-pot' or Bill-and-Jill party. Only condition: Everyone had to bring a good guy for the taking. So, they had a selection of eligible singles with the best possible seal of approval. And it had worked. Stella had found her Jon. While obviously no one had thought of arranging a blind date for them, they were made for each other – maybe not despite but rather because of their very different but complementary strengths and weaknesses. Stella, the power woman full of energy and joie de vivre, seizing life with both hands, and Jon, the scientist who went missing in his own world, from time to time. As it turned out, he was the first one who did not only see and love the gorgeous woman in Stella but also her intelligence, her humour and everything the other men had missed. Stella used to say that he was not perfect but perfect for her. Two great lucky ones. And this was all that mattered. They now lived near the sea with their daughter and a dog, and I visited them when I needed friends, good discussions and a substitute family.

Unfortunately, Stella's friends were all in relationships, by now, so that there were no more Bills nor Jills no pots without lids.

My own version of this lid and pot story had not really proven fruitful. For years, I had invited friends and offered them to bring friends. They had done that and brought all their – female friends. Great! Of course, I did not want to discriminate against my consexuals, but secretly, I had hoped for the home delivery of love. For that purpose, women just happened to be of lesser use.

The pool of friends and friendsoffriends had dried out1.

Choir. In theory, a great idea: You sing together, get together regularly and slowly but surely get to know and maybe to love each other. In practice, however, choirs were like real life: A good man is hard to find. Most choirs were chronically short on men (apart from gay and pure men's choirs, of course, but this realization did not really help, either), and at least in my choir, all men were already taken. And I would never leave my choir to choir-hop for the purely academic chance to sing a duet.

Travel. For the longest time, it had been clear to me that I would explore the world with my beloved partner, one day. Until I realized that it made no sense to wait for someone who might never show up. Or who might not enjoy travel. Or maybe, I would even find my 'Someone', on a journey. Like Lars had stepped into Tina's life. I had to admit to myself, though, that the typical male-female-quota on group tours did not really raise hopes too high. Even on my only single trip, there had been 21 participants: 19 women, two men, one of them gay. The truly singular man had hit his way down the hit list until number five had answered his prayers. I wondered whether they were still together.

However, there was evidence that things could work out: On a journey through Vietnam and Cambodia, I had met Alexandra, another strong woman, and a tall one at that. Too tall for most men. Lady Diana syndrome. For years, she had been searching for a partner on websites such as 'GrandIsGrand'. When we crossed the border river to Cambodia, she spotted a man in the crowd waiting for us onshore. He looked back at her, not flinching. He turned out to be our local guide. On the journey, they had sufficient opportunity to get to know and like each other, but they only realized that they belonged together when she had returned back to Germany. Despite all hurdles (yes, Cambodia has a different idea of proper documentation than Germany), she brought him over. Now, they were married. Even though he initially spoke hardly any German and was permanently one foot shorter than her. He gave up a decent career in Cambodia, because his skills as a tour guide did not really come in too handy when living in Germany. We talked on the phone, every now and then, and she was still deeply in love with her Arun, 'Finally a real man who knows his priorities and does not freak out over nitty gritty.' Life could work out this way, too.

Conclusion: In principle, travel was a good option, but the lack of men was chronic and evident. A single man could hardly avoid coming back non-single. But that did not really help me. And with my luck, most travel guides were women or retirees.

Hobbies in general: Next. A hobby with male surplus? Fishing? Extreme ironing? Boxing? Maybe the Harley Davidson Club? Unfortunately, it would quickly become apparent that I was not really interested in the motorbikes but in those sitting on them. And equally unfortunately, my relationship with high speed had to be labeled as aggrieved, at best. I was even challenged by the speed when biking, sometimes. I very much preferred flat courses and had to change my brake pads, at least once a year, because I was creeping down even comparatively flat hills. Once, when riding down a hill, I heard a child ask why I was riding so slowly. 'She is scared, Kevin.' That was doubly deplorable, both what was said and the fact that I could hear the complete conversation while riding – crawling – standing downhill. In other words, I was a speed non-kie, so that typical male hobbies such as motor biking, speed boating and all forms of skiing were not really made for me. In Switzerland, this aversion against speeding down mountains automatically made me an outsider. Why, oh why had my parents raised me so consequently in the flatland? In the end, it was always the parents' fault. Anyway, it would not really serve the purpose to spend my life with a speed junkie and his best buddies 'Horror' and 'Terror'.

Which other male hobbies were there, maybe slower ones? Knittingstitchingcrochetingknottingbatikingsilkpaintingpottingcandledipping and so on were off the list. I was not feminist enough to expect that as a distinctive feature in a man. Colouring-by-numbers Anthony was excluded.

Maybe swimming? My friend Mary had met her Leo and his son Carl at Lake Zurich and immediately fallen in love with both of them, not only because of their wide grin but also because Leo treated Carl the way she wanted her future children to be treated. But when Leo had told her about his deceased wife and his work as an engineer at the Swiss Railway Company SBB, everything had gone wrong: Carl had slipped and fallen down, broken his arm and been rushed to the hospital before they could exchange telephone numbers. Normally, this would have been it. But what is normal when you know that this is the one and only? Mary hired a private investigator who placed an ad in the employee magazine of the SBB. 'Looking for Leo, engineer in the train department. You have forgotten something at Lake Zurich, on 15 July 2007. Please call…' Et cetera. While that had helped Mary, it was of no use for me, here and now. It was September; the swimming season was almost over.

Newspaper. What about an ad? This had worked for Steve and Florence. Steve had been browsing through the classified ads in his local rag, looking for a motor bike, and had then closed his eyes and randomly pointed at an ad in the personals section. 'Fun and flurry scratching-cat looking for a durable scratching post up for the challenge and interested in a lasting co-operation' When he finally wrote to her, a month later, Florence had already worked through the first responses. Steve's letter fell out of the usual time frame straight onto fertile soil. By now, they had been married for 22 years and were scratching, purring and challenging each other and the world with so much perfection, love and dedication that it was a pure joy watching them. Yes, maybe I should try that.

Apart from that, there were speed dating, online dating and generally the Internet to weave the electronic threads of love around the world. At home, my computer would likely become my best friend. Hopefully, this would be just an interim solution.

The plane landed. At home, I realized that I had not watched our cutie pie go through customs with her whiskey. Too bad, this could have been fun.

Udo

Back in Zurich, I set off to tackle my annual plan. Fortunately, things were rather calm at work. Usually, I had 12-hour-working days. When we started our day, our colleagues in the US were still fast asleep. When they turned up, we had already addressed the most pressing issues. Following some hours of peaceful co-existence, they kept us busy so that we eventually left the office shortly before they did. Unfortunately, they found it perfectly normal to sign us up for endless conference calls starting at 8 pm or later. Yes, the 'international work environment' was by far less glamorous in real life than in my student fantasies.

Still, I enjoyed working with my foreign colleagues. I was always amused about how they lived up to the respective national stereotypes (of course, this was not true for us Germans – we were all individualists); from the French who preferred staying in adjacent rooms on business trips and built their days around lunch, through the Brits who could kill my yearly alcohol intake on a single evening, and the Italians, who seemed to enjoy mastering their self-inflicted chaos, to the Americans who were always 'more-er': more important, more stressed, more demanding, more expensive, more productive as far as PowerPoints were concerned, louder, bigger, but also more open.

As a lawyer, I found a country existing under a system as strange as the US law dubious. Not only the lawmakers set the rules, but when someone takes an odd question to court, the court decides and the rule applies to everyone. Allegedly, it was not allowed to walk the streets of San Francisco if you were 'ugly'. Whoever was positioned to define that. In times of Botox-bloated millionaires' wives and actresses (and their male equivalents), this question was obviously in flux.

Naturally, my work heavily contributed to my single status, a fact that surfaced in my conscience and then receded into oblivion, in intervals. Until Klara's wedding, I had actually ensconced myself quite comfortably in my single life. This state did have its undeniable advantages; I was flexible, could do what I wanted to do when I wanted to do it. If only it wasn't for this stupid, empty heart. Everything else could be arranged. I had come to terms with the fact that no one would demonstrate his manliness by fixing the drain, painting the walls or mounting the shelf. Instead, I had taken a course 'Basic repairs in the household', which had actually made me (more) independent. By now, I could change plugs within minutes. But admittedly, a fixed snap-lock also did not really make my life complete, so that my content was shattered at a shattering speed. For example by a wedding.

Whatever, I told myself that I would not go on the manhunt at all price but just create opportunities. In practice: I booked the course 'Running a single household'. This would come in handy, in any event. And it just had to have a male overload.

When entering the classroom, on the following Saturday, I quickly realized that men were obviously the better housewives – or at least thought so. Well, or they just did not care. Anyway: Ten women, three men.

I started a discussion with the guy sitting next to me, 'Hi, I am Johanna. So, why are you here?'

'Nice to meet you. I am Udo. I have just moved to Zurich. My wife is still in Berlin with the children. Worrying that I will end up a total slob and that she will have to recivilize me, again. So, I am here for the sake of civilization. And you?'

'Now, that's what I call a coincidence. I have been living in Zurich, for a while, but I am also from Berlin. I hope to learn some tricks, here. Laundryironingcleaning is not really what I call fulfillment.'

The instructor interrupted us. 'I see that you have already started the introductions. Why don't we do that together, then? My name is Eggerswiler. And for me, Laundryironingcleaning is a passion. I hope that this will rub off a little on you, today.'

My big gob and me! Fortunately, Ms Eggerswiler seemed not to be vengeful.

We also had a boy of maybe thirty years with middle parting, horn-rimmed spectacles, beige-brown shirt, brown slipover and matching corduroy pants. He murmured softly into his hands, kneading them so violently that seeing it caused cramps of solidarity. 'I am Marcel. My mom said that I should take the course. Because, once she is no longer with me, I can then at least take care of myself.'

That would take more than just a day course in housekeeping, it seemed.

The last armed knight's self-introduction was also no more glorious. 'My friends all chimed in to give me this course for my birthday. So, I thought I might well take it. Even though I do not need it.'

A cursory view at the state of his clothing, his hair mop and generally at him, however, leisurely revealed to the unbiased spectatress why his friends had had this glorious idea. They were real friends, and the training was necessary. Sorely necessary. However, it did not quite tackle the right spot. Obviously, there was no class 'Body hygiene for beginners'.

The rest of the day, the two of them were not heard of, again.

The course was interesting, but it did not transform me into a maniac for housework. My personal revelation of the day occurred in the ironing section, when Ms Eggerswiler interrupted me. 'No, really, you no longer start ironing the back at the yoke. That's no longer done since World War II.'

Not only had I not known that this piece of the shirt had a name to be called by. No, I also felt like a stick-in-the-mud – and much older than 39. And it was all my mom's fault. She had missed the brave new world of pressing and raised me in the ironing spirit of World War II. Of course, I could not see any difference in the result, but being classified as an antique pressionista … that hurt. I decided to be dignified about it.

After cleaning and pressing through the day, we were released into a new and better life of sparkle and shine (and flawless yokes). Udo suggested to go for a drink. He did not know anyone in town, I might be able to give him some tips.

At the bar, I dutifully started writing down addresses for him. 'Well, if you want to meet people, you should check out Meetup. They organize events. You know, like going to a bar or playing soccer or so. How do you like to spend your time?' Boy, I was good at getting to know people, as long as it was about friendship.

'Gymnastics. But, you know, I think I have already found what I am looking for.' He did not quite look like a gymnast, but so be it. 'So, why don't you put away the paper and we just chat a little. What do you do, these days?'

Surely, someone could figure that out, but not me: First, he wanted tips, and then he didn't. And then, men said that we were the fickle gender. Yes, sure. Well, it did not matter. I had no big plans for the evening, so we could also have a talk.

'I am a lawyer. At the Blau-Weiss Insurance. And, what do you do?'

'Psychiatrist. Mostly couples counseling. Even though I have to admit that I find that rather superfluous.'

'What, you offer couples counseling, even though you find therapy unnecessary? How does that go together?'

He laughed, 'I think that life as a couple is not necessary. This relationship model has outlived itself. And this also renders the therapy designed to save the model moot.'

Obviously, the question marks in my eyes were clearly visible. He continued, 'I am just writing a book: 'Me, myself and I'. It shows that the human psyche is not made for togetherness. Monogamous relationships are so foreign to our nature that they suck up disproportionate amounts of energy and keep us from individual fulfillment. This is why monogamy is primarily an instrument of control and power, initially used by the church, now by the government. A well-embellished one, though. The only way to find emotional and intellectual freedom is polygamy. Honestly, how many people do you know who are really happier in a relationship than they would be on their own?'

That was not really in sync with my current mindset. 'Well, I do know quite a number. Just last week, a friend of mine got married. And they are very happy.'

'And how long do you think this will last? At the latest when the children come, he will start roaming, while she is tied to her home and is yearning to throw him out. The order of events does not matter. The outcome remains the same. At first, women race against their own 'best before' date to find a partner. Then, they race against the 'best before' date of their relationship to keep him. But every 'best before' date kicks in, eventually. Just like milk: If you keep it in the fridge, you can delay it, but in the end, the milk will always rot.'

Well, I could also be a stinker, 'That sounds like a severe case of déformation professionelle. You only see the ones who have a problem. A severe one. But that does not mean that the model doesn't work. If you want to make a different choice for yourself, that's your decision, but that is not the next step in sociological development. It's just your personal choice.'

'And still, you are single. So, how can you live like that if you believe that life is only complete and full of happiness with a partner? You must be feeling totally unhappy and incomplete 24/7.'

Well, that was certainly one of the many, many things that were none of his business. I took the next exit. 'Well, if all odds come to ends, I go to a course 'Housekeeping for singles', learn how to cook single menus, and that should cover the problem.'

He smiled with the full knowledge of his presumed superiority. 'Seriously, you don't need a partner. Every now and then, you need a real man in your bed to do some gymnastics. That's it.'

'No, I disagree. Sex is not bedtime gymnastics, it is the result of attraction plus trust plus affection – in whichever order.'

'It is bedtime gymnastics. Not more. Our society has just mystified, tabooed and glorified it. What you are looking for is not a soul mate but a sports buddy. What we consider love is actually the expectation or exchange of good sex. You should try it. We are in our prime for it.'

He seemed to have very precise ideas of who I could try it with. Eventually, this was irrelevant, though, as I would neither test 'it' nor him. 'I am wondering whether your wife shares your view on that.'

He waved my question aside, 'Jesus, no. No, she is so old-fashioned, she does not get that.'

'I am sure she will be thrilled to read your book, then. It must be very educational for her. You know, I have to leave, now, I want to call a friend.' We had said it all, anyway.

Obviously, the housekeeping class was not the place where HE was hiding. And it would look quite stupid if I took this course, again, week after week.

What else was on the list?
Speed dating.
Back at home, I started my computer. The website promised droves of young, beautiful, smiling people in wonderful places, obviously captured for eternity just in the very moment when Amor's arrow had hit them and they were stepping onto the path towards a glorious, evidentially together-ly future.

Next departure of the train to bliss: Friday. I signed up. Let's see.

I had hardly submitted my application when I started

feeling queasy. Had I unchangeably crossed the line into the crowd of the sempiternal leftovers?

I called Mary.

As usual, Mary brought things into perspective. 'No, you are doing absolutely the right thing. You know, Leo and I would not be together if I had not sailed in back then. Sometimes, a woman has to leave her comfort zone. The worst that can happen is that you have to spend a boring evening. That would neither be the first not the last time. But I wanted to call you, anyway. Are you around, tomorrow night? Leo and I are meeting some friends at Il Centro. Wanna come? At seven?'

'Yes, of course. Thank you so much. You are an angel. I needed that, now.'

'Cool. See you then!'

When I woke up on Sunday, the sun was beaming, and I decided to go biking. Fortunately, the biking routes in Switzerland are signposted in a foolproof manner, so that I could daydream – and much to my surprise, Mr Right soon no longer played a role in those dreams.

I stopped at the church in Klosterfelden, and as I was all by myself, I practiced a little for our next choir concert. At home, I would never do that to avoid disturbing the neighbours. In the streets, I would have felt weird singing. Empty churches, however, were built to be sung in. When singing, I was all myself, all with me. And I did not care that there were millions who sang better than me. Let them go to the TV shows and prove their talent. Here and now, it was just I.

Sunshine, biking, singing – I was happy. Mr Right had to wait.

Even when I reviewed and sent the wedding pictures off to Klara in the afternoon, it did not throw me out of this wonderful state of Om.

In the evening, at Il Centro, Mary, Leo – and five women were already at the table. Plus two free chairs, one for me and one for 'Hans will join us later. He is still at the gym.'

Ah, yes, the male part would only join us later, because he was still defining his six-pack. Well, the purpose of priorities is that you set them. And, obviously, the people around the table were not a priority. My inner eye saw a testosterone evaporating, tanning-booth tanned muscleman prancing through the room, only handicapped by his exuberant potency, throwing a different pose with every step and kissing his bicep, tricepses and everything else he could reach.

The real Hans turned out to be a rather wispy, pale tot. Admittedly, compared to my imagination, even Schwarzenegger would have seemed a wimpy kid. In hindsight, Hans was probably just average and had not let us wait to perfect an astral body but to build up the tension. Not a lucky move.

Hans sat down, checked the tender and started hitting on the woman sitting opposite him: Tania – tall, blonde, attractive, legs down to the ground. He did not notice that he was not graced with the slightest discernible sign of interest. Or he studiously avoided noticing. This did not change during the evening –which, however, was not a problem, as our rejected group had much more fun than the poor object of desire who repeatedly and unsuccessfully tried to include us, especially her neighbour, in her communication. So did Mary, but she was equally ignored. Hans had smelt a rat. One rat.

And what did five single women and a couple talk about over good food and a glass of wine? About the world, his brother and their family and at some point –

men, precisely: incredible dates. If there were a world championship in this discipline, the title would be mine. While this obviously caused its moments, it also provided for good stories.

While we were going through our collections, Mary confessed that she and Leo had convened all the singles they could muster to finally help Hans find a partner. 'He is such a good soul, you know? But it seems that this doesn't really work. Well, it was worth a try.'

I only understood what she meant when Hans asked Tania for her plans on the weekend. The response was sobering. 'My fiancé is coming from Munich.' Hans's jaw dropped so abruptly that I was worried it could hit the table. The object of desire was not designated prey but co-organiser of the hunt, which was why she had continuously tried to redirect the chase to her neighbour. Well, lousy briefing, I would say. Hans's immediately instituted attempts to discover the treasure in what he had considered trash were moot – we did not appreciate being considered trash.

Too bad, so sad.

M1 – M10

Very much to my surprise, Hans called me a few days later. He wanted to join a hiking or cineaste group, and apparently, Mary had mentioned that I might help him with some Internet addresses. He suggested that we could have dinner together.

An evening appeared to be a rather flexible time frame, though, and I suggested lunch on Saturday. Hans agreed. 'Yes, why don't we go to the self-service place in the department store in Bahnhofstrasse? Whoever comes first can then already start eating.'

Another one of those 'Did he actually say that?' moments. He had not really proven to be equipped with the best of manners, but meeting up in a self-service place so that he could start eating before I would arrive, that was really advanced non-manners. Given that I was not fostering any romantic intentions, I had to be late to give him the opportunity to pull this through. It was not a date, so I classified it as a social experiment.

Fortunately, I had more exciting plans for Friday: Speed dating for expats and English speakers at the Honolulu Bar.

Scientists say ... a lot; amongst other things that one needs seven dates to find Mr Right. Statistically. The speed dating website promised ten dates for the evening, so I should go home happily in love. If not, I would call upon Churchill and henceforth only believe in statistics that I had doctored myself.

Upon arrival, I was immediately led to the ladies' waiting area, 'to make sure that you do not see the gentlemen, yet.' I would not have considered that too much of an issue on a dating night but I trusted that the organizers knew what they were doing. Obviously, a certain level of alcoholic intoxication was, if not a necessity, then an advantage. Prosecco was handed out generously.

When ten men and ten women had gathered, the master of ceremonies introduced us to the art of speed flirting.

Each lady would sit at a table with a number. The gentlemen, carrying a badge with a number, would join them. Every seven minutes, the gentlemen would change the table and hence the conversation partner. We got lists with potential topics for discussion, 'but of course there is no right or wrong in what you discuss, only the chance to meet extraordinary people.' As always.

So, this was the land of male and honey, and all I had to do was wait for the good stuff to land on my plate. Finally, Tarzan would swing by and land right next to me. Nice.

'After every round, you write down the number of the person you spoke to and check whether or not you want to meet him or her, again. At the end of the evening, we will analyse the data and if the other person also wants to see you, again, we send you both a text message with each other's telephone number. You can also check our website, tomorrow. All right? Great, then I may ask the ladies to take a seat and off we go.'

I sat down and morphed into F8.

M8 sat down at my table. 'Hi, I am Dominic.' Obviously, he found this as bizarre as I did. 'This is my first time. Strange, somehow, this whole thing. Don't you think?'

'Yes, I also feel a bit strange. Reminds me of a supermarket. Even though the steak does not pick the buyer, of course.' Dominic kept a straight face.

What followed was the usual small talk on job, hobbies, non-family – non-committal and pleasant. We did not have to revert to the questions we had been provided, but I was also not struck by a lightning, I did not feel butterflies, and the world kept turning at its usual pace. But can you expect that after seven minutes? I felt that this was asking too much, and I ticked the box that I wanted to see him, again. Maybe, the second encounter would feel more relaxed.

Same experience with M9. Seven minutes were too short to make up my mind about the rest of my life – with or without him? Maybe because I had never experienced love at first sight. Or because I no longer believed in it. Or maybe, the whole problem was that, deep down in my heart, I did in fact believe in love at first sight and waited in vain for it to happen. Or was I too undecided? Did I know what I wanted?

At least, I decided quickly that I did not want M10. That was better than nothing. He was a paediatrician. When I uttered the admittedly not too original platitude 'Oh, that must be a wonderful job, to be working with children!' he barked at me how much these spoiled little brats were getting on his nerves, only surpassed by their constantly googling parents who kept coming up with the most exotic diagnoses and therapies. And how he hated his job. And, actually, pretty much everything. What a cutie pie!

Well, in all fairness, I did understand him to some extent. The medical dramas on TV with their antiseptic diseases, telegenic and angelic children and jubilant parents who gratefully shook the noble saviour's hands with tears in their eyes, choked by gratitude ... well, those were not documentaries. Frustrating but true. I had dropped my dream of becoming a vet upon the realization that nothing and no one scared our dog as much as the vet did. That had been at age six or seven, so it was surprising that M10 had not seen that. And if he was so unhappy with his life, he had to change something. And with that, I did not mean that he should find a partner to bleat at.

M1 also dropped out before entering the competition. He slouched all over the chair and fired off. 'I am Roger. Not married. No kids, as far as I know. I am a mechatronics technician. From Klosterfelden. But you don't know that, of course.' Actually, I had just been there, but M1 was too occupied with himself to have time for a communication. 'Primary school, secondary school, technical school – all as it should be. And I do motocross. After all, life's not just work. Last year, I even drove in a race in

Germany. Well, amateurs, of course. But still. But no worries about the pit babes. I prefer curvy women. Like you.'

So, was this a compliment? Was it baseness? Or just blabber? I switched off until he hit my hand. 'So, my three-and-a-half minutes are over. Now, it's your turn.'

Oh, my gosh – seriously? He had taken exactly three-and-a-half minutes, to the second. I had not prepared a three-and-a-half minute biography. I gave it a try, nevertheless. 'My name is Johanna. I am a lawyer. Originally from Berlin, but I have been living in Zurich, for a while, now. I love it here, especially the mood at the train station on a Sunday morning, when everyone is heading for the mountains. I always say that I am lucky to live in a place where other people would be happy to spend their vacation. Even though, Berlin is also great. Do you know Berlin?'

'Well, I have never been to Berlin, but to Blackpool – so cool. This is why I am here at the English language speed flirting, you know. I spent a weekend there with friends. Boy, we were so trashed. Alcohol is practically free, there, you know, at least compared to Switzerland. And the women are – wow!' Lucky me, I could go back to standby mode. I refused to even try to find out more about the obvious mystical connection between Berlin and Blackpool. Obviously, it was all in the 'B'. The remaining three minutes, M1 enlightened me about the virtues of British women with a particular emphasis on those women who tended to attend hen nights in Blackpool. Which did not quite include me. I nodded absent-mindedly, every now and then, but Roger did not notice.

I glanced at the list of questions. 'Do you believe in eternal love?' 'If I allowed you to blindfold me, what would you do with me?' 'What was the worst thing you ever did?' 'What was the best day of your life?' 'What does your perfect day look like?'

Unfortunately, none of that information was of any interest to me as far as M1 was concerned. But eventually, that did not matter. M1 was content with himself, as it was.

M2, too, lived in his own world. He was wearing a quilted, tight-fitting pink jacket with a Porsche emblem. There are few men who can wear pink. M2 was not one of them. He banged his keys on the table. With the Porsche pendant on top. Yes, I got it: He was a real cool guy. I did him the favour. 'Hi, I am Johanna. I see you like Porsches.'

'Yeah, of course. Steve. Yes, I have a Porsche. What a car! You wouldn't believe how the women dig that car. You never know if the chicks really want you or the Porsche. What car do you have?'

He was right, actually. I really could not believe that women were craving for such a car. 'I do not have a car, actually. I don't think I need that in Switzerland.'

He took my hand and looked me in the eyes understandingly – had someone died? 'Well, I understand. Not everyone can afford a car.'

I took my hand back. 'Well, if I wanted a Porsche, I would go to a store and buy one. But I don't want one. What else do you do all day when you don't drive your Porsche?'

'Investment banker. But, seriously, you must drive a Porsche, some day. Then, you'll know what you've been missing. Just like real good sex. You cannot imagine that if you haven't experienced it. Talking about that: Do you know the blonde at the next table? Can you give me a hint on how to score with her? Has she told you anything before you came in? You know, my last girlfriend was so prudish. Really annoying. I gave her the Kama Sutra for Christmas, a coffee table book, with all the pictures. Really expensive. But the stupid cow was just too dumb to sort that out. Boy, how I struggled to get that done. And she just said 'Darling, wait a second, I have to check whether we are doing it right, here.' Bullocks! And she really should have known, and should have been much cooler with it. After all, she is a vet. Her practice is in …'

'Steve, I really think that this is none of my business.'

Anyway, Steve giggled on about the good joke he had apparently just cracked.

Porsche, sex talk, investment banker. Did I see a golden necklace and a bracelet? No, really? Why do some people have to impersonate every stereotype? I did not feel comfortable discussing his sex life. At a first not-even-date. And I did not want to become material for his next round of bitching. Setting aside the fact that I was apparently Quasimoda, with whom one could safely discuss the other, obviously more interesting women. The only escape was – well, to escape, if not from the room then at least from the subject.

'Say, Steve, what kind of movies do you watch?' That should signal clearly that I had no intention of working through or discussing the Kama Sutra, here and today.

'Well, I totally dig action movies, like Lethal Weapon or Rambo or so. But, you know, about my ex, she was also really ungrateful. I mean, I gave her the cool book. And it was so expensive. With the paintings and all. I mean, I was entitled to great expectations. And then, she just said that this was all too complicated and that if she wanted to do Yoga, she would do so at the gym, not in bed. What a frigid cow.'

On the upside, he was not a porn addict. I was sure he would have said so had he been. On the downside, he had not swallowed the red herring. Another two minutes. Had someone manipulated the clock? All clocks?

'Rambo and Lethal Weapon. An acquaintance of mine also likes those. He is Korean. Do you like to travel?'

'Absolutely. Berlin, New York, Thailand. Thailand is so cool! It's all happening there. The women there absolutely dig European men, so I feel like a king. I cannot even fend them off, that's so cool. And it's almost for free. No comparison with the hookers here. Say, have you ever had a threesome?'

Gong, rescue me! What had I done to deserve this guy?

'Well, this is too personal for me. I hardly know you.'

Finally, the gong! Bell-like sound of salvation! Steve murmured 'What a frigid bitch!' and waddled off. Porsche-Man ran definitely a different race.

M3 was British – and a lot of it, as far as volume was concerned. At least, there was more of him than the shirt had been designed for. It was a little, well, very tight on the belly, it had also surrendered two buttons to the superior powers of mankind, uncovering unknown territories that I really did not fancy exploring, and stressing the lunch leftovers near the empty button holes. Tomato sauce. Enjoy!

M3 was insurance mathematician and freelance theatre critic, and unfortunately, he fulfilled all associated clichés. Cynicism and tartness, coupled with underdeveloped social competence; that was really not a felicitous combination. He lamented at length about all the idiots surrounding him and complained about how difficult it was to find someone who was even remotely able to follow him intellectually. And if there were an intellectual match, then it would be a man, because women spent their days talking about shoes, makeup and fashion. And they would not understand his job, anyway.

Well, he was obviously living testimony of the fact that one could also care too little about clothing, and most women would probably have sent him to the car wash, first. Without a car. But I felt no urge to tell him. I did not care that much about him, really. I also kept my little secret that there were actually numerous interesting topics for discussion between the extreme poles of insurance mathematics and makeup.

But I did not want him to die ignorant. 'Well, I do know your probability models, in principle, that is. I work for an insurance company, too. But eventually, life is a series of butterfly effects, anyway, Sheldon.'

'Well, that's a coincidence that you know about that. But why are you calling me Sheldon? My name is Ernest.'

Ah, he had no TV. I decided not to drag this higher life form down to the lowlands of trivial non-culture and asked which theatre productions had recently caught his interest. That turned out to be a mistake, too, unfortunately. To make a long story short: None. Productions were boring, actors incompetent and the plays arbitrary. And seven minutes were a long time.

Wow, I had run into a little ray of sunshine. Maybe, I could tweak out a smile, anyway. 'Do you remember the black and grey period all over Europe in theatre in the eighties? Dark stage designs, the bad guys wearing leather coats and Nazi boots. No matter what you saw, it was black, grey, leather. And each and every director considered this concept truly unique and himself a genius. At some point, the spook was over. Fortunately. And then, I went to the Magic Flute with a friend and told her about that theatrical leather & latex phase. The curtain went up and everyone was wearing light green judo suits. We had to laugh so hard.'

M3 did not have to laugh.

I did not give up so easily. 'That was a weird evening, anyway. First, we had to wait outside half an hour past the original opening time. And then, two men with a hearing aid were sitting in front of us. We were really impressed that they went to the opera despite their handicap. The director entered the stage, greeted the Prime Minister of Norway in the audience and apologized for the delay and the security measures. Only then did it dawn on us that the men in front of us were not hearing impaired but bodyguards. We laughed until they turned around, and I explained to them why we were laughing. Really funny.'

So, would this confession of my own dopiness tickle out a smile from him? No. Instead, a tirade about the lack of inspiration on the part of the directors. Why would someone spend so much time and energy on something he did not enjoy?

Anyway, I would not spend more time and energy on M3, for that exact reason: I did not enjoy it.

At least, I seemed to fit into his predatory pattern, and he went off saying, 'It was really great to meet you. I absolutely enjoy dating women your age. It's just so much more relaxed. Kids are no longer an issue, and no one holds ticking biological clocks of any type to your ear, all the time.'

Yep. That was exactly what I wanted to hear. What any woman wanted to hear, actually. Well, he probably had a point, though. I would not have wanted to feel like a potential sperm donor under assessment, either.

My joyous expectation had transformed into anxious apprehension. How many more were to come? Four. That should be feasible. Survivable, that was.

Surprisingly, I really hit it off with M4 (Tony), even though he was not my type. He looked like my old physics teacher. But that was not his fault, so I faded out the optics.

M4, Tony, was a recycling advisor and loved his job. His enthusiasm was highly contagious – old plastic cups were exciting! For years, I had been fighting a lost battle against my colleagues' bad habit of using disposable cups, as if china and glass had not yet been invented. In my missionary zealousness, I had even given them mugs for Christmas, which were now being used as pencil holders. 'You know, Jo, the mugs are much work, having to rinse them all the time.'

So, I was sitting in the Honolulu Bar with Tony, raving about hikes in the mountains, long bike trips, the Rigi, the Rhine, the Aare and of course the Matterhorn. He told me about the cow (as in 'Mooo') that had joined him on a hike, I told him about picking blueberries in Ticino. And all that without any disposable dishes.

When the gong separated us, I had to tell him. 'Tony, that was real fun. Thank you so much. I was almost ready to give up.'

He also ticked 'Meet again'. 'Yes, I enjoyed talking to you, too. But why give up?'

'Well, I just could not click with some of them. One only talked about his Porsche and sex. That was really unpleasant.'

'Are you talking about Stefan? He is my best friend. Well, then things will not work out for us, I'm afraid. Too bad.' He changed his choice to 'Not meet again' and left.

Dangit! What an idiot I was! Why could I not keep my big mouth shut? And why were the Swiss so damn loyal? Well, it was a bit too soon for a theatrical 'I cannot live without you!' scene.

Could things become worse? I had enough but felt that I could not just leave.

M5, Daniel, turned out to be a real surprise, though: He

smiled. That won him extra points. I was easy to please by now.

Daniel generously spread his smile and his enthusiasm when telling me about his encounters. Apparently, there were some real characters among the ladies, as well, and we laughed together about our experiences. Not too loud, of course. He, too, loved traveling and told me about his trips so vividly that it felt like I had joined him. Seven minutes were way too short, and I would have loved to ask him to stay. Unfortunately, this was not possible, but at least, it was a very clear 'Meet again'.

M6. A man who knew what he wanted. 'Hi, I am the one you've been waiting for. And, what do you think about all of this? Quite lame, isn't it? Say, do you have plans for the evening? My apartment is right around the corner, and I'm sure that we will find something to excite us.'

Yes, that was exactly what I needed. I had not thought that someone would so casually top Steve. I claimed a case of emergency and waived not only the remaining six minutes but also the chance for an encore with M6.

I wanted to go home.

But I still needed to meet M7. And, indeed, M7 really made the evening complete. Green corduroy pants, brown-green checked shirt, all buttoned up, leather tie, brown slipover. The dressing twin of mom's darling from the housekeeping class. I had wondered where such clothing came from and whether one could buy it or had to knit it oneself, but apparently, that was a real business.

M7 – Francis – was one of those specimen who appear like professional actors, because they just cannot be for real. But Francis was for real. I was sure that he would have been a sweet guy if only his shyness had permitted him to look me in the eyes or at least to respond to one of my questions with any other response than an aspirated 'Dunno'. He smiled at me appeasingly, like the bunny at the snake. I gave up quickly. I did not want to torture him but to get to know him, and that obviously made him feel very uncomfortable. Francis evoked motherly feelings. However, I was not looking for a mission but for a partner.

The last gong. Another experience made. Fine. I hoped that I would see Daniel, again. And, indeed, he approached me at the exit, smiling. But why the camera? 'Johanna, I have a confession to make. I told you that I am a journalist. What I did not tell you is that I am working on an inside report about dating. And you are such a nice person that I thought you might want to be the peg for my story. Then, the whole story would be about you and your quest for love. With photos. Oh, and I would like to introduce you to my wife. Here she comes. Darling!'

I felt sick. Really sick. 'No, please don't, that's not necessary. And I don't want to be in the newspaper, either. I have to go.' What a finale!

I was happy that neither he nor anyone else followed me into the streetcar. My eyes were under water. No one had to see that. Half an hour later, 'Your happy speed dating team – the place where love comes with a bang' sent me Daniel's number. I deleted it.

Hans

Just for the sake of completeness, I checked the next morning whether anyone else had uttered the desire to see me, again. But, again, only Daniel with his investigative interest was smiling at me. Becoming the figurehead of the partner-less was not my aspiration.

I would have loved to tell M8 and M9 that I had not fancied them that much, either, but that I had given them a chance. Because this was what decent people did. I felt like watching a dating report, where beer-bellied, greasy haired men in sweaty Hawaii shirts who could hardly form a sentence with more than three words, were looking for a wife. Preferably an Olga from Kazakhstan. Said Olga was then supposed to fling herself around his neck or, better even, to his feet, swept away by a tempest of passion, desire and lascivious devotion, because some Bernd would redeem her from Kazakhstan to his janitor-bedsit in some basement in Craptown. Said Olga is a molecular biologist with model features whose only mistake in life was to have been born in the wrong part of an unfair world.

All of that, I would have loved to yell or even just say to someone. But there was no one. I had served myself on a silver platter and been rejected.

I had to re-direct my energy to useful purposes, and went to the gym. Usually, I wondered why there were so few men in the classes, but today, I did not mind. Right now, I considered this part of mankind highly dispensable.

Even the Greek god in the back row, kicking and beating, panting and sweating away, generously showering his Greek goddess by his side with his charm … I only casually glanced at them. Couples! But I had to admit that it was nice to see two people in such casual harmony, at ease with themselves and the world.

By noon, I had fortunately calmed down and recovered emotionally. Honestly, I was not in the mood to see Hans, but given that I would not be in that mood, either, on any other given day, I arrived on time, with the planned delay of two minutes. And, Bingo, I found Hans, munching away his cannelloni. He had obviously come early, which had resolved the obnoxious issue of who pays with finality and the desired outcome. I did not want a date with him, but it would have been nice to invest minimal courtesy. I would have paid myself, anyway, as was the norm in Switzerland, or probably I would have invited him to avoid any sense of obligation on my part. Men! Taken, only for men – or Hans.

Lunch was over just as quickly as Hans had arrived. I gave him some tips and Internet addresses for meeting people, but that did not even provide enough material for fifteen minutes of chatting. The elderly lady sitting next to us at the long table intervened and gracefully shared all details of her recent cancer check-up. What did it say about my love life that I preferred the field report on a stranger's proctoscopy to a non-date with Hans?

In this mood, I was not even too surprised about a rather bizarre experience, in the elevator on my way home. Upon entering, I heard a voice. 'Don't worry, just go.'

I looked around, even though I knew that I was alone. 'Where are you?'

The voice insisted. 'Up here. No worries. Just enter.'

Indeed, the voice came from above. Well, not THAT above. The close above. Apparently, someone was sitting on the elevator – or kneeling or whatever one did up there.

I only knew extraordinary elevator use situations from the movies, and there, they tended not to end well. 'Actually, I don't think this is a good idea. Can't you just come down?'

'No problem. Just go ahead. I do this, all the time. Regular maintenance.'

So, the time had come that men did not even want to share an elevator with me, any more. Somehow, that made sense. I pushed the button, and – Eureka! – my travel companion was still alive when we reached the ground floor.

Coming home, I found a letter from Klara in my mailbox. She thanked me for the photos from her wedding and invited me to her Halloween party. On a Thursday, six weeks from today. Cool, I would add a long weekend and see some friends in Berlin. That was exactly what I needed. Good friends are there for you when you need them, even if you do not even know that you do.

I called her. 'Hey, sweetie! How is the married couple Dobberin?'

'Great! You know, I had not expected that, but somehow, it does feel different when you say 'This is my husband Konrad.' He is such a darling. You know, when we meet somewhere and I see his wedding band, and I get all disappointed that he is married so that I cannot flirt with him. And then, I remember that he is my husband and that I can flirt all I want with him. And that just makes me so happy. The only thing is that he works too much. But look who I'm talking to, you are no better than him. Hey, tell me, are you coming to our party? You know most of our guests, anyway: Desi, Sinéad and Bernd, Mark. All the good ones, you know. We will be at least 30 people.'

'Sure. I would not want to miss out on that. And, do you have to go as a pumpkin, already?'

'Naa, cut it out! Why is everyone asking me that? We married because we wanted to, not because we had to. And, anyway, nowadays you do not even have to marry if you have to marry. And, seriously, with Konrad's working hours, the stork is off duty, anyway. Counter question: What will you come as?'

'Oh, I have not thought about that, yet. Maybe as Quasimoda. Or as the Invisible Hulk. For that, I would not even have to dress up.'

'Do I sense an undertone, here? Tell me!' Klara knew me, and I graciously accepted the shoulder that she had offered.

So, Klara learned all about the housekeeping class, the 3.5 minute dater M1, Porsche Man M2, Cynichub M3, the hiker with Porsche appendix M4, our literary hope M5, Sex Machine M6, shy M7 and the social miracle Hans. And about the fact that the 7-date-rule apparently did not apply to me.

Klara was appropriately sympathetic. She confirmed that this was really not my fault but the lack of supply. 'Who knows, maybe something happens at our party. The only confession I have to make is that we will have a full house, that night. Can you sleep somewhere else?'

'Yes, sure. And about the somethinghappening: The only one I picked up at your party is green, fluffy and stuffed and dangling from my backpack. Maybe, I should come as a princess and check out whether I find a nonfrog for kissing, this time.'

'Cool, we do not have a princess, yet. Promise you come as a princess.'

'That was a joke. I was not born to be a princess. My father always said that I might become gentle if I worked on it, but never genteel. And certainly not elegant.'

'You know, your dad could be quite mean, I must say. Well, he probably thought this was funny. I guess that was the way he was. Best regards from my dad, by the way. He was so happy that you sat next to each other.'

'Yes, that was really nice. Your dad is a sweetheart. The only thing he may have to work on is his timing when it comes to speeches. Well, on the other hand, he will not have to do another father-of-the-bride one. How is he doing?'

'Do you remember the elderly lady with the violet

dress? The one with the big straw hat? Konrad's aunt Ruth. From his mother's side. You know, they are just getting together, still in the trial phase. Not her and Konrad, of course, but her and my dad. They are happy like teenagers freshly in love. I knew that widowers his age are not in the market for long.'

'I'm happy for him. Great that he is no longer alone.' Again, happiness by proxy. Why did everyone find love in a flash while I was still searching for my first big love? Wasn't it my turn, finally? Well, life was not fair, and it was certainly not Mr Miller's fault that I was the only un-Bill'd Jill on this planet. Or felt like it. Still, it started getting at me.

'And, how do you feel about it? Isn't it strange that your father is with someone else?'

'Well, they are very happy together. And that makes me happy, of course. But in the beginning, it was weird to see him with another woman. Probably a bit like him seeing me bringing home a man, for the first time. Just that now, I have the protective instincts and hope that she will not hurt him. And of course, I feel like I would not even exist if he had met her before my mom. I feel a bit like a mistake. But that's totally unwarranted, of course. If this works out, that's great for him. And it makes things much easier. He has already told me that he will go on vacation with Ruth, for Christmas. For us, this makes things much easier, too. That's quite pleasant. By the way, what are your plans for Christmas?'

'Nothing special.' Since the death of my parents, Christmas had been an iffy subject.

'What do you mean, nothing special? Aren't you going to your brother's? Why don't you come here? Konrad's family is coming, but you know them, anyway. They would sure be happy to see you. They really liked you.'

'Klara, you are a darling. That's really sweet of you, but Christmas is family time. I do not want to spoil your party. It's not your fault that I am alone. You know, last year, it was actually quite nice. I went to Christmas service in the *Grossmünster*. But I must admit it was weird to be praying for the people who were alone and to know that I was one of them.'

'Lady, you are exaggerating. Think about it and let me know if you change your mind. And what about New Year's? Don't tell me that you were all by yourself that night, too?'

'No, I was at a New Year's dinner at a hotel. Just to avoid the crappy moment at midnight, when everyone kisses the most important person in his or her life, and you as a single stand there all by yourself until everyone else has returned from cloud nine to the here and now. Once, I went to the New Year's fireworks at Lake Zurich: 100'000 couples doing lip service of almost all kinds. And me.' In the moments that counted, singles were alone.

'Shit. Yes, I had almost forgotten that feeling. Not that I would have cared to remember, I always hated that. And, was last year's party fun?'

'Well, they had told me that they would have a table for singles. But when I arrived, everything was geared towards couples. With a price for the most beautiful couple, the best dancing couple and what not. With the singles nicely spread all over the place. One for every table. The couple next to me then insisted on having a separate table, so that I spent the night next to two empty chairs on one side and a flirting couple on the other. The only remotely funny moment was when the couple complained that there were no fireworks in the neighbourhood, at midnight. Well, they had obviously failed to notice that the hotel was situated next to the cemetery.'

Klara giggled briefly. 'I see, we have to discuss that when you are here. I will not allow you to celebrate Christmas by yourself and New Year's Eve, on the cemetery. And if you do not come here, we come to you. But first, you come over for Halloween. Jo, I gotta go. Huggies, my dear! See you, soon, Prinicpessa! You promised.'

I called Tina – deal, I would stay with her and Lars. My mood improved. Then, I called my brother Christian. I poured my basked of unhappiness over him.

'Jo, come over. We would love to have you. Always. You are part of our family, and the children have asked already if you are coming. We love you.'

Fortunately, he could not see that I was close to tears. 'And I love you. And I miss you. You all. Why can't you at least live on the East Coast? Then I could come for a long weekend. Or for Christmas. But San Francisco – you know, I cannot go on leave around Christmas. That's the privilege of the people who have children. They take priority. And I cannot spend two of three days on the plane.'

'Why do the people with children come first? They have their family close. Singles have to travel to be with their loved ones, not families. Don't you think that you can get that arranged?'

'No, I can't. Christmas is family.'

'Shit. And your friends?'

'Yes, they have invited me, too. But I don't want that. Christmas is family. And I happen not to have a family of my own. Yes, I know I have you, but you know what I mean. And it is not your fault that I am alone.'

'Jo, please think about it, again. I am sure that Klara or Stella or Mary would love to see you. You have us, and you have them, and you know that you are always welcome. We mean it, and so do your friends. I cannot bake a partner for you, but still: You have a family, and that's us.

Say, do you want to talk to Larissa?'

He called my niece Larissa to the phone, and we talked about school, the fact that boys were stupid (in America, too), that guinea pigs were great, and about her last concert. Christian knew how to cheer me up.

An hour later and in a much better mood, I booked my flight for the long weekend in Berlin. Christian was right. I was not alone. Not all alone, that was.

CHM7K5KW

On Sunday, even though and because speed dating had worked sub-optimally, I sallied out into the beautiful world of online dating. While national and international media announced that it was socially accepted, I still felt like a bargain on sale, waiting for a taker. Even though I knew perfectly normal people with no obvious deficiencies who had met their partners, online. I pulled myself together. It was worth a try. Definitely. Probably. Probably definitely.

But the Internet had placed an inquisition between myself and success. I had to fight my way through an hour of psychological testing. Many of the questions that would now guide my way to happiness, I had never thought about. Was I a morning person or a night owl? I considered myself relaxed, friendly and just likeable around the clock, really. Well, maybe I was a tiny bit biased, in this regard. Would I mind if my partner smoked? Here, too, the response was not easy. After all, smoking is not smoking. A cigarette on the balcony impacted me only peripherally. A pipe, lit in the living room, lingering for days, was a whole different story – especially as pipe aficionados generally believed that it was incredibly homely for everyone else to drown in clouds of smoke. You were expected to collectively feel reminded of your old, Santa-like grandfather and enjoy. I did not feel that sentiment. But, anyway, I did see the nexus between these questions and the viability of a partnership.

As for other questions, I was slightly concerned that my future felicitousness was to depend on my responses. 'Do you sleep with windows open or closed?' Well, that would depend on the noise level and the temperature outside. 'Which interior design style do you prefer?' Comfortable, I guess.

The real psychological questions, however, were spooky. 'Which square is darker?' 'Which shape do you prefer – the circle or the oval?' I would have loved to see these deciphered. Did a preference for the circle expose me as a bore? Or were ovalists potential mass murderers? I would probably never know.

The result surprised me. Allegedly, CHM7K5KW was a completely different person than the Johanna I knew. She was not at all controlled solely by the brains but rather she was a bundle of emotions driven by the heart. Crap! I had always been a head person, not a heart person. Period. And I had no intention of always compromising my own wishes for the sake of a relationship like the person I was reading about. I stood my ground at work and would do so in my private life, as well. I should have ticked the circle!

If I could not recognize myself in the description, then potentially interested parties would hardly find the person from the description in me. Not good. And why did the program in its eternal wisdom decide that I, an independent spirit, desperately needed a clinger by my side? In all likelihood, this would neither make him happy nor me. But then, I had decided to give it a try. And now that I was in it, I had to trust – well, a machine, it seemed, and go with the rules. And maybe, it was time for me to meet another side of myself.

But first, I had to describe the side that I knew: Hobbies, music, sports, that part was a piece of cake. But subjects like 'Three things I do not want to miss', 'Traits I do not like in others', 'My perfect day', 'My feel-good oasis', 'What / who would you want to be if you were reborn?', 'My favourite vacation', 'A weakness of character'; all of this was quite personal. So, I either had to bare my soul, serving myself on a silver platter – or keep a low profile that would perish in the masses. I tried my best to hit middle ground.

'Three things I would not want to miss' – That was easy. My bike, my photos and my spectacles. Being short sighted, my life expectancy in a world without glasses would have been extremely limited, and I would have had to thrust myself into the arms of the first visually gifted guy coming my way, hoping that it really was a man and not a bear. Well, maybe this conundrum would have made finding a partner easier…

'Traits I do not like in others' – Arrogance, egoism, people who permanently interrupted others. Allegedly, one tends to particularly dislike one's own bad habits in others. Were those my weaknesses? Nope, I did not think so.

'My perfect day' – Easy. Get up early, grab my bike or the hiking boots and bike (by myself) or hike (never alone) all day, stop at a church on the way to sing a little bit, have a good dinner with friends.

'My feel-good oasis' – The mountains. Considering that I had grown up in the flat surroundings of Northern Germany, I was remarkably mountainesque.

'A person I would like to meet' – „The Pope' could be misunderstood, just as „Leonardo di Caprio' or „Angelina Jolie'. Even though I really found all three of them truly interesting. So, it was Leonardo da Vinci.

„What / who would you want to be if you were born, again?' – Fortunately, I had given this some thought, before. A blackbird. Sings beautifully, is not on the middle European menu, and black makes for a slender complexion. And who else has his own Beatles song, of course.

'My favourite vacation' – Namibia. Sleeping under a sky of glistening pinheads. Watching the elephants taking a sun downer at the water hole, the giraffes sounding out how the land lies for hours before they drink, the zebras racing off at the slightest commotion, and the reason for the whole caution: the lions lying next to the water hole, pretending to be cute little pussycats.

'A weakness of character' – Did I want to dissect that and put it on the table even before the first date? Not that I considered myself perfect, but I simply did not always think about how great or not great I was. Should I write something completely meaningless? No, that would be false labelling. Like Jack the Ripper saying that he sometimes tended to be slightly impolite. So, what would get on my nerves if I weren't me? 'I am quite extroverted and this is probably strenuous at times.' This was accurate and should suffice. A rocky road.

'How attractive do you find yourself?' – Well, just like one finds oneself. Some pounds too much but other than that, quite okay. Unfortunately, 'Quite okay' was not one of the available categories, only 'Extremely attractive', 'Very attractive', 'Attractive', 'Likeable' or 'No comment' were on the list. I hoped that 'Likeable' was the code for 'Quite okay'.

After the compulsory exercises, I turned to what I hoped would be the freestyle: The men of the day.

A presumably impressive data processing centre had compiled a list of prospective partners. Awarding points. The Grand Prix d'Eurovision de La Liaison. „Johanna – Sept Points'. I could sort the men by points, by location, age, and, and, and. Frightening enough, most of them considered themselves 'Extremely attractive'. I had not known that I was living in the land of male beauty.

The point system had a distinctly surreal touch. After generations of poets, musicians and philosophers had tried to decipher the inner soul and the secret of love, our generation had gone ahead and replaced poetry by a value. '107'. Efficient. Sobering. I was no longer Jo, I was CHM7K5KW. And I was not funny, friendly, feisty, outgoing or annoying, I was, depending on the counterparty, a 122. Or a 103. Or a 58.

If there was a 122, should I even look at a 105? Or would 53 be the love of my life, because a computer is just a computer, after all? And if I were the 121, would someone who had a 122 'at hand' even respond to me? What was the potential maximum value, anyway? The illusion of unlimited availability of eligible partners.

I refused to let numbers bully me around and checked

out the profiles – age, profession (usually, 'financial sector' – I was in Zurich), children, hobbies, relationship status... Surprisingly many were 'Separated'. Were they just in it for an adventure? Or were they hoping to hop into the next relationship, without a stopover at themselves? Wouldn't it be better to first conclude history? What would they do if the old relationship was revitalized, after all? No, I did not want to be the fall back solution in case things did not work out with the not-yet-ex. One click and they were ex.

On the other hand, I gave bonus points to the fathers. I had always known that I would have children. Slowly, time was running out – even though I had never believed in the urgency of biological clocks ticking. Stella had told me to just buy the required ingredient. Or check out what or who was available at the disco. A viable path, but not mine. I wanted children, but I wanted them with someone I loved and respected, with whom I would share the joy and the burden. Single mothers seemed to fight for survival, for sleep and for the air to breathe. I did not want that. Of course, one could never know whether a relationship would last, but at least I wanted a chance at having an old fashioned family. And if there were children, already, so much the better. Or did I want too much?

So, I clicked through the male supply. While browsing through the lives of others, I felt like pulling down the shades. Just like me, these men had tried to describe in an almost public market place what constituted their personality. That required courage. Most of all towards oneself, admitting that one did not find a partner in the free hunting ground, for whatever reason. And they, too, had struggled. With varying success. They all enjoyed time with friends, hiked, biked, usually skied, went to concerts and the movies and were looking for someone to laugh, discuss and go to bed with. Like me. Of course, after all, those were men with whom I supposedly made a good match.

But their self-descriptions, too, were rather uniform. Statistically, I, or 'You' was extremely popular. The person most of them wanted to meet was 'You', the perfect day was a day spent with 'You', and the one thing on Earth nobody wanted to miss was also 'You', or rather me. But, naturally, the individual candidate could not know that this was basically a standard response. Probably, my responses were also not as exuberantly individual as I found myself. But I would never know that. Hopefully.

One by one, I worked my way down the hit list. Like everyone, probably.

I picked four men:

- A communicative, fun-loving chemist from Berne, who loved classical music just as much as good food and long hikes with his dog;
- A doctor with a child in Zug, who shared my love for the movies and traveling, in particular in Asia and Africa;
- A musician from Zurich, who enjoyed cooking and photography and wanted to meet the Dalai Lama;
- And a teacher from Basel, who did a lot of biking, sang in a choir and wanted to be reborn as a bird.

I concluded the contract with the dating platform so that I could really start communicating with these men. Without payment, all you got were the teasers. The contract would run for half a year and then automatically renew if I did not terminate in time. What was that to tell me about my chances of success? That I had no chance of finding anyone within half a year, anyway? Or that I should reconsider my options if I had not found anyone within six months? I determined to terminate the contract, the next day, to avoid it silently slipping into prolongation while I would hopefully indulge in the joy of love.

No risk, no fun – I wrote a brief note to all four. There would be time to get to know each other, later. I also uploaded photos of myself to the website, so that they would know how I defined 'Likeable'. And now, it was no longer in my hands.

To satisfy my purely investigative interest, I also checked whom the system had categorized as a nonmatch. And I had to admit, computers or rather their programmers were not all that dumb. I immediately saw that I would not really come into play with a 25 year old whose only hobby was 'Sex', whose feel-good oasis was 'My bed – or any plac were on can have sex' and whose outstanding (pardon) characteristic was that he was 'horny 24/7'. The 49 points for the two of us were clearly more than I would have given us. On the other hand, this increased my confidence that my four candidates might actually be the right ones. Or at least one. One would be enough.

The doctor was online. Brutally honest, the whole thing. Once you were in, there was no cheating. 'I didn't see your message' or 'My computer didn't work' were no-go's. And Mr Sex Machine would also see that I had visited his profile. Fortunately, he would not be able to read my thoughts.

Speaking of the devil – I received the happy news that Mister 49 points had checked my profile. And, Bingo, a few seconds later, the boy with the horizontal life plan sent a message. My first message on a dating platform! Not from one of my candidates of choice, but still, the inner fanfare could not be overheard.

'Hey you! I have sent hat you checked me out. And we have money points. Do you want two meat? At my place?'

Long live the spellcheck! The fact that 49 points were 'money' for him shed a very positive light on the women of Switzerland. I gracefully and gratefully declined – thankfully; the platform provided the appropriate platitudes for that. 'I have concluded that we do not really make a match.'

I had spent almost the whole day at the computer. Online dating was eating my time even before it had started. When I just wanted to shut off, things became exciting. A message from Martin, the Doctor. As far as looks were concerned, not my type – category blonde scrag. But this was not what mattered. After all, I was here to meet the true person and not just the outside. He had sent a complete CV. Two pages. Exciting. He loved classical music, arts, good food, had travelled the world, and I liked the way he wrote. Fun, easy-going – and only a good father could describe his daughter so lovingly. My heart beat faster and I was curious. Of course, this was his standard response, else he could not have sent it so quickly. But I did not care, really. You had to start somehow.

I responded immediately. Spoke about me, dug deeper and hoped to evoke his interest, too. The games had begun.

Martin

I dreamt that I was trapped inside a Chinese terracotta

warrior. I fumbled a tiny pebble out of my clay arm, and saw my own arm underneath, miles away. I also twiddled a small, heart-shaped gem out of my armour, but underneath, there was just clay.

In the morning, I wondered just briefly what this dream wanted to tell me, before checking my email. Martin had not yet responded. Well, it had been quite late in the day, really.

But I had received my first request: Pedro, a Spaniard living in Geneva, had written to me. Investment banker and model. With photos. Black-and-white, with a cool retro look. Wow! It was obvious that he was a model. A little young, maybe. I would have estimated him at 25 years at most, but could be wrong. After all, models build their careers on not ageing visibly, and he had unfortunately forgotten to indicate his age. Well, in any event, the „Extremely attractive' was, by regular standards, an understatement.

I wanted to take time for my response, so I would write in the evening.

Fortunately, my working day was no more eventful than usual – emails, telephone conferences, meetings, everything ASAP. The usual.

In the afternoon, however, a surprise landed on my desk: A file from our corporate archive. It dealt with a life insurance from 1927. Our archivists had actually found this file I had not even dared hope they would find. Carbon copies, handwritten drafts of letters and notes to file in Sütterlin, a handwriting I had not seen since my grandmother's death. Exchanges of letters that took months in the making. Formal protocols instead of some bullet points in an email. And no PowerPoint presentations.

Unfortunately, the quality of our communication had decreased even disproportionately when compared to the increase in quantity over the past decades. I received copies of copies of copies of emails that had no link with my tasks and me. Buried in communication, I sometimes did not get to do any real work, any more. And everything was urgent. Some colleagues had set the flag 'Urgent!' as a standard. Also when they sent the lunch invitation for next month.

How pleasantly different this file was: A time in which only bank employees were even more boring than insurance agents. Well, and all male.

Maybe, life had generally been easier, at the time. You lived in a village, knew the potential partners or at least their children since childhood. And when time came, the families got together and made a match in the village, not in heaven. That appeared much more manageable than millions of singles with a score on a virtual marriage market.

However, this system likely only worked in the given context, with the existing gender roles: The man brought home the dough, got the big piece of meat and dealt with the children only inasmuch as punishments needed to be handed out. The woman was in charge of house, home, hearth, hungry children and husband and frequently had an external job by the side, on top of it all. And church propagated marriage as the glue that kept this symbiotic community together, not as a promise of eternal bliss.

Now, the roles were in a constant state of flux. While we women were constantly claiming new areas, the purported certainties of the male existence had gradually eroded, without having been replaced by new ones. The fact that boys were allowed to play with dolls and that men were allowed to iron could hardly be considered a value added when compared to the opportunities we women had won from the social revolution of the last decades. If I were a man, this would unsettle me. To keep it all together, we probably needed a new type of glue.

Granted, there were still some islands of manhood. In Zurich, those were the guilds, the members of which naturally were no longer armorers, blacksmiths, weavers or tanners, but bankers and other service providers. On the third Monday in April, the day of the six-o'clock bell ringing, the *Sechseläuten*, they dressed up in medieval costumes and paraded down Zurich's main street, with pomp and circumstance, by foot or on horses. At 6pm, they burned a paper snowman, the *Böögg*, more than 3m tall. The faster his head, stuffed with firecrackers, exploded, the better the summer would be. If you wish, a public execution light. The women were allowed to buy flowers and present them to their proudly marching hubbies.

A colleague of mine had once been invited 'to the *Sechseläuten*'. She had taken this as a date, but it had turned out to be a disaster when her proud 'cobbler' had asked her to celebrate the day in the ladies' room, while he would have a ball with his buddies. Granted, this was not your typical ladies' room but rather a hall in the basement where the wives and other women had dinner, but still... she was not amused, and he did not only take the biscuit but also permanent leave from her life.

I had lost myself in my thoughts and in the file. When I left the office, it was dark outside, of course – only the light from our deserted meeting room lit the pavement. I briefly struggled with myself: Should I ignore it? Like my colleagues? No, I went in and shut off the illumination. Why was it always just me who noticed such things? Or why was it always just me who cared? I had to think of Tony, the recycling advisor from the speed flirting. He would definitely do the same. Dang it that I had not managed to keep my big mouth shut! Looking back, striding from my deserted office to my equally deserted home in the cold of a dark night, he and the other speeders appeared in a more benevolent light. Was I too picky or did I apply the wrong criteria? But no one had wanted me, either. What was wrong with me?

Coming home, fortunately, an email from Martin triggered more positive sentiments. He was also happy about my message – well, that was a start! It would be a while until we could meet, though, as he was at a conference in Sydney for a week. He learned a lot, met colleagues and enjoyed the good food, the sunshine and the blue sky. Especially on this internally and externally grey day, I wished to be there, too.

I sent him a message, sharing some of my thoughts on the past. And I wrote on the weather in Switzerland.

Now, let's talk Pedro. I liked the way he described himself. Originally from Barcelona, now in Geneva. He wanted children, as long as he was still young enough to romp around with them and enjoy them. He still had not a single grey hair.

I responded:

'Dear Pedro,

I was very happy to receive your message. I am also a (happy) expat in Switzerland, but from Germany and in Zurich. But I also like Geneva and Barcelona. A town that is situated near the water is automatically beautiful. Do you also go swimming in the lake, in summer? In Zurich, people even do that during lunch break. I love this relaxed atmosphere.

I bet that being an investment banker is very strenuous. And to be a model on top of that – wow! I am heavily impressed. And I am also impressed that you are so clear in your wish for children. I feel the same. I am a dedicated aunt and love children. Do you have any nieces or nephews?

What about meeting up? Are you in or near Zurich, any time soon? I come to Geneva, every now and then, so I am sure that we can get this sorted out. And until then, I look forward to getting to know you better in writing.

All the very best,

Johanna'

Pedro responded promptly. Unfortunately, he had no plan of coming to Zurich, any time soon. He had just washed his hair – which, by the way, was pitch black. Other men his age would colour their hair, but not he.

I could not have cared less. I responded that I was, in fact, beginning to grow shades of grey. But this was to be expected, at 39.

I had hoped to bury the topic with these remarks. But when he presented me with new aspects of his truly unremarkable hair care program, in the next email, I became curious. I knew that I was not vain enough, but how often could a man wash his hair, and why was it so important that he had no grey hair?

I went online. There were not too many investment banker Pedros in Geneva. In word and deed, „my' particular sample was actually over 50. The photos he had sent dated back almost 30 years, to his student days, when he had actually worked as a model. By now, he was a very good-looking, grey-haired man.

I had to discuss this with Klara.

I described the situation to her, 'You know, for me, the

age is not an issue, at all, and he looks great. Wait, I send you a current picture. Did you get it?'

Klara agreed, 'Yes, he does have a George Clooney touch.'

'Exactly. And all women on this planet agree that George Clooney should not colour his hair. But if this is such a problem for Pedro, I will spend the rest of my life carrying the can with his complexes. I don't get that, anyway. A receding hairline, bald patches, hairy patches, no hairy patches – that's just a problem if you make it one.'

Klara laughed. 'You don't know how right you are. Do you remember our dog, Hasso? Always bunking off because of some seasoning bitch somewhere. I can't count how often we had to pick him up from the animal shelter.'

'Sure, I remember Don Hasso.'

'Well, when he turned older, he developed a bald patch on his tail. The vet then told us that on top of the tail, there are glands. When a dog is sexually hyperactive, these glands swell, so that there is virtually no more room for hair. From that perspective, baldness really is no issue at all.'

Now, I had to laugh, too. 'At least when you are a dog.' I had never looked at it this way. Pedro neither, I assumed.

'But seriously, Jo. How much trust can you have in a man who deludes you from the beginning? I mean, what kind of photo did you send him? And do you really want to be with someone who has such an issue with getting older, even though he is much older than you are? That's *so* unlike you.'

Good point. My photos were two months old and not even benevolently blurry. I said farewell to Pedro.

With Martin, however, a steady penpalship developed. He wrote about his journeys, the sunrise in Angkor Wat, the Holi festival in India, about hiking in Scotland; of the satisfaction and happiness to be able to help people, and time and again of his daughter. I told him about my bike ride along the Elbe, choir concerts and Africa. And with every email, I felt closer to him. The butterflies awoke.

I also got mail from the chemist in Berne. Bernard was not as talkative as Martin and suggested a meeting after an exchange of 43 words (from us both). We were to meet this Saturday, for a walk in Berne. How had Mr Miller said? 'Suit the action to the word, and all of that.' Willie, you know.

Meeting Bernard – was that cheating on Martin? He knew I was on the dating platform. I told myself that I would not mind if he wrote to other women. Not yet. And it was not even clear whether the whole thing would ever go any farther. My curiosity prevailed, and I accepted.

Two – well, what? 'Beaus' would be too much. Takers? Fish on the hook / approaching the hook / in the pond? Anyway, two whatevers! I spent the rest of the week humming and prancing through the office, until my assistant Lilo asked if I had won the lottery. No, I had not. Not yet.

On my way to Berne, I concentrated on being calm. With varying success. After all, this encounter might change my life.

Maybe, I would finally be struck by the lightning, which would pull away the ground from under my feet, and I would faint like Scarlett O'Hara. Of course very theatrically and preferably with a slight sigh. I did not quite know why everyone was always fainting with this little sigh, but it appeared to be the most unambiguous indicator of successful wooing. Sigh!

Or Bernard would turn out to be a crazy scientist who was building Frankenstein's monster, in his spare time and more interested in my liver than in me. Unlikely, but still more likely than the possibility of a theatrical sigh-fainting scenario on my end. I had a very stable constitution.

Or Bernard was actually Pedro, and we would go to the hairdresser's, together. To have our hair dyed.

Bernard was waiting in front of the station with Wummy, his St Bernard's dog. What a sight! Giant Wummy, tiny Bernard, connected by an umbilical cord. So much dog to cuddle! I loved Wummy at first sight.

While we made our way through Saturday's shopping crowds, Bernard defined the scope within which a potential partnership could be initiated. His partner would have to move in with him, in Wankdorf near Berne. She would have to have a job that involved no travel, left the house after him and came back before him. After all, he was not marrying to be all by himself, eventually. But he was a modern man, so it was fine if she would make more money than him. Of course, she would stay at home until the two children-to-be would go to school. Then, she would work, again, so that the family could afford stuff. At least as long as his parents could still live by themselves. Later, she would take care of his parents who conveniently lived in the same house.

The man had a plan.

Wankdorf? Would I want a man living in a place with that name? I did not quite see myself in such a regulated life, not with a man who claimed the right to make all decisions. I was speechless.

Bernard took this as consent.

Well, I should first learn a little more about him. This would also allow me to look behind his fixed ideas. He elaborately answered my questions, raved about Wummy, told me about his work, his siblings, his parents and his travels. 'Well, I have travelled all over, you see: London,

Paris, Munich, Davos, Arosa, Constance – actually, I go to Germany, quite a lot, to do my shopping. Toothbrushes are incredibly cheap, there. I always take the car, then I can load the trunk.'

'With toothbrushes?' He seemed to be a very dental person.

'No, I don't buy just toothbrushes! What do you think?'

So far, so good.

'And, what do you do when you travel, I mean, what are you interested in?' I inquired.

'Well, this and that. I like many things. Last month, I was in London, and I went to the opera.'

What a pleasant surprise. 'Wow, great, I love the opera, too. What did you see?'

'Well, I did not see anything, but I took a tour of the building.'

It took me just a few minutes to recover from that unexpected response. Unexpected but admittedly unique.

While we were walking along the river in the autumn sun and I inquired about him, not the slightest hint of curiosity developed, on his end. There was no 'And you?' nor any proactivity. More and more, I felt like a talk show host. While at the same time mastering an obstacle course. It had rained, and Bernard tended to circle pits closely. We had linked arms, so this tendency on his part unfortunately steered me right into the pits. Arduous. I de-linked.

After a while, I had reached the end of my questions. Where were the cheat sheets from the speed flirting now, when I really needed them? Without this reserve, however, I had shot all my arrows.

So, I started talking about myself, even though no one had asked me. 'You wrote that you like classical music. We will soon sing Orff's Carmina Burana with the choir. I love that.'

'Yes, this piece suits you fine.'

'O, thank you.'

'That was not meant as a compliment.'

Well, great! Wummy was following us at a distance. I turned around and headed back. Bernard followed. The farewell was short, friendly and final. Too bad, I liked Wummy. But I could not marry a man just because I had fallen in love with his dog. But then, this went out of question, anyway. While I was on the train to Zurich, Bernard struck me off his contact list. 'Sorry, you are just not my type.' Well. This *ius primae finis* seemed to be a special kind of home turf advantage.

I had to realize that, eventually, online dating also tends to lead to a first date. Only accentuated by the fact that you always wondered whether you wanted to live with this laughter, this voice or this whateverisannoying as long as you both shall live. After all, this was not just an encounter but rather potentially the initiation of a life relationship. So, the stakes were high.

And so you meet, Amor is on vacation or otherwise busy, and the date passes by just as uneventfully as in real life. Even though the computer system had concluded that Bernard was my one-and-only. So, did he not match me or did I not match him? Or did I not match myself? Had the program been hacked? Or were we the ideal couple, after all, and just too blind to see?

Well, not everyone was able to realize what was good for him. On my way home, I met my neighbour. I estimated that she was more than 80 years old. Bent forward after too many decades of hard work, she was carrying home her way-too-heavy shopping. I took her bags from her and chatted a little, when our discussion took an unexpected twist. I suggested her to buy a little caddy, as I really appreciated mine.

'No, no. My children have also suggested that. But this is absolutely not an option. These granny-caddies are only for old people. What would the neighbours say?'

'Well, I suspect they would not say anything. At most that this is a really good idea.'

We walked the rest of the way in silence, and I decided not to carry her bags, again.

Fortunately, Martin had sent a mail. He would come back, on Wednesday. His daughter would spend the weekend with him, but we could meet in Zug, Sunday evening. Of course, I accepted.

I also had a message from the Basel teacher. Guillaume wanted to meet for a drink, as this was the only way to test our chemistry. While I had to grant him that, I had not expected that someone would so casually undercut Bernard's 43 words.

Guillaume had also sent photos. Maybe, he should not have done that. Did I really want to see him staring into the sky with an open mouth and twisted eyes moronically, as if a golden giraffe was flying by? Or how he divulged the one cocktail that was definitely one too many, after the obviously gaudy night he had already had? Admitted, there was also the hiking photo (fortunately), but I doubted that there was actually a bike on the market that would not crash under him. Where did the head end and the body start? Was there something like a neck? At least, I knew now why he hoped to be reborn as a bird. If there was any sort of continuum between lives, though, he would be an emu and not a hummingbird.

Again my internal debate started. Should I meet him or not? After all, Martin and I had arranged a date. On the other hand, we were still miles away from having a relationship, when you really looked at it. Butterflies or not. I decided that I was completely free until the first date. This led to the second question: Did I want to meet Guillaume? I did not want to go by outer appearance, but this was about me, and I was allowed to want (or not). I felt threatened by his physical presence, as captured on the photos. I could not imagine falling in love with him. So, I took the liberty to say no. And I felt good doing it, even though I had just gone against my conviction that only the intrinsic values mattered.

I had Martin. I would meet him in one week. And see whereto the butterflies would flutter.

MomInZurich

Martin's emails became the highlight of my days. I no longer cared for the new proposals from the website. I had Martin.

Until Saturday morning.

'Dear Jo

Unfortunately, I have to cancel our appointment, tomorrow. My daughter had high fever, yesterday, so we had to take her to the hospital. When we sat next to her bed and saw her there, so small and fragile, my ex wife and I realized that there was more connecting than separating us. Not just but also our daughter. So, we want to give each other another try. I am sorry that I will never meet you, but I know you understand.

I wish you all the best for your search. I know you will find the right one.

Affectionately,

Martin'

A man like a toilet. Occupied. The butterflies died and lay heavy in my stomach.

I told myself that we might not even have liked each other. I would never know. Such was life. So, off to the gym - Saturday appeared to turn into the weekday when I needed an outlet.

Even the Greek god in the last row was back, with another goddess, though. Still, he embraced her just as intimately and lovingly. What was this about? I had relished in the delight of witnessing a happy relationship, and now this? Was there no love anymore between people? In the shower, I considered approaching her to let her know that I had seen him with another girl, just two weeks ago. I decided against it. I did not even know her.

When I left the changing room, he was standing there, talking to Greek goddess 1. Greek goddess 2 passed me by – and gave the two a hug. The threatening thunderstorm in my head only cleared when Peripety, Greek god 1, joined them. Twins! Two Greek gods! Too-beautiful-to-be-true in a double pack. I toddled off.

In the afternoon, upon recovery, I approached my next project: For years, I had been a member of an Internet platform for foreigners in Switzerland, sent tips for trips and answered questions. Maybe, my Mr Right was a Monsieur. Or a Señor. Or so. Let's go!

'Single? No plans for Saturday, October 19? Want to meet other singles?

Why don't you join us at the Bar on the Lake, directly at Bellevue, at 7pm? I send the link and a map to make it easier to find. The more the merrier.

I will wear a jeans jacket with a smiley button so that you can find me. Please let me know that you are coming so that I can make sure we have enough space and can look out for you.

See you Saturday!'

Send.

Would anyone sign up? Or maybe many? Men? Women? Would I end up with thousands of people, like the poor teenagers who had pushed the wrong button on Facebook? A little nausea set in. Why did I think of that only now?

I escaped the tension and walked to the Rigi view funicular. A funicular in the middle of town, where else do you find that? I rode up to the forest and walked along the path to the zoo, enjoying the view over Zurich, to the mountains. My resort. Too bad the sun did not set behind the mountains. That would have been lovely. Well, you cannot have everything. The only irritating thing were the many cooing couples, whispering sweet nothings and holding hands, kissing and being two. Gosh, did there have to be violins dancing through pink skies, everywhere?

At sunset, I always had to think of a New York friend. A guy had taken her to the coast on their first date. They had a picnic and cuddled, but he became more and more nervous. Until it was dark, and he mumbled that this was not what he had planned. He was from California, and for him, the sun better kindly immerse spectacularly in the sea. Unfortunately, this tends to be a rather rare occurrence, at an East coast, cuddling or not.

Anyway, I came home grounded and checked my

email. Five people could not make it but thought that it was a good idea, hoping to come, next time. Fifteen had responded 'Maybe'. Two would come. A beginning.

There were other responses, though, which drove me out of my inner Zen garden.

A 'Tinkerbella' wrote, *'It is utterly disgusting that you are searching for a guy, so publicly. Can't you leave any space where our husbands do not get hit on?????? If you cannot get your act together in real life, at least leave us alone!!!'*

And 'MomInZurich' seconded, *'Who gives you the right to exclude me, just because I am married with kids? This forum is for everyone, not just for singles. I also enjoy going out and meeting new people, and just because I have children, that does not mean that I have to spend my evenings by myself in the kitchen. It's always about singles, I am sick of it! We mothers also have rights!'*

'CoolGuy' felt the irresistible urge to share, too. *'All day long dating ads, that's making me sick, already. I really don't wanna read about it, on the forum, too. Leave me alone with that crap!'* Obviously, he was not cool enough to just ignore my message.

And so on. Overall, I had received more such mails than reactions on the actual subject.

Once more, I was speechless.

Where did all this aggression come from? If MomInZurich wanted to organize something, I would not be in her way, and if she were to invite me, I might come. But if I wanted to invite only violinists from Watchamecallit who made their living taming pink hippopotami, or if I wanted to limit things to full body tattooed refrigerator salesmen from the North Pole, that was my choice. And when an email annoyed me, I deleted it and went on living.

To press down the dust, I answered, though.

'Hi, everyone,

I have received some quite negative reactions regarding the singles night. I did not want to hurt anyone and apologize if I did. I just wanted to address other singles to do something together. Next time, I will organize something for everyone.

To avoid burying people with unwanted and irrelevant emails, I ask those who are interested to send me an email so that I can set up a separate mailing list. This way, I will not get on anyone else's nerves. ☺

Again, sorry if I have offended or hurt anyone. This was not my intention.'

I also wrote directly to MomInZurich.

'Dear MominZurich,

You may have seen my response to all, but I also wanted to write to you, directly. I find it awesome if you have a happy relationship and children. I am single, and I want a family – so I want for myself what you have found.

This is why I am trying to meet other singles. I was hoping that everyone else would understand or at least tolerate that. This assumption turned out to be wrong. I will take this offline and no longer use the mailing list for invites.

Enjoy your relationship, your children and the happi-

ness you have found while I am still searching for it. And please excuse me if I have hurt you. That was not my intention.'

I hoped that this would resolve the situation. Else, I would have to live with it that there was one more person walking the face of the Earth who did not like me. As long as this was the whole of my non-fan-club, it was still a good quota.

I called Nandika, an acquaintance from the fitness club. Telepathy, she had wanted to invite me for dinner on the next evening, anyway. Of course, I accepted – not expecting the discussion that was to follow.

'Very good, Jo. Whom are you bringing?'

'Bringing? What do you mean? Whom should I bring?'

'Well, a man. After all, there have to be as many men as women, at the table.'

'Really? And why?'

Nandika sighed. Obviously, I had just asked a very stupid question. 'For the flow of energy. For the Hatha, the opposite energies have to be balanced. So, where there's a man – there's got to be a woman. Just like Yin and Yang in China.'

Nandika was a passionate yoga fan – or was it Yogan? Yodista? Yoda? Anyway. 'Nandika, I am really sorry, but you know that I am single. And I cannot steal someone's man just to get the Karma swinging. In particular as this would create a whole lot of other negative energies.'

Silence on the other end of the line. Was I such an exotic beast?

'Hatha, not Karma. You really don't know *anyone*? There must be *someone* you can bring along.'

Well, I certainly did not want to bring just *anyone*.

'Nandika, I am really, really sorry, but there simply isn't anyone. I don't have a rib to spare, I cannot bake him, that's just how it is. If this disturbs the – Hatha, then I cannot come.'

Deep breathing. Nandika was in touch with her Om to digest this shock. I did not want to upset her, but where should I get a man from, just because she ordered it?'

'All right, we will try to find someone. And if you can come up with someone, let me know. Take care.'

Shoobidoo! I ended this weird evening and went to bed. Alone. Of course.

I woke up when someone called me from the living room. But I could not understand what he said. Besides, what was he doing in the middle of the night in my living room? I jumped out of bed, ran to him and woke up from a cracking noise. My little toe hurt. There was no one in the living room. It was two 'o clock. I went back to bed.

Nandika

Sunday. Hopefully a perfectly normal day and a perfectly normal dinner at Nandika's.

I got up. Nope, this would not be a perfectly normal day. My little toe hurt, and it was not really a little toe any more but rather a blue-and-red prune. Yeiiii!

I had been sleepwalking for as long as I could remember. I was used to it. Usually, it was not a problem. When I had guests, I warned them and asked them to send me back to bed if necessary. When alone, I sent me myself. It was all a matter of practice. But tonight, something had gone wrong.

Fortunately, the foot still fit into my hiking boots, so that I could drag myself to the emergency doctor's. Not being the most urgent case was totally fine with me. I enjoyed waiting and had both reading material and slippers on me.

So, I had established myself rather comfortably when, a few hours later, a doctor, freshly hatched in a US medical drama, turned his attention on me. The only thing missing was a walk down the aisle in slow motion, but he did not do me that favour. Even though this would have made it much easier for me to limp after him.

The serial dream come true inspected my tow with due sensitivity and ordered x-rays, which he then mustered, beaming a smile at me and uttering 'How cute – how did you manage to crack this little fellow?'

I mumbled something along the lines of 'Sports'. That sounded much better than 'I slammed it against the door frame during my nightly hallucinations.'

'All I can do here, really, is tape two toes together and give you some painkillers. You should not walk too much for a few days, but you will be all right. Wait, I will write you a prescription. ... Oh, you are living right around the corner from my place, what a coincidence.'

He gave me the prescription, and off he went. Adieu, thou God of the bruised!

I trotted home and put my foot up.

When I called Nandika, she surprised me with the happy news that she had actually found a male counterpart for me, so that her eveningly micro cosmos would be fully hatha'ed. Well, I could obviously not cancel after these efforts. So: Foot up, painkiller in.

At least, I was busy, both with the Internet in general and my single meeting, in particular. The yield was sobering. While 60 singles were interested in principle and general, only five had accepted in particular and the given case. 32 would decide spontaneously. Of course, after all it made no difference whether I needed space for six or for 38 people.

What was so difficult in checking your agenda and deciding? Of course, sometimes this was just not doable. 'I am nine months pregnant and may be giving birth, then.' Yes, this would have been a very comprehensible reason. But maybe not the right time for a night out, anyway. I found it inconsiderate that the non-committing maybe had turned into the standard response. Once more, I wondered whether modern communication was a blessing or a curse. Most Maybes would not even endeavour anything exciting but simply merge into their sofa. Unless Tarzan or Jane landed next to them, on the sofa. But we have discussed that.

Apart from that, there were more unfriendly emails from non-singles. Among them MomInZurich.

'How do you know that I am happy? That is a typical single attitude and likely the reason why you are single. Marriage is not cloud-cuckoo-land; it is work, compromise and sacrifice up to self-abandonment. Permanently. Every day. 'Happily ever after' exists only in fairy tales.

And then, you get excluded from all fun activities, because the snotty singles want to be amongst themselves rather than descend to the hollows of true life in which we mothers raise your pension payers, change diapers, wipe off slurry and read the same bedtime story 1000 times.

But I do not think that you understand that. You are Single. I do not want to meet someone like you, anyway.'

I had obviously sparked an existential crisis and had to hope that MomInZurich would not throw herself off a skyscraper. Fortunately, buildings in Zurich tended to be flat.

So, let's see what was going on regarding online dating. The musician still had not responded. But I had two new requests. With photos. The first was from – Udo, the gymnast from the household class. Status: 'Single'. The course had been less than a month ago, and not even the Germans were efficient enough to get a divorce so quickly. His email also made no mention that he was married and just looking for a training partner. What a … well, why should I bother? 'I have come to the conclusion that we do not really match.' So long!

And then Jacob from Wintersingen. A village that sang in winter, I quite liked that. According to the Internet, 619 inhabitants. Cute. But a little far for the commute. But why was I thinking about that, now? At first, have a look at what he writes.

'Dear stranger,

I have seen your profile and fallen in love with you. The stars have aligned their paths to bring us together, and now it is for us to wage the adventure and walk the path together. Yes, I do believe in love at first sight. I am a very sensitive person. My heart has been broken, over and over again, and I am looking for that special someone who will pick up the pieces, mend them and keep it. Could that be you?

Yearningly waiting for your response,

Jacob'

Phew, this was a bit too much for a first mail. I knew myself well enough to know that I tended to be rather direct. And ironic. Sometimes sarcastic. Definitely not the ideal fare for sensitive souls.

I responded.

'Dear Joseph

Thank you very much for your open and warm message. As a sensitive person full of soul, you deserve an equally sensitive partner. Unfortunately, I am not what you are looking for, I know myself well enough to see that. I wish you good luck in your search, though.

Yours fondly,

Johanna'

I thought that I had written that nicely and took off to Nandika, the pure energy of hatha'ed couples and of Samuel, the Yang arranged to even out my Yin, a colleague from Nandika's office.

As a welcome, he squeezed my hand as if he wanted to prove that he had enough Yang for – let's say a travel group of singles. A determined handshake is certainly a good thing, but you should not mangle anyone's hand with a vice like grip. I only knew this from men who had a particular need to demonstrate their manliness in a G-rated manner. And for one day, I had had enough bruised extremities.

After this demonstration of strength, Sam was obviously too exhausted to participate in the ensuing conversation. It was not until the parting that he said anything, asking to see me, again. Strange. To get to know me, he could just have spoken to me. I did not really find him dislikeable, rather neutral. But I was not really into the great mysterious guys. Sam noticed my hesitation. 'Oh, because I am so small? I thought you were different.'

I had not even noticed that, we had been sitting most of

the evening. Or was I unconsciously driven by prejudice? This left me no choice. We agreed to meet on Tuesday. Maybe, he would be more talkative, on a – yes, this was probably a date. And if not, it would be just another boring evening. Sam was satisfied.

Samuel

Tuesday evening, we met up at *Paradeplatz* – Sam had insisted on deciding spontaneously where to go. It was raining, and I found 'spontaneous' extremely stupid, especially as Sam was more than half an hour late and I could not find any dry place to sit down anywhere. And chasing away an old lady with reference to a broken toe did not seem appropriate. After all, I was not a Valkyrie. Even though – with the bandage, my foot no longer fit into the hiking boots so that I was squirting through the October rain in flip-flops. At least, the weather could not harm the shoes. Only my emotional state.

Sam showed up and gave me a brief hug. This seemed the lesser evil when compared to another squeeze. He beamed at me. 'Hey, Jo. Cool. This works out perfectly. I had a quick drink with a colleague. Great that you are so cool with the time. I like that.'

I forced myself to nod. Even though I had no clue what made him think that I was cool with him being late. I found that disrespectful, actually. Especially given that I neither wanted the date nor the meeting place.

To escape from the cold and the wet quickly, I recommended several restaurants nearby, but Sam refused all of them. 'Too expensive.' 'Too plain.' 'Too posh.' 'No, I do not like Italian food.' 'I can get better African food elsewhere.' 'Indian? No, I had that for lunch.' 'Swiss? That's boring. No, I want something special.' I had to confess that I found this date rather special, as it was. But not especially good. 'Fish is a no-go. I am allergic.' I began to feel a little allergy creeping up inside, as well. 'Vegetarian? Of course not. A man needs meat.' Maybe to increase his ability to make a decision? I expanded the scope. Finally, the Chinese place at Stadelhofen found his benevolent approval.

There were two Chinese restaurants there, though.

'Just to make sure we are on the same page, Sam. Which Chinese?'

'The little restaurant in the passage, which also has takeaway. The Chinese noodles are my favourite dish. Do you know that?'

So, it was not the Chinese restaurant but the takeaway. Well, that would speed things up. 'No, I have not tried the Chinese noodles, yet. Good, so I will get to try something new. The tram should come, any minute.'

'Come on, let's walk. It is just half an hour.'

'Sam, my foot hurts, and it is raining. I don't want to walk. I will pay for you, too. No problem.'

'Come on, that doesn't hurt you. And I'm sure you are on painkillers.'

So, I teetered through rain and darkness, a bulk of ominous silence by my side. I resorted to small talk. 'So, what brought you to Switzerland? Work, love or skiing?'

'I went to a boarding school in Geneva and met all the sons of totally important people. They are all totally important themselves, now. For example…'

What followed was a listing of all the totally important men in Sam's orbit. If I had cared, I would probably have felt totally unimportant. Not only did I not know any of them, I had also not even heard of them, and was therefore unable to appropriately savour their importance and the undoubtedly deriving importance of Sam. My toe hurt. Totally.

In the takeaway, Sam ordered two servings of his noodle dish. 'This is really totally great.'

Outside, an elderly lady walked her hopping dog in the rain. He was hopping back and forth so swiftly that it took several closer looks to recognize that he was missing his right hind leg. That did not seem to bother him, though. He was hopping and wagging and sniffing around to find the ideal spot for lifting his – wait a second, that would not work with just one hind leg. I nudged Sam. 'Look at the dog, he has only…'

'Disgusting. Just look at the old woman how she runs after him to clean up his shit. He lives like a prince, and in Africa, the children are starving. If all this money were sent to Africa, there would be no hunger, there. I could throw up.'

By now, the dog had found his ideal spot. He went into a handstand, neatly bent the only hind leg and did what dogs do. I suppressed a smile. Sam was not the right company for happy moments. Still, I had to defend the two.

'Sam, if she had no dog, the child in Africa would still not have anything to eat. As long as I can remember, we have been donating for Africa, and many countries there are actually rich. And still, children are starving. I think we first have to find out why things are the way they are. I would really like to know how you see that.'

'You don't understand that. That's an extremely complex issue. That's what my dad says, too. Say, where do you have your apartment, by the way?'

'I have an apartment near the university. And if this is so complicated, then do help me understand.'

'How many rooms?'

Ah, temporary partial deafness. Too bad, I would have been interested to have this discussion. 'Three rooms.'

'Very good. My dad cannot move in with me in my shared flat, he is 83, after all. But in your apartment, he can have a room. That's perfect.'

I had obviously missed key moments of this evening. In particular the part where we fancied each other, fell head over heels in love and rode the rainbow to cloud nine, on a white unicorn. What a pity, I somehow found this bit important.

'What do you mean, your dad lives with me?'

'With us, Jo, not with you. That's the way we do it in my family. We stick together. You will get used to that. One more thing: Your clothes, you have to change that. Your stuff is way too cheap. I only buy Armani. The way you are dressed now, I cannot introduce you to my dad.'

That was certainly unexpected. Granted, I did not wear Armani, but I certainly considered myself appropriately dressed. For the money Sam spent on befitting clothes, one should be able to feed many children and even more dogs. If it really was Armani. Or finance an appropriate apartment for Sam and his dad. At least, he had told me the way out. All I had to do was to become a rag doll, and he would be gone. Perfetto!

Food came, and Sam was obviously hungry. Between, actually during two bites, he inquired, 'So, what do you think about Pope Benedict?'

Holla? So, I was also to discuss religion, now? This was such a no go; it did not even qualify for consideration.

During the next ten minutes (or what felt like it), Sam stared at me silently, probingly and incessantly, so that I had to say *something.* 'Well, I think he is a man with convictions. But I am not Catholic, so I do not always share his opinion.'

Was this diplomatic enough?

'Well, once you have converted, you will see what a fantastic man he is. I read everything he writes. Go, ask me something.' Sam leaned back, folding his hands behind his head.

Slippery slope! 'You know, I do not really enjoy discussing religion. I think that's an iffy issue.'

'Come on, don't be yellow-belly! We are friends, after all. I really want to know what you think.'

'Okay, if you really want to: What do you think about his stance on contraception? Especially with AIDS and hunger in Africa?'

Sam did not hesitate. 'When God gives you a child, you accept it. Contraception is a sin.'

My vision became clearer but not more attractive: I would live in a three-room-apartment with Sam, his old, needy dad and every year a new baby. Add in a man who spends his time with his important friends. All of this in style, though, or rather in Armani. And without a dog. Hallelujah, praise the Pope!

Fortunately, we were finished, so I could initiate my departure. I called the waitress and she placed the bill in front of Sam. He calculated, put 17 Swiss francs on the table and said. 'It is 16 francs 80 each. I rounded up.'

I added 20 francs. 'Yup, we can go.'

'And your change?'

'I also rounded up.' In Switzerland, one does not pay American tips, but it is also not right to be stingy.

We left the restaurant. It was still raining. Sam tried to kiss me. I became stiff. To kiss me, he would have to break my spine, first. He gave up.

We said goodbye with a short hand gesture (no handshake with this Rambo), and I took the tram home. I would probably not see Sam, again. That was not a major loss.

Lilo

Wednesday. The middle of the week. A balanced day in every respect. Nandika called to inquire how things had gone with Sam. I just responded that the spark had not sparked. Nothing one could do.

But this wonderful sense of smoothness ended when my assistant Lilo came into my office with a bouquet of long red roses. That bode ill. In an envelope, I found a photo of the Pope with a note on the back: 'You're simply the best! Love, Sam' I was quite certain that this referred to me rather than Benedict. What did that mean? And, anyway! I dressed Lilo down. 'Lilo, why did you even accept these? I never get any flowers, certainly not to the office. If someone brings flowers, then that's a mistake and you don't accept them. You send them away. And where did this guy get my address from, anyway?'

Shit, I must have mentioned where I work.

'He called and wanted to talk to you. And you were not in, so I ... but they are so beautiful. And he said that you are engaged and that he wants to surprise you.'

'What a creepy little bastard!' That felt good. But Lilo was fighting back her tears. No, that was not what I wanted.

'You know, Lilo, I am not engaged. And I would much rather marry the Pope than him. But I should not have let that out on you. I am really, really sorry. And I promise you will be the first to know if ever I get engaged. But never to him'

I distributed the flowers amongst my colleagues, including Lilo. So, the flowers Samuel Prince had so graciously offered *did* spread love amongst men, eventually.

It was 11pm when he called. Great!

'Hi, Jo'

'Hi, Sam'

'So, anything special happened today?'

'Yes, thank you very much for the flowers. They are beautiful.'

'Just like you. So, when will I see you, again?'

'Well, you know, Sam, I have a lot going on, these days.'

'What about next week?'

'No, I mean really busy. You know, I hang out with friends, a lot.'

'But I *am* a friend.' He had poured a whole bottle of Snuggle softener over his words.

'Sam, I use the term *friend* very carefully and rarely. And I don't think that we are friends.' Breaking up was never easy, I knew, but we had not even been together! I just lacked experience in these relationship thingies.

'So does that mean you don't want to see me, again?'

'I'm afraid so.'

'Do you mean forever?'

'I'm afraid so.'

He hung up.

Another experience made, leaving me neither happier nor wiser.

On Thursday, my boss told me that I had to hold a presentation on US class actions in London, the next day, as the US colleague who had signed up for it had fallen ill. Well…

I called Stella and was lucky. They were at home, so I

would spend the weekend with them. I looked forward to seeing them. And Cordelia, my goddaughter.

In the evening, I went back online. No, the Zurich musician had still not responded. Well, he had not been online, for weeks. But I had a request from Andy, a banker from Zurich. He looked like a nice guy, even though neither his photos nor his message kindled any fire of passion in my heart. Well, this was probably asking too much. I suggested that we meet for a coffee, one of these days. I did not want to spend weeks exposing my soul and building up a dream just to be told off, at the first date. In the end, it was the chemistry that mattered, no matter how often everyone stressed that only the inner values were important. I was old enough to know that they came second – unfortunate, but true.

Klara had sent the thank you notes for the wedding presents. Her party was just two weeks away. My friends were scattered all over Berlin, so the preparation of a visit required military precision.

I sent them an email.

'Dear friends,

Some things in life are recurring: Easter, It's a Wonderful Life, traffic jams on the first day of the holidays, real estate bubbles – and me! I am coming to Berlin, for Halloween, i.e., on October 31 (for those who have no kids) and the weekend after. I hope that you can still squeeze me into your schedules, somehow. Just let me know how and when it would work for you. Once I am haunting the town, you should not escape me.

I am looking forward to seeing you!

Big hugs from –li land.

Love, Johanna-li'

Just like the US was the '-er land', my friends knew Switzerland as '-li land', as this was the commonly used diminutive. I loved the Swiss consistently speaking dialect, even though many did not appreciate it when I tried, too. At least, some Germans thought that I actually spoke Swiss German. My favourite Swiss word was 'Füdli'. That sounded so much friendlier than 'arse' or worse terms. And when I looked at some back ends (my own did not participate in this assessment, due to technical reasons), I considered it an expression of utmost amicability that the Swiss used such a gentle-sounding word to describe them.

Klara called immediately. 'Great that you are staying for the weekend. We must see each other, then. Perfect. We have to get you out there. And who knows what this might lead to?'

'Klaaaaaraaa! We have discussed that, so many times. You know that I am a hard one to place.' After all, I had met her friends at the wedding, so I was not expecting anything in this regard.

'What is that supposed to mean? Just because you have met a bunch of duffers? You can't be serious. You don't even want those guys. You come over and we will see. Principessa, right? So, ciao, cara mia! Konrad is waiting, we want to leave.'

Classic Klara. Unfortunately, I realized only now that I did not have a costume, yet. Neither princess nor anything else. Fortunately, princesses were no longer what they used to be. The common high nobility no longer had to run around with voluminous dresses with ruched skirts and puffed sleeves in the Sleeping Beauty style. My reference point when it came to nobility, Desi, would have fainted had she been forced to wear such a dress – a very elegant, sighing faint, of course. No, candy-coloured puffed sleeve atrociousnesses of ruche were only to be found in American weddings, these days. Apparently, American brides harboured an inane, quench- and merciless desire to put their bridesmaids into the most unflattering dresses they could find.

I was drifting off topic. So, where should I find such a dress?

Tina! She had bought a belly dancing costume, in Egypt. Baby blue with glitter – and a belly top. Who said that a princess had to be European? And the one thing that was for certain was that Tina would not be able to wear belly tops, for the time being. I gave her a call, and the costume issue was resolved.

So, the only one missing on my schedule was Desi – as had to be expected, she was still at the office. We arranged to meet for lunch, on Friday. I would pick her up at the office. Afterwards, I would visit my uncle. I left Saturday free for Tina and Klara – the long weekend in Berlin was well under way.

Cordelia

But first, I left for London. The lecture I had to give went well, and so did the small talk with my colleagues – but then, what should go wrong in superficial communication? I actually quite enjoyed it, as I deemed a superficial friendliness preferable to a non-superficial dislike.

Lilo had filled the afternoon with appointments. Obviously, she had decided that I should meet the whole company, that day. And she was right; I had to use the opportunity to meet people in person, even though the sun was shining on a bright London day. Older colleagues were always raving about their business trips, with sightseeing, exquisite restaurants and the best hotels. Those days had long since gone by. When traveling, I saw the airplane, the airport, the metro, meeting rooms and hotel rooms, sometimes even a restaurant. But still, I enjoyed the travel, meeting the colleagues live, getting to know their mentalities and approach to work right there, and simply breaking away from my daily grind. And this time, I would actually have the weekend for myself. But first, I had to take the train out to Stella and Jon's – one and a half hours, a perfectly normal commute for a Londoner. Wow, I was lucky living in Switzerland.

Of course, Cordelia was in bed, already, but when she heard me, she came down the stairs, once more, and thrust herself into my arms. She installed herself in front of her parents the way only four-year-olds and Henry VIII can, thrust her fists into her side, and stated, 'Well, Aunt Jo is not here just for you, you know. So, tonight you can have her, but tomorrow, she is mine.'

I loved this confident little person, but fortunately, Stella sent her back to bed, immediately. Otherwise, we could have run very late. Instead, we went to bed. We still had two days to talk.

When I came down to the kitchen, in the morning, Cordelia was already having breakfast. She did not want to lose a single minute and felt strongly that we could hurry up a little more, too. When that did not help, she bunked off.

The way people raised their kids was the strongest expression of their own personality, in my opinion. Some (former) friends were rotating around and above their children until they not only merged into their role as parents but actually became submerged by it. In Switzerland, the gender of 'Mami'/'Mom' was neutral, and when I looked at those friends, I knew why. The agendas of their kids were brimming. When the parents were not entertaining their children, they were just tired. I had once read that scientists believed children were programmed to keep their parents busy so that their parents would not make any siblings. That seemed plausible.

Other parents, such as Stella and Jon or Mary and Leo, remained full-fledged people, even though they lived by the rhythm set by their children. But it was never an issue to see them. By now, I knew the playgrounds in the area and took off with the children, by myself – with full parenting rights. Cordelia had started to correct my English. Fair is fair, especially as I usually spoke German with her, like Stella.

I gave Stella a quick run through my efforts of the last weeks. I even showed her my online candidates, which she summarized, 'What do you expect, Jo? The good men are all in England. What do you think why I moved here? Right, darling?'

Jon gave the only response that was appropriate for a gentleman, 'Of course, my love. Whatever you say.'

'Yes, but I like living in Switzerland. And I don't want to move just on the vague hope of finding the man of my life, here. After all, you also moved for work, not just for trust in Amor. And Jon was the luxury icing on the cake. With sprinkles and all.'

'Bene. Well, Jo, let us approach this professionally. I will write an ad on MySingleFriend.com. This way, you don't have to put yourself on a silver tray, because your friend does that for you. This would be me. And on your next visit, I will get all my friends together for a Bill-and-Jill party. But I do need some advance warning for that.'

So, while Cordelia and I undertook a little pilgrimage to her favourite playground, Stella delved into marketing me. Two hours later, I delivered a manky but happy Cordelia to her parents. Stella showed me her work.

'Jo is an amazing woman, a loyal friend and a gift to her friends, including us. She is spirited, intelligent and not only gifted with her own opinion but also with an unbeatable sense of humour, which allows her to find the comical side to every situation. With her, life never gets dull. Whether you want to hike, visit a museum or the opera, go dancing or on a trip around the world, whether you want to cook, sing or just hang out, it will be twice the fun with her. At least. She is a successful lawyer, tough at work but one of the most loving and loveable people I know in her private life. Most of all, she loves children, and our daughter, her godchild, loves her. There is nothing she would not do for her friends. If you have her for a friend, you have hit the jackpot, and the man who marries her one day is the luckiest beggar ever.'

I hugged her, unable to speak. Stella had saved the day.

'Hey, I did it! Jo speechless. Let me take a note in my agenda! Say, are you crying? Stop that! I mean every word. Don't let the bastards get you down. The men are just too stupid to see what they could have in you. Or too blinded by the light from the blonde poison across the room. Jon said he would marry you immediately if he wasn't married, already. And, do you want me to upload it? Here, this is the picture I want to post with it.'

'Gosh, everyone can see this on the page, right? Including colleagues and neighbours and my family and everyone, right?'

'Yes, of course, this is for the international site. But

what would they all be doing on the website? You just told me that everyone you know is married.'

Her finger hovered over the enter key, 'So?'

I pulled myself together. The photo was as good as it would get, and the text was just lovely. 'You are right. And even if they read it, they know that I am single. Yes, do it.'

I felt hot.

Stella called for help, 'Cordelia, could you come here for a sec, please? Please push this key, just once and gently, please. And then, Auntie Jo needs a big kiss from you.'

Cordelia delivered promptly and in abundance.

This stage was no longer under my control. My heart beat faster but also tighter. I did not want to check for responses, every five minutes. I wanted to escape. Usually, Jon and I would have gone for a long walk. The green of the meadows soothed my eyes, just like our long discussions about history, politics, current affairs soothed my soul. As did the presence of Stella and Cordelia. But after romping around with Cordelia, my toe hurt again, so we went to the movies, instead. Cordelia was happy as a honeybee.

On Sunday, Stella and I controlled the inbox.

Three responses.

One from a man in Ghana who had fallen in love with my smile and urgently needed someone who would advance the money for his hospital bills.

The second response came from Paris, Texas, 'Hi, I saw your profile. Do you want to meet for a coffee? Bill'

What on earth was that? He could not be serious. Had he even read my profile? Probably, he just wrote to every woman who was new on the platform. Well, great!

And then Michael, programmer from Baden. He also sent a link to his website: A caterpillar crawling up a rose, biting a heart into the top leaf, pupating and hatching from the cocoon with a heart shaped pattern. Really cute. Carefully done. Talented. A lot of work. Quite desperate. Did he have a life?

Fortunately, I had Stella with me. I was beginning to question whether I was too picky, but she shook her head, 'Nope, he will just be sitting in front of his computer. You can meet him for dinner if you want, but I would not expect too much. In the end, it comes down to a numbers game: The more men you meet the bigger is the chance that you meet the right one, some day. So, why not, check him out.'

Hallelujah, I was not completely off.

I quickly checked my other love box. Andy, the Zurich banker, felt pressured by my proposal to meet. Things went way too fast for him, and he yanked me off his contact list. Oops, now I was a stalker.

After the morning roll call, we let dating be dating and drove to the sea for some fresh air. Stella and Jon walked along the beach hand in hand until Cordelia thrust herself into Jon's arms, thus ending her parents' tête-à-tête. Jon whirled around Cordelia and then Stella. Cordelia cheered, Stella was happy. I would have loved to throw myself into his arms, too, just to feel how it was to be caught, to be held, to be embraced and to be loved. But it would not have been the same. And quite embarrassing at that. Luckily, I was handicapped, anyway. Would I find someone like that?

My phone rang. A Swiss number.

'Hi, there! Hans speaking. Guess where I am.'

'Hi, Hans. In Zurich, I guess.'

'Yes, exactly. I am lying in my bed, all by myself, and

have nothing to do,' he oiled along with a voice that he apparently considered sexy, 'What are you up to?'

Oh, shit! He couldn't be serious!

'I'm in England, on the beach with friends. I hope you also have good weather in Switzerland, so that you can get out, a bit. Have a good one!'

Obviously, the good men were really all taken.

Saying farewell to Stella, Jon and Cordelia was hard, as always. Why did the people I loved have to be spread all over the globe?

On the flight home, I took stock. The search for a partner was a full time weekend job. So far, nothing had emerged. If this had been one big lid-on-the-pot party, I would have had to admit that most lids were dented. Probably, I was damaged, too. Well, I shouldn't be too tough on myself. The way things had gone with Tony was bad luck. And it was not my fault that Martin and Daniel were in relationships. It seemed like I had to continue wading through ponds and kissing frogs.

Tim etc.

During the following days, I received several dozen standardized responses from all over the world on mysinglefriend.com, and despite all efforts, I was and remained unable to figure out what could have moved the senders to write to me. Obviously, some of them focused on the numeric aspects of this game and indiscriminately showered womanhood with emails. The fact that they lived on the other side of the globe did not really matter to them, it seemed. Or it may have been the reason for their efforts, as several of them were about to die of cancer if they did not find a loving soul to pay for their treatment. Or they had always wanted to visit Switzerland. Or they had a dying uncle. Of those living nearby, several seemed to have gone through a similar process like me and proposed an immediate meeting.

I limited my hunting grounds to Zurich and arranged lunch with the Lord of the Caterpillars and one of the disillusioned, but for both parties, the relationship synapses seemed exhausted by permanent test runs, so that they were unable to connect to anything or anyone. The rest of the week, I took off from the dating business. I deserved a time out.

After all, I had planned the single night for Saturday. Eventually, ten people really signed up, another 45 booked tentatively. By now, I was relaxed enough – or was it already indifference? – to take things as they came. In the afternoon, I got emails such as 'How do I get to Bellevue? I do not have a car.' Half of Zurich does not have a car, and seven tramlines stop at Bellevue, this problem seemed solvable. 'I do not drink alcohol. Can I still come?' 'Please send you telephone number so that I can call you if I get lost.' 'What is the name of the bar?' 'What is the address?' 'When do you start?' 'Can I bring my fiancé?' or „Jeg taler ikke tysk. Kan jeg stadig komme?'

Singles appeared to be high maintenance – and too lazy to read the invitation. Of course, they were. It was a long email, after all.

At 7pm, I showed up at the Bar on the Lake, with a jeans jacket and a smiley pin, as I had said. I occupied a big table in a corner. And waited. After half an hour, the first two showed up — a Finnish and a German girl. And that was that. Nice, but not what they and I had hoped for, both regarding numbers and diversification. Apparently, the Zurich sofas had had a scrumptious supper and swallowed everyone else. After two hours, we determined to relocate to a disco.

The dance floor was still deserted. The youngsters would show up around midnight, at the earliest – I was too old for that. Had I ever been so young? Dragging myself through the evening in order to get going when I started to get tired? No, I would have considered that quite stupid, at all times.

As always, the men were ridiculously outnumbered, but luckily, we had three dances with the professional dancers hired by the disco – one reason why we had picked this disco. José and I gracefully graced the dance floor – or rather, I felt like Ginger Rogers and José had to do what he had to do. He was a good sport about it, and probably used to such grace. After exactly three dances, I had to release my hostage and descend from my cloud to the reality of life. In ballroom dancing, this truth meant that the room belonged to couples.

I went on the hunt. Yes, this guy could be something. Standing at the table all alone, tapping the beat. In sync! Good basis! I asked him if he wanted to dance with me. He denied. I trotted off. No more success with the next two guys, either. That was even worse for the ego than speed flirting! Three nays in three minutes. I headed towards our corner to lick my wounds and met: 'Udo! Hi, that's a surprise!' Udo from the housekeeping course.

He smiled, but in hindsight I have to confess that it was not a smile of delight, 'Hi, Johanna, right?'

The woman by his side had to be the person standing between him and a life in happy polygamy.

'Oh, so you are Udo's wife? He has told me about you.

I thought you spent the weekends in Germany. Pleasure to meet you.'

Udo rolled his eyes. His company stared at me, then at Udo, and off she went.

Udo took a deep breath. 'What gives you the right to interfere with my personal life? Of course, this is not my wife. Thanks a lot for spoiling it. I almost had her laid, and now, I have to start all over.'

The darkness in my brain was illuminated by a thousand lights. She had thought to have found the entrance door to the wonderland of eternal love and happiness. And he wanted to do gymnastics. And a guy like that was a psychologist! I turned around and left without a word, like she had done.

I found the others in the best of moods, 'So, how is it going?'

'Three rebuffs. In one dance. That's just not normal. And then, I caught an asshole in the act cheating on his wife. Well, not in the act in the act, but quite in the act.'

'What do you mean rebuff?' Mette laughed, 'Don't you know how this works? If a man denies you a dance, he has to pay for a drink. That's how it works, here. So, this was not a refusal to dance but an invitation for a drink. All three of them wanted to get to know you. And what act are you talking about? I'm lost.'

Yes, me too. If this was not about dancing, why was this a disco? And why did the men not say that they wanted to invite me? Then, I would not have run into Udo, either. Which would have been fine with me. This was too complicated. I gave them a short run through the history of Udo and wandered off home. The evening had taken quite a different route than expected.

On my way home, I got a message, 'At the bar. Where are you? What is going on? Tim'. Yet another Prince

Charming. I responded that we had gone home.

Again, I needed a time out from dating and went to bed not only by myself but also looking forward to being by myself, on Sunday, talking to Klara, Stella and my brother on the phone.

My spirit thus having been re-built, I had a relapse on Sunday evening and started wondering: Where were the good singles hiding? And why and from what? And why had not one of the 'Maybes' shown up? Was it too much to ask that they had to commit? Or was the 'single' label a deterrent? Good, I would try it, again – without any signup. I wrote to everyone, single or not.

'Who would like to see the Picasso exhibition in the Kunsthaus museum? We meet on Sunday, November 10, at 11 am in the entrance hall of the Kunsthaus, to the right from the entrance. I will hold up a sign saying 'Expats forum' so that you can recognize me. Please get your own tickets.

The Kunsthaus is situated right next to the tram stop Kunsthaus, on lines 3, 5, 8 and 9, bus 31. Map attached.

The Kunsthaus also offers a workshop for kids so that children are taken care of. If we feel like it, we can go for lunch, afterwards. No sign-up required.'

And, indeed, no cry of outrage. MomInZurich remained silent, and I even received some friendly mails – almost registrations. Wait and see...

Only one response was a little unusual, given that this was not a dating event.

'Johanna,

How R U? I hope very well? You have a beautiful

smile, angel. What a beautiful woman you are! Please, do you allow me to get to know you better, angel? I am a chemical engineer and have been a widower for three years. My pastor said that I should join. Your profile attracts me, you have such a beautiful soul, and I want to become your friend.

I will go to bed now, to dream of you. I am excited to hear from you. You are beautiful, and I hope that we will be friends forever, because I have been alone much too long.

Earl Thomas
Austin, TX'

I would have been willing to ignore that I had not even published a photo of myself and that my profile ('Berlin girl in Zurich') could not really have helped him to explore the beauty of my angelic soul. But good old Earl was also a member of a group called 'Gay single men in New York', as shown on his online profile. That was beyond limits.

Anyway, I stayed in take-it-easy mode, as far as dating was concerned. Fortunately, the initial flood of senseless emails from MySingleFriend had ebbed off so that I could look around a bit, myself. But soon it felt as if I was reading the same profile, over and over again. Apparently, I had to extend my time out, a bit more to be ready for intake, again.

One evening, I went shopping for a nice homemade dinner. The lady at the cashier inspected me, 'You were in the newspaper, today, right? In the Arts and Entertainment section, right? That's you, no?'

I denied.

'Yes, yes, I am sure. Well, almost sure. Just don't be shocked when people ask you about it.'

I bought the newspaper, but I could not inspect it right in front of her, of course. This would have looked too eager. On the way home, I wondered. I was not famous, I did not know any journalists, I ... Daniel! Had he made me the poster child for his article on speed dating, after all? And taken a photo? I felt sick.

At home, I dropped everything and looked through the paper. No photo of me. Fortunately! On the arts and entertainment section, the photo of an Andrea whatever. Well, maybe the haircut was about right, and the beret maybe. But other than that? I read, 'Andrea whatever, son of ...' What? SON? So, once in a lifetime, I was mistaken for a famous person, and then it was a man? Going back to the cashier would not really have improved the situation. My fifteen minutes of fame were not even mine.

Well, still better than being the symbol of un-lovedness.

I continued reading and found – Daniel's article: 'Lonely heart in Zurich'. He had, indeed, taken one of the participants as a poster child. Francis. Daniel benevolently but joyfully elaborated on all aspects of Francis's social incompetence. Francis had been looking for five years, and had done speed flirting, hobby courses and Internet, just like me, but had also put adverts into the local newspapers and consulted with the TV astrologist. Fortunately, I was not (yet) at that point. All to no avail. If he could not fill seven minutes of speed flirting, how should he survive a real, full date? Maybe, an Uber-Mom would react to the article and adopt him. As much as I was hoping for that – for his sake –, as hurt I was that life had stuffed me into the same category as the Francises of this world. On the other hand, at least Daniel had not mentioned me. Only as part of the indifferent masses. 'In today's speed dating, too, none of the women wanted to see Francis, again.

'Yes, that does hurt me, of course', says Francis, who could have imagined a future with one or the other of the ladies, and sighs.'

I would have liked to console him. But I did not have his number, and I did not know how to give him peace of mind, either. Fact was: Dating was a shitty game. Sometimes for men, too.

Sunday promised to be a glorious day, probably one of the last of the season.

I joined a public hike at Urnersee. No, I was not prone to any illusions that Mr Right could be hiding in this sea of grey hair. Usually, I walked with elderly widows who told me the stories of their lives. And some of them had great stories to tell.

Of course, there had to be an exception to this rule, as to every rule. Today, a man accompanied me: Boris, a psychiatrist, father of two and, of course, married. But friendly.

Inevitably, we discussed singledom, and I was happy to see that he did not share Udo's opinions.

'You know, many of my patients wonder whether something is wrong with them, because they have been single for so long, even though they feel like they do everything to find the right partner. But in the end, it is always the same: Open issues from childhood. Or they just want it too much. Or simply bad luck. At least you still have a chance if you were just unlucky thus far. Otherwise, you need a pro.'

'Well, I hope to be unlucky, then.'

'To find that out, there are two options: Either we meet up professionally, or you apply my bad luck Chuck strategy: Go to the gym, look around and talk to someone. You have time and a shared interest, and it is extremely non-committal. And apart from that, stop checking every man out whether he could be the one, just let things happen. If he is not the right one, maybe his brother or a friend of his is Mr Right.'

Well, this undoubtedly well-intentioned advice could have been obtained by a quick look into any woman's magazine. Unfortunately, it was as ubiquitous as useless. Everyone but me was buttoned up, when going to the gym, especially in their ears. I had hoped for a brother or friend of a friend, for years – in vain. I thanked him and diverted the discussion to his children.

Bernd

I had booked my flight to Berlin for Thursday afternoon, allowing for sufficient time to leisurely pack my bags, in the morning. As had to be expected, this did not work out. Life, or rather the office, called. So, I packed my bags with one hand, held the telephone with the other and took notes from the call with the … whoever. After all, I was to be gone, for a whole working day.

In the end, I was relieved when I made it to the plane, just in time and ready to enjoy my gift of the day: No emails. No calls. Just quiet, reading and maybe even some thinking.

The flight attendant read my thoughts and ended the security announcement, 'We now kindly ask you to switch off all electronic devices. Enjoy a whole hour without email, telephone and Internet!'

The world would keep turning. Just as it had turned before the introduction of total communication. Blessed days when 'cc' meant 'carbon copy' and not 'copy as many people as possible to demonstrate your importance'. Too bad that the flight was so short. And the airline magazine featured an article threatening the introduction of wireless LAN on long distance flights. Another oasis lost.

Anyway, I even had time to read my horoscope. I was staggered: 'Singles will meet the love of their lives.' Now, that was a message. I had some doubts as to whether all Aquarius in the world would hit the jackpot in the lottery of life, today, but I had to admit, it was a nice thought.

In Berlin, I first took the train to Tina. Despite the news about violent youngsters beating up unsuspecting passers-by – news which had even made it to Zurich. Actually, the train was quite full, and the feeling of un-safety passed.

Opposite me, there sat a man in his fifties, his long grey hair held back by a bandana. I ate an apple, and he began synchronising my chewing.

He addressed me, 'You won't believe how good it feels to see a woman who likes to eat. Finally a woman who is not a bag of bones. After all, a woman has to be a full woman.' He placed his hands around an imaginary bosom.

I decided that I had to get off. Immediately.

'Oh, my God, how much I would love to unwrap what I see there. May I touch it, just fondle a bit?'

Had he really just said that, on a train, on a Thursday at 3pm, to a complete stranger? Yes, his hand touched my knee. And I had no room to avoid his touch.

'Leave me alone, please,' I raised my voice, 'I don't want that. And apart from that, I have to leave now.'

No one reacted.

He did not seem to mind, 'Well, just take my card, then. You can call me any time, then we can meet and fondle a bit. That doesn't hurt anybody. And if it turns into more – well, that doesn't hurt anybody, either. Just call me. Any time. Or I can come over. And a friend of mine has a house in Spain. We can also go there.'

What a dirty old man! He shoved a card into my pocket, but I was too busy getting my suitcase, my backpack and myself off the train to fend him off. Fortunately, he was no gentleman who would have helped me with my luggage. He remained seated.

'Singles will meet the love of their lives.' Thanks a lot, Fortuna! Nice try. Horoscopes were no longer what they had never been.

On the platform, I became sick and started shivering. The shiver only ceded when I got to Tina's. I told her what had happened, and we jointly engaged in our disgust for a while. Another thing that only happened to me.

Tina had already laid out the oriental costume, and I got dressed. In my memory, there had been more cloth to it, but, anyway, the main thing was that it fit. We postponed our chatting session to the evening or the next morning. We had enough time.

I hesitated whether I should take a cab, but eventually refused to change my behaviour for the sake of a pervert. I hoped he had made it home and was busy doing whatever his type was doing at home. A line of thought I had no desire to pursue.

On the way to the train, a man approached me, 'Know where the Drinkbar is?' Obviously, he had given the drinking a head start.

'Sorry, I don't know this area.'

'Oh, so you don't know anyone around here, either? Why don't you come along? We can look together and get drunk.'

Had he really said that? And why were all the loonies let loose just on the day when I came to Berlin? And how could the Horoscopist know that? Questions upon questions. I kindly rejected the friendly invitation.

Klara had not promised too much: They had transformed their apartment into a scary den with skeletons, cobwebs, pumpkins and candlelight. She had even organized a short-skirted waitress who smiled at everyone and silently offered drinks.

Some people just knew how to throw a party.

Witches, vampires and zombies, surrounded me, but also less scary creatures – and a 5.5 feet frog with a crown. I was not really sure whether I found him scary.

I knew many guests from the wedding. Desi had shown up befittingly as Dracula's, no, Count Dracula's daughter. She was just talking to Sinéad, an absolutely flawless Morticia Addams. Bernd was an undeniably pitiful version of the associated Gomez, but I had to give him this much: He had no issues with stepping back to let his Sinéad shine.

Klara, or rather the snow queen, was in her element, scurried around and made sure that everyone was feeling well, usually having the waitress on her coat-tails. And on the waitress's coat-tails a visibly jingled guest who seemed magically drawn to her barely covered butt. No matter how often she fended him off, his hand still kept reaching out. I stepped closer to intervene, but she gave me a sign that I need not worry. I wished that someone would go after that guy, the same way, but I did not quite feel like being that someone. This would have borne an unbearable risk that he would feel flattered and use the putative opportunity.

I looked around for Konrad – maybe, he was the frog? The frog, however, was a bit too tall and a bit too massive. Apart from that, he approached every woman, opened his arms and shouted, 'Aaah! Princess! Finally!' and tried to kiss the target. This was definitely not Konrad. But the voice sounded familiar. Deep, very deep voice, tall, massive and annoying … the Doctor! I initiated a French leave – but not French enough to go unnoticed. He called after me, 'Don't run away, oriental beauty! Your frog is waiting!'

Dang it! He was really the last thing I needed. Even though – in a way, it was quite heart-warming. Somehow. Clearly calculated but still quite charming. I turned around and kissed his frogmouth in turning. He had obviously not counted on that; he lost his balance and held on to me to avoid stumbling. I had to laugh, and so did he, it seemed. That was difficult to tell, under the mask.

'And, where is my prince?' I asked.

'Well, that hasn't worked out, it seems. But you mustn't think this is easy for me. To the contrary, my dear. Life as a frog is tough, indeed. You are constantly canoodled by wannabe princesses, you hope, you tremble, you kiss, you wait – and then, nothing, again.'

'I would say the princess is right, but the frog just isn't a prince.'

'Well, I'll not comment on that. Anyway, I am happy to see you. Say, I cannot live only on flies. Have you had dinner yet? I assume that there is a buffet in the kitchen.'

As usual, half the party community was stranded in the kitchen. We blazed a way through the masses – or rather the Doctor did, I followed. Such a giant frog came in handy.

Klara had excelled herself on the buffet. Everything was appropriately bloody and gory, apt for a comfy evening in ghostly and vampire-y company. Klara had even thought of cutting veggies for the… well, let's say weightly challenged. A real friend.

The frog heaped stuff onto his plate and pulled off the mask, revealing a slightly deranged and heavily sweaty Dr

Kinsey.

He tasted and smiled, 'A delicacy. Spaghetti brain. Of course, real pork brain would be preferable. I love brains. Just like all innards. But unfortunately, it is hard to get that, these days. So, my princess, have you flown in for this party from Switzerland?'

'Yes, of course, I can't miss a party of Klara and Konrad. By the way, have you seen Konrad?'

'No, I have to disappoint you on that. But what do you think about brains? A delicious Turkish lamb brain soup?'

There were things in life I did not have to try. 'I prefer the brain in the head to the brain on the plate. But each to their own.'

He seemed disappointed and dug deeper, 'Well, most women find innards disgusting. Would you give it a try? I see that you are munching away on green stuff. I did not think you were so frigid.'

Frigid?!? Well, whatever. What a little terrier. 'As I said, I prefer brains in the head. And I eat what I want to. And right now, I want to eat this.'

'Ha!' he shouted triumphantly. 'So, you are one of those finicky women who find everything that nature has to offer disgusting and only eat anonymous meat where you don't see what it is? You don't know what you're missing. Go to Mongolia, they eat the whole sheep's head, with brain and eyes and all. Very tasty. The locals were all disappointed that I ate all of it and did not leave anything for them. You should have seen how they admired me. The eyes are a delicacy, you know, but the normal tourists don't eat that, of course. In the old days, our people used to eat everything, as well, not just the fillet. But, as I said, all of this is getting lost, now. Unfortunately.'

He was on a roll and obviously expected storms of passion or an eruption of disgust. Or maybe both. But all of this was not so important to me, and I did not quite understand why he insisted on putting me into a box as a friend or enemy of innards. 'If you like that, that's great. Chacun à son goût.'

He seemed disappointed but recovered quickly, 'So, how do you spend your days in Zurich?'

'I am a lawyer, at an insurance company.'

'You mentioned that. And apart from that?'

'Just the usual: Meeting friends, movies, theatre, concerts, hiking, biking. And I sing in a choir. And you? What do you do if you are not working or hopping after innocent princesses?'

'Just the usual: Cooking, biking, concerts, playing the piano, gardening – the things an elderly gentleman with little spare time does.' He winked at me and obviously expected protest.

As it seemed to be important to him, I decided to do him the favour, 'Well, well, you make it sound as if you were geriatric.'

I had obviously pushed the right button; his tiny eyes were beaming, 'Just because you mention the term *geriatric*. Did you know that the German term for an old man, *Greis,* used to be a title of honour? Immanuel Kant was actually addressed as 'honourable *Greis*' from his fiftieth birthday on. Today, people would protest against that. But you are right, I certainly don't belong in that group.'

What a peacock! I was probably supposed to be impressed by the casual way in which he had brought up Kant. On the other side, I could not ignore the wonderful groundwork he had done for my punch line, 'Just to make sure: Which group don't you belong in? That of the polymath or that of the honourable *Greise*?'

Obviously, this was not the right button to push. He snipped back somewhat choked, 'We are talking about age, not about genius.'

So, did that mean that he considered himself a young genius? I steered towards calmer waters, 'Well, that's good then. What do you like to cook? Only innards?'

This was the right button, again. He raved about roast saddle of venison, braised squab and scallops, about Italian trattorias and Chinese backyard restaurants, showing photos of his creations. I liked people with the capacity for passion, and I almost took to him. His enthusiasm for his ultra light racing bike was also infectious. He biked every weekend, in every weather, as fast as possible. I was not as zealous, being more of a steam train than a fast train: Steady and enduring.

I had not noticed how time flew when Klara struck a gong, 'Dear guests and Halloween fans! As befits any proper costume party, we have not shied away from cost nor effort and offer a prize for the best costume. Nominations, please.'

I nominated Morticia Addams – Sinéad grew two inches. Countess Dracula was also mentioned, and so were the economic crisis and the property shark. I had not even noticed those. The frog king brought up Scheherazade and looked at me. Oh, that was me. I was pleased but of course did not say anything.

And then, Klara let the bomb explode, 'Not only but also because I am his lovingly loyal wife, my favourite is my beloved husband Konrad, of course.'

Obviously, I was not the only one who had not seen Konrad, yet, for everyone started looking around. Until the frog king shouted, 'That's great, but where is he?'

The waiter-ess stepped forward, and his voice did not sound female, at all, 'Dear Doctor Kinsey, dear guests: Welcome! And I can tell you one thing: Never again a woman. These shoes are killing me.'

A muted but in the silence clearly audible 'shit' escaped the lips of 'her' fan, before we broke into applause. No doubt, that was the best and most deprivation-ridden costume of the night – not only had Konrad sacrificed his beard, he had also put up with high heels and unwanted admiration of a votary patiently and silently.

There was no need for a vote. Still, it was nice that the frog had nominated me. But the prize was more geared towards Konrad than me, anyway: A kiss from Klara.

Sinéad consorted with me, while Desi occupied the Doctor.

Sinéad was interested, 'Hey, Johanna, that was really nice of you to nominate me. Is the frog who nominated you one of your admirers? Dr Kinsey, right?'

'Well, if he was an admirer, he would be very fickle. Look, he is with Desi, now. What is much more important, though: Sinéad, you look really – how would Bernd say: a-ma-zing! But he doesn't seem to be too well. Something wrong with him?'

Sinéad hesitated but could not hold back, 'We had a fight. Again. Again about his snakes. I don't even recall whether I mentioned that, but Bernd breeds snakes.'

'Snakes! No, you did not mention that, I would definitely remember. That's unusual. I have to admit that I do not really feel comfortable around snakes.'

'I feel the same, I am also scared of these slithering beasts. I tried so hard to find them likeable, but I just can't. All I want is for them to be gone.'

'I understand. I don't know if I could warm up to that, either.'

'You know, it would be fine if he would at least take care of them, himself, but he cannot see them eat, and this is why I have to feed them. But I also don't enjoy throwing such a poor little mouse into the terrarium. Especially as I breed the mice and the rats, myself. And then you throw them in there, and the mouse has no chance and the snake gobbles it down, and then it lies there and digests. And you know that the poor little mouse is in there.'

Sinéad was close to tears, 'I am so scared that one night, one crawls out of its box and strangles me. I know that this cannot happen, but that doesn't help me when I lie awake at night. The beasts are really huge, you know, his boa is 2metres. It's called Sweet Tooth.'

'Sweet Tooth? How cute. Isn't this illegal?'

'No, all that you need is a licence from the veterinary department, and you have to demonstrate that you know how to treat them. And Bernd has this knowledge. He just can't feed them.'

'I can't believe that you have to feed them and even raise the food. I wouldn't want to do that. And I couldn't do that. You develop a relationship to the animal. The mouse, that is.'

'Exactly. But Bernd says that I just don't want to like the snakes. He says if I loved him I would also love what makes him happy. But I can't help it if I'm scared.'

I gave her a hug. 'What an idiot. If you are scared, you are scared and this is just no hobby for you. Period. That has nothing to do with love. Else, you could turn it around and say that if he loved you, he would get rid of those critters. Either he has to look away when he is feeding them or he has to give them away and agree on visitation rights.'

'Bernd says that this is the survival of the fittest. That's how nature works. But still, I am scared when they stare at me with their eyes open all the time. They cannot blink, you know. And we have not been on vacation for 15 years. We can't, who should look after the snakes?'

'Well, I would not say that lying in a glass box, having

your food thrown at you has a lot to do with Darwin. If Bernd is so much into survival of the fittest, then he can be fit himself and feed them, but it cannot be that you do the dirty job and live in constant fear. I would book a nice vacation, just for you, hand him the mice, and then let him do what needs to be done. Just leave, you have to get out of there.'

Sinéad sighed, but before she could respond, I heard a deep voice behind me. 'Well, well, little princess, who is meddling with other people's relationship issues? And that as a single.' He smirked. Annoyingly.

I did not know what the Doctor had heard, but in any event, he was a crude bloke. After all, no one had asked his opinion. I tried to stay cool, 'Well, well, little Doctor, who is meddling with other people's conversations? Hasn't your mom taught you not to eavesdrop?'

He stopped smirking. 'I was not eavesdropping. I just happened to hear what you were saying. On the merits, I have to agree, though. I also believe that a couple does not have to be glued together, at all times. In particular as a man, you do need your freedom.'

Well, this would be something we partly agreed on. 'I would have to agree, also from a female perspective, even though I am not quite sure that we are referring to the same type of freedom, at this point. In any event, I find the notion of staggering through life like a Siamese twin frightening. And, Sinéad, if you are constantly frightened because of his hobby, then that can strangle the biggest love. But you have to decide for yourself how bad it is for you. After all, there must also be good sides.'

'Yes, that's right. I really have to think it over. Thoroughly. Thank you. But, say, …'

Sinéad was interrupted abruptly when someone pumped up the volume of the music to the max. Time to dance! Sinéad, Desi, Klara, Konrad, me – and the economic crisis and whoever else was around. The Doctor was watching.

At midnight, I became tired, as behoves a real princess. When I put on my street shoes, Kinsey approached me. 'I also want to leave. May I drop you off, somewhere? Or do you have a car?'

At this time of night, the offer was just too good to be declined, 'No, I don't have a car. If you could drop me off at the train station, that would be very kind, indeed.'

'Where do you have to go?'

'I am staying with friends in Tegelort.'

'Well, that's almost on my way. I live in Heiligensee. So, please allow me to take you home. At this time of night, the train is just not the appropriate place for a princess.'

He could not be stranger than my train acquaintanceship. And admittedly, he seemed like an arrogant but interesting conversationalist. Especially when you were tired and preferred listening to talking.

I was right on that. On our way to Tina, he told me about his journeys to France and Italy, Spain and Egypt, his grown-up children and his late wife. And he seemed actually likeable.

The ride almost went by too quickly. When I gave him the hand to say farewell, he pulled me towards him, held my head with the other hand and kissed me. On the cheek.

Tina and Lars were sleeping when I came in. Luckily, I was too tired to ponder for long whether this had been a real kiss. I fell fast asleep.

REX

Fortunately, the night was uneventful – which was a relief, as I could never be quite sure of that and had warned my hosts accordingly.

When I woke up, it was almost nine, and Tina and Lars had left for work. I got dressed for breakfast – in my family, we did not laze ourselves into the day in our pyjamas, we showed up for breakfast all ready, even if no one else was around. Prussian Huguenots.

I called Klara to give her first feedback on the party, in particular on Konrad's costume, of course, and to arrange a meeting for the evening. I did not mention Kinsey. And off I went to the next gym.

For lunch, I met Desi at the office. The receptionist in the lobby was tense: REX was in. The choleric who was so preoccupied with himself that he did not even realize that he took the centre stage, wherever he went, expanding the centre into the stalls and leaving no space for anyone else, depriving them of the air to breathe. Or who just did not care. When I passed his office on my way to Desi, he yelled through the open door, 'Hey, you, bring us coffee!'

He hadn't known me when I was still working at the same law firm. Of course, he had no clue who I was, now that I no longer worked here. But I was a woman, so I was obviously able to make coffee.

'Good day, Mr Xavier. I am a potential client, not your employee. Have a nice day.'

His visitor got up, 'Don't worry, Richard, I will take care of this.'

It was – Kinsey. His small mouth displayed an as-wide-as-possible grin when he approached me, 'Hello, little princess, that was quite a statement. Kudos! Say, do you have plans for the afternoon? I will have lunch with Xavier, but maybe afterwards? I'll be around.' He smiled, turned around to ask the receptionist to bring coffee and went back to REX. Without waiting for a response.

'I'll be around.' What kind of a statement was that? Presumably, he was not going to linger around aim- and senselessly at the office and wait for me.

Desi had been right. I knew hardly anyone at the office, so that I walked almost straight to Desi with hardly any disruptions.

Desi thrust her news at me, 'Do you remember our bet, at Desi's wedding? I think I am going to win. I have a date, today.'

Actually, she had refused to bet, but I felt that one should not ground someone who was hovering three inches above the floor, so I went along, 'Really? Tell me all about it!'

'Well, it is not a real date, yet, but I am sure it will turn into one. And I cannot tell you more.' She giggled like a teenager.

Desi stayed firm, also during lunch. So, I told her about my adventures of the previous weeks: About the speed flirting, the online dating, the housekeeping class and the 'normal' dates. When listening to myself, I felt like I had spent all my time chasing men. But then, no pain no gain.

When dropping Desi off at the office, I ran into the Doctor. Literally.

'Hello, Principessa! Great, that works out splendidly. So, where shall we go for a coffee?'

'I have just dropped off Lady Kestrell, and have to leave, again. I have an appointment.'

'Oh, that's disappointing. This would have worked out so nicely. My next appointment is in three hours only. Where do you have to go?'

I explained that I wanted to visit my uncle.

Kinsey's response surprised me, 'A former colleague lives at the same place. May I take you there? Then, I can see my colleague while you visit your uncle. Please, you cannot deny me that. I promise that I will behave. Behave well, that is.'

Well, it seemed like he would come along.

After a few minutes in the car, he asked, 'Would you be very mad at me if I fibbed a tiny bit, before? I have to do a short phone call. Don't say anything.'

He dialled, 'Mrs Bromstedt, could you please connect me with Mrs Kestrell?'

Desi!

'Lady Kestrell, this is Dr Kinsey. Unfortunately, I will have to cancel our appointment. I have to attend to something unexpected. Could you please talk to Mrs Bromstedt for a new appointment?'

Desi's, 'Yes, of course, Dr Kinsey,' was very short.

I felt miserable. So, he had been her almost date. And now, we were sitting in the car on our way to my Uncle Walter. Shit! Shitshitshit! Why did he have to put me in such a weird situation? 'You said you did not have any appointments. I could have taken the subway, no problem.'

'Don't worry. That's not a problem, really not. After all, I am the client. And she is the mistress of noble countenance.'

He grinned at me, 'I have the time, now, and we go on our visit.'

Kinsey was a strange mix: Friendly towards me, disrespectful towards Desi, caring towards his former colleague. Full of himself, but still leaving enough room to adore his children more than anything or anyone. And on good terms with REX.

The ensuing enactment of 'My GPS and me' disclosed his (non voluntary) talent for comedy. After he had ignored the instructions with comments like, 'To the right? Why should I go to the right? We have to go straight.' 'What are you talking about? God, this thing is really crap!' we found ourselves somewhere in the sticks of Berlin. This led to more comments, 'Where has she led me, now? Sometimes, I wonder who builds these things.'

At some point, we passed by a signpost leading us the way towards the highway. From there, I knew the way and took over the navigating.

At the senior home, Kinsey dashed off to meet his former colleague, but came back a few minutes later when he could not find him. He decided to join my uncle and me and remained a silent onlooker, not even playing with his phone. Which I appreciated a lot. This would not have been appropriate in the environment. Uncle Walter was happy to see me, greeted my company, but fell asleep quickly. In particular as I had no cake to capture his attention.

The doctor offered to drive me wherever I wanted, but that was too much for me, 'That's very kind, but you are over qualified as a cabby. I cannot accept that.'

'Maybe misqualified, but not over qualified. Michael Schumacher would be overqualified.'

'Well, you are right, actually, but still, that's not an option.'

'Well, that's fine, but at least take my card. Call me if you need a cabby. I'll be around.' He beamed at me. Again, this 'I'll be around.'

'Thank you, that's very kind. I presume that you have more exciting things to do on your weekend, though, than driving around in Berlin.'

We shook hands to say goodbye. He squeezed my hand

firmly, but not uncomfortably.

On my way to Klara, I tried to call Desi to check how she was doing, but she did not pick up the phone. In a way, that was good. After all, I did not quite know what had happened, myself.

Klara diverted my train of thought to more useful areas of life: cleaning up the den, eating leftovers and talking about things that have nothing to do with dates, singles or men. I needed that. She asked only briefly what was going on with Dr Kinsey – she had seen us leaving the party together. I told her that he had been so friendly to drop me off at Tina's, as it was on his way home. I did not mention today's excursion.

Even before Konrad came home, I had to leave for Tina's. I would have loved to see him without the beard – and without make-up. Good, we would have to postpone that to Sunday. We arranged to meet at the flea market in the *Straße des 17. Juni*. By then, he would only have a designer stubble, anyway.

Rodolfo

On Sunday, Tina, Lars and I started into the day with a long and scrumptious breakfast. Tina seemed happy like a cat lying in a basket of fresh laundry. I would not have been surprised had she started purring. They had a very relaxed and joint approach to the pregnancy. Lars insisted that we stayed away from his household chores, 'Jo, we hardly ever see you, just relax. You have so much to talk about, just pretend that I am not here.'

Well, that was a statement, 'Say, Tina, what has become of your boss? What was his name, again? Ricardo?'

I vividly remembered him, even though I had never met him: Italian, strictly Catholic, married, four children. Latin lover type with an extra serving of class. He invited the female colleagues for lunch and kept digging like there was no tomorrow, but he never went further than that. He always concentrated on the singles in his team who then uncomplainingly did his job while he enjoyed wife and children in his home sweet home. His special promotional program for women.

'Rodolfo. Rodolfo de Cropolati. Yes, he is still my boss. But I hardly ever see him, now that I am working at the Berlin office. But I don't mind. When I told him about our engagement, lunches and coffee breaks and drinks were over, anyway. And so was the unpaid overtime, doing his job. And I was no longer sitting next to him in the meetings, that seat is taken by the head of accounting, now.'

'Single?'

'Of course. She is his head errandess, now. And the way she works, she will keep that extra job. She doesn't have time to meet anyone. And as long as she does his job, he stays her boss. I am so happy to have met Lars.'

I had to agree, 'Hooray for the Egyptian touts and their insistence. And of course for Lars.'

Lars gave word from the off, 'In particular for Lars!'

'Yes, of course, my little teddy bear. But unfortunately, I cannot send all the Duracell bunnies that Rodolfo has gathered around himself to Egypt. And Lars is taken. It's just difficult for successful women to find a partner. But who am I talking to? Most men don't dare getting near someone who can say more than 'Yes, darling,' and who actually uses this ability. Unless she can make up for this flaw by external values.'

'I have just read that two thirds of German women

would give ten points of their IQ for better looks. It was not clear, though, whether they would have perceived the loss of IQ as a loss or as an extra bonus.'

'Crazy. There are only few real men. I think I have picked the last one off the market. Right, Lars?'

'Yes, my darling.'

We had to grin, 'Well, you don't score a brownie point for this answer, my darling.'

I had to laugh, 'Well, you do get one from me.'

Lars joined us, 'Anyway, from what Tina tells me, Rodolfo is still playing this game. Flirts like a trooper, but would never go a step further than that. If you are single and that's all you can get, then you work yourself to death for this little bit of attention. Even though you know that that's all.'

'Well, that's still better than if he tried to go further. In the end, he will always stay with his wife, so anyone else would always be a spare wheel.'

Lars insisted, 'Have you never considered an affair? I mean, of course this wouldn't be my cup of tea, but for many men, this would be the logical step.'

'No, not really. I am just not interested in a married man. I want the real thing, not part of it. And I do not want to ruin anyone's marriage. Well, of course, flirting is fun and perfectly fine, but the way Rodolfo uses it… A colleague once proposed in all seriousness that I should look for a stallion and enjoy my freedom as a single, lucky me. And he was not talking about riding lessons.'

'Let me guess – he was married, and he had a particular stallion in mind.'

'I think so. I thanked him, said goodbye and asked him to give my regards to his wife.'

Lars laughed, 'And that in Switzerland. I thought the Swiss were so overly correct.'

'Well, the rule, the exception and all that, you know…'

I changed the subject, 'Say, what are your plans for Christmas, this year? Egypt does not seem to be in the picture, no?' Usually, they had spent Christmas in Egypt, 'following their own steps,' as Tina called it. She did not appreciate the exquisite humour expressed in Lars's description, 'Refreshing the memories of the last days in freedom.' His buddies never ceased to laugh out loud when he said it, though.

'No, we are in the middle of the negotiations with our parents. The Middle East Peace negotiations are nothing compared to this. By now, I hope that HeShe will be born on Christmas Eve. This would solve the issue. For this year, at least. What about you?'

'Don't know yet. I'll see.'

'Really? You have no plans, yet? Otherwise you could come here, and our parents would then have to come here, too. But with HeShe… Dang it.'

'No worries, that's no big deal. I will find something.' I did not want to be sad. Once again, I realized what I was missing in life, but also what I might find. At some point and with lots of luck.

While the two were planning their weekend shopping, I went off to the gym. They needed some private time, after all.

At the gym, I saw some familiar faces from the day before. Maybe, they were single, too. Theoretically, a good opportunity to start a casual chat. Boris the psychiatrist was right about that. In reality, though, everyone was fully plugged up, listening to music or watching TV. Or they were debating loudly, preferably in Russian. Berlin had really changed a lot since I had moved away.

Today, however, they had to speak louder if they wanted to hear anything, for the groaner was back – a fully trained power pack of muscle who sugared his training with a coating of languorous expressions of endless delight, 'Yeah, Baby, that's it! Yeah, that's so good. Uuh – yeah – keep going, Baby. Uuuh, Baby, you're so good.'

Setting aside the fact that 'Baby' did not really seem to be an appropriate nickname for this lump of muscle, as well as the fact that full-throated soliloquies were embarrassing by and of themselves, this was not really a soliloquy but rather a one hour sport-induced solo coitus non-interruptus on an uninhibited level of intensity. Good for him. Bad for the remainder of mankind, at least to the extent mankind was present. Shamefulness-by-proxy, for a change not in front of the TV. Still, I felt that I was doing something wrong. I pulled out my choir notes, plugged up and started learning Carmina Burana. O Fortuna.

When I took a little swim, afterwards, Moany approached the pool. He looked relaxed. Again, good for him. But no matter how elegantly he slid into the basin, I could not help but wonder how far he was distributing his manhood. And given that I wanted to get on the way, anyway, to meet Tina and Lars at the movies, I escaped to the changing room – where I had to acknowledge to myself without any mercy that the Russian ladies around me, freshly ascending from the pool, looked more stylish than me after I had spent what felt like an eternity on styling. Some people just had it. And I let it be.

Tina had chosen a romantic comedy, and it followed the usual structure, thanks to Jane Austen: Woman searches for love, falls in love with asshole, while her soul mate is lingering around in the corner, ready to rescue her when she realizes that the asshole is an asshole and falls into the good guy's strong arms. Alternatively, the hero and the heroine fight like Godzilla vs. King Kong until they fall into each other's arms. Of course, I had realized by now that life did not work out this way. But still, seeing these portrayals of allegedly normal people allegedly falling in love like normal people allegedly do made me feel as if something was wrong with me. When everyone found someone, even the people in the movie, Mr Miller, Steve and whoeverelse, why not me? Maybe, I was too picky, after all?

In the evening, I quickly checked my mailbox. A mail from Samuel.

In many words, he explained that something must have gone wrong. And no matter how deep he dug in his memory of the evening, he had no clue what this could have been. Obviously, it had been a misunderstanding. No woman had ever rejected him, and we were such a good match, also from an objective point of view. He had also spoken to his dad, who was very pleased with our relationship and coming to Switzerland for Christmas to meet me and give us his blessings. So, we should meet ASAP to clear the little mishap out of the way.

Clearly, a lack of confidence was not one of his weaknesses. Good for him.

'Dear Sam

Thank you for your mail. I very much appreciate your openness. You are a great guy, but love and life go their own ways. In my case, this path unfortunately does not lead in your direction. I am sure, though, that you will soon find someone who loves, appreciates and values you the way that you deserve.

I wish you all the best in love and in life

Johanna'

After all, I did not want to bring him down but only end

something that, on my side, had never even started. Tina and Lars agreed that this was no loss.

Nefertiti

On Sunday, I met Klara and Konrad at the *Siegessäule*. Konrad really looked somewhat ragged, without his beard. If I hadn't known, I would probably not recognized him.

I liked the *Tiergarten* area in the early morning hours, when the mist was not the smoke of barbecues but rather morning fog hanging low above the grass. Only rarely, a jogger would cross your path, so we had all the time and opportunity to talk.

A loud snuffling behind us did not seem to stem from the running guild, even though it was very rhythmic and slowly came closer. When it had almost reached us, it uttered, 'Principessa, is that you?'

No way! We turned around – yup, the Doctor. Where was he coming from, now? And why? Klara read the question from my eyes and shrugged.

'I knew this was you. A wonderful good morning, Klara - Konrad!' He smiled at one after the other and tried to get his breath under control.

'Good morning, Mr Kinsey. Well, that's a surprise.'

'Yes, Principessa, who would have thought? I wanted to enjoy the *Tiergarten* in the morning mist. But of course, I would not have dared to hope for such charming company.'

'You come all the way from Heiligensee to go for a walk, here?' I was surprised.

He nodded. Klara invited him to join us. Well, fine, now he was here. I let Klara and Konrad have some one-on-one time and chatted with him.

There was not much going on at the flea and arts market we had aimed at. Probably, the tourists were still sitting at the breakfast buffets in their hotels. The artists were putting up their stands. I did not mind. I did not want to buy anything, anyway. I had everything I needed and more, especially as I had not moved in years. It was amazing how stuff amassed. I absolutely loved and admired decorative thingies when they were collecting dust in other people's homes, not in mine, and I often wondered who bought all those things. Klara and Konrad also just wanted to browse. We assured each other that we would just look. The times of flea market bargains were over, once and for all.

Eventually, we still went into relapse. It started drizzling, so that the purchase of a hat turned from superfluous into a necessity – especially as the specimen I chose reminded me of Sinéad and thus of Klara. I knew that I would probably forget my purchase in the overhead locker, on the flight back to Zurich. But such was life. Klara and Konrad proudly purchased L's featuring artists we remembered from blessed childhood days. So, it was just the Doctor who had not contributed to the welfare of German economy. Of course, we could not leave it at that, and I found the ideal object to purchase: Two Frog King mugs. He could not object to that, and so it turned out that we all purchased things that we had not really sought. Well, those things could not count on surviving if we were to move our respective homes.

The drizzle turned into rain, but the market still attracted more and more people. Klara and Konrad had to go home. And I still had half the day to spend before I had to be at the airport.

The Doctor offered me to take me to my uncle, again,

but one visit was enough. For Uncle Walter and for me. So, I decided to pay my respects to Nefertiti. Not that she would have expected me or appreciated my company, but it was still always a pleasure to see her. Kinsey asked if he could join me. I was beginning to wonder if the man had no life of his own. After all, I was not his entertainment committee. And he was not my personal chauffeur. On the other hand, he did not really bother me, so I agreed.

On the way to the museum, he told me about his trip to Egypt with his late wife, again. My subtle hints 'Yes, you told me about this at the party' vanished unheard or at least to no visible effect. So, he unstoppably lectured about pyramids, obelisks and sphinx until I re-directed his flow of narration towards food. On my trip with Tina and Lars. we had been exposed to extremely repetitive tourist cuisine, in Egypt. One-pot-unluck, day after day – another mysterious method to repel tourists. So, I was curious to hear what he had to say. As it turned out, however, the Egyptians had gotten the better of him, too. He had not experienced any Lukullan joys, either.

In the museum, however, I had to stop him. It is nice to have broad knowledge of everything, but one should carefully avoid presenting it on a platter. And one should avoid even more carefully thrusting it down the throat of a fiercely struggling victim. You just don't do that. It is not nice. In particular if you don't even know if the forcibly blessed victim knows more than you do.

I slowly made my way from tiny hints via sticking the message on a baseball bat and waving it in front of him to beating it over his head. 'I know. – Yes, I've read that, too. – Yes, we learned that in school. – Wasn't that in all the tabloids, recently, maybe? - Yes, my little niece was very impressed by that, too.' When all of this failed to stop the cascade, I stood in his path and looked straight into his eyes, to the extent possible, given the difference in height, 'Mr Kinsey, I have been to Egypt, I have read many books about this, you are not telling me anything new. Could you please just stop and allow me to enjoy the exhibition?'

'Yes, well, but did you know that Akhenaten…'

I turned around and left him where he was. After a second of shock, he followed me and continued lecturing. I felt like I was in kindergarten. The appropriate reaction would probably have been to close my ears with my hands and sing 'lalala' to avoid hearing him, but then, I did not want to go that far. Given that no earplugs were at hand, I had to internally shut him off. It took a few minutes to get to that state, though. What a chatterbox! Eventually, even he realized that I had mentally reduced his constant sound production to an ambient noise, and he gave up. So, by the end of our then peaceful and almost silent tour, I was almost reconciled with life. He suggested having lunch, together, and given that I actually had no plans and felt a bit bad for shutting him off, I agreed. I had never really liked eating by myself.

We drove to his favourite Chinese place, where he was 'actually part of the family'. The restaurant was almost empty, and we were seated at the table between kitchen and loo. The restaurant was about as snug as the waiting hall in a train station – genuinely Chinese, indeed. And the dishes that the Doctor chose were actually not only authentic but really good. Good food was a good thing.

The Doctor had reached his next favourite subject: His job. He told me about a mega deal he was just getting lined up. The Maienwald group would buy 100 hotels in Bulgaria, with attached nursing home units, to care for German seniors. This was obviously an extremely complex but equally lucrative deal that only a true genius could get under control. I felt uncomfortable. These internal details were none of my business. Myself, I hardly ever talked about work, certainly not with a casual acquaintance. Unfortunately, he did not react to my attempts to end the subject.

It was getting late, and I interrupted, 'Mr Kinsey, it is really nice talking to you, but I have to get to *Bahnhof Friedrichstrasse* to pick up my suitcase, and then on to the plane.'

'Well, princess, I can drive you. The train station is on the way, and so is Tegel airport. That's no problem at all.'

That was accurate, geographically. 'Okay, then I will invite you for lunch, though.'

He did not protest. So, this was not a date. That was reassuring, because I shared this assessment. I paid, and off we went.

I was a little surprised, though, when we got to the airport and he asked, 'Say, I will be in Basel for a convention, next week. I could stay in Zurich, for the weekend. I heard it is a nice little village. Are you around?'

'Oh, I do not really know off the top of my head. I would have to check my agenda.'

I got off and opened the trunk. When the usual chorus of hooting kicked in – yes, I had held up traffic for a full 10 seconds –, Kinsey shouted, 'Gotta go. Call me or write me, you have my details. See you next week, Principessa!' He took off. And that was good.

I checked my agenda. I had planned the visit at the museum, for Sunday afternoon. Well, he could come along, if he wanted to, so I responded accordingly.

He responded immediately.

„Dearest Principessa!

I am truly delighted! The convention ends on Friday at

4 pm. Shall we meet in Basel, or should I come straight to Zurich?

Looking forward to Friday

Yours sincerely,

Dr Mark Kinsey'

This old fashioned formality was somehow endearing. On a regular working day, meeting him at 4 pm in Basel was not an option. So I set for a meeting in Zurich. I would organize a hotel room nearby.

As much as I enjoyed seeing my friends, I also liked to return to my regular life. While I enjoyed our intimate three-getherness, I knew that those 'getthernesses' were temporary, and that I was the temporary part.

When I dropped my empty suitcase in the basement, water was dripping from the ceiling. Dang it – where did that come from?

While I looked for the number of the property management, the telephone rang. It was Samuel. He asked how I was, and lacking even the slightest intention of discussing water levels with him, I decided 'I'm fine'.

Silence.

He asked, again, how I was.

Still, 'I'm fine'.

Silence.

'And, how are you, Samuel?'

'I'm feeling bad. Very bad.'

'Oh, I am sorry to hear that. Why that?'

'Well, you know, there are people who make up their minds about people. And then, they do not give these people another chance.'

I did not have time for this discussion, given that the

basement was just being flooded. And I knew that I would not be up for it, later, either. 'Samuel, I am afraid I am one of those people. I gotta go, I'm really sorry. Farewell.'

I felt like a death squad with a license for verbal killing, but I could not help it. If I did not watch out, his father would show up at my place out of the blue, with all his stuff, ready to move in. I did not want that. And apart from that, right here and right now, I had another, more pressing problem.

The plumber on duty had a look at the damage and concluded that the source of the problem was located in my neighbour's bathroom. When he got ready to pry open the bathroom wall, I intervened and told him that my compartment in the basement was situated on the other side, really.

'Young lady, why don't you leave that to the expert? I have done this for a while, you weren't even born back then.'

Yes, sure. I still inquired whether it wouldn't be a good idea to consult the floor plan, or maybe just go into my basement compartment and knock on the ceiling. After all, such a hole in the wall was not only unpleasant but also expensive.

The pitiful look he cast at me told me that I had not the slightest clue what I was talking about. The situation was in dire need of a Y chromosome. Fortunately, the person in whose bathroom we were standing disposed of this proof of competence. When he suggested that he would go downstairs and the plumber should knock on the floor, the plumber felt that this was an excellent idea. While I did not quite see how that differed from my proposal, I had to admit that it was a good idea.

Putting this idea into practice, we quickly determined that the problem was located in the apartment on the other side. Woohoo! Manhood had solved the riddle! Having witnessed such remarkable success, I almost regretted having rejected the chance of binding such an outstanding Y chromosomist as Sam to me. Only almost, though. No, not really.

Yes, I had had enough for the week.

Downing

I spoiled myself with another week off dating. I even managed to deactivate my ring view, the automatic look at the ring fingers of the male part of the population. I did not like myself when doing that. The pause was and did me good.

I was beginning to wonder whether there really was such a thing as big love, the perfect harmony and the ecstatic explosion of overwhelming shared happiness. Was it just a myth, maybe, which had been perpetuated for thousands of years by poets, singers and painters but was not true nonetheless? Had we all been fooled into collective self-deceit? And all those who had so splendidly described this feeling, were they just searching themselves? Were they singing about their own dreams, louder and louder to convince themselves? Like a child whistling in the dark so that it would not feel alone? Were they describing what they had searched for, or was it what they had found? Maybe, arranged marriages were the answer. Marriage as a multipurpose vehicle, primarily an economic and social community to raise children. And if you were lucky, you got along well and lived on cloud three or four. But no one would expect cloud nine. At least, the rules were clear. This seemed to work for some of my Indian acquaintances.

Anyway, I was on a dating break. So, it touched me considerably less when one day, I saw my personal god in white from the casualty department, again. He actually lived around the corner from me, on the ground floor, with a window opening right to the boardwalk I was passing on. He was smooching around with his girlfriend or whatever in plain sight. While it was innocent and sweet by objective standards, it was still not a sight I wanted to see.

When my colleagues suggested a visit at an after work party, I went along. Given that I was not looking for anything or anyone, I could come along and be relaxed.

As had to be expected, the occasion was mainly populated by those who found regular disco nights too loud and too late. The early evening tea of our generation. When we were young, the night started when the sun came down, not at midnight…

Not marred by my own desires and longings, I noticed the men who were dancing ostensibly casually while scanning the women, looking for prey from above. That was really disgusting. In particular as none of them approached me. Men!

Obviously, I was not the only one who had noticed this hunting game, for a hefty dispute emerged among the young lawyers from our department. Which gender had the better prospects in the dating game? Each side considered itself severely disadvantaged. One had to wonder how mankind had made it, given that it was obviously a mission impossible to find a mate.

'Just look at the poor lads! Pure despair! They know exactly that there is nothing going on. You women play us like puppets on a string.'

'And whose fault is that? Just look around at all these amazing women – and, what do these glorious samples of the pride of creation do? Wait for Claudia Schiffer to throw herself on them. Even though they are far from perfect, themselves. Why don't you ever take the first step, guys?'

'Gimme a break! Have you never seen *A Beautiful Mind*? We know that we cannot all get the blonde beauty, we are not that stupid!'

'So, why do you do it, then? Because all of you think that they are the hot stallion who gets the blonde bombshell!'

'No, really not, but if I get rejected, I want it to be worth the try. Who wants to be rejected by the ugly sister?'

'Well, maybe she wouldn't reject you!'

'Yeah and maybe the pretty sister also wouldn't reject you if you did not just look at her boobs.'

'Guys, if a man actually makes a decent move, every woman will be happy. Unless the chat up line is really, really stupid. But today, women do not only have to take the initiative, we also have to give you the feeling that you are in the drivers seat. That's really exhausting.'

'I can't believe it! Which dream world do you live in? It's the other way round: When a woman chats up a guy, every 500 years, she can say what she wants, and bingo, she gets it. But we have to walk on eggshells, and every word is weighed and inspected. And, by the way, what is a stupid chat up line, anyway?'

'Well, the most annoying line that was ever whispered at me was 'So, it's your fault that it's raining. The angels are crying, because the most beautiful angel has come down from the sky.' Yuck! How long did he take to learn that?'

A colleague chimed in, posing theatrically, 'Another classic, 'Oh, the sun is blinding me. But, no, it's your eyes. Has your father picked the stars from the sky?' My gosh! That makes me so sick. Really, you cannot pull this off. No, really not.'

'Ladies, you don't know what you want, do you? First, we are not romantic enough. And when we try, you don't like it, either. Really, I would love a woman saying something nice like that.'

'C'mon, you can't be serious. This is dripping slime so badly that you can slip on it. No, really.'

The discussion of male and female courtship culminated in a competition of its own kind. The one who would collect more telephone numbers of the opposite gender would get a drink. Each side appointed a representative.

While our female colleague triumphantly waved her first card at us after what felt like two seconds, it took the chosen him a while to come up with a good chat up line. Once this had been established, things went smoothly. Apparently, men and women both pitied the opposite gender enough to not want them to lose the battle of sexes. Or they really hoped for a call. After half an hour, they were on par. 47 cards each.

I was truly flabbergasted, though, when I saw the cards they had collected. Not only the expected (male and female) bankers, IT nerds, consultants, web designers and representatives of all kinds, but also a scientist from CERN and someone working at 10 Downing Street. He had immediately offered her a job ('*We always need people with guts like you*') and then proven that the English do know how to chat up a woman. The male colleague, too, made similar experiences. No job interview, though.

It was amazing how much could happen if one let down one's guards. For today, though, this approach had been exhausted. And I was on vacation from my dating job, anyway.

Alma

I was yet unsure whether I would have a date with the Doctor on Friday, or whether he was just planning on using the opportunity to get a guided tour of Zurich for free. Of course, that DID make a difference. I settled for the latter. After all, we were still Mr Kinsey and Ms Lenné. I booked a hotel room around the corner and sent him the address, asking him to give me a call upon arrival.

He did, and we met in one of my favourite restaurants for dinner. I usually went there for lunch with my colleagues, and the owner had obviously misinterpreted the shift to the evening and the request for a table for two. He brought us champagne and whispered in my ear, 'This is on the house.' What a lovely gesture! What bad timing!

Kinsey liked it, 'Well, Principessa, that's what I call a welcome. What did you tell him, if I may ask?'

'That I need a table for two.' The tone was obviously lost on his selectively deaf ears, as demonstrated by his absent smile.

After some back and forth and long descriptions of the various dishes on the menu, he settled for the chitterlings. I had almost expected that. Then, he beamed at me, 'And for you, we will take the *Züricher Geschnetzeltes.*' The traditional Zurich veal stripes in a creamy sauce with hash browns.

'Yes, they make great, *Zürcher Geschnetzelte*s. But I think I will have the fish, though.'

'Oh, DO take the *Geschnetzelte*, please.'

'Thanks, but no thanks, I do prefer fish, today.'

'But I want to try the *Züricher Geschnetzeltes.*'

'Why don't you have it, then?'

'No, I'm having the chitterlings. I want to try from your

plate.' He pouted, bowed his head and looked up at me. Someone must have told him that this was irresistibly cute. Maybe his mother. I did not think this was cute. And not irresistible, either. Only childish. Men are not supposed to be cute. Women neither. Not even children should consciously be cute.

'You can order a small portion as a starter. Or you have it tomorrow. Seriously, you can get this anywhere in Switzerland. Or we come back here. Anyway, I prefer the fish.'

He pouted on. When the waiter came, Kinsey ordered, 'I get the chitterlings, and the lady gets the *Züricher Geschnetzeltes*.'

'Chitterlings and the *Zürcher Geschnetzeltes*,' the waiter repeated, elegantly stressing the non-existing 'I' and ignoring the fact that Kinsey had just ordered in the most German and rudest way possible for Swiss ears. In Switzerland, one did not state what one would get – one asked nicely.

Kinsey looked at me in a manner that was presumably meant to be 'whimsically dinky'. Men are not dinky. Had I mentioned that?

I corrected, 'The lady would like to have the fish, please. And a big bottle of sparkling water. Could we have a small serving of *Zürcher Geschnetzeltes* for the gentleman, as a starter, please?'

'Of course, Ms Lenné.' Of course.

'But on two plates and with two forks! And a bottle of Merlot.' He smacked self-contently.

I waited for the waiter to leave.

'Mr Kinsey, why don't we just say that you eat what you want to eat, and I eat what I want to eat. This way, we both get what we want, and life is good.'

His grin vanished. 'Oh, I did not know that you take

this so seriously. I am sorry. Of course.'

After a minute, he continued, 'You know, I have to decide all day, it has become a habit. Please don't hold it against me. And thank you for your help. That was very, very kind. So motherly.'

'No problem. I just like to decide and control what I eat. I have just lost a lot of weight, and I do not want to jeopardize that.'

'But you don't have to lose weight, really not. You are a woman in every sense of the word, and that's wonderful. I would never have guessed that your weight is an issue for you. Trust an elder gentleman with a lot of experience in life and love: You are perfect the way you are. And a few kilos more would not change a bit.'

Now, that was sweet to say and even sweeter to mean. 'Well, you are exaggerating, but I thank you. I just don't want to carry so much extra weight with me.' He had just delivered my yearly quota of compliments.

The waiter returned with wine and water.

Kinsey tried. 'Waiter, the wine is corked. We need a new bottle.'

I did not even know how corked wine tasted. I had obviously been lucky thus far. Fortunately, the second bottle met his taste.

The doctor raised his glass, 'A toast. To a nice evening and an even nicer weekend.'

'To a nice weekend.'

Apparently, it was for me to get a conversation going. 'So, how was the convention? Was it worth the trip?'

'Well, it was interesting. The best part was the social program, though. I mean, with my experience, of course, I cannot benefit from such a convention, any more. It is rather the convention that is benefitting from my participation. Do you know the *Kunstmuseum Basel*? I had not expected such a beautiful Holbein collection in the deep backwater. And now guess who knew the answers to all the questions the guide asked?'

He raised his arm and clicked his fingers like a primary-school pupil. How embarrassing!

'Me, of course. Well, I bet no one will say that old Doctor Kinsey did not pay attention in school. Today's children don't even learn the things anymore which my generation already forgot. Did you know that Hans Holbein, the younger that is, painted the portrait of Anne of Cleves for Henry VIII? Henry did marry her, but she was so much uglier than her portrait that Henry annulled the wedding and basically fired Holbein.'

'Well, good for her, I guess. Yes, I knew the collection, Holbein was a citizen of Basel. But Basel was and is certainly not backwater.'

'Oops, it seems like I hurt the Swiss national pride. But I really did not mean to be offensive. Time and again, I am pleased and amazed to see the treasures to be found in, let's say, hidden places. In Zurich, for example.' He looked at me, took my hand and kissed it. He smiled.

The waiter interrupted. The *Zürcher Geschnetzeltes*. It disappeared fast and without help.

'Did you notice Kokoschka's *Bride of the Wind*? My favourite painting,' I wanted to know.

His eyes told me that he had no clue. How could a man with such a keen interest in arts not notice this painting? Especially as it was hanging at the head end of a long suite of rooms, the best spot in the whole museum. Well, maybe he had not read the title.

'You must have noticed. On the upper floor, way back in the end. You walked towards it, the whole time. All in shades of blue. A man and a woman lie in a boat, like in a pair of big protective hands, in the middle of a storm. The two are Oskar Kokoschka and Alma Mahler. She sleeps, all snuggled up to him, and smiles. So peacefully. The waves are surging behind her, but they pose no threat, because she is with him. They are like the wings of angels. He stares into the void, his hands cramped on his belly. She is all with him, but he is still alone.'

'You really like the painting, don't you?'

'Yes, a lot. Really, a lot. Whenever I am in Basel, I visit Alma and Oskar. And I wonder whether they were the only ones for whom it was like that.'

'For whom what was like what?'

'Well, that the woman is fully committed to the relationship while the man does not even notice and wolves on.'

'Wolves on?'

'Yes, dwelling in his role as a lonely wolf. I mean, he does not even see her, because he is so preoccupied with himself and his life rather than feeling her and loving her. She is all here. He is not. And that's how it really was with these two. He was so jealous and possessive that she eventually left him.'

'If I may say so, you are contradicting yourself. If he was so jealous and possessive, then he was not preoccupied with himself but rather his world was revolving around her. Especially as you said that she had wings to fly away.'

'Well, for starters, the wings, or the waves rather, are not for flying but more like a blanket or a shield. But I know, you haven't seen the painting. And second, jealousy has nothing to do with the other person but only with oneself. After all, one does not set out to do what the other person needs or what is good for that person, but rather, one expects and forces her to fulfil one's own desires. That's not about the other person, the other person is just the trigger.'

'Objection, your honour! If I did not love a woman, I would not care what she does where and with whom.'

'But that does not mean that it is about her. It is mainly about wounded pride and ownership claims. Not about the partner. And that's what the painting shows. Which is really interesting, for Kokoschka to paint himself in this manner.'

'Well, I will have to look at it, again, then. But to get back to Holbein, I just thought of something else. A nobleman once complained to Henry VIII about Holbein. Henry responded, 'I'll tell you frankly: if I had seven peasants, I could make seven lords. But if I had seven lords, I could not make ONE Holbein.' Of course, this was prior to the Cleves disaster. I always liked this story. You don't expect that of old Henry.'

'Yes, that's true. That was almost a republican approach, or a meritocratic one.'

'Yes, I think so, too. And now, would you believe that the guide did not even know this story?'

So, he had also had a go at outsmarting the guide. What a dish! With him in a travel group, one would not even need a retired professor for a good load of shame-by-proxy.

No, it was better not to comment on this masterpiece. 'We have drifted off. So, how WAS the convention? What exactly was it about that made you come all the way from Berlin?'

What followed was a review of the convention (which had not brought him any revelations), the presenters (who were not really very competent), the participants (who had not even noticed that) and the open discussion round (in which he had apparently not only asked the questions but also given the answers – a dish, a dish, a dish-a-dee-dish).

Well. Eventually, he ended up discussing art in Basel, Germany and the world. That was actually quite interesting, every now and then interrupted by an 'Ah' or 'Interesting' on my part. Apparently, he needed that. And it was nice not to have to do the whole conversation. We just had to find a better balance.

When he was more or less done, I wanted to sort out the next day. 'Have you thought about what you want to do, tomorrow? Mountains, forests, lakes, Zurich, another city, museums? The weather forecast is promising.'

'I thought you would have a suggestion.'

'Yes, of course. But I need to know what you would like to do, generally, to make a good suggestion.'

'I have complete trust in you.'

So, it was up to me to guess what my guest would be interested in. If the weather were good, it would be a shame to go to the museum, especially as my quota of arts lectures was exhausted. Hiking was difficult, giving his knee issues and his weight. Apart from that, he seemed to be short winded. My guess was that he was in his early to mid sixties, and like most men of that generation, he was obviously living in a happy symbiosis with his. So, it was time to go for the geriatric program. 'What about a train ride up on the Rigi? There's already snow, up there, and the view of the mountains is staggering. Then to Vitznau with the funicular and back to Lucerne by boat.'

'Well, if you want to do that, I will come along."

'No. I know the Rigi. For me, we do not have to go up there, I am trying to find something that you would like.'

'Whatever you like. I am flexible,' he insisted.

'Okay, then I would like to go on a hike. I can search for a place that has snow already, then we can go snowshoe hiking.'

'No, I cannot do that, I have never tried.'

'Well, what about dog sledding, then? Hardly anyone has done that, before, so you don't need any experience.'

'Is that sitting in a sled and the dogs pull?'

'No. You stand in the back and drive the sled. You have to run along when it goes uphill, and slam the brakes when it gets too fast. It's real fun, and the dogs are amazing. It's in Muotathal, just two hours from here, so it would be a nice and full day.'

'No, that's not for me.'

'Regular hiking? Somewhere flat, near a lake?'

'No.'

'Well, what IS for you, then?'

'You decide. I don't want this to be all about me,' looking 'cute', again.

Whatever other non-sitting activity I suggested, it was not his thing. So, back to square one, 'Okay, then we go to the Rigi. That does not involve much walking. There is snow up there, but there are handrails.'

'See, I knew we would find something that is fun for both of us.'

Again, I paid the bill. He just let it happen without commenting. So, it was not a date, after all, kissing of hands or not.

I dropped him off at the hotel, a brief goodbye with Swiss triple air-kiss and ciao.

All in all, this had not been one of my worst evenings.

Dr Kinsey

When I arrived, he was already waiting in the hotel lounge. Wearing jeans (okay), a new outdoor functional jacket (okay) and shining office shoes (absolutely and utterly completely not okay). I should have thought that he was really old enough to choose his clothing, himself. Still, I asked, 'Did I mention that there is snow, up there?'

'I may assure you,' he replied indignantly, 'that I am fully aware of what a mountain looks like.'

'Good, so we can go, then.'

On the train, he pulled out his phone and started torturing it; highly concentrated, mouth open and biting his tongue slightly, breathing heavily. Obviously, this was hard work. The way he looked over the rim of his glasses reminded me of my grandmother. The difference being that, of course, she never wrote any emails. And even if she had done so, she would never have been so impolite as to do it when riding on the train with someone.

Anyway, I got the message. I joined in the electronic communication with third parties. Within not even two hours of peaceful parallel existence, we arrived at the snowy top of the Rigi. Almost at the top, that was. And I had done a full weekend's worth of email. Very good. The path leading to the top, not ten minutes in summer, was a bit muddy. Fortunately, it was not frozen, so that the ascent was not an issue. Unless one was wearing office shoes, of course. I offered to skip the way to the top, but the Doctor refused brusquely, 'You go, and I will follow. I am fully capable of going up there. Go, why don't you go, now?'

Every step required his full attention. His tongue worked strenuously between his lips, and when going up, I heard him wheeze behind me, for a while. But, as mentioned, he was a grown-up, and if he wanted it like that, that's what he got.

We waited on top of the mountain until the Doctor could breathe properly, again. Even though I had been up here, many times, the mountains always offered new perspectives – this time, blue sky, snow, and a view of the lake way below. And it was definitely a value added that my company did not want to waste his breath on educating me.

After the – no swifter – descent, we took a break at the restaurant near the station, before heading to the boat by train and funicular.

Slowly, the Doctor started melting. He told me about his childhood in post-war times and his youth in the fifties, of his infatuated mother, marinated beef with potato dumplings, every Sunday, of the return of his father from captivity as a prisoner of war. My parents had also told me a lot about this time, so that it had always been present in my life. They had also maintained certain habits from the war. My dad had always bought chewing gum in bulk for the next ten years, 'because you never know'. As a child, I had thought that chewing gum had to be a crumbly, tasteless thing only adults could like. And when watching documentaries from that period, I still felt the fear crawling up from my stomach to my heart, the fear that my parents had experienced as children. But I also realized that the few years' difference between my dad and the Doctor had protected the latter from the worst experiences that my dad had gone through, or at least the memory of them: bomb nights, evacuations and hunger after the War. Let alone the horrific fate of those boys who had been conscripted

in the last days of the War. So, he had grown up in a world where the only way was up.

His generation was probably the luckiest in German history. While they had lived through the post-war period, they had been too young to have their lives thrown at the front. After the War, economy improved constantly. There was enough work for all who wanted it, and as long as one did not steal the silver cutlery, one kept his job. When they hit university in the 1960s, they pushed the old elite out and replaced them, never to give up their positions, again. They raised us under the heading 'anti-authoritarian', which actually meant that they let us do what we wanted and had the freedom to mind their own business. Then, they benefitted from the boom of early retirement, and now they were receiving pensions for decades, which my generation did not even dare to dream of, regularly increased by new pension and other support plans which we would only know by the contributions we paid. And on top of it all, the generation of the Rolling Stones was now considered cool – even though hardly any of them were Mick Jaggers.

The perspectives of today's rookies were depressing. Maybe this was the reason why my generation tried so hard to give our children everything we could, most of all: a chance in life.

Somehow, my generation had fallen through the cracks.

While I was just musing about the injustice of the intergenerational contract in its actual application, rescue came from an unexpected direction.

'You see, my dear, I truly had a rich life. And a lot of luck. Of course, I have worked hard, but I also had a lot of opportunities. I am 62, now. Next year, I will go into early retirement. Then, I want to do something for others. Give back to society. Maybe a charity for children. There are so many issues, there. Many children don't even learn how to read and write, these days. They don't go to school, because the parents cannot show them that work makes life richer. The children have mobile phones, computers and the latest TV's, but they don't have a chance in life.'

He spoke straight from the bottom of my heart. And

straight into my heart. 'Yes, you are right. It hurts me, too, to see this.'

He was not done yet; the issue was near to him. 'You know, as a society, we have a responsibility to show our children the right way. I am a father, myself, and the most important thing has always been to open opportunities to my children. I still remember the moment I first held my son – such a little human bundle. You want to put the world at their feet. And you want to lock them up in their room or wrap them in cotton so that no one can ever hurt them. I wish I could experience that feeling, again. There is no greater happiness than children.'

I looked at him. No, no smug smirk, no trying to catch my attention. This was the real Dr Kinsey talking, and not his image of himself. I liked the real Dr Kinsey. So much more than the educational long-playing record from the evening before. I placed my hand on his, 'Dr Kinsey, you surprise me. I wished there were more people like you.'

'Well, well, you're exaggerating. This is not all altruistic. You know, I'm wondering a bit what I will do after retirement. Going from 150 to zero, that's just not me. I cannot do that. And I don't want to do that. With my charity, I would have something meaningful to do, but still enough time for a partner. Maybe, I am lucky and find a woman who wants to build that together with me and then continue our work when I am no longer around.'

'That's admirable. Maybe, you can also support an existing organisation, too, then you don't have to establish the whole administration and wouldn't be responsible for everything. I think a lot of charities would be very grateful to be supported by a man like you.'

'Yes, of course, obviously, they want old Dr Kinsey. But I want to decide what is being done and how. Together with my partner.'

He held my hand tight. My hand prickled, then my arm, then my belly. I tried to catch his view, but he looked out the window. We remained silent until the boat reached Lucerne, watching the mountains all around the lake. Was he smiling?

In Lucerne, we visited the Lion Memorial honouring the Swiss mercenaries who had been killed in the French Revolution. The sight always made me sad, but even more so now, after hearing so much about the post-war period. How horrible to die like that, for something completely unrelated to one's life. Hard to imagine that Switzerland was so poor back then that her sons had to sell themselves as mercenaries. And now, it seemed like an island of the blissful.

Unfortunately, we were not alone when we visited the Jesuit Church, afterwards, so that I could not sing, even though I felt like it. But I did not want to disturb anyone. I also interrupted the Doctor's lecture on Jesuits. While he struggled to believe it, I actually knew more than Kinsey about that topic. Some years before, a friend's friend, a Jesuit, had declared out of nowhere that he intended to leave the order to marry and have a family with me. He had naturally assumed that I wanted that, too. Naturally but inaccurately. After all, I had not even known that he was participating in that whole side of life, at all. The books I read to better understand the Jesuits and him did not really reveal much with respect to the topic of love (not surprisingly). But at least they had helped me to choose the right location to solve the problem: His brains. He had to separate the two topics 'order' and 'partnership'. If he came to the conclusion, regardless of me, that his future was outside the order, then he had to quit. And afterwards, he could search for a partner. But whether this would be me, that would be a different question. An unanswered one. But I did not want such a mortgage in my life, without even knowing him. Yes, I had seen *The Thorn Birds,* on TV, as a child, but it had never been my plan to be in the sequel.

Of course, I did not tell Kinsey about all of this. Instead, I directed our path to a nearby restaurant.

I went to the loo. I had to clarify something. I could not call Klara, so I phoned Mary. I told her about the whole situation, eating out, the flood of words, the bills I had paid, the human being showing up here and there, the hand, the silence – and the return to the flood. As well as the fact that we were still on a last name basis. At last, I asked the question I seriously had no answer to: Was I on a date or on a friendly field trip?

Mary was certain, 'Date, obviously a date. He wants to impress you. And maybe, he is also a little nervous, that's why he is talking so much. Wait a second.' She shouted, 'Leo, my love! Say, Jo is out with a man who is talking about himself, the whole time, including personal stuff. They are still on a last name basis, though, and she has paid most bills. No real physical contact. Date or no date?'

'You mean real personal? Men don't talk a lot if there's no reason to do so. Did he talk about children?'

'Jo, did he talk about children?'

'Yep.'

'Yes, he has. And, what do you think, darling?'

Leo was sure, 'Definitely date. Go for it, Jo.'

'Jo, did you hear that? So, he is on a date. The question is whether you want to be on a date. With him. Be open. It's just a date. It doesn't mean that you have to marry him. Talk about yourself. Show him the great woman you are. And most importantly: Hang up, now. Else he has left when you get back, or he sends you a rescue squad.'

'Wow, bummer, you are right. But thank you so, so

much. Well, then, let's get back in there!'

Yes, he was waiting for me, 'Hello, Principessa, I was beginning to get worried. I have ordered champagne, already, so that we can switch to first name basis, finally. I have been waiting for a while for you as the lady to offer me that. But now, I am beginning to believe that if I don't take the initiative, we will still say Mr and Ms when we are in bed, together. So, I am Mark.' He took my hand.

'And I am Johanna.' I could have skipped the telephone call, it seemed.

'Pleased to meet you, my dear Johanna.' He bent towards me, pulled my head to him and kissed me on the mouth. Demanding access. Wet. Too wet. And for a long time. A very long time. Wheezing. I let it happen, but did not prolong it. Actually, I did not like his way of kissing.

As Mary had suggested, I then talked about myself and, really, he was interested, charming, polite, listened, inquired, supplemented without talking in monologue. I liked him. More and more. Maybe, I had just been too hesitant. And he too nervous.

On the way to the station, he held my hand. It was prickling. My telephone rang. It was Christian. While I gave him a recount of the week, carefully avoiding the weekend, Mark's hand landed on my *Füdli,* and he kissed my neck. I had to prevent myself from giggling, and told Christian I would call the next evening, when I would have more time. On the train, we sat opposite each other, again, because Mark did need some space. He pulled his iPhone out, and started to write emails. Well, fine. He obviously needed a break.

In Zurich, I said goodbye, 'This was a truly lovely day with you, Mark. Thank you. Your hotel is right over there. So, when will I see you, tomorrow?'

'Oh, this is…I thought…So, tomorrow. Yes, would you like to join me for breakfast at the hotel?'

'Yes, that works. I am looking forward to that. 9 am?'

I approached him, held his face and kissed him on his mouth. Not wet. He kissed back. For a long time. Still too wet, but it felt good and tickled. Good enough for today.

'See you tomorrow,' I turned around and left. When I looked back at him, he had already gone in.

Mark

Another one of those nights. The doorbell woke me up. There was nobody at the door. No response on the speakerphone. No one in the street. Back to bed.

The same game: Wake up – door nobody – outside nobody – look out on the street nobody – bed.

Again, and again. Tonight, sleepwalking definitely got on my nerves more than usual. Or maybe my nerves got more on the sleepwalking than usual.

When I showed up in the hotel's breakfast room, Mark welcomed me with a hug and did not seem to have spent the night waiting at my door in vain to be let in. And I was quite sure that he would have let me know. I was glad I had not gone downstairs to check.

Mark kissed me (definitely a noticeable improvement in quality). He had ordered champagne. 'To us!' He smiled and leaned towards me, whispering, 'My dear, I must confess that the way you left me yesterday was quite hard, I must admit. Especially because I was also quite hard.'

He grinned. Did I really want to know? No. I chose to ignore it. We went to the buffet. He was hungry. Or he just wanted to explore everything.

Unfortunately, he did not really enjoy the booty from his culinary crusade. 'Say, where did this guy learn how to cook? Have you tried the omelette?' A sneak peek at my plate would have revealed the answer, actually. 'He added flour. I don't believe this. I thought that in Switzerland, a cook would know not to put flour into an omelette. If I wanted that, I would have ordered an *Omelette à la farine* or a *farinette*. Or a pancake. How can a cook in a self-proclaimed global city like Zurich not know that? I am really getting mad, now. Waiter!'

It was good for him that he knew three different words for an omelette with flour, and such fancy French words at that, but that did not help him much. I pulled down his accusingly raised arm. 'Mark, does it really matter that much? This is how omelettes are made, here. If you don't like it, just don't eat it. Or order a German one, as you like it. I am sure they will do that. We are old enough to solve this without such an uproar.'

He was not amused. 'What does this have to do with my age? If you want to refer to yourself, feel free, but leave me out of this. And if you think that I am too old, then just tell me. Anyway, I don't like it. If you like it so much, then you can eat it.'

'No, I cannot eat eggs in the morning. That makes me throw up. Just leave it, that's fine. Too bad for the omelette, but that's life.'

'What do you mean – that's life? The cook should have asked me if I wanted flour in it. After all, it is obvious that I am German and not Swiss.'

I sighed and took his hand, 'Mark, it is an omelette. It is not an atomic power plant, not a spaceship and not even rack of venison.'

'Why are you talking about rack of venison, now?'

He had taken the bait. Presumably, he was not even aware of the drama evoked by the impromptu speech held by the father of the bride. Maybe, the story would cheer him up. So, I told him all about Klara's despair when she thought that rack of venison for 100 people was just dying a second death in the oven, about her killer looks, about the photos – and the rescuing soup.

Now, the Doctor had to laugh, too – fortunately. I gave him an emotional valve and asked him how he prepared his omelette. As expected, he spread all details of the (only) accurate omelettation right in front of me. Of course, flourless. And while I was really not interested in this topic, it did elicit the personable enthusiasm that I had liked in Klara's kitchen. And then he started recounting how he had made omelette and scrambled eggs and pancakes and French toast for his children on the weekends, before heading off to hike or bike, to the zoo or to the museums. And I actually enjoyed listening to him.

'But they always liked my omelette most. Well, I will make that for you when you stay over night.'

'Like I said, egg in the morning makes me sick.'

'Aah, note to self: Overnight stay has been booked.'

He grinned. Strange enough, I really did not feel any rejection – even though it was already the second remark of this type on the first or second (who knew?) date. Maybe, this was really an option. Maybe even today, before he would leave.

But first, I had organised the excursion to the *Kunsthaus*.

'Mark, I think I told you that I have organized a visit at the Picasso exhibition, today. You are joining us, aren't you? We will have to set off, soon. Have you already packed your stuff?'

'Ah, yes, the museum. I have hard hopes that this plan

has been cancelled. I only have to check out from my bed at noon.' He took my hand and grinned, again.

'Mark, I cannot miss my own event.'

'You do not even know if anyone shows up. And I find this hard – very hard.' He tried to pull my hand towards his crotch. I pulled it back.

'Mark, I am quite sure that this is neither the first nor the last time that life is hard. I would be happy for you to join me, but if you don't want to, that's also okay. I planned this before I knew you were coming. And, please, stop talking about things or other that are hard. I do not like that.'

'Then I will go home, now.'

He let go of my hand, left the room – and did not come back. Not after one minute, not after five minutes, not after ten minutes.

Granted, I was somewhat baffled about his brusque reaction, but it seemed that this was just not his day. Well, that was his decision.

On my way to the museum, the sun had fought its way through the morning haziness, and I enjoyed the free space to think.

I waited near the museum entrance with a sign 'Expats Forum', feeling rather ridiculous.

And really, by 11, six art lovers showed up, including the Finnish girl from the dance night and three men. So far, so good. Unfortunately, I had not counted on the curse of modern technology. While I had conscientiously gathered information on the exhibition to facilitate a discussion, the group had telepathically agreed to use the audio guides. Thus, the topics 'Getting to know other people', 'Discussion' and 'Together' were automatically struck off the agenda. Dang it, I should have thought of that.

While walking through the museum on my own, I suddenly realized what would attract masses of people, no, of men – masses of Super Bowl-esque dimensions: A gathering on a military training ground with Harley Davidsons and tanks, decorated with illustrations from the Kama Sutra, where the participants would gloriously save our and other mankinds and the universe with light sabres and tomahawks. A beautiful image. Too bad that I did not really see myself participating. Well, good luck to the guys organising that.

Back to this reality, on a November Sunday in the *Kunsthaus Zürich*. We ran into each other near the exit, more or less coincidentally – 'more' because we had not arranged for that, but 'less' because we were all listening to the same emission. We bid each other farewell, because everyone had important plans. Wow, great! Another lesson: Technology wins.

My telephone beeped. A text message.

'My dearest, please forgive me my abrupt departure. For me, it's all or nothing, and I want all of you. Alone. I promise to behave better in the future. Cordially and hopefully more, love, Mark'

He knew what he wanted. Me. No one had ever said that to me. Or shown it. He seemed certain of his feelings. I was obviously slower, even though I had liked the tickling. Maybe, I was just not the type for love to hit like a lightning. But was this it? Was this how love felt?

Another beep of the phone. A text message from Mary.

'So?! What's up?!? I want information!!!!!! In breathless antici…. pation, Mary'

Not being sure of what I felt, I left things vague. 'It was a nice weekend. More or less. Big huggies, Jo'

Mary responded promptly, 'Hunnybuns, don't worry! The right one is somewhere out there. Love ya, Mary'

I had lied a little, but another little, I had not lied. Was he Mr Right? Or did he just think he was? Or did I just want him to be? I decide to postpone the answer, together with the answer to his text message.

It was late when Mark called, 'Hello, Johanna, did you receive my message?'

He sounded tired and fragile. No wonder, he had been driving all day, the poor guy. I turned very mild.

'Hi, Mark. Yes, of course. Thank you. Too bad that you did not stay. I would have been happy to have you. And essentially, we would have been by ourselves, anyway.'

'I only go on dates that are exclusive. By the way, when will I see you, again? And where? Are you coming to Berlin, any time soon?'

'Well, actually, my uncle will be celebrating his birthday, on Friday. I was still wondering whether it was really worth coming to Berlin, because he forgets it as soon as I leave. But then, if it makes him happy now, I simply mustn't care if he forgets, five minutes later. So, to make a long story short, I could come to Berlin, on Friday.'

'Oh! Oh, now, that's good news. Very good news, indeed. I'm almost a bit overwhelmed, now. A woman who makes fast decisions, I like that. Actually, I love that. Let me check what my weekend looks like. But I think that should work. When should I pick you up?'

'Well, his dinner will be over by seven, I guess. His bedtime.'

'Good, I will pick you up at seven, then. At the retirement home? Or do you want me to join you for dinner? After all, he already knows me.'

'No, he won't remember you, he forgets everything, right away. So, I will see you on Friday, at 7pm.'

Mark smacked. 'Well, I doubt that he really wouldn't remember me. But you are right. It would be weird if you turned up at your family event with your new lover. So: I'm looking forward to it.'

'Me too. See you on Friday.'

'See you on Friday, my dear.'

I had obviously just arranged a cohabitation date. I would have to digest that.

I booked the flight and went to sleep. Would I dream of Mark?

Uncle Walter

No, I did not dream of Mark.

Instead, a butterfly landed on my hand and flew away, again. I looked at it, and I knew that this was my soul, my heart – me. I had to catch myself to stay me. Carefully, so as not to break my wings. But time and again, I escaped from myself and danced through the air in the deep dark night, fleeing from me and chasing me.

When I asked myself whether this chase through my dark room in the middle of the night actually made sense, I had to acknowledge that it did not, and I sent myself to bed.

But still, I did not dream of Mark. Not in this night and not in the following nights. Despite our telephone dates, every evening. I left the office in the early evening to talk to him, and took some work home to continue working, after our call. Of course, this was a bit strenuous, but I did not mind doing that for Mark. I felt as if I had overtaken myself, on the fast lane with my trip to Berlin. So, spending hours on the phone with him gave me much needed comfort.

My job appeared easy when compared to what poor Mark had to go through. From the outside, those major concerns always appear very professional and organized. But the closer one looks behind the scenes the clearer it becomes how much time is consumed by useless power games and administrative nightmares. This was also true for the Maienwald group, where apparently everyone not only fought for himself but also against everyone else. Vain peacocks who wanted to seem more than they were. Employees who demanded more responsibility (and a promotion), as soon as they had worked an hour of overtime, even though they could not even manage their current job. His secretary whose professional skills were limited to the preparation of tea and fruit plates. 'Very good tea, but still tea.' A CEO who never took any decisions for fear of having to bear the responsibility. And in the thick of all of this: Mark. He was the only one who did not focus on his own interest but on that of the corporation, the jobs, the shareholders and the customers. In changing order. But, in any event, it was not just about himself. He constantly had to turn around to check whether someone was trying to stab a knife into his back, and he spent half his time with internal politics. Even though he hated it. Every day, new intrigues and machinations. He clearly enjoyed to have someone who listened to him and who was there for him. Even though I did not understand how these men could act this way, and even though I did not think it was appropriate for me to have all this insider knowledge.

Sometimes, he sent me emails following up on topics we had discussed in our calls.

'You mentioned the *Klausjagen* in Küssnacht am Rigi. Did you know that this tradition has existed since the modern age, and that the men carry so-called *Iffelen* through the village? *Iffelen* are made of carton board and thin coloured paper, and they look like a Bishops mitre and are lit from the inside. They can be up to two metres in size.'

Indeed, I had told Mark about this tradition, which could have been perceived as an indication that I had actually heard of it. And I did know how to Google. 'Mark, I knew that. I told you that I have seen it. And you really don't have to go through the trouble of sending me such things from Google, I am totally capable of finding that myself if I want to.'

'Yes, but I just found this so interesting and wanted to share it with you. I feel so close to you, then.'

In a way, this was quite sweet, even though I did not really need these lectures. After some rounds, I gave up on this discussion and started to only browse his messages.

On Friday, I did, indeed, leave for Berlin. I had not informed my friends. Not even Klara. I needed an empty agenda and a rather empty mind. I would tell her later. She would understand. And I would take things easy.

In the elevated spirit of pleasant anticipation, I started chatting with an American couple waiting in line in front of me at the check-in. Someone had stolen their backpacks with all documents, in the morning, and since then, they had been traveling all over Switzerland to get temporary passports and new tickets. Now, they had no money left and a long stopover in Frankfurt ahead of them. This was really mean. I gave them some Swiss Francs and the Euros I had on me, so that they could at least buy something to eat, and ran off to the *Sprüngli* for some truffles. For Mark and for the couple. I did not want anyone to leave the country I loved with such a bad feeling.

Just a few minutes later, life switched me back from nice to normal, though. On the long escalator ride down to the gate, I heard a rumbling behind me. I turned around and saw people clearing the way for a suitcase coming down the stairs, faster and faster. Well, great! The family in front of me tried to gather their children. I stopped the suitcase and waited for the owner, a blonde loaded with another suitcase and a handbag, which would have been totally sufficient for an average household relocation. But somewhat over the top for hand luggage. She forced out a 'thanks', and graced away.

Fortunately, my side only hurt a little. The bruises would show later. Hardtop cases. My pleasure.

I met our little angel, again, on the plane. Yippee, she sat next to me. I had the aisle seat, she sat in the middle. After filling up the overhead bin with one suitcase and her handbag, she switched up one gear on the 'Help me, I am the helpless little Bambi' scale and asked if she could quickly shove her suitcase under the seat in front of me, just to see if it would fit. I let her, and it did.

She switched to the next gear and trilled, 'Well, now that it fits there so nicely, why don't we just leave it there? This would be so much easier.'

Too bad that I was not a man and therefore not really into helpless Bambis. Apart from that, I did not like people who took along all their belongings as hand luggage, while idiots like me stuck to the rules.

My syrupy voice informed her that I was quite convinced that the suitcase would fit under the seat in front of her just as nicely.

So, Bambi had to spend the flight with knotty legs. I was such a mean green mother! And was punished with contempt. That served me right. Yes! I could have sworn that the women around us were smiling, while the men's hearts were bleeding silently. What a bitch I was.

The birthday party was much smaller than it used to be: only the closest family and friends. Obviously, I was not the only one who was determined to spend a joyful evening, even though we all felt like crying. So we first celebrated Uncle Walter and then the blessed memories of better, healthier times. Uncle Walter seemed to smile when he dozed off.

As expected the evening ended at a child-friendly time. I needed a hug.

Mark was waiting outside. 'Hello, my love. Your lover is waiting, just as ordered.'

This was not what I needed right now. 'Actually, I need a friend, now, not a lover. This has made me sad.'

'Oh, I'm sorry, my dear. Yes, of course. I could have thought of that, myself. Yes, I also feel sad when visiting my old colleague. And I know how lovingly and motherly you feel for your uncle. Motherliness is a virtue that underrated. Even though...'

I interrupted him, 'Mark, please don't. I just want to digest for a little bit. Just give me five minutes for myself. And afterwards, you can tell me everything you know and think about motherliness.'

'Yes, of course, my dear. Really, I should have thought of that. Did you convey my regards? Did he remember me?'

'Maaark! Please! Five minutes.'

He prepared a response but swallowed it down and remained silent. For five minutes. Exactly five minutes.

He inquired, 'May I?'

I had to smile. The way he was sitting there, like an oversized and overweight schoolboy, he was kinda cute. Not quite as cute as he thought, though.

'Yes, you may. Thank you. So, what did you want to say?'

'So, motherliness. I think that motherliness is totally undervalued, these days – and wrongly so. I mean, it is the nucleus of the family, no, of life. Did you know that the oldest figure of a mother goddess, the Venus of Hohle Fels, is 35'000 to 40'000 years old and was found in the Swabian Alb? I was born not too far from there. Personally, I am a profound admirer of motherliness.'

I was not in the mood for a lecture. 'Mark, being a SINK, this is not really my ballpark.'

'SINK? You are a spout?'

'Single Income No Kids,' I had to smile.

'But the fact that you do not have children yet, that does not mean that you are not motherly. I have seen you with your uncle, and that really made my heart melt. You so reminded me of my mother. Ah, my Mutti. She loved me so dearly. No matter what I did, no matter what I needed, she always had my back. She was always there, when I came home. Food was on the table, and she wanted to know all about my day. And that despite all the work on the farm. I was her life and her happiness.' He looked at me, 'That was the moment when I fell in love with you from head to toe. You will be a wonderful mother. I am really looking forward to that.'

'Whoa, whoa, hold your horses, doctor!' I had to laugh, and I felt a warm feeling growing in my heart. After all, I wanted children, too.

'Well, not right here and now, but just you wait. And, did he remember me?'

'Well, I did not mention you. It was an evening with the family, and my uncle lives in the past, anyway.'

Mark swallowed his response.

We arrived at his house, a light blue art deco villa, white columns framing the entrance, large, white-bordered windows and a steeple. What a beautiful house!

He looked at me, 'I cleaned the whole day, but I don't think that it's really clean. Please don't be mad at me. You will see that it really needs a female hand.'

Indeed, the door window was so dirty that I did not even recognize that it was made of glass. After fidgeting for a while with the key, he finally managed to open the door. 'You don't expect me to carry you across the threshold, do you? That's what I like about you emancipated women.'

'Well, we are not married. As I said, hold your horses.'

But somehow, it touched me that he thought about this.

We entered, and a surge of insipid smoke embraced me, mixed with cabbage stench. I fell into a coughing fit.

Mark came to me, 'Did you catch a cold? Oh, you poor thing. And I opened all the windows upstairs to get in some fresh air. Wait a second, I will close them.'

I held him back, 'No, Mark, fresh air is good. Why don't you open the windows downstairs, as well? We are here, now, no one will come in.'

Dried foliage all over the hall. Bachelor dilapidation.

'You know what? I made us a vegetable broth. The food at such places really isn't much good. I am sure that you want to eat something proper, now.'

That was really sweet of him, and the way he stood in front of me, full of pride, I just couldn't disappoint him, even though I wasn't hungry, anymore. I just had to swallow it up. After all, I did not want to spoil the evening. 'That's sweet of you. Yes, why don't I give it a try.'

Mark led me to the dining room. He had set the table, with a blotchy tablecloth, chandeliers and flowers. Sweet. While he was pottering around in the kitchen, I had a look around. I liked art deco houses with their high ceilings, the stucco decorations and the fluxionary lines. The dining room even had an oriel with ornament glass. So beautiful!

I took a closer look – and had to realize that even timeless beauty and elegance are substantially hampered by a swarm of dead insects. Flies, bees, in the middle a butterfly, dusted in grey, like a moth. Sad. Hopeless. Like a quote from a French art movie. This did not call for a female hand but for a cleaning squad. But that could be changed.

Mark returned, and saw my look, 'Oh, yes, I forgot that. The windowsill. And the window. You know, after my wife's death, I left everything the way it was. That was ten years ago. And I think it is quite convenient, actually. Every burglar thinks that this place is not worth breaking into when he sees this.'

'And you believe that helps? Dirty and poor are not necessarily related, really.'

'Well, so far, no one has tried it. Come, sit down.' Despite my protest, he poured me a glass of wine and filled my plate to the rim.

He urged me to try, and, true, the soup was good. 'Wow, that's delicious. Praise to the chef. Say, did you add fennel to it?'

'Yes, that's my special recipe. You know, I have never had such a delicious soup, anywhere else. And you know that I am a real gourmet. But you don't say a thing. Say, don't you like it?'

'Yes, of course, it is really good. As I said. Really, very good. What spices did you use?'

'Well, if you don't know what it is, then I won't tell you, either. As I mentioned, it is a secret recipe. But you can guess.'

He pursed his lips, slightly tilted back his head, looked down on me and shook his head slightly, humming.

Actually, I was not that utterly fascinated by a soup. But given that it gave him so much pleasure, I gave in.

'My guess is that it is fresh coriander.'

He was disappointed. 'That's right. How did you know?'

'You know, I cook, too. I invite friends, and we eat and drink and talk late into the night. In English, German, French or sometimes in languages that I do not even understand. And when I feel like it, I choose a country as a motto, and then everything I cook is from that country. And there is always coriander in the Indian or Asian cuisine.'

'Oh, I want to be part of that. So far, I just cannot fit that into my life. If you and I get together, I will not only have you but also friends. This will be wonderful. Very much so.'

'Yes, I am only available as a package deal with my attachments. Kind of a family tradition. My brother married my sister-in-law as a package with her little daughter, as well. Her daughter then climbed on his arms during the wedding ceremony. This way, she married him, too. But don't worry, my friends won't climb on you.'

'Yes, this would be a bit heavy. But as long as they don't climb, it's fine. You know, I can go into early retirement, soon. Then, I will move to Switzerland, to you. We buy a house, I take care of our kids and go biking, and when you come home, I have already prepared dinner. And on the weekends, our friends come to visit. We will be so happy.'

He had taken my hands and pulled them towards him to kiss them. I let it happen. Actually, this went way too fast for me. Being here went too fast for me. But I was also touched. He let go of my hands and directed his attention back to the soup.

'Would you like some more? Or more wine?'

'No, thank you. You know, I had dinner at my uncle's.'

'So, you don't like it? Of course you don't, you took hardly a spoonful.'

'Yes, of course, it really IS very good, especially with the coriander. But I simply cannot eat any more.'

'And the wine?'

'The wine is equally good, but I just don't tend to drink a lot.'

'Well, I will have another serving. And I will empty the bottle. I like it, you know.' His voice had cooled down. How could his voice and his mood tip over so quickly?

When he returned from the kitchen with more soup, he had cheered up. 'What a wonderful evening with you, my Principessa. I am so grateful that you are here. And I look forward to getting to know you better. I hope you are fit. When your lover gets into his stride, you will need that. Especially now that he is fully invigorated. Don't you want some more soup, after all?'

'No, please just let it be. I just don't want more. And apart from that, I have brought something for us.' I got the truffles, 'Try this. *Truffes du Jour* from *Sprüngli*. The best chocolate in the world. You have to eat them fast. They are so fresh, they don't last long.'

Mark did not expose the expected enthusiasm, 'I don't believe this. You refuse to eat my soup, and then you want to eat chocolate? No, chocolate is not allowed in this house. Well, now that you have bought it… But, anyway, in principle, this is a no-chocolate household. It only makes you fat.' He took a piece and grimaced with visible pleasure. 'Wow, these are really amazing.'

'Well, everything is possible in moderation. We put them in the fridge. Just you wait how good they are, then.'

'Well, a bowl of soup won't kill you, either. But, fine, if you don't want it, then that's fine, too.' He did not sound as if he thought that this was fine.

We took the plates to the kitchen – a culinary battlefield. I had not known how many pots and pans were required for the preparation of a soup.

He engulfed me in an embrace and kissed me. The nape, the mouth, along my neck. His hands touched me, caressed me, up and down and back, touched my hands that explored him, as well. It was only now that I realized how massive he really was. I could not reach around him. But that did not matter. The energy flowed through my body like gentle shivers. He pulled me into the bedroom, and we made love.

Unfortunately, this did not touch me as deeply as I had hoped. Shades of Grey sex. One shade. Of grey. Very grey. Apparently, I had expected too much and wanted too much that this would be the night of nights. Well, maybe, there had been too much soup discussion.

And I would have to get to know him, first.

Mark smiled like a huge, content giant baby.

When I turned to the side, he embraced me from the back, his head right behind mine. 'I love you. Thank you for being here.'

He droned languorously and began to snore. Somewhere between jackhammer and starting jet. It felt like a starting jet, definitely.

The more I tried to wriggle out of his embrace, the tighter he held me. I woke him up and asked him to let go of me and turn to the other side.

He grumbled, 'No, I sleep very well. I want to hold you in my arms. I love you.'

I waited forever until he unfastened his grip enough for me to squirm free of him and move to another room, where a mattress was lying on the ground.

Quiet.

When I woke up, I looked straight into Mark's small, deep, pale blue eyes. They were smiling gently. 'Hello, Principessa. Did I expulse you? I am sorry. Look, the sun is shining. What do you want for breakfast? An egg? Two? Omelette?'

'Good morning! Yes, you bellowed quite a bit. No eggs, please, that makes me sick, in the morning. Why don't you let me get up, first?' Prussian-Huguenot morning routine.

Mark had already set the table. A white dog rose was lying on my plate, 'The last one of the year. I don't know how it survived up to now, but I think it waited for you, my angel.'

Next to it, the two frog mugs from the flea market. How sweet of him! Mark embraced me.

'So you are sure you don't want omelette? Another one of my secret recipes. Really delicious.'

'No, Mark. I told you that eggs in the morning make me sick. Enjoy, but enjoy it for yourself, please.

Indeed, the mere smell made me feel like throwing up, but I did not want to ruin his morning and instead tried to calm down my stomach by filling it. 'Say, is this green tea with mint leaves? That's my favourite tea. What a coincidence.'

'You had that at the wedding, after dinner. And you looked so happy, just like a little Buddha. I remembered that. I was watching you, that evening, you know?'

'You did? That sounds kinda creepy. Anyway, that's sweet of you. Thank you so much! This tea is really good.' Even though – I felt the far-reaching shadow of surveillance right into the here and now. And I did not like it.

'The preparation of green tea is an art, you know? The water must be no warmer than 90°C. I made it in a water bath.' He beamed with pride.

A glance into the kitchen showed me that the proper preparation of green tea obviously required the installation of several pots, an immersion heater and a thermometer, as well as the flooding of half the kitchen.

'That's really sweet of you, but you don't have to stress out like that, just for my sake. My tea is not used to frills.' I had never talked this much about food.

'That's no stress. I enjoy doing that. Very much so, indeed. So, what shall we do, today? For tonight, I have tickets for the Berlin Philharmonics. The German Requiem by Brahms. Shall we just hang out a little bit? Or maybe a walk along the former border? We can also take the bike.'

I hugged him. 'The Philharmonics? With Brahms's German Requiem? And the Rundfunkchor?'

He nodded.

'That's amazing! I love the Rundfunkchor. The best choir in the world. Have you ever noticed how they get across the consonants? You understand every word, every T, K or F. And the dynamics, just ingenious. And Brahms! I have their recording, and we have also just performed that piece. And you have tickets? Great, I'm excited. But, you know, I do not have anything to wear.'

'I have never seen anyone who can be as genuinely happy as you, my little frog,' he laughed, 'and you can wear whatever you want to, I will always love you.'

'I mean, I cannot go to the Philharmonie with jeans and a sweater,' I insisted.

'Of course, you can. Everybody does. Or we go to the *Ku'damm* and buy something. I also need some sweaters. But first, let me give you the grand tour of Casa Kinsey.'

He had not exaggerated – eleven rooms on three floors. A house, way too big for one person – and also for two.

Most rooms were more or less empty, apart from the clothes, books and CDs, computer cables and bags piling up on the floor. A house, built for a big family, inhabited by a messy nomad.

'I have left everything the way it was when my children moved out. I feel almost a little embarrassed, everything is so empty and so untidy. But now, you are here. Look, that's the highlight of my household – well, apart from myself, of course.'

A grand piano. It was shimmering.

'Mark, what a beautiful piano. My dad had one, too. One day, you will have to play something for me.'

I placed my hand on the smooth, clean surface. I loved the cool but warm, tangible elegance of the shellac.

'Don't scratch it,' he burst out.

Why would I do that? Obviously, an iffy issue.

I changed the topic, 'Say, your house is really huge. But you don't have a sofa or anything to snuggle on, do you?'

'My god, a sofa. Please don't tell me that you want a sofa! My wife always wanted one, but I just refused. That's so square! No, such a thing won't get into my house. Absolutely no way.'

'And where do you want to sit and cuddle, then? I like that.'

He shook his head and breathed out loud. He was not convinced. But actually, that didn't matter, I would not move in here, anyway. And in Zurich, I had a sofa.

Mark took me to a door and lowered his voice, 'Okay, and now I will show you my sanctum. But you must be very quiet.'

I was curious. We entered the conservatory, a bright room full of savaged potted plants, divided into twelve sections the size of a bath sheet, each with a shoe box in it.

Looking more closely, I saw that each of the boxes had an entry hole.

'This is where my hedgehogs live. I found them at the feeding spot in my garden. They were still far too small and would never have made it through winter. So, I took them in. Now, I coddle them up, and when they reach their hibernation weight, they will relocate to the basement. Everything is prepared and waiting for them. You want to see?'

He led me down to the basement and presented the room for his prickly house guests. My heart wrenched. I kissed him.

In the afternoon, we drove to the *Ku'damm*, West Berlin's former shopping area. Childhood memories flashing up here and there – just rarely, though, because the area had changed as much as the whole city of Berlin.

So, sweaters for Mark. I was amazed at how quickly we found what we were looking for. A woman his plus size would have been better off setting up a cotton plantation or a sericulture if she wanted to get her hands on clothes that fit. I wished I were a man! Once again.

I hadn't bought any new clothes in ages and was delighted to find out that I fit into a size 10. I could have embraced the world – or kissed Mark, for lack of a world at hand. I did not tell him why. I wanted him to see me the way I was and would be. He turned out to be a good kisser, just too wet.

'Wow, Schatzele, you cannot leave your hands off your lover, can you?' He whispered into my ear.

'Mark, please quit that lover business. That sounds so trashy. I don't have a lover. I have a partner, a soul mate, a friend. Not just a lover.'

'Well, of course, if you don't like it. That's what I love about you. You say what you think. You are the love of my life. Do you know that?'

I was not at that point yet. I did not respond and kissed him. If he took that for a response, so be it. I kept my size 10 dress on, we drove to the Philharmonie and wandered through the foyer, arm in arm, me in my new dress, he big and cuddly. A good, fulfilled feeling.

The concert was moving, exhilarating and gripping as expected. Was this love or was my heart just warming up in the wonder-, hope- and love-ful music of Brahms, melted into the memory of our own concert and the warming feeling of not being alone in a perfect moment?

I looked at Mark He was beaming. Me too.

I sat here, listening to the most beautiful music in perfect rendition, next to the man who loved me. Reason enough to be happy.

My neighbour coughed, and I handed her a cough drop. The usual scene: With every disease, you go to the doctor's, only with a cold, you go to the concert. Fortunately, I had come prepared.

On the way home, Mark said, 'I could have done without the concert, actually. I looked at you, the whole time. That was enough of a performance for me. You love this music, don't you?'

'Yes, I love Brahms. And hearing his music like that, sung by this choir and shortly after singing it, myself, that was such a gift, you cannot imagine how big a gift it was. Thank you, my darling.'

'What, you sang that yourself? Really? Are you that good?'

Why did he have to sound so surprised?

'Yes, of course. Most choirs sing it. It's a standard. It was fantastic. Standing ovations and very good reviews. The only sad thing is that you practice for months, and then you sing the piece just once and it is over. But that's worth it. It is as if my heart was singing. When I sing, there is so much more than the here and now. Then, I am all myself.'

'Well said, my dearest. I hope I can witness that, myself, one day.'

At Mark's place, I pulled him into the bedroom. We kissed and made love, but for me, things remained Grey. He saw the rainbow. It must have been my fault, but I would manage to get that straight, as well.

He was facing me, eyes closed, mouth open, tongue sticking out slightly, waiting for mine. He reminded me of an alligator snapping turtle I had once seen at the zoo. A big, dark lump of turtle. It is lying in the mud, prefers not to move at all and lets its tongue spin in its open mouth. The fish that mistakes its tongue for a tasty little worm and takes a bite is an unlucky fish. Not very eroticising.

When I left the bedroom to go to sleep, Mark opened his eyes and moaned, 'Don't leave me alone, my love! I want to hold you in my arms when I fall asleep. Please stay with me.'

I turned around, 'Mark, I am tired. I am sorry, but your snoring is just too loud.'

'When you love someone, that doesn't matter. Come on, stay with me.'

'That doesn't have anything to do with love. I just want to sleep. See you tomorrow, my dear.'

I left.

Granddad

Mark sat at the breakfast table in the kitchen, with a

view to the garden. 'My favourite place in the house. I sit here for hours and watch the birds. And the hedgehogs, of course, but they only show up at twilight. And in the summer, I sit outside with my pipe. See, there's my personal little feeding ground. I built it so that the jaybird cannot get to it. Last year, I had 23 breeding pairs. And I still put out something for the hedgehogs, just in case one of these little guys strays over and needs a hibernation home for winter.'

He emanated endearing bliss. Just because he was happy. A happy, affectionate, compassionate human being. Normally, I would have responded that one should not feed animals as long as there was no snow so that they could still find food themselves, but one did not have to comment on everything.

'You know, Johanna, I am so looking forward to summer, when we both will be puttering around in the garden. And then, I will repair the swing. We set it up for our daughter when she was just a little toddler. And soon, there will be another little Kinsey sitting on it, and I will push it to swing high. I'm so glad to have found you. I had almost given up.'

He was describing days like those I had spent with my granddad. I was too young for that, I just did not see myself living the life of my grandmother. And besides, we would live in Zurich. But he looked so happy, and I did not want to ruin this moment for him. On the other hand – no, this seemed important.

'Mark, I'm just not there, yet.'

'Where?'

'In a garden with children and swings.'

'But why not? You know, I'm absolutely certain. I can hardly believe how lucky we are. We are already like an old married couple. On our second weekend! Others have to work long and hard to achieve this. I have never felt as natural as I feel with you. When you find someone like that, you have to take the bull by the horns and grab the chance.'

I had never seen it like that. Routine as the ideal for a relationship. Really? Maybe, I was just expecting too much. Or the wrong thing. Maybe, there were no fireworks and violins of love flying through the air, in real life. Maybe, it was just a feeling that one could get along with the other person, and every now and then a little butterfly passing by. I liked him, even though his patronizing know-it-all attitude got on my nerves, sometimes. But then, there was also this feeling of being safe with him, his soothing certainty that we belonged together. Was this love? Was I feeling comfortable with him? Certainly not in his house. But maybe, just the very fact that I stayed in this house was a sign of love. Or maybe my willingness to somewhat accept his know-it-all attitude? And that I built my faith on the hope that sex with him would become more colourful over time? Was he the man who was not perfect but perfect for me? Or should I not only have accepted but rather not noticed or approved of all these things? Maybe, it was time to say farewell to my girlish dream of an irresistible love that would take me over like a tsunami. Maybe, I had just not allowed myself to fully fall for someone, yet, and now had to – what had Mark said? – take the bull by the horns, to see where this would lead. And maybe, it really wasn't a bad choice to do this with someone who was so certain and seemed to know what he wanted and what he was doing. Maybe, affection would grow.

Mark looked at me expectantly. Obviously, I was supposed to say something, 'Yes, maybe you are right.'

'Of course, I am right. We belong together, and there is

nothing more relaxing than gardening. What do you think of a little bike ride?'

That was a little abrupt, and when I looked out the window and thought of the hedgehogs preparing for hibernation, I lacked the appropriate enthusiasm. 'You know, I am more of a good weather cyclist. It's just ten degrees, outside. And apart from that, I do not have a bike or a helmet. Another time.'

'No worries, we will just go for half an hour, just a little warm-up. You can take my daughter's bike. Why don't you just have a look at it?'

We cleared the table.

'Mark, where can I put the empty yoghurt glass?'

'The trashcan over there.'

'No, I mean where do you put the glass for the recycling?'

'Well, into the trash. In the end, they just throw everything together and burn it, anyway. This whole recycling myth is just deceit and flim-flam. I always give the binmen some extra money for Christmas, and they take everything. Yes, you just have to know how to do it.'

Mark's look shouted, 'I am so great!', but my look denied the obviously expected expression of admiration. I considered the limited sacrifice of personal convenience required to recycle a glass highly reasonable. It would be a long way for me to understand him, but I did not want to discuss that, now.

Off to the bike!

Mark's daughter had a heavy mountain bike, he preferred a racing bike, 'A custom bike, extremely light and fast. I will change and be right back.

Mark returned in tight, black racing gear. It was the first time that I saw him in daylight sort of naked. Like a huge spider, with a massive body, scrawny legs and arms and a yellow helmet. He was about 150kg, unevenly spread over two metres height. I pitied his bike a bit. And a spider on a bike did, indeed, look somewhat ridiculous. But of course I did not say anything. After all, it was good that he did some sports. Over time, he would also lose weight.

We headed towards the forest, him first, me following. With every treadle of the pedal, the distance between us grew. It started drizzling. Which did not improve the situation. We had left 20 minutes ago, and I had no clue where we were. I hit the pedal until I heard my heartbeat drum like lashes in my ears. I managed to catch up.

'Mark, we wanted to go for half an hour. Are we on our way back? It is drizzling, and it's cold.'

'Oh, Schatzele, we are not made of sugar, are we? We go a little longer. I am just having such a good run, and the motion is good for my heart. You know what, I will wait at the lake. Just keep going straight ahead!'

He raced off, I followed slowly. The mountain bike was heavy and hard to handle. The drizzle turned into rain. This was not the little tour I had envisioned.

After another hour, I found Mark, sitting under a chestnut tree near the lake.

'So, Schatzele, what do you think? Quite a fast liver, your lover, right? See, you will have to switch to another gear if you want to keep up with me. Let's see who can beat that – faster than my thirty-year-old mistress.'

He looked so proud that I could not hurt his feelings. So, I refrained from mentioning that I did not want to defeat him but to spend the day with him. That men on a racing bike were always faster than women on a mountain bike. That he had just done what he wanted instead of what we had agreed to. And also that I had already told him that I found his reference to himself as my 'lover' highly ridiculous. I also did not object to the 'mistress'. I let him beam with happiness and stayed silent.

The way back was no more pleasant, and when I finally arrived at Mark's home, I was drenched and frozen to the marrow.

He had prepared a hot bath for me. 'My poor Schatzele! You are all frozen. Hurry! Get in the tub. Relax. I will make a nice cup of tea for us.'

Actually, hot baths were a waste of water, but today, I did not care. It felt good. Really good.

When I came into the kitchen, Mark pulled me away, into the bedroom, and whispered, 'Let me show you how couples make love. Real, true love. The best thing ever.'

We kissed, and our hands explored each other's bodies. We dropped on the bed.

'Turn around, Schatzele!'

I turned my back on him. He put his arm heavily on me, moved closer, much closer, sighed and fell asleep. And snored.

So, this was it? Pure ecstasy? Wow, cool. Again, I was trapped. His arm smothered me. After what felt like hours, he finally turned on his back, and I took the chance to escape. He was lying with his mouth open and snoring, like a huge, content bear.

I went to the kitchen and had a now cold tea. The truffes du jour were gone. Obviously, Mark had enjoyed them, after all.

I called my brother. The feeling of trepidation vanished, and it remained gone when I spoke about Mark.

Christian was surprised, but most of all pleased. 'Finally! I'm so happy for you. You know how much we've been wishing for a partner for you. So, when are you coming over so that we can meet him?'

'Oh, I don't know. It's still brand new. It's only our

second weekend, you know. But if things go well, I will present him, of course. I'm curious what you think.'

'Okay, but for now promise me that you will be careful. You are right, it's all good and nice, now, but take it slow, you are not in a hurry.'

'No worries, I am getting to know him, now. That's why I'm here. And I have no intention of eloping to Las Vegas. By the way, I don't even like Elvis impersonators.'

'Jo, just promise that you will look after yourself. And I want to sound this guy out. I know that you are grown-up and all, but I am your brother. I don't want him to hurt you. You had no relationship for such a long time.'

'Christian, he is not a tot. He is in his early sixties.'

'What? You are dating a retiree? Jo, did you really think that through? I mean, sixty!'

'Well, he doesn't sit in a wheelchair. Promised, I will take care and won't do anything that you wouldn't do. I love you.'

'Love you, too, Jo. Take care. And give me a call if something's wrong. Or just come over.'

I loved Christian. As children, we had quarrelled 24/7, but now he was one of the few people who would always back me and be by my side. It was cute of him to be so worried – but he didn't know Mark. After all, he was a good guy, despite his little weaknesses. Certainly, I had my flaws, too, and just didn't notice them because they were mine. And if he could ignore mine, I should be able to reciprocate.

I decided to give him, to give us a chance.

In the late afternoon, Mark came downstairs. 'Thank you, Schatzele, for staying with me until I fell asleep. Wasn't that wonderful? Much better than sex, wasn't it? You know, once you've been married, you realize that sex is totally overrated. Cuddling is so much better and also much more important. And the female orgasm doesn't have a biological function, anyway.'

This could have been my granddad speaking. Even though he would ever have used the word orgasm, of course.

'Well, without it, there will be no more sex. And that's not good to preserve the species.'

'Oh, I never saw it this way. Well, next time, I will give it to you so that you stick under the ceiling.' He embraced me and kissed my neck. 'Good, and now, I will cook a nice little something for us.'

'Can I help you? Peel? Slice and dice?'

'No, no. I prefer cooking by myself. I have my own ideas, you know.'

Mark kissed me and left for the kitchen. I was a little surprised to be alone, yet again, but then, I knew that he wanted to treat me. So, I went back to the study and worked a little.

Two hours later, Mark was done. The fish was exquisite. Remembering the soup disaster, I praised every bite, hoping that Mark would really understand that I enjoyed it. It worked. 'Oh, stop it! You're making me blush!'

Actually, he could not have blushed any more. He was sweating.

After dinner, Mark took me to the airport. 'Thank you so much for this wonderful weekend. I hope that you are not too shocked by the house. Of course, it's impossible not to notice that this is a bachelor's den. You come back next week?'

I kissed him, 'Yes.'

My belly was tickling.

The tickling continued on the plane. Good. I dug deep down into myself not to miss a sign of being in love.

Apparently, the tickling was visible, and my neighbour

asked, 'Wow, you seem to be happy! Are you going on vacation? I saw you waving at your father.'

He looked nice. Very nice. Out of an old habit, I noticed that he was not wearing a ring. But that was none of my business, really.

I had to laugh. Mark would have said that he was my lover. 'No, I'm going home, actually. But that was not my father.'

'Oh, *äxgüsi,* I guess that I've just dropped a major clanger.'

'No worries. You are a German living in Switzerland, as well?'

After a while, we all adopted certain Swiss-isms, and '*äxgüsi',* a Swiss version of the French *excusez,* was definitely one of them.

I was right. Alex was an IT specialist from Berlin who had been living in Zurich, for five years. He loved Switzerland just as much as I did, loved bike riding, played tennis, went to the movies, cooked for friends and went hiking. We raved over our recent excursions, exchanged film recommendations and recipes. The flight passed in a flash, and I was a little disappointed when we landed on time. We exchanged email addresses. Maybe, we would have dinner, at some point.

At home, a message from Mark was waiting on my answering machine.

'Schatzele, I hope I told you and showed you, but just in case it is not absolutely clear by now, I just wanted to make sure you know. Because I will be in bed by the time you get home. I am so happy to have found you. I thank you for every minute, and I cannot wait for the next weekend. Schatzele, I love you!'

The message made me happy. It was good to be loved. Too bad that he was already asleep; else I would have called him. Good that he was already asleep. What would I have said?

Xavier

I wondered whether I should tell my friends about Mark. At least Klara. But if Desi knew, ... I did not want to hurt her, at least not as long as things were not certain.

In the evenings, I had no time to talk to them, any more, anyway. Every day, Mark's reports from his working hell became more detailed. I did not envy him. On paper, he had accomplished everything. But what is 'everything' if every day is a fight for survival?

He also told me about his daughter Marie, though, who was studying medicine in Cambridge, and who was very homesick. I suggested a CARE parcel with childhood memories, and every day, Mark told me about a new treasure he had found: effervescent powder, rice paper, pumpernickel, a DVD with reports from Berlin and his favourite sweater which she loved to snuggle into. What a loving and caring father! I liked that. I liked him.

On my end, I kept things short. There was no room for confidential information outside my work. And I did not want to burden Mark with my issues.

On Wednesday, a call from Alex interrupted my daily routine. We arranged lunch in early December. In Switzerland, planning was a serious matter.

Apart from that, my week was pretty normal – until late Friday afternoon, when things became somewhat bizarre. An Armenian family came by and demanded a meeting, even though they had not made an appointment. Else, they would set up camp in front of the main building. Well…

They had written to me several times, claiming that the Tsar had given their ancestor all his gold in 1915. The ancestor had allegedly deposited into a life insurance contract with *Blau-Weiss Versicherung.* We had searched our archives over and over again, but not found anything. And now a meeting. Friday afternoon, at 4 pm.

The group waiting for me in a conference room was, indeed, remarkable: The mother of the tribe had been designed as a *Matrjoschka* – outer layer, that was. But unlike the Russian doll, she did not contain any pleasant surprises but rather, she was nasty through and through. At least, this explained where her son (type Armenian gigolo with a white suit, white shoes, sun glasses and enough styling gel for the whole tribe) had acquired his extraordinary taste. The brother / uncle was comparatively non-descript. The interpreter greeted me and asked whether the two bodyguards should wait outside the building, given that they were carrying weapons. Yes, please, I would indeed appreciate that.

The meeting proceeded as I had seen many meetings proceed. The mother wordily explained that her relative had been given the gold, indeed. If it was no longer there, it was obvious that I had stolen it. Amazing how much shorter the translation was than the avalanche of words that had just gone over my head. When I started explaining that we had searched for the gold all over and in vain, the son's telephone rang. *You're my heart, you're my soul* by Modern Talking. He threw a surge of words at the interpreter, who forwarded a shorter version to me: A neighbour had called the police because of the bodyguards, who were being interrogated just now. Could I help?

I ran from the building, explained to the police that the two little sweetie pies were with me and picked them out of the police car. Was this an act of freeing prisoners, already? Whatever. I deposited the two at our reception and asked for our security service to be called in and watch.

Back to my intercultural intensive course, I explained that we had not found the supposed riches, and I asked what had driven the family to believe that this gold should exist, and exist with us. Was there any documentation? As expected, this truly outrageous question was countered by ranting and raving, which did not sound any nicer in Armenian than in any other language. It was slightly irritating, though, that the uncle / brother winked at me and sent air kisses my way, while his sister went off at me. His slimy smile put him at risk of sliding out in his own slime puddle while sitting. Why did these things always have to happen to me?

The rant culminated in an announcement, 'Many people have died for this gold. Now, it's your turn.'

When shaking hands to say goodbye, the interpreter inquired, 'Did you understand what I translated? Mrs Alzerian said that she will have you killed. Sorry about that.'

The fact that the brother / uncle said 'I loaf you' for a farewell also felt more like a threat than anything else, especially as he was accompanied by two men who were in a position to obtain such love by means other than romantic wooing. I was happy that I had called for our own security guards and would therefore not have to meet the bodyguards by myself. Unfortunately, life did not quite catch up with my expectations, at this point: Our security guys had called it a day at knocking-off time. How comforting.

So, I stayed at the office until the very last minute, hoping that they would not wait outside. I was right, no one followed me. It was a true relief when I could finally travel to Mark. And then, when he picked me up, he even had a surprise for me: Tickets for the Philharmonics, again!

'Mark, that's fantastic. Where did you get those? Do you have season tickets? For two?'

'Richard has invited us. After the concert, we're having dinner, together. I'm sure it will be lovely. After all, Xavier wants business from me.' He smiled at me, and his eyes were yet bluer.

On the way to his house, my phone rang. It was Klara. I kept things short and hung up. 'Stop it, Mark!' Mark's hand was exploring the area and specifically on its way to the area between my legs. I did not like that. The hand landed where it belonged. On the steering wheel.

In Mark's house, warmth and the smell of – smoke and soup were waiting for me.

Mark hardly left me the time to get out of my coat and pulled me into the kitchen. 'You know, I made a soup for you. I am sure that you haven't had anything decent to eat, yet. Have you?'

Mark and his soup. Surely, he meant well, but actually, I was just not hungry. Still – I remembered my last soup experience and decided to bit the bullet and whatever else there might be in the soup. 'That's really sweet of you that you did that. But really, you shouldn't have.'

Mark served and slurpingly pitched into his soup, 'You know, you have to slurp the soup so that the taste can fully unfold. Don't purse your lips like that. Just like wine tasting. The real connoisseur knows that, of course, but I am sure your parents have de-stilled that from you. Give it a try! Feel free!'

Unfortunately, my ears and my tongue were too close to function in such complete separation, and I preferred a much-reduced level of sound.

I tried. Without sound effects. The soup was good. Soup, it was. Mark beamed with pride and expectation, and I was ready to deliver, 'Mark, the soup is even better than last week's. Excellent. Really. And the herbs, again, really delicious.'

Mark was smiling blissfully. He continued slurping, and looked at me after some spoons, 'You don't say anything. Don't you like it?'

'Mark, I did say that I liked it, a lot. And I really do. It is really good. What else am I supposed to say?'

'Well, if you don't like it, then you can just be honest and tell me up front. That's still better than pretending you do half-heartedly.'

He obviously expected to be drowned in praise. I hoped that this would balance itself out at a bearable level. After all, even children were only praised up to a certain point in time when they used the potty.

'Mark, the soup is really extremely good. Like in a restaurant. Or better. But I really said that, already. Just imagine me saying that with every spoon I take. Even if I don't actually do it.'

Mark was proud, 'I taught myself all of this. My mum was an amazing cook, but she did not cook as well as I do. The soup is really good, isn't it?'

I nodded. I knew that my capacity for enthusiasm relating to a vegetable soup was limited.

'Mark, the soup is really good, and you are a fantastic cook. I am sorry. It is almost midnight, I had a busy week and I really just want to go to bed, now. Why don't we do it like this going forward: You just don't cook for me when I get in this late. I am just no longer receptive. No matter for what.'

'Oh, my poor Schatzele! Yes, of course, you must be tired, and your lover is keeping you up with food. Come, my dearest, let's go to bed. Just leave everything, I will clean up, tomorrow.'

Now, this was sweet of him.

We went to bed. I just remembered that this was the night he would be nailing me to the ceiling. Well, I did not see any signs of that, though. Mark was just lying there. I kissed and caressed him until he turned towards me, and we made love. However, I did not see much of a difference compared to our earlier attempts. The same shade of Grey. Mark was satisfied. Interestingly, he did not request any feedback, on this aspect of life.

I got lost. We needed separate bedrooms if I did not want to hate him before ever having really loved him. He protested with a faint, 'Schatzele, pleasepleaseplease, don't leave me alone! You love me, don't you?'

Well, I wanted to be able to, at least. I left.

At breakfast, we observed the birds, again, and Mark showed me the side of him that I was here for. He greeted every bird full of joy and with shining eyes, it seemed like he knew each one of them. I wondered how much of this warm hearted, loveable person there was in him.

This question posed itself with an unexpected urgency when I placed a box of truffes du jour on the table.

Mark moaned, 'Johanna, I told you that I do not tolerate any chocolate in my house. Why are you doing this?'

'But last week, you killed the truffles practically all by yourself. So, I assumed that you enjoyed them, and wanted to do something nice for you.'

'Well, you assumed wrong, then. I had one or two, just because they were there, but that certainly doesn't mean that I want more of that. I don't want to become fat.'

'Okay, then I will eat them, myself.'

'Great, do that if you want to become fat. And don't

bring chocolate, again. I don't want that crap in my house.'

Well, I would have to deposit a secret stash for chocolate emergencies. The next morning, the truffes were gone. When I asked Mark about this strange occurrence, he grinned down at me, said, 'I am a little rascal, I guess,' and pursed his lips.

Who on Earth had told him that women liked 'cute' men?

The lips remained unkissed.

On Saturday, we went shopping.

'You know, the shop owners all know me. They are having a blast when dealing with a real connoisseur. Most people do not even know what they are buying. So, when I come, it is almost like a family reunion, or maybe an expert convention. By the way, my specialty is quail with liver stuffing. I will make those for you, too, some day.' His grin seemed even wider than his face.

'Well, no – no worries. I don't like liver, it is so smudgy. But what I like is to see you so happy.'

I kissed him. It was tickling in my belly. Good.

Unfortunately, all of Mark's fans were absent, today, so that we were treated with the same friendliness as everyone else. Mark seemed a little disappointed.

Near the market, a honking convoy of cars passed us by – a wedding. Mark moaned theatrically, 'Dear God, the poor guy, another unlucky man on the path to his misfortune.'

I did not comment. My dad had made this very 'joke' for decades, and I had not found it funny at all back then – and neither had my mom.

We had not managed to find everything from his shopping list, so we made a quick detour to 'my' old area, to the shopping street where I had gone as a child with my mom. I was happy to see all the old familiar faces, and they were obviously glad to see me.

Mark seemed puzzled, 'Say, they all know you, by name and all. Have you worked here, before?'

'No, but my mom took me shopping, here, even when I was a baby. Of course, I know everyone. And they know me. By the way, I still have to do some shopping. Why don't you drive home, and I will come back, later.'

'But we can do that, together, my dear.'

'No, no, that's fine. Just go back, and I will come, later.'

I did not quite know how to explain to Mark that I wanted to buy cleaning equipment. I had seen a broad range of hygienic standards, on my journeys around the world, from a squat toilet in Italy or China to a privy in Okaukuejo National Park in Namibia, separated from the lions by a flimsy fence, accompanied by the sounds from the worried and worrying travel companions, 'C'mon, hurry up – the way the lions look really worries me.' In Central Europe, however, I had never come across a bathroom that had not been cleaned for at least a decade. I had to take measures if I wanted to feel even remotely comfortable. And given that Mark obviously did not feel this way, I had to dig in the dirt. And, obviously, I could not count on the availability of the appropriate tools. So, I bought mop, cleaning stuff, a scrubber, rags and whatever else I would rather not have used, let alone bought on my free weekend.

When Mark opened the door, his grin shrunk instantly to the width of his nose, 'What, cleaning stuff? I thought you were getting a surprise for me. And I have cleaned, already.'

'I know, my Schatzele, but I want to do some final fine

tuning. No worries.'

I cleaned like I had never needed to clean, before. After a while, I heard the piano playing – playing well. Obviously, this was Mark. After about an hour, he stopped playing and came to me, 'My angel, what are you doing here? I thought you were sitting somewhere comfortably and reading. And I felt so close to you. Me at the piano, you reading, connected by the bond of music. And then, I find you cleaning up our dirt, up here. That can't be. Don't do that. I told you I had cleaned up. That really suffices.'

'You know, I just don't feel comfortable with a sticky bath. See, I have changed the cleaning water, the third time, now, and already, you could sell it as solid food.' I had not expected to lead a discussion about cleaning water.

His already thin lips disappeared completely. He turned away, 'Well, if my house is not good enough for you, then do what you need to.'

I let him go. I just wanted to get this done.

A little later, the smell of soup spread through the house. Warmed up. I denied. He protested. I stuck to my choice.

The evening with REX was approaching. I was a little nervous, 'Say, Mark, does Mr Xavier even know that I am coming? And who I am?'

'Johanna, that's no problem. I have known Xavier ever since we were young lawyers. Those were the days! We were young whippersnappers, working like crazy. Only Richard was just observing, always being there when things got important, but never for the real work. And somehow, he managed to convince everyone to believe that he was a top-notch lawyer. Simply by virtue of sitting at the table and nodding when things became important, no matter what it was about. He is one of those people who can hold a presentation on medieval rocket science on five minutes' notice, and he will do it so well that you believe at the latest Leonardo da Vinci went up to the moon. He is the one who got me the job. And I like to mandate him, because I know that he doesn't do the work himself but delegates to people who know what they are doing. He is the one to go for lunches and stuff. And he is really good at that.'

'Wow, I had no idea of all that. But now that you say it: Right, I have never even read a single sentence that he wrote himself. But, say, where does he take his arrogance from, then?'

Mark laughed, 'He is a lousy lawyer, but he can win over people, he has an excellent network, and he can send Leonardo to the moon. That's a special talent, too. That's even much more rare than good lawyers.'

'Still. He should sit quietly in his office and thank his fate, his karma or his whateveritmaybe, rather than throwing his weight about and into everyone's face and folding up people. Setting aside that no one should do that, anyway.'

'He has the right to do that. After all, he's the boss. And this is not about the legal expertise, and it is also not about the client. It's just you women who believe that. When you have the choice to work all night to make everything perfect, or to go for a drink with the client, until he doesn't care any more, then you will choose the all nighter and work. That's why you don't make a career. At least half the day, I do things that have nothing to do with legal work. When we talk in the evening, I am already past the drinks with my colleagues, but then, that's part of the job.'

All of a sudden, his fate seemed by far less deplorable than it had seemed before. Even though I had to admit to myself that he had a point, there. 'Okay, I see that that's a talent. And I see that it is not always about the cause. But still, it's not right.'

'Schatzele, that's how life is. You women are happy to stand in the second line. You deliver impeccable work, really, but when it comes to standing up and selling it, it's a man who does it. You then wonder why everyone feels that the man who stole your work is the genius in the room rather than you. But in the end, it's good that the genders are different.'

Mark got up, pulled me up and held my head with both hands. He looked into my eyes, 'Schatzele, I love you. You are the love of my life. My one big love. I don't know how I lived without you and how I could live without you, now. But you have to know one thing: I could not respect you for what you do professionally. The stuff that you do, anyone could do. Don't take it personal, that's just a fact. But it doesn't matter, because I love you. I love you as much as a man can love a woman. But not as a lawyer, rather as a woman and soon as the mother of my children.'

He pulled me closer and kissed me fervidly. I was too surprised to fend him off, and I had not quite processed the statement he had just made.

On the way to the *Philharmonie,* I got a chance to think about it a little more. I was a full-fledged lawyer with a PhD, I headed a team of 15 people in an international insurance, I held speeches in three languages at international conferences – and he could not respect me for that? Did he not know about all of this? Had I not told him enough about my work and my professional accomplishments? Or had he not listened? And why did he feel the need to tell me? To demonstrate how gloriously honest he was? Or that he loved me so much that it did not matter what I did? Or was he just clumsy in interpersonal relationships? Or callous? I was convinced that every job had its challenges and deserved respect. I would have found it very difficult to sit at the cashier at a supermarket, to care for patients, to look after children or to take away the trash. Every person deserved respect in his or her profession. I really had to take this up with him, again. But not now. I could not distract him when driving. And I did not want to spoil the concert for myself, either.

At the *Philharmonie*, Mark pulled me towards the stairs.

'Mark, that's entrance D. I think we sit in section A Right.'

'Schatzele, I do know where to go. After all, this is not my first time here.'

For the knowing look he cast at me – yes, I could have killed him. But I had decided a long time ago not to hinder people who thought they knew where they were going. They found out themselves, sooner or later. Mark, too, eventually had to turn around when the usher sent us to section A Right. There, REX and some doubtlessly important persons had already gathered.

Mark switched on his most beaming smile, 'Wellwellwell, Richard! It's good to see you, old man! May I introduce: Johanna Lenné, my,' he chuckled as if making a joke, 'my arm candy.'

'What a pleasure to meet you, my dear. Say, do I know you? Somehow, you seem familiar.'

What weird movie was I watching, here? Or was I in it? No, not that, please. It felt like a black-and-white movie. Old and seen through gaze. I was certainly not arm candy, definitely not his dear – and, yes, we had met more often than I needed. Fortunately, he did not seem to remember our last encounter.

Mark seemed to sense my uneasiness, and he interrupted, 'Yes, this must have been at the firm. Johanna worked there, years back. But I think we have to sit down, now, the concert is about to start, any time. We will have time to talk, later.'

We squeezed through the row, Mark shoving his butt along the line of the people who had got up to let us pass through. I usually expected impeccable manners from older people, but this was obviously also just a prejudice.

Unfortunately, my neighbour seemed familiar, but I did not really recognize him. And given that he meticulously ignored me, I did not really stand a chance to solve the riddle. Mark was talking to his neighbour – Susan. I thought Susan had quit. She saw me and smiled. But not really in a happy, amused or content manner.

Fortunately, we had not come together to conduct a fun name quiz but for a concert, so I concentrated on that rather than on my neighbour. As had to be expected, it followed a coeducational approach: The first part featuring a composer on the verge of noise pollution for whom probably none of us would have come, and in the second part Mozart.

During the break, we stayed with REX and his guests. He introduced us, and it turned out that my neighbour was the son of the former Home Secretary. Hence the halfway resemblance. A C list politician, in a sense. I pulled Susan aside for an update. She was working for REX, again. He had raised her salary by 50% and invited her to the concert to celebrate her re-entry – in particular given that he needed a female accompanist. So, this was how she had ended up, here. But she did not really feel comfortable, at all.

'So, my dear, how did you like it?'

Apparently, I was REX's 'dear'. 'Well, this was what we usually refer to as 'interesting', I would say. I think'

Mark interrupted me, 'Well, Schatzele, such a response of politeness is not appropriate. I consider the work outstandingly inspirational. But to see that, one has to have an advanced comprehension of music, of course. With all due modesty, I may claim to have that understanding, I have been playing the piano ever since my early childhood, after all.'

REX laughed.

'That's lovely for you,' I responded. 'The question was how I liked it, though. And that's something you cannot comprehend or apprehend. Only I can.'

'Well, Schatzele, what I mean is that I have a much more advanced understanding of music than you do. And on that basis, I can provide a much more profound assessment. One has to jump into the unknown pond to find the hidden treasure. After all, there is not just run of the mill music like the Mozart and Brahms you like to sing.'

Didn't he realize that every word brought him deeper and deeper into a verbal no-go area, or did he just not care?

'Mark, I have been singing sine my childhood. So, I am fully capable of assessing and justifying whether and why I like a piece. And if you want to know more, I find it arrogant when a composer expects his audience to do a Master of Musical Arts degree to find access to the sublime spheres of his music. Mozart had exactly one chance to convince the people. And he used it. The day after a performance, people were singing his music in the streets. That impresses me. Not the mind games of someone who breaks down overwhelmed by his own genius every time he hears a note he has written.'

REX laughed, 'Well, Mark, that kid really is a character. I hope she is always so agile.'

'Mister Xavier, I...' 'am not a kid, and whether I am

agile or not is absolutely not the slightest bit of your business', I wanted to say, but Mark ushered me to my seat, 'Darling, the gong has been struck.' Indeed, and in so many ways.

Who did this idiot think he was? Disgusting. Sure, I had not expected anything else from REX. But what was going on with Mark? First, this thing about respect, and then this arrogant behaviour, finally this open insult. Not only towards me, but also towards himself, for REX had also put him into a drawer in which a man of our times really could not feel comfortable. Didn't that bother him? He pulled me close and placed a kiss on my cheek, 'Schatzele, you have to ignore this. He just doesn't get it. But he is a friend. Old men, you know.'

He was probably right. The important thing was that we got along. An old man like Xavier could not be changed any more, anyway. A discussion with him would be love's labours lost. And Mark had only put a good face on a bad story, but he knew what was right. That was comforting. I concentrated on the concert. Mozart. So beautiful. Me, the simple mind.

Mrs Andersen

With some luck, we managed to get through the interim phase between concert and restaurant without further embarrassment. We took Susan to the restaurant. Mark asked her about her son, work and how she had liked the concert. At dinner, he also sat between Susan and me. On her other side REX, then the politician's son's wife and her husband, next to Mr Andersen, an American lawyer who closed the circle.

When hearing that I worked for the Blau-Weiss Insurance, Mr Andersen lapsed into a knee-jerk sales pitch and described his countless-fold lawyerly achievements – which, however, did not encompass a Swiss law degree nor any knowledge of insurance law nor any other capability that could be even remotely of use for me. Unfortunately, he still felt strongly that we urgently needed to discuss 'whether we could do something together,' and did not permit any distraction from this glorious idea. Unfortunately, Mark was no help. He was completely calibrated towards Susan – as was Mrs politician's son's wife, crossing over REX. The raising of plants and children, washing machine repairs, the advantages of frozen vegetables, Tyrolean vacation and similar topics. Surely, the evening was paid for by the law firm, allegedly making rain for the company. And then, all these commercially important people were discussing frozen broccoli.

The restaurant was known as a hot spot for politicians, even though that was not quite apparent, tonight. But even if one took it to be true, I still did not get why it would be true. It could not be because of the food, even though Mark praised it almost as much as his soup. Well, I would have preferred licking away on some frozen broccoli.

REX ordered wine. One bottle after the other. With the raising level of alcohol, Mr Andersen lost sight of his commercial intentions. Well, that was something.

He had long been stationed in Japan with the Air Force – and, obviously, he had accomplished amazing things. Or rather, his wife had changed the foundations of the country, based on Mr Andersen's tales.

'You know, most Americans just stick to themselves when they are abroad. But not Mrs Andersen and I. We always want to get to know the country and the culture. And in Japan, we really took to the sumo wrestlers. Have you ever seen that?'

He obviously could not see my nodding, 'They are real human warhorses who wrestle in a sand circle with a kind of underwear. Well, actually, it looks a bit like a nappy. And, anyway, they try to push each other out of the rink. Following ancient rules. Every Sunday. The best seats are right near the rink, in booths, on cushions, like at the opera. You drink tea, eat cookies and have appetisers; it's all very distinguished. You make your bets, and chat to your company. But the audience is still fully engaged. At our first fight, Mrs Andersen was absolutely shocked, because everyone was so quiet. Well, but then she took to a wrestler, a really young guy. And then, she went to all his fights and cheered for him. Really cheered, I mean, the way it should be. With getting up, shouting, clapping, whistling, the full program. The first time, the people around her looked at her as if she had turned mad. But of course, Mrs Andersen didn't care at all. You don't know Mrs Andersen, of course, but that's the way she is. Every weekend. She went to the fights and screamed her head off for him. And slowly but surely, the others joined and started cheering for their wrestlers, too, and when we left Japan, after three years, the rink had become a madhouse. Just like in a U.S boxing fight. And this is how Mrs Andersen single-handedly changed thousands of years of Japanese wrestling tradition. Well, that's my wife for you.'

He looked proudly into consentaneous faces. I was the only one spoiling the party, 'I'm sorry to hear that. You must be so embarrassed that a tradition has survived for thousands of years, and then you come and destroy it.'

This notion was obviously so foreign to him that he preferred to ignore it. Mark kicked me under the table, and sent killing looks at me, above the table.

The American gentleman generally seemed a stranger to the wonderful world of international habits and customs. After dinner, he crossed knife and fork on his plate. The waiter poked along our table like a dog along his empty food bowl, but the cutlery did not move. After what felt like an eternity, Mr Andersen became impatient – and handed out. For starters, 'We have finished fifteen minutes ago, and here we are, still sitting in front of our empty plates. And this is supposed to be a top notch restaurant?'

I intervened, 'Why don't you place fork and knife in parallel, like everyone else at the table has done?'

After the expected opposition, he gave in and did as told, and, voilà, the waiter thrust himself at the plates like the falcon at the mouse, and the problem was solved. Yes, the knowledge of local customs tends to come in handy.

Unfortunately, the lawyer was not the only one in sales pitch mode. The politician's son, too, tried to jump through the perceived window of opportunity, and he unloaded an infomercial on tax-privileged property acquisition over the men around the table, 'Well, this basically finances itself automatically. Fully financed with a loan, and the costs of the loan are tax deductible. This way, the government pays for my real estate. The quota of self-financing is minimal. And when I retire, I can live off the rent. But the best is that I won't have to pay for housing, any more, because I have the apartment. I have recommended that to several friends, and they are all very satisfied.'

I had encountered people being ruined by such supposedly good deals, so I did not like the expression of interest on Mark's face. Well, questions are one of the few joys in life that tend to come for free (even though not all answers do), so I hopped on the boat, 'Excuse the question, but I don't understand that. Either you can live in the apartment, or you can derive income from the rent. You can't have the cake and eat it. And apart from that, to get tax deductions, you first have to pay the money. And then, the government waives the taxes on what you have paid. But no one pays the apartment for you. It's you who pays. And usually, these apartments are sold at double price compared to what they are really worth. At least. These are not called junk properties for nothing. Can you explain to me what it is that I'm not getting?'

Obviously, Mr politician's son had followed me until about word eight, and chose the way forward, 'Well, of course, this is hard to understand. After all, it is almost too good to be true.'

I ignored Mark's staccato kicking against my leg, 'Well, I do believe that I understand quite right. If it sounds too good to be true, it probably isn't true. Why should the government make you such a gift?'

Mark could not bear it any longer, 'I am sorry, Mr Miller. My friend here actually does lack real experience and insight in financial matters. Maybe, we should change the subject.'

Prompt for REX. 'Well, it's not so long ago that she has caught such a big fish. But she will get used to it.'

Going by the reaction around the table, this was a real good jest. Actually, a real roaring joke.

Mark showed me his back; I could not see his face. So, I was alone, 'Yes, I really don't know much about loans, because I always pay immediately. This is why I am so happy to have found a partner who does not only love me for my money.'

Kicking staccatissimo. What a musical night!

Mrs politician's son's wife took control, 'Well, let us not spoil this wonderful night with business discussions.

Susan, you were just telling us about your splendid vacation in Greece. Say, have you also been to Turkey?' The holy triad of a good wife: children, vacation, and kitchen. I went offline.

The restaurant was emptying; the waiters prepared the tables for the next day and ostensibly put up the chairs. Obviously, the staff in a politicians' restaurant was not used to late nights. It took Mark a while to react to my request to leave. Our departure marked the end of the evening.

REX protested, 'Susan, please stay. Come on, the bottle is still half full, and the night is still young. Almost as young and beautiful as you are.'

Susan hesitated, but Mark came to the rescue, 'Richard, Susan lives right around the corner from my place. I think I just give her a ride, that's the safest and fastest for her.'

We left, dragging along a truly relieved Susan. REX stayed behind at the empty table, with half a bottle of wine and himself for company. I did not envy him the company. Nor anything else.

Anyway, this had been a nice gesture of Mark. To end the silence in the car, I put on a CD of our choir. Rutter's Requiem – a mix of Disney and Schönberg. And simply beautiful. This should be the right choice for a man with a taste for musical experiments such as Mark.

He switched off after a few seconds, 'What kind of noise is that?' and changed to Mozart's *Little Serenade*. What a musical adventure! Well, it gave me time to calm down.

When we had dropped off Susan, I approached Mark, 'What a strange evening. You know, I pity REX. He has…'

'You pity WHOM? REX?'

'Well, REX – Richard Ernst Xavier. REX.'

'You call him *Rex*? Like a king?'

'Well, also a very popular name for a dog. You pick. Didn't you know that? Everyone at the office calls him that.'

Mark laughed, 'Well, I have to tell him that. He will like it. King Richard. And how does everyone call me?'

'I guess you would have to ask your colleagues that. But what I was about to say is that I pity him, in a very weird way. You know, he has money, a domicile on Jersey to avoid taxation, a vineyard in Tuscany, every thinkable credit card and mileage status, countless people around him to serve him, and thousands of telephone numbers in his address book. But to such a dinner, he shows up with his secretary. When he dies, there will be an amazing funeral service, and maybe, one or the other will be sad. But no one will grieve. No one will miss him as a human being. He is so successful on paper, but he has such an empty existence.'

Mark took a deep breath, but swallowed whatever he was about to say. It took him a moment, 'Yes, Richard is definitely not as lucky as I am. A miracle happened to me when you stepped into my life. A chance. My last chance. You are my big love. My last love. You know that, don't you? You must never leave me. This would be the end.'

I fought a silent battle. Should I tell him now that he had a strange way of showing me? That he had spent the evening ignoring me or presenting me as a little pretty birdbrain, like a true macho? Or would I thus destroy a moment that could be wonderful? No, silence could not be the basis for a relationship, 'Mark, you haven't talked to me all evening. I don't understand that. And I don't see this as an expression of love.'

Mark concentrated on the street ahead, 'And I don't see

it as an expression of love that you ridiculed me in front of my friends. But as you have noticed, I am not holding this against you.'

'What? When did I ridicule you?'

'The discussion during the break was extremely uncomfortable. Answering back *coram publico*, no woman has ever dared giving that to me.'

I was speechless, but I could not give into that, here and now, 'Mark, when I say that I don't share your opinion, that does not mean that I am ridiculing you. That's a normal exchange of opinions among adults. If you are looking for someone who admires you like a god, then I am not the right one. Then, you have to return to one of the lovely women who never dared talking back.'

'Schatzele, I did say that I forgive you. It just shouldn't happen, again. And now, I have to concentrate on driving.'

'There is nothing to forgive. And it will definitely happen, again. The one thing that must not happen, again, is that you treat me like a bimbo.'

'Schatzele, not now.'

After a few minutes, Mark interrupted our silence, 'One thing, though. After all, I had to entertain my neighbour. And I am really good at that. That's one thing you have to admit. After all, your lover is a gentleman.'

'Mark, don't give me that lover thin, please. It's ridiculous. And a true gentleman would be fully capable of being a gentleman towards two people on the same evening.'

This *lover* thing was becoming annoying. Someone carrying this title on a silver platter had to deliver. And Mark didn't. He should be grateful that I was not constantly holding that against him. At least, I could sleep well, tonight, despite the jet that took off next to me immediately after lying down. Thank you, dear wine!

Don Camillo

Mark woke me up with a kiss and a good mood, 'Schatzele, breakfast is waiting!'

I decided to follow his example. Blue sky, sunshine – let's go!

After breakfast and an intense albeit unilateral exchange on birds and hedgehogs, Mark announced that he would go biking. I let him go. I did not feel like participating in a race only he would be riding. If a bad mood could be avoided so easily, I would do just that, use the home trainer and call Klara. After the usual HowareyouHowislifeWhat'sup, I let the bomb explode, 'Klara, you will never guess where I am. At Mark's. Mark Kinsey's.'

Klara shrieked, 'Great! So, it has worked? Wow, I'm <u>so</u> happy for you two. Wow, Jo, I <u>so</u> hope it will work out for the two of you!'

'Wait a second! What do you mean, 'So, it has worked'? Klara?'

'Well, he is a family friend of Konrad's, and after the wedding, he had pumped Konrad and then me for each and every last bit of information about you. No worries, I did not tell him everything. And then, we arranged Halloween and the market and all. But he hasn't told me that you are together, now. I mean, are you together? How serious is it?'

'Well, now I get it, Mr Frog! But why didn't you tell me? I could have prepared myself for this, then.'

'Exactly. You could have prepared. I know you, Johanna Lenné. When you realize that a man is interested, you dissect each and every word he says and everything he does to be sure that he is Mr Absolutely Perfectly Eternally Right. You don't even give the guys a chance. And then, it is bound to go wrong, of course. For there is no Mr Absolutely Right. Everyone has his little imperfections, even you do. Even Konrad isn't perfect. He's just perfect for me. And that's what matters.'

'What? Am I really this bad? Really? But, I mean, if it doesn't fit, and if you see that from the beginning, then it does not make sense to spend three months dating just to have the inevitable happen a bit later.'

'See, you are doing it, again. There is no comprehensive collision coverage in love. You have to buy into it and work on it. The foundation has to be right, not every detail. But, anyway, that doesn't matter, now. After all, it has worked out. Hasn't it? You are with him. So, say, how does it go? I was a little uncertain, because he is so much older. On the other hand, he seems very active for his age, and you need a strong man who is a match for you. After all, you are quite a bundle to handle, my love. So, how is it?'

'I think I have to digest that, for a bit. Well, anyway, where are we? You know, he can be so sweet, like when he talks about his children or smothers his hedgehogs. And he keeps telling me how much he loves me. And he is interested in the same things I am interested in: music, cooking, biking. That is nice. But on the other hand, he is constantly teaching. And that while he is the one acting in a childish way. He is expecting hours of heavenly praise for his cooking. And biking is not about being together but about winning. No matter whether I am even competing. And the house is so dirty, it's simply disgusting.'

'Okay, so in summary, he is a man. Last things first. I have never been to his place, but that lack of cleanliness, that's rather common. They just don't see it. Even when they see it, every day. And if they see it, they don't see the point in cleaning something that will turn dirty, again, immediately. The upside is that they don't interfere. And the competition thingie, that's genetic. Men are like that. Let them win and tell them that they are doing marvellously and that they are so cute and adorable, and they are happy. Have you ever noticed that there is a child-man but no child-woman? The woman has to be the adult in the relationship without letting him feel it. That's just the way it is.'

'Klara, I am not looking for a child but a partner. I mean, I want children, but I want to have them with a man, not in the shape of a man. Mark is in the top management of a DAX company, I cannot praise him like a little boy, all the time.'

'Oh yes, that's exactly what he needs. Big shot or not. Look, who else is lauding him? At work, he is admired and maybe feared, but no one tells him how great he is. The other bigwigs also consider themselves the greatest invention since square chocolate, they will not say anything nice to each other.'

I interrupted, 'Klara, that doesn't have anything to do with man or woman. No one comes to fix laurels to my curls, either.'

'Yes, but you are genetically used to that. It's always been like that, for women. If that's all it takes, then go for it. Nuzzle and cuddle him, tell him what a hero he is. That's what we all do. And remember one thing: Men marry women because they think they stay exactly as they are, and then the women change. And women marry men because they think that the men will change. Until they find out that the men stay exactly as they are. Those are the general terms and conditions of marriage. The man you see is the man you get. For good.'

'Oh, blimey! I have never looked at it like that. But I guess you are right, it does make sense. My dad was just like that. Well, to some extent. But I just don't know if this is the only issue. Shouldn't I be thinking of him, all the time and get butterflies and all when doing so? You know, I have moments where I really like him, and where I want to hug him and kiss him. And then, I don't. And when I look at our weekend, I feel like an old couple. Already!'

'Well, you must listen to your heart, of course. But I can tell you that this romantic 'You, you, and only you' doesn't last forever, anyway. In the end, you are not looking for a hot lover or for an object of adoration, but you want a partner to spend your life with. And if you have this casual familiarity and closeness from the beginning, then that's good. At that point, you must be willing to compromise, too. You make such a good match. And you don't want the man who rows you across the lake and sings heartfelt songs to the lute while the water is running into the boat. You want the man who takes you back to the shore.'

'Well, I had hoped that there were men who can play the lute without sinking boats. But maybe, this is asking too much, after all.'

'Jo, you are an independent woman, so a man just assumes that he doesn't have to do all the romantic crap. Take Susan. Do you remember her husband? With darling here and precious there and love and opening the door for her and carrying her bags and the whole shebang?'

'Yes, vaguely. Very vaguely.'

'Well, he pulled off the whole program from little girls' dreams. With picnic in the forest, boat ride, proposal at sunset, huge engagement ring, white wedding, horse-drawn white carriage, several metres of wedding cake, blah blah blah.'

I had to grin, 'So, like you and Konrad?'

'Well, Konrad is different. With him, it's real. He is an exception, anyway, but we know that. Anyway, Susan's husband realized when their child was born that he was no longer Number One, so he switched to plan B. Or rather plan Y – Yvonne. Yvonne did not know about Susan. Now, he is married, again, Yvonne's Number One, and Susan is a single mom. And paying off the loan for the wedding. And for the ring. He had overdrawn their joint account. Well, then I would rather have the pragmatist. You know, all those butterflies and the feelings flying high up to the sky, they do not tell you whether you function as a couple.'

'Function' – if that meant a routine, then we definitely functioned. 'Thank you, Klara. You are probably right. You have really helped me.'

'No problem. What are friends for?'

'Great, my love, I will call you, again. Oh, before I forget, one thing: I think that Desi…'

'Desi knows. Yes, she had laid an eye on him, but that's not a problem. You see, you have made a really good catch. You just have to stop always dissecting everything.'

Klara had given me food for thought. She was right, I did not really need a lover, even though it would have been nice had Mark's self perception been closer to the truth. At least a little. And objectively, we did have very matching interests, which was good. I was almost 40 and definitely had my quirks. Maybe, there was no perfect lid for my pot but rather one had to take one that at least didn't fall off and harmoniously rattle through life, together.

I fetched my choir material to practice for our concert. Singing creates room to breathe, and I was back in equilibrium.

When Mark returned, sweaty and happy, I put Klara's advice into action. Praise! Admire! 'So, my hero, how fast did you go? Were you faster than everyone else, again?'

Really, 'You – won't – believe – this! Well, of course you will. You know me. I left all the young guys behind, one after the other. Easy. Well, true grit, your lover!'

I bit my tongue not to comment on the lover, yet again. Obviously, this was something I would have to get used to.

The question he popped during lunch (no, not soup) came somewhat unexpected, 'Say, Johanna, why don't we marry in January, before you turn 40? This would really mean a lot to me.'

Was this a proposal? The white knight in the shining armour kneeling down before me, placing his eternal love at my feet, making the birds sing and the violins play cheesy tunes?

Despite all rationality, this was definitely not what I had envisioned as a girl. And I did not want to wade my way through slush on the way to the altar. Even setting aside that this would not allow my friends and family to plan. After all, it was mid-November, already.

'Say, was this a proposal, now?'

'Well, as a fully emancipated woman, you will not expect me to fall on my knees and beg for your gracious hand. Essentially, marriage is about providing for the children in case something happens to me. I have an extremely generous retirement plan and several life insurances.'

Actually, this was supposed to be one of the most beautiful moments of my life, of our life. Instead, I unsheathed my claws, 'Well, first of all, it is very well possible to propose without the kneeling but still not sound like the initiation of a merger. Actually, even a merger can be more romantic than this. Second, we don't have kids. Third, I don't see any need to rush. Fourth, I will not marry you because of your retirement fund, let alone for the widow and orphan's annuity. Thank you very much.'

'Schatzele, you don't have to give me such a strong reaction. The children situation can change, any day. Only on the weekends, of course.'

'Well, not now, actually.'

'What? What do you mean by that? Are you taking contraceptives? You don't want my child? Did I get that right?'

I nodded.

'Wow, that's unexpected. Seriously? You don't want my child? I never had sex with a woman who was locked down there.'

I was baffled. Which century was he a product of? 'Mark, if you apply a broad definition, we have been together for a month, now. Of course, I don't want a child with you, yet. And a wedding is much too early, too. We don't really know each other, after all. We are only in the testing phase.'

'Why testing phase? I know that you are what I want. And just imagine what my colleagues will say if I marry a woman in her thirties!'

'No way! You can't be serious. Are you telling me that I am too old for you when I am 40? May I remind you that you are 62?'

He bit his upper lip like a hamster chewing away on a carrot, giving away that he was absolutely serious. 'Well, age is different for a man.' He did not find any trace of consent in my eyes and changed strategy, 'Schatzele, you are right. It's not urgent. I just want you to be taken care of if something happens to me. And you are gorgeous. You know that. At 39 or at 40, that doesn't matter. It's just that this would mean an awful lot to me.' He bent his head down and looked up at me with his *I-am-so-cute-am-I-not?*-look.

It took a while for him to realize that this did not have the desired effect.

'Say, what are your plans for Christmas? Anna and Frank are coming so that you can meet each other. Does this work for you? Or are you with your brother?'

'No, he lives in California, that's too far. Being single, I am not the one who gets the vacation time over Christmas.'

'Very good, then you come and celebrate with us. And maybe, you can get some time off, after all, given that you are engaged, now. Anyway, I am happy. You will get along great. That's really important to me. Children are the most important thing in life, after all. And my children are wonderful.'

Here he was, again, the caring, loving Mark I could fall in love with. Finally! 'I see it the same way. I am looking forward to meeting your children. And I promise you that I will never make you choose between me and them.'

Mark smiled fondly, and it slipped my mouth, 'I love you.' Had I said that? It seemed like it, looking into his beamingly happy face.

I became emotional and changed subject, 'So, what shall we do with the afternoon? Shall I call Klara and Konrad whether they have time to meet up? After all, they are not completely innocent when it comes to our situation, if I get that right?'

'Well, it is so much nicer if we make it comfy, just the

two of us, right here. And in the evening, I will make you a soup and take you to the airport.'

'No, no, I don't need soup, today. That's too much trouble. And please don't go through all that trouble when I come in the evenings, either. I eat…'

'But, Johanna, such a soup is…'

'Please let me finish. I simply don't eat that much, in the evenings.'

'Fine, if my soup isn't good enough for you.'

Why did a nice moment have to evolve into a soup discussion? 'Mark, I didn't say that. But you don't have to extend the effort, because I am not hungry, in the evening.'

'Well, that doesn't matter. I am not cooking the soup for you. I would also cook it just for myself.'

That didn't improve the situation, 'Mark, if you want to cook soup for you, then that's perfectly fine. Enjoy and rejoice. But I will not eat it, and that must not hurt your feelings. This just has to be clear.'

I did not want to talk about soup, any more. He seemed hurt, but that appeared inevitable. It obviously took two to hurt someone. I had not said anything mean, really. I had just not afforded due admiration to the greatest soup in the history of mankind and its creator.

It took a little while, but he got hold of himself, 'Okay, whatever you say. Let's watch a movie! Do you come to the bedroom?'

At first, I did not really expect him to want to watch a movie. In bed. At noon. But that was exactly the plan. Of course, he did not have a living room or any other comfort zone. No room to retreat, no comfy corners. And stuff lying around, everywhere.

Mark suggested watching Don Camillo and Peppone. I hadn't seen this movie for at least 25 years. It started in

French. Mark hammered on the various remote controls, 'Shit! Either the DVD is broken or the player or both. Or the TV. You cannot even switch the language.'

'Really? I don't think so. Why don't you give it to me?'

'No, you can't do anything about it, either. The goddamn thing is broken. I mean, of course it is not a problem for me to watch the movie in French, but for you, German would be easier, obviously.'

'Oh, French is not a problem, don't worry!' This sentence tended to have a rather different meaning at our current location, but I was not unhappy that this was only apparent to me.

After a few minutes, another eruption. 'They are just mumbling, who on Earth is supposed to understand them? Something is broken. What a shitty piece of crap!' Mark pressed all buttons, one after the other, time and again, and did not find the language menu.

My advice to go via the submenu was ignored. 'Mark, do you want me to give it a try?'

'You can't change that, either. The piece of junk is broken, Or the idiots didn't program it right.'

'Mark, things are not necessarily broken or junk, just because they don't work the way you want them to. So, when you are done, please just hand me the remote, and I will also give it a try.'

Every mom knew: Stay calm when the children's emotions overtake themselves. I let him fiddle around for a while, until he gave me the remote, not failing to point out the uselessness of my endeavour.

I chose the submenu and clicked on the language selection.

Mark tried to grab the remote, 'Yes, and now, you have to press *German*. Just give me the remote, I can do that.'

I turned away, 'Mark, don't be childish. I did not intervene when you tried. And now, please let me do what I want, as well.'

Mark took refuge in his inner sanctum of sulking, and we watched the movie. In German.

Unfortunately, Mark was quick to forgive me, and I got to enjoy his commentary. 'Yes, and now, Peppone's wife will come into the church, and then she wants the child to be baptized. Lenin. And Don Camillo does not allow that. And then, Peppone comes, and then,...'

'Please don't, Mark, I want to watch the movie.'

'Oh. Sorry.'

'See, here comes Peppone. And now, he fights with Don Camillo. And Don Camillo wins, and...'

'Please don't, Mark, I want to watch the movie.'

'Oh. Sorry.'

Obviously, my communication lacked clarity.

'See, and now, Don Camillo says that the baby can have Lenin as a middle name, provided he is also named Camillo, because the Camillo outweighs the Lenin.'

I stopped the movie, turned to Mark, held his big face with my hands, and looked him straight in his small eyes, 'Mark, please listen to me. I want to see the movie. Please stop your announcements. If you rather want to tell me the movie, then we can switch it off and you can talk.'

'Oh. Sorry. But the movie is just so funny, and the dialogue is so witty.'

'I get that. Totally. And that's why I want to watch the movie and hear the dialogue. Which is impossible if you talk the whole time. So, please no further recitals.' Kindergarten teacher might be a good job option for me, after all...

That worked for a bit. But unfortunately, not forever, 'Do you see the bulletin hanging there? Someone wrote 'Donkey' on it, because Peppone had made so many mistakes.'

I got up and left the bedroom. Mark shouted, 'Can you get me a sparkling water? And is there any of that delicious chocolate left?'

I brought him a glass of water and left. He had had the chocolate. All of it.

'Schatzele, don't you want to watch any more? Don't you like the movie?'

'Mark, I've told you a zillion times that I am not enjoying the movie like this. Obviously, you cannot respect that, so I will do something else.'

'Oh. Sorry. But I couldn't know that you are so serious about that.'

I left, and he followed me. He came closer and embraced me, 'My Schatzele, little Mark really wants to apologize hard to you so that you are no longer mad at big Mark.'

'Tell little Mark that this is between big Mark and me.' I turned around, 'Mark, I don't know how else I could have put it. If you didn't get that, then we have a real communication issue. What should I have done for you to understand? Have it tattooed on my forehead? Or on yours?'

Mark realized that I was serious. 'No, Schatzele. You know, at work, it's me setting the pace. I just have to learn to listen to someone. Just like our CEO. You be my CEO.'

'More than your CEO. Mark, I am not one of your subordinates who pluck every word from your lips gratefully and full of admiration. I know that you are used to setting the tone, but so am I. If you want us to work out, I am your partner. On the same level.'

Mark got into interruption mode, but I closed his mouth with my hand, 'A relationship can only work if both partners respect each other, listen, and really appreciate what the other one says. You are a great guy, intelligent, funny and all, else I would not be here. But I will not unconditionally admire you.'

He embraced me, 'Darling, please forgive me. Give me another chance. I need you. My life is so much better with you. I sleep better. And I take better care of myself and do more sports. I eat less, and I have already lost weight. And I drink less. I have become by far calmer and more relaxed. Even my secretary has noticed that. Please, Schatzele, be good. I will do my best, really. But I am not a young rooster, any more, and I cannot change everything over night.'

His remark triggered the realization that with him, I slept less, ate more, drank more alcohol and had no more time for sports, had already gained weight and was generally more stressed.

But then, I had to admit that he was right: At his age, such a change was complicated. Well at least he realized that he had to make some change. And given that he was an intelligent man, he would manage. 'Mark, that's why I said it. Because I care for you and for us, and because I want to give us a chance. Else, I would be gone, now. But it is not enough to tell me that you love me, you have to live it. We have to be eye to eye. Shall we have a little walk? The sun is shining.'

'I will first lie down for half an hour or so. Come, let's go to bed. I sleep so much better when I can hold you in my arms.'

No, I certainly did not feel like that, and I also resisted when Mark tried to pull me away. He trotted off and started the roaring engine. And I cleaned the bathroom.

When I tried to wake him, he did not flinch, no matter how loud I shouted and how often I buffed him. He kept snoring. I gave up.

When I entered the bedroom, again, in the early evening, I found him sitting naked on the bed, glazing out the window. I coughed, trying not to startle him. He twitched but did not turn around. Seeing him like that touched me, and I took a picture of him from the back. When I showed it to him, he said, 'What a wonderful photo. You must send it to me. What a wonderful, symbolic picture: The wise man, thinking, contemplating. His bed all messed up, after a night spent with his lover. Truly beautiful.'

I found the photo quite sad, actually. An old man, all by himself, turning his back on the woman he called the love of his life because he was so thrilled to see himself as the poet and thinker. Kokoschka. But maybe, I interpreted too much into it. Why did I only see the negative? Literature and movie theatres were full of couples that found each other after initial turmoil. I should be able to do that, as well.

On the way to the airport, we discussed the following weekend. Mark would come to Zurich. He was in Frankfurt for business, anyway, and this would also allow him to join the Christmas concert of my choir. In the *Tonhalle*, Zurich's main concert hall. I was looking forward to that. To the concert and to Mark.

For Friday evening, though, I suggested that he stay in Frankfurt to spend the evening with his son. After all, Frank barely ever saw his father, and we would have the whole weekend for us.

'And before I come, you go to the jeweller's and pick an engagement ring. I want everyone to see that you belong with me. An emerald would be lovely, to match your eyes. And like this, we do not have to run around searching, forever.'

Apparently, this meant that we were engaged. And would get married. Not in January, though. And it seemed like the question of questions would never be popped to me. Maybe, it was good that he was so sure of the situation and dragged me along.

At home, I called Christian to tell him that, apparently, I was engaged.

'Jo, I am happy for you. If this is what you want. I mean, it's an obvious decision for him. For him, you are the best thing that can happen to him. I hope he knows that.'

'I think he does. At least he said so.'

'Well, that's a start. You know, Jo, I have no right to advise on that. He seems to be a good guy, and he seems to love you, based on what you say. But I do have to say it once. After all, I am your brother, and I have loved you longer than he ever will. His age worries me. You always wanted children. He will not want that, any more. And even if he did, he would be a grandfather rather than a father to them. Is this what you want in life? A few years from now, he may require care. Then, you will not only be a single mom but also caregiver and for all I know working full time, on top of it all. I mean, he would be lucky and should be happy to get you, so I fully get what is in it for him. He cannot get a better insurance for his old age, so shortly before that gate closes. But what does he give you? It cannot be the money. You are not the type for that, and probably you have more than he has, anyway.'

'Trust me, Christian, I have thought about that, as well. Many times. But, you know, he is the first man who wants me. Really wants me, that is. And I am almost forty.'

'Jo, I know how much you yearn for a family. But fear of being left behind is not a good advisor. He comes from a completely different era, and if I get it right, he is not even like our parents but much more like our grandparents. Plus you will always be Number Two after the children. At least, this is very often the case.'

'Well, being the Number Two after the children is fine with me. That would be the same with me. You can divorce a partner, but the children will always be yours and always in your life. They should come first.'

'Well, before you take any decision, you first have to meet the children. And I have already told you that I want to meet him, as well. As a man, I do have a slightly different perspective, you know. And have you introduced him to your friends, yet, apart from Klara and Konrad, that is? Your friends know you well enough to have an opinion, and they also just want you to be happy. And what are his friends like? That also tells you a lot about a person. Get all the information you can about him. You know how to do that. This is the most important decision in your life. You must be absolutely certain.'

I didn't know if he had heard my sigh when he continued, 'But it is your decision. I can only raise questions. Of course, every relationship is work and compromise. And if you believe that you can build up such a relationship with him, then do what feels like the right thing to do.'

'I love you. And you are right. That's exactly what I am trying to do. And I will introduce him to my friends, that's a good idea.'

Despite all the concerns he had raised, our discussion had put my mind at rest. My doubts and inner disputes were probably normal. I just had to try a little harder. And look a little closer.

On Monday, I also informed Lilo that I thought I was engaged. After all, I had promised her that after the disaster with Samuel.

'What do you mean, you think you are engaged?'

'Well, it seems like I will get married.'

'How, when, to whom?'

I gave her a short version, and describing her the situation as a fact rather than an option gave me a strange feeling of certainty. It just felt a bit odd when Lilo asked for his birthday, given that he was so much older than me. But, well, it was what it was.

At lunch break, Lilo approached me with a piece of paper and a big grin all over her face. 'Do you have a minute? Great! Well, you know that I do numerology and astrology, as a hobby. I have compared your data, and when I take it all together, everything looks really great. In summary, the stars are on your side.'

Actually, I did not believe in the power of the stars over our lives. But on the other side, it was too good a prophecy to not believe in it. What if it was really fate? Despite my strongly enlightened roots, Lilo's transcendent support made me feel good.

If my life were a movie, that movie would probably end here. The credits would show scenes from our wedding in a sunny garden somewhere in Italy, us happy amongst our equally happy friends, us cutting the cake, a bouquet flying through the air, us parting for the honeymoon. This was what the movies taught us. Always. I was curious to see if my life would keep the promise the movies had given me a thousand times.

Florence

1st December. A whole weekend with Mark, a from his house and thus without cleaning, dead insects, spiders and long travel. No soup. I really liked life much better like this. And our Christmas concert at the Tonhalle. We had practiced for several months, just for this day. I knew that, due to Mark, I was not as well prepared as I usually would have been, but our conductor Philippe would guide us safely. I liked Philippe. He lived music, knew exactly what he wanted and usually also how to get it. The worst degree of criticism was 'Good improvisation. Now let's try the composer's version. And then, we decide which version we prefer.' All of this said with a smile and French accent.

Of course, Mark stayed at my place, this time. He arrived in the morning, fully equipped with coins for the parking meter and instructions on how important it was to use them. The Zurich meter maids always noticed when my visitors parked for two minutes without paying. I did not know how they did it, but they invariably did.

I had placed an advent calendar, on Mark's pillow, hand made: 24 cards, each of them with a quote or saying about love. I had enjoyed making it, thinking of Mark and relishing in the idea of love. Plus this was so nicely tangible. He was very happy and then told me about the evening with Frank and his partner, the evening before. 'Well, it was a really nice idea of you. Frank was truly thrilled. He also introduced his fiancée to me. A very nice girl. Very well equipped. Short skirt. Of course, I like to see that as a man. But also not stupid. She reminded me a little bit of you, even though you beat her by miles, of course.' He placed a kiss on my cheek. 'But after all, it's logical that Frank has a similar taste like mine. A Kinsey man, you see... You know, I was always sceptical when he wanted to study law. It is always tricky when people compare you to your father, all the time. In particular when he can only lose such comparison. But now, he is actually doing quite well. And so is Anna, by the way. But I find it more surprising in Frank, I must say.'

As a father, Mark was obviously quite a challenge.

'Well, the main thing is that your children have found a job that they like. I am looking forward to meeting them. I hope things go well.'

'Oh, don't worry about that. You are important to me, so you are important to my children, too. They will love you. How could anyone not love you, my angel? You are wonderful. Come, let us get the ring that you told me about.'

On our way to the jeweller's, we came by Mark's car – including the parking ticket. 'I don't believe it! They want me to pay a parking ticket. 60 Franks!'

'No, I don't believe that, either. You paid for the parking, they cannot give you a ticket for that!'

'No, I did not pay. I do not see why I should pay for parking. They see that I come from Germany, and they should be happy that I come here and spend money. And I already paid the highway toll. That's absolutely outrageous, and I will definitely not pay for that.'

'But, Mark, I had given you the change for parking, and the rules apply to...'

'I don't care, I won't pay this.'

He threw the ticket away.

I picked it up when Mark did not look. Well, I would pay, then.

At the jeweller's, it was a fast pick. Mark liked the ring, paid and I was engaged. Visibly engaged.

Mark wanted to celebrate with oysters and champagne. I did not like the thought of eating a living creature, but Mark said that this was the same in nature. And that oysters did not have a fully developed brain and therefore would not feel anything, anyway. I was not quite convinced, and, actually, did not taste that much. Really, al I tasted was salt water. Mark, on the other end, visibly enjoyed, and that made me happy.

On our way to the tram station, we passed by a group of Christmas singers from the Salvation Army. And, who was singing his life away in the back row? Francis, number M7 from the speed dating, Zurich's loneliest heart. He seemed to smile at the world, benevolently. I did not know whether he had recognized me but preferred to move on, rather quickly. He did not fit with oysters and champagne.

I had to go to the final dress rehearsal, anyway. Mark would go to my place and take a nap. I had written down what ticket to get and where to go, nothing could go wrong.

When I got on stage with the choir, a few hours later, my eyes found Mark in the audience, he waved at me, I smiled back, and I was happy. It was always a special moment when, after months of rehearsal, everything came together – the choir, the orchestra, the music, the venue, and the audience. And now, also Mark. Someone I sang for. Every note I sang made me happy, even though it was one note less that I would have left to sing.

The music did not fail to move everyone. Standing ovations. A full success.

After the concert, the choir, the orchestra and the audience gathered in the entrance hall.

Mark embraced me, 'A nice concert. Very interesting.'

'Mark, I'm still somewhere on Cloud Nine. It was so beautiful. And to know that you were in the audience – yes!' I embraced him. I could have embraced the world. I was happy.

'Darling, I looked at you, the whole time. Only at you. Your confidence is amazing. Even though you were singing completely different than your neighbour, you just carried straight on and did not let her confuse you. You see, of course I am sure that she was wrong and not you.'

I avoided the verbal bucket of cold water, 'Of course, Sieglinde sang something different than me. She sings soprano, I sing alto. The dividing line has to be somewhere, after all. And when the alto is divided, half of us sing something different, yet again. And you are absolutely right, you must have confidence and know exactly what you do to be on the line.'

Before Mark had a chance to respond, an elderly gentleman approached us. 'There you are! I saw that you really enjoyed the concert! It was like you were just beaming with joy, and you smiled at the conductor, the whole time. I could not keep my eyes off you. What do I have to do for you to beam at me as you did at the conductor?'

Now, that was a sweet compliment! Today was just the perfect day, despite Mark's needles.

'Aw, how nice of you to say that! Yes, it was a wonderful concert. And if you want me to beam at you like at our conductor, there is only one solution: conduct!'

The gentleman laughed, winked at Mark, shook my hand and left us.

Mark had reunited with his own self, 'Darling, it makes me happy to see you so happy. Enjoy it!'

I introduced Mark to my friends from the choir. As expected, they were happy for me. They congratulated me, admired my ring, and made Mark feel welcome and good. He radiated charm, chatted and made jokes, and the more my friends seemed to like him the happier I was to have him by my side. Sieglinde took me aside to tell me how happy she was to see that I had found someone, after all the years as a single. And, of course, she promised me that the choir would sing at my wedding.

Philippe also joined us and listened to conversation a bit, before addressing Mark, 'Wow, we could really use you as a bass. Why don't you come to one of our rehearsals? We have the nicest singers of Zurich. Especially the altos. But I think you know that, already. I am so happy for Jo that the long wait has paid off.'

He laughed, and so did Mark. My (un-)marital status appeared to have been of interest to more people than I had thought. And all of them were happy with me about Mark.

On the way home, he said, 'Darling, your co-singers are really a great bunch of people. And they really like you. I am looking forward to meeting them once I have moved to Zurich. And I understood every word they said. Swiss German really isn't that difficult. But that was clear to me, all along, if you understand that, then I understand that, anyway. That's obvious.'

'Mark, that was not Swiss German. That was high German with a strong 'k' and 'ch'. Not Swiss German. But setting that aside: The choir really is special. A special bunch of great people, that is. You heard Philippe: Why don't you join us when you have moved to Zurich? You do have a nice...'

'Well, when I do something, I do it right. So, I would definitely not sing in a choir. I would sing properly.'

'What do you mean with 'properly'? We all take singing lessons, we all sing off sheet, some of us also do solo projects.'

'Well, I would only sing solo.'

'Mark! It's not that we CANNOT do that, we just don't WANT to. We prefer social singing.'

'Still, if I was to sing, it would be solo,' he mumbled.

'Oh, like Florence Foster-Jenkins. Sure.'

'Florence who?'

'Florence Foster-Jenkins. The worst singer of all times.'

Mark's deep breathing showed me that he was hurt.

'That was mean. I'm sorry, Mark. I have never heard you...'

'Yes, that was really mean. But today is such a beautiful day. I forgive you. But why was she the worst singer of all times?'

'Well, she was really pants and didn't know. She couldn't hear herself. Her husband organized a concert in Carnegie Hall and carried her torch while she was torturing the Queen of the Night. It sounded like a pig being passed through the grinder. You must check it online. But Carnegie Hall was sold out, because the people wanted to have some fun, too.'

'Oh my God, how embarrassing! He should rather have locked her up. If this was my wife!'

'But, you know, the whole thing also has a very touching side. He loved her a lot, after all. And his love did not only make him blind but also deaf. And if it was her big dream and worked for both of them, why not?'

'Big dream, big dream! She made a fool of herself and of him in public. And this is how the world remembers them. Even you know them! Horrible!'

'You know, Mark, life is not only about doing things perfectly, but also about why you do things. For example, when Klara sang, that was beautiful, even though she will definitely not win a golden record.'

'You think so?'

'Yes, I think so. That was a declaration of love and cost her almost superhuman effort, but she did it for Konrad. That's what you do when you love someone.'

'Well, if you insist on warbling a ditty on our wedding, feel free to go ahead.'

Wow, there was really no limit to his enthusiasm.

Well, let's change to another topic, 'Mark, just imagine you could do anything you wanted and had every talent you desired. What would you do, then? What would be your dream?'

Long silence, then, 'That's a stupid question.'

'What, you don't have dreams?'

'No. Seriously, no. Why should I? After all, I have accomplished everything in life. And now, I also have you.' He took my hand.

'But everyone needs dreams. I mean, the life of Florence and her husband was definitely much more exciting, and much richer, this way.'

'You mean richer in embarrassment. No, I don't need that. Come on, let's have dinner. Didn't you say something about a Chinese place where you like to eat?'

'Well, then I take note of the fact that we simply don't float the same boat on this. My favourite Chinese is back there, on the right, in the hotel. But, say, we had quite a good lunch, I would say.'

'Well, I am a lucky child. Wantlessly happy. Just a little hungry, right now. Come on, let's see if your Chinese is really so good.'

Mr Jian welcomed us, or rather me, as always: With a big smile, open arms and a table in a quiet corner. I let Mark go ahead and choose the dishes. And he had to admit that it was better than at his 'friend's' in Berlin.

I didn't have anything for Christmas, for his children, and as Mark had no ideas, I asked him to tell me a bit about them.

All lawyer, Mark approached the topic systematically and started with the pregnancies, 'There is nothing more beautiful than a pregnant woman in the house. A woman is never more beautiful, never more woman. And the sex is fantastic. I noticed the pregnancies even before my wife did. You know, I am a living pregnancy detector. I see that immediately, this womanhood. Somehow, you are fuller then, and you are glowing with hormones.'

But even the time after the pregnancies seemed to have sprung from a commercial of the Minister of State for Families and Children: Little children's feet tapping on the wooden floor, shooing to the parents' bed to cuddle on Sunday mornings, the father caringly and protectingly carrying his feverish child through the night. Mark loved his children, and my heart felt warmer.

When we came home, I kissed him and pulled him to bed. And while Mark saw the stars, I remained in the mist. A few minutes later, he snored, and I cleared away into my guest room. The smoke still stood in the air. Mark had smoked in my apartment. Great!

Ariane

Mary and Leo had invited us for Sunday brunch. I was looking forward to seeing them, Leo's son Carl and their daughter Ariane. And to showing off Mark. Sprouting pride of ownership.

On our way to the streetcar, we met my neighbour, also a Berliner – pregnant to the max. The baby was due, any day, and she had also chosen a name, already, 'Maurice with a - whatchamacallit?'

'Whatchamacallit? What's a whatchamacallit?'

'Well, a dash on the E.'

Her finger drew an *Accent égu* in the air.

„But then, the baby will be called Mauricé, with a long Eee in the end. Mauriceeeeeeee.'

„No, no, that's just because it looks prettier. My husband has the same, so we want to start this as a family tradition.'

Well, her husband's name was André. With a long Eee in the end. The whatchamacallit actually made sense, there. My family also had such a tradition, but with the last name Lenné, that was a given. I had full confidence in the Swiss authorities to capture that and exercise their authority, protecting the poor kid from life as a whatchamacallit. I did not pursue this discussion any further.

Mark looked satisfied, 'See, of course I saw immediately that she is pregnant. A man sees that. And a pregnancy detector sees it, anyway. So, tell me, isn't that extremely erotic?'

Nope, no comments on that. That was beyond comments.

When he punched his ticket, I saw that he had bought the wrong one – at four times the price.

'What's that ticket that you got there, Mark? And why?'

'That's a ZürichCard. That's so much better than the ticket you wanted me to get. The lady at the ticket booth was from Ticino, so I spoke Italian with her, of course. And when she noticed that I was practically a compatriot, she gave me the insider tip to buy a ZürichCard. You know, she really liked me.'

'Mark, you don't need a ZürichCard. That's the all-inclusive card for museums and stuff, that's why it's so expensive. We don't even have time for any of that. That was not an insider tip, you got the wrong ticket.'

'WHAT? You mean she TRICKED me? What a weasel!'

'No, she did not trick you. You got her wrong. Ticino dialect is different from regular Italian, you know. That's all.'

Mark bit his lip. Apparently, I had just questioned his

Italianità. Ouch!

On the streetcar, Mark – quite voluminous, as he was, anyway – sat down like two Clint Eastwoods, taking up almost the whole bench. I squeezed in next to him, and he put his arm around me.

When I almost fell down, in the first curve, I got up.

'Oh, we have to get off, already? Then, we did not have to…'

'No, it will be a while.'

'Well, then stay right here with me, Schatzele!' Mark took my hand and pulled me down.

'Well, it's a little tight, there.'

'What's the matter with you? I am sitting very comfortably.'

Exactly.

At the restaurant, Ariane came dashing towards me, 'Hi, Aunt Jo! Who's this?'

'This is Mark. Mark is a very dear friend of mine.'

Mark was more direct, 'Well, I would not quite say 'friend'. I am Johanna's fiancé. We will get married, soon. And you will be our flower girl.'

Ariane ran to Mary, 'MommyMommyMommy, Aunt Jo is getting married. And I will be the flower girl. Will I get a dress? In pink? And with ruffles? Mommy, I want a real fluffy one, like a princess. And flowers in my hair? Please, mommy! Carl, I will be a flower girl!'

Carl was seriously under impressed.

'Slowly, slowly, Ariane! First of all, I have to talk to Aunt Jo. There will be enough time for dresses and garlands and flowers. Jo? Is this true? Or did Ariane misunderstand?'

Mary peeped at my hand, and I turned a bit for her to see the evidence.

She embraced me, 'Jo, wow, that's amazing! Why didn't you tell me?! Was this your loo date? Tell me! Leo, Jo is getting married!'

'Well, if you could let go of me for a second, I could introduce you,' I laughed, 'Mary - Mark. Mark – Mary.'

Mark offered his hand for a shake, but Mary embraced him, 'Mark, I am so happy for you both! Jo, you must tell me everything, right here and now. Leo, you squeeze out Mark, and afterwards, we compare notes.'

Mary knew what she wanted.

So, I reported how we had met at Klara's wedding and got to know each other a bit better at the Halloween party, I gave her the details of the loo call – 'I knew it! Leo, he is the somehow date! Okay, keep going!' – About Uncle Walter's birthday, and about Mark's decision to get married.

Mary was delighted, 'Johanna Lenné, I am happy for you. Just happy. See, I always told you that the right one would show up. You just had to wait a little longer. I am happy! So happy!'

Time for hugs. Feeling that all my friends were so happy for me made me feel good, myself. And their confidence in Mark's decision gnawed at the lump of doubt sitting on my chest, sometimes bigger, sometimes smaller. But then, it was normal to be concerned and to have doubts. After all, it was a big decision, and I had never done this, before. So, how was I to know whether I was doing the right thing?

It seemed that Mary's jeans was a little tighter than usual. And her face seemed fuller. There were no embarrassing questions among friends. 'Talking about big events and congratulations, am I right that I will have a reason to congratulate you, soon, as well?'

'How do you know? Is it that obvious, already? Really?

Please, Jo, it's not official, yet. Promise you won't tell anyone. We want to announce it at Leo's birthday, when the first half is over. Before that, it's bad luck. Promise! Is it really so obvious?'

'No worries. I think I am over-sensitive to that, at the moment. Mark is constantly raving about pregnancy.'

'Oh, that's really nothing to slobber over. It is a rather limited pleasure. Spending the mornings hanging over the toilet, that's really nothing to rave about. Some men enjoy it, of course, with the big boobs and all. Pride of ownership. After all, they don't have to carry the ball. But does that mean that you want a baby with him? I mean, that's all very new. And he's getting a bit long in the tooth. I mean, no offense, I'm sure he's a great guy, but…'

'No, no, you are absolutely right on that. This would be way too soon for me. First of all, we have to get our things together. Of course, we cannot wait forever if we want to do it, we're both too old for that, but at least until we are married and live together. He is moving to Zurich.'

'Oh, that's a relief. I was getting concerned I would have to go to Berlin to see you, all the time.' Hug. 'And, do you have a date, yet?'

'He wanted to marry in January, but that's too soon for me. I mean, I hardly know him. And I don't see why we should. Maybe in summer. Actually, he is much more certain about all of this than I am. I mean, I am sure he is right, but I am a bit slower. After all, I have never been in this position. That's just the way it is.'

'Jo, it has to be right for you. Not just for him. But does he know that you have some doubts? See, he is already hiring flower girls. You know Ariane, she will start searching for that perfect dress, as soon as we get home.'

'Yes, that wasn't too smart of him. I'll tell him. But you are right, we have to sit down and discuss that. Maybe

Christmas. The weekends always go by so fast, and this needs some thought. But I have definitely told him that I won't get married, in January and that I need more time.'

'You'll manage, Jo. Just listen to your heart. Anyway, I am happy for you. And always remember how lucky he is to get you.'

Well, that seemed to be part of the problem; my heart was rather tight-lipped, these days.

Leo came over, 'Congratulations, Jo! He seems to be a really nice guy, your lover. And he is head over heels into you – gosh, I did not even know what an honour it was to know you.'

Mary buffed him, 'Well, Leo, I trust that you sing my praises just as he sings Jo's.' Leo kissed her. Yep, that counted as a response.

We turned to other topics and the buffet.

On our way home, I asked, 'Say, don't you think it's a little early to hire flower girls? We don't even have a date, yet, and Cordelia and Leanna will want to do that, as well.'

'Oh, Schatzele, I only said that to make her happy. Children forget such things, on the spot.'

'Not Ariane. She will start working on Mary about the dress, every day, starting today. And in her situation, that's really not what she needs.'

'No, the kid has already forgotten all about it. And your friend should really be able to take that.'

'Please don't make any promises you cannot keep. Certainly never ever to children. For children, it is much worse to be disappointed. And if I should ever be pregnant, I also expect more consideration on your part.'

'Schatzele, now you are exaggerating. Besides, why are you mentioning pregnancy, now? You are not pregnant, are you?' His smile sent question marks all over his face.

Obviously, the pregnancy detector had not detected. So be it. 'No, I'm not. But if I ever become pregnant and we have children, you must never make false promises to them. If we ever have children.'

'You mean when, not if. Anyway, I promise, my darling. But, you know what? Maybe it's good that the issue came up, now. We really have to plan the wedding.' He pulled me close and kissed me.

When we kissed, things were alright.

In the afternoon, we checked agendas, booked flights and made plans. The contemporaneous version of cosy togetherness. I would come to Berlin, on the remaining weekends of the year, and of course for Christmas. And from then onwards, it would be two weekends in Berlin, one in Zurich and one off. After all, we both had to get stuff organized in our respective homes, as well, do laundry and all of those fun things. Squeezing them into a normal working week had proven difficult for me.

Mark had already made plans for the wedding, 'Well, we publish our year-end results, in May. On 15 May, we have our annual general meeting. Until then, it's a no-go, I am absolutely booked. Let's get married, on 16 May, that's a Friday. And on Saturday, we take off for our honeymoon.'

'So, you are fully booked until 15 May. You want to get married, on 16 May, and leave on honeymoon, on 17 May.'

'Yes. Wouldn't that be cool? Wedding, and off we go.'

'And how do we organize everything?'

'Well, I don't need big preparations. As far as I am concerned, we can go and get married, just the two of us. Anything above and beyond, you have to organize, if you want it.'

'Of course, I want more than that. After all, I intend to marry just once. Christian and his family will fly in from the United States, and my friends will fly in from all over. I am not gonna kiss them good bye and get lost, the day after.'

Mark's tortured soul made its way to his face. 'But this is my wedding, not that of your brother,' he moaned, 'If they come just for this, that's not my problem. After all, I don't expect strangers to entertain me, either. We can have a party, on Friday, if this is so important to you, but leave, on Saturday. Just like any modern young couple. They will manage without us.'

'Mark, they are not strangers. They are friends and relatives. Yours, too, by the way.'

'What kind of friends are these people, anyway? Are they somebody or are they just feel-good-friends?'

'Feel-good-friends? Of course, they are feel-good-friends. I feel good with my friends. That's what friends are for.'

'No. The most important thing is that friends further you. To feel good, all I need is you. If we start inviting people and spending all that money, there has to be a benefit.'

'Well, maybe that's the reason why you don't have friends.'

'I DO have friends. It's just that I don't talk about them and don't have to see them or hang on the phone, all the. I have even made a list for the invites, already.'

Obviously, I had hit a sore spot.

'Well, that's great. So, you don't want to go and get married, just the two of us, after all. See, and we will manage the other questions, too. We just have to plan well. So, where do you want to marry? Zurich, Berlin or somewhere else?'

'That depends. Where can you contribute the better guests?'

'The BETTER guests?'

'Well, your business contacts will be in Zurich, and I presume that your Berlin friends are generally friends from school or so – feel-good-friends.'

'Please don't say that. You make it sound so negative. I care for my friends, and they are all great people – each and every one of them. And they will come wherever I invite them to. After all, they feel good with me, as well.'

'That's what I figured.'

'I hope you did. After all, that's what makes a friend. What about that: civil marriage in Berlin, church in Zurich. And my friends and your strategic alliances come to where they want to.'

'Church? Do you mean white and horse drawn wedding carriage and all the shebang? No, there is no way we do a white wedding. I already had that. And it's ridiculous, anyway. I went to a wedding, recently, and they also christened the couple's child. They called it a wedstening. And the bride and mother in virgin white. Absolutely ridiculous. I'm not having that.'

'Mark, I will not have a child by then, and I will also not be pregnant. Of course, I am marrying in white.'

Mark was visibly unhappy. 'I thought you young people were much cooler. Come on, let's do it casually. We go to the wedding in jeans and have a party in a pub with a garden, somewhere, and then we just bunk off. None of all the traditional hoopla. If you really love me, you don't marry in white. You are no longer a virgin, anyway.'

'Mark, the 'traditional hoopla', that's stuff like the white wedding carriage, kidnapping the bride, dance under the veil, garter and all that. The things Klara and Konrad did.'

'Well, that's a no-go, anyway. Their wedding must have cost a fortune. I will not finance such a luxury event for strangers. No, we will do it only with a few chosen people. Ten people max. You and I. Only we are important. It will be our day.' He stroked my hand.

'Mark, I don't need luxury, and I don't need all the 'traditional hoopla'. But I want to share it with the people who are important to me. And that's more than ten people.'

Mark switched on his puppy dog eyes. 'But the most important person, that's your Mark. Don't you want your Mark to be happy?'

Puppy dog eyes had always had a sobering effect on me. Even an attempt at blackmailing should have a certain finesse and style. Even the mob was more subtle. 'Mark, you have been going on and on about how much you look forward to meeting my friends. And this is the logical consequence of having friends.'

Mark was tense, we were at a dead end.

'Mark, we don't have to make that decision, now. Now, we both know where we are starting from, and we can think about where we can meet. In any event, I am not going to pick a date based on your general meeting. I will not do all the organization work, all by myself. And I will not run off, immediately.'

'So, it's you who makes these decisions. And where am I in all of this?'

'That's not a decision, those are logical parameters. As you will have noticed, I have not mentioned any shebang, not even the wedding gown. So, I am compromising up front. The only thing I would really like is the wedding dance.'

'That won't happen. My knee. Schatzele, I'm tired. What do you think about a little nap?'

The ultimate escape. Well, maybe the discussion had been too intense for him.

'I'm not tired, but if you want to, why don't you just lie down, for a bit?'

'Schatzele, but I want to sleep with you in my arms,' switch on puppy dog look, 'That's my little piece of heaven. Come on, Schatzele, I sleep so much better when you are lying next to me. If you love me, you come upstairs with me.'

The thought of having 160kg body mass lying behind me, snoring directly into my ear, with a leaden arm on top me, preventing any escape, overwhelmed me. 'I see, but I cannot sleep at all. See, you have just had almost a bottle of wine, already.'

'Well, I like it.'

'Yes, but the more you drink the louder you snore.'

He seemed seriously surprised, 'What? Where did you get that from?'

'Have you never talked to your doctor about the snoring? Alcohol, overweight and sleeping on your back, all that makes it worse. And now look at yourself and do the math.'

'Why overweight? You don't mean to say that I am overweight, do you? When I look in the mirror, I see a portly, stately, real man. And when you're not here, I tell myself that.'

'WHAT? You stand in front of the mirror and give yourself compliments?'

Women, even the most beautiful ones, inspected themselves and criticised every kilo. And he considered his belly 'portly'?

'Yes, of course. Sure, maybe I could lose five kilos or something like that. But in principle, everything is how it should be.'

'Mark, you're scaring me. Add a zero to the five, then we are slowly approaching the right realms.'

When he had raved about his weight loss thanks to myself, I had not thought that he basically saw himself near the finishing line rather than barely off the starting block.

'Okay, if that's how you feel, then I will sleep alone.'

He sounded hurt. He turned around to leave, but I held him back, 'Mark, I did not want to hurt you. Really not. But I want to be with you, for a while, and with the weight and the smoking and the wine, I am worried about you.'

He turned back to me, 'My weight is my business. Topic closed.'

My dad had taught me when I was four years old that his 'nagging' was a sign of his love and caring for me. I had understood that. But telling Mark that now would help neither him nor me. He adjourned to the bedroom and began snoring. The discussion had been too much for him, obviously. Had I overstrained him? Was I asking too much? He was right; it was our wedding, not Christian's. But then, it was ours, not just Mark's, as well. And even when I excluded Christian from the equation, Mark's autistic wedding with a career driven attendance list did not match my idea of a whooshing party with friends. And I could not prepare everything by myself – nor did I want to do that. Especially not when he had a list of invites in the backhand who I was apparently to cater for. Essentially, all of this was way too fast for me. First, we had to test living together. A wedding would be the icing on the cake, in the end. It's not the eggs and the flour you start baking with. I would let the subject lie. Searching for a house or an apartment in Zurich would be much more important.

I called Klara. And was surprised when Sinéad responded.

'Hi, Sinéad, that's a surprise.'

'Hi, Johanna. Didn't Klara tell you? I'm staying with her and Konrad. Just for a while, until I have found something. I have left Bernd.'

'What? You have left Bernd? How come?' Obviously, the real question was how she managed to stick with him for so long.

'Well, I told you about Bernd's snakes, didn't I? There was just no room for a second human being in our marriage. Just for him and the creatures. I don't deserve such a life. And then, my father died.'

'Of course, you don't deserve that. And I'm sorry to hear that about your father.'

'Well, thank you. Anyway, Bernd immediately started browsing catalogues, because he wanted to finally buy a venomous snake. And the whole equipment is quite expensive, so he could not afford it up to now.'

'What? Do you mean he wanted to use your inheritance to buy another snake?'

'Yes, and he drove off to Holland, because it is so much easier to get the beasts, there, apparently. I begged him not to go, but he told me not to be ridiculous. He had wished for that so long, and now he finally wanted to do something for himself.'

'A poisonous snake. In your apartment. Bought with your money. No, that would send me off, too. You were so right to leave him. That's really phat. And then, you just left.'

'Yes. When he returned, I was gone. I fed them all, one last time. After all, it's not their fault. But I took the remaining rodents to the animal shelter.'

'And, how did he take it? I mean, he was more proprietorial than a possessive pronoun.'

'Well, with him, everything is always bigger and better and now worse-er. And possessive. He will get over it. He can cuddle his viper.'

'Well, that's fine, then. But how are you dealing with this?'

'You know what? I haven't felt so good, in years. Actually not since our wedding. I can do and not do what I want to, I no longer have to look stag-ge-ring, all the time, I…'

I had to laugh out loud. Sinéad continued, 'And I am no longer called SinHead. So, all in all, I am doing great. But, of course, I know that I am more than lucky to have Klara and Konrad.'

'Yes, you are right. Those two are amazing. You know what? Do let me know if I can help you, or if you just need someone to talk to, or if you want to emigrate to Zurich, for a bit. I have a guest room.'

'That's sweet of you, Jo. Klara and Konrad take good care of me, I'm fine. And I have to organize everything for my dad, you know. But you probably wanted to talk to Klara, right? I'll tell her that you called.'

Having some time to myself, I called Christian, and then Tina. The baby had not made an appearance, yet, but there were news, still, 'Say, Jo, do you remember my boss? Rodolfo de Cropolati? You won't believe it, he's been fired.'

'No way! Tell me! DetailsDetailsDetails, please!'

'Well, I had told you about our head accounting, his busy little working bee, Adele Schmittke. Well, recently, our company started filtering all emails to prevent sexual harassment. And good old Rodolfo didn't read the memo. Surprise, surprise. Well, no surprise, actually, he's never in, actually. Anyway, they are now looking for words like 'sexy' or 'horny', and also for very specific verbs. And so, the correspondence from their work emails with Adele.Labelle@whatever.de and HotRod@dunnowhat.com popped up. And that was that.'

„My gosh, what a dumbass would use his work email for such correspondence? Well, a sexy and horny one, I guess. Yes, he should be fired for pure dumbness, anyway.'

Tina laughed, 'Yes, he was. All of that. I mean, Lars would never write such stuff, anyway. But if he ever did, he would not use his work mail for that. Who can be so stupid?'

'No, I cannot imagine Mark doing such stuff, either.' And I was quite certain that he would not cheat on me, as well. We did have our differences, but that was to be expected, given that we had only known each other for such a short period of time.

In the evening, I deposited a little St Nicholas package in the outer pocket of Mark's suitcase. With exquisite white tea and a sticker, 'Please open on 6 December, only.' I knew he would love this little surprise.

Before taking off, next morning, Mark hugged me and murmured, 'I am so happy to have you. I know that you are right. I am wrong. Always. I love you so much. All I want is for you to be happy. If things don't work out between us, then I will find someone who will make you happy. And I will stay alone, forever. After you, there cannot be anyone else.'

'Mark, don't say that. Let's try to work this out, together.'

'That's all I want my darling. The whole thing about the wedding, we will get that sorted out. Exactly the way you want. I want this to be the best day of your life. I am an old hermit, but I want a life with you, your friends and your family. And our children. You are my butterfly, so happy and colourful and alive. That's why I don't want to marry you in white. But we do what you want. From now on, everything will change. And if I fall back into my old patterns, you must kick me.'

He could be such a sweetheart.

We kissed and started into our single-everyday, knowing that we were not singles.

Mark called in the evening. He had found the parcel and opened it, 'But I don't have anything for you. I didn't know that I had to give you something for St Nicholas. Are you mad at me?'

'Mark, giving is not something you have to do. I just wanted to make you happy. That doesn't…'

'Well, anyway, I don't have anything for you. And, to be honest, I don't like being put under pressure, this way.'

Wow, that had backfired. 'Mark, I did not want to put you under pressure. If you feel that way, just put it aside, and we will consider it a Christmas…'

'Nonononono, I will not return my present. A present is a present. Only thieves get back.'

For someone who did not want any St Nicholas presents, he was remarkably firm in defending his. I steered the communication to topics that were less controversial than well-meant presents. Things like mass murderers or so.

Alex

A few days later, I had dinner with my co-passenger Alex, relaxed and without any relationship-related afterthoughts. Even though I didn't really care, I could not help but notice how attractive he was. Clear, deep green eyes, full lips, a warm smile that even showed when he did not smile, and an athlete's body – and under the shirt, there was definitely a six-pack. He was a compassionate tennis player, and despite my repeated warning that I had not played in 20 years and would definitely not make a good partner, we picked a date to go and play, together. He laughed, 'No need to worry, at all. As long as I can be in the court and beat up little yellow balls, I'm good. You know, men are made after a simple pattern, we are unpretentious.'

And, yes, a few days later, we were really standing in the court, and Alex was beating up little yellow balls. Well 'beating' was not really the right word, actually. He carefully deposited the balls right in front of my racket so that we actually managed some longer rallies. To get us there, he had to run a lot – which was, unfortunately, solely due to my lack of control over these mean little buggers, not to any plan or skill on my end.

After our exchange, we let the evening wind down slowly, and it became later than anticipated; we chatted and laughed through my regular telephone time with Mark, unbeknownst to me. Unfortunately, I had left my phone in the dressing room. So, I was already on the bus when I saw that Mark had tried to reach me, fifteen times, and had also sent me two texts. 'Schatzele, where are you? I cannot reach you. I'm worried. Please call, Mark', and, half an hour later, 'Darling, I cannot reach you. Please call. Who are you with? Mark'.

At home, I immediately called him. Fortunately, he was still awake.

'Hi, Mark, this is Johanna. I'm sorry for being incommunicado. I was out playing tennis. With Alex. I thought I had mentioned it. I'm really sorr…'

'Who is Alex? How old is he? Be honest! You didn't just play tennis with him, the whole evening. And apart from that, it is incommunicada. You are a woman.'

Lord almighty. Now, that was important. I decided to ignore the head master and tried to reach the person, 'Darling, I told you about him, I am absolutely sure. My seat neighbour on the plane. No, we played some tennis, first, and then sat together for a little chat.'

'Ah, so that's what this is called, now. So far, everything sounded perfectly innocent, and now…'

'…it's still innocent. I have nothing to blame myself for, and you don't have anything to blame me for, either. After all, I don't inquire every evening who you go out to have a drink with, while I am still working.'

Click. Mark had hung up.

Fifteen minutes later, the telephone rang.

'Schatzele, I'm sorry. Don't be mad at me, please. That was stupid. I was stupid. You know, I am just so worried to lose you. You are my love. My big love. My one and only. You must never leave me. Promise me!'

This was not easy for him, I could hear that. I was sorry for him. 'Schatzele, when I have made up my mind, I have made up my mind. There's no need for you to worry. Alex is nice, and I like him, but you have to trust me. After all, I trust you, too.'

'What do you mean? You are not jealous, at all?'

'No.'

'Do you think I can't have another one? Because I'm too old? If that's what you're trying to say, …'

'Mark, this has nothing, absolutely nothing to do with your age. It doesn't even have anything to do with you. I trust you, because you are my partner. That's the foundation of our relationship, I don't question that. And if you ever abused my trust, this would be it.'

'What, you wouldn't fight for me?'

'No, I would leave. I would be gone. Period.'

'What – leave, just like that? You would not fight for

me?'

'No. Not at all. I am either with you or I'm gone. But I'm not jealous, and I'm not fighting. That's for the movies, not for me.'

Obviously, Mark had expected a different reaction. Well, at least that put the subject of Alex to rest.

The next morning, my neighbour passed me by in the street. With a baby carriage. The child had surprised everyone by being a girl, after all. Her name would be Doreen. Without any whatchamacallits. So much for that. Unfortunately, reality of life with a new-born did not quite match the young mother's (much more positive) expectations. 'We have been back home, for three days, now, and she hasn't slept through a single night. I don't think I can bear this much longer.'

Was it for me to break the news that this was what she had signed up for, for the next years? No, life would assume this task. After all, this was what made life so exciting. Always new things to learn…

For example, on my next flight to Berlin, I read the results of a survey, 'I love being single, because…' That sounded promising – but unfortunately, the responses were not really surprising. Apparently, hard core single women mainly enjoyed not putting on any make up, eating what they wanted, and no longer getting upset about things – exactly those things which hard core single men enjoyed most. The men had happily abandoned any 'exaggerated' bodily or other hygiene, enjoyed the full range of bodily noise and other emissions, and had removed everything green from the house, be it edible or decorative.

I hoped that these responses were not representative. Well, they reminded me of a date that had ended in his apartment – and that had really ended when I saw his underpants dangling happily from the ceiling lamp. I had not checked, though, whether they were in a before or after state. I had to admit that Mark was pleasantly out of the ordinary regarding the veggie issue. From that standpoint, even vegetable soup seemed somewhat appealing. Somewhat. From the distance and in theory.

Mark's week had been so strenuous that I took a cab from the airport. The house welcomed me with the intense smell of soup. Why did my life seem to revolve around soup, as of late? I gracefully declined, despite Mark's insisting, and even more so when he started slurping through his whole range of tones. He responded monosyllabically to my questions and did not even show any reaction to the anecdote about my neighbour and her baby, so I was happy when we went to bad. As a favour, I went to bed next to him, but when he started snoring, I left for my mattress. My favourite piece of furniture.

When I woke up, I looked straight into Mark's face. I smiled at him. He smiled back. After a few minutes of silent smiling, I got up and went to the bathroom.

At breakfast, Mark asked, 'Say, don't you want your lover any more?'

I decided to let the 'lover' reference go unnoticed.

'Why?'

'Well, when you came to bed with me, last night, I was expecting make-up sex, of course. And then, you were just lying there. And I waited like a parcel at the post office that no one picks up. And the same, again, today.'

'Well, you could have taken the initiative, as well.'

'No, that doesn't work. I need to feel desired. I need the feeling that you are really hot for your lover. Else, it doesn't work.'

True. Apart from our first time, it had always been me

who had taken the initiative. For no satisfactory reason, actually.

'But that means that I will never feel desirable, right?' I concluded with some consternation.

He pulled out his 'What a little rascal I am'-face, 'Yes, if you love your Marky, that's the way it is. And apart from that, you know how sexy you are. Otherwise, I would not go to bed with you, in the first place. Just imagine: My boss's wife is almost 60. I couldn't do that. The mere thought – the wobbly skin, and the wrinkles... disgusting. No, I could never do that.'

And, once more, he had managed to casually surprise me. For me, a man more than 20 years older than me, with a belly, wobbly skin and wrinkles was a desirable gift of God. For him, a woman some years younger than him and doubtlessly in better shape was a disgusting imposition. I had thought that he knew I was not kissing the prince but the frog, permanently, but that I was accepting that, because sometimes you win, and sometimes you lose, in every relationship. Apparently, I had been wrong. While I was still thinking about that, Mark left the room.

Just a few minutes later, I heard a jolly 'I'm going biking, my dear! See you, in the evening!'

I had not expected that. Of course, I did not mind. We were not one of those Siamese couples joined at the hip, after all. But if I had known, I could have made plans with friends. And naturally, they all had plans, now.

But I was lucky, there was a workshop on the opera 'The Tsar's Bride', at the *Deutsche Oper*. I didn't know that one, so that worked out well.

Using public transport, the way to the city seemed even longer than it had been, on the car. Wow, Mark really lived in the middle of nowhere. But then, we would move together, in Zurich, soon. We hadn't discussed it in a while, but we didn't need to. Everything was clear: Mark would go into early retirement and move to me in Zurich. And knowing how much he loved his garden, I had started searching for a house for us – which was quite an endeavor, given the difficult real estate market in Zurich.

At least, the ride gave me the opportunity to do some reading. The story was as it should be in a Russian opera: tragic. Marfa, a young and beautiful merchant's daughter, is about to marry her beloved Lykow, when the Tsar orders the most beautiful to be presented to him so that he can choose a wife. Of course, things evolve as has to be expected: He picks Marfa, and in the love pentagon that develops, not only Marfa dies but also Lykow, as well as her rival. And things don't look good for the rival's lover, either. Sometimes, life sucks.

At the opera, the situation was no different than at any other typical cultural event: Two men and twelve women. Well…

In the next few hours, we read and listened to excerpts from the opera, performed and danced – and, yes, danced a little. Admittedly with limited artistic value. The view behind the scenes and the singing on stage was exciting, indeed.

Things turned a bit odd, when half the male participants of the event decided to impersonate Marfa. After all, this was a borderline experience, and if you get involved in such a thing, you really have to leave all borders behind. 'And as a man, it is important to be in touch with your female side, after all.'

If you say so, buddy! Of course, women like us regularly got the chance to explore our male side, for example when we wanted to dance. I realized that we were clearly privileged when compared to the poor men caught in their male roles.

His Marfa turned out to be a timid, shy creature with narrow movements who barely lifted her eyes off the floor and only became so bold as to whisper. Why all men near and far were falling in love with such a truly expressionless girl remained a secret forever buried in the bosom of the comely male maiden.

When most of them were dead and I on the way home, I received a message from Mark. He had spent the day on the bike and on a bench near the lake – to think. Now, he was sitting in one of his favourite restaurants and asked whether I wanted to join him. I responded that I had been to a workshop at the opera, and was still on the train. I wouldn't be able to make it in time. Mark responded that I should not stay up. He would be late. When he came back, he first took a shower and then went to bed. And started snoring, immediately.

The rest of the weekend went by quietly. If not to say on mute. I had obviously made a mistake. Even though it was not quite obvious to me what that had been. Was this my life, now?

Urs

Only two weeks to go until Christmas! I strolled through the shops and hoped to find things that yelled the name of their future owner at me. Of course, this was the easier the better I knew the person. For Mark's children, it was a challenge. For Mark, it was easy.

I concentrated on electronics: A water boiler with variable temperature settings for his tea; a solar power station for his phone; a gadget for saving his SIM card data. Plus cycling maps for the Berlin area, and a Swiss knife with his name engraved. A tablecloth which my great grandmother had crocheted; after all, we would soon be family. And a little bit of this and that. And definitely no chocolate. While at it, I bought some of the presents for Christian, as well. When it came to technical gadgets, all men were the same.

With every gift, I felt closer to Mark and imagined how he would unwrap it and be happy. I pushed aside the memory of his reaction to my St Nicholas gift. Presumably, he had not received any real presents, in such a long time that he had to learn that, again. But I would manage. And I would also show him that no other man could put our relationship at risk.

I was surprised and relieved when Mark asked me for my wishes for Christmas. So, Christmas was an acceptable occasion for presents.

Spontaneously, I had only one idea, 'I want a professional cleaning team to come and clean the house. For a week. Top to bottom. At least four people. I will pay for it, I will organize it, I will supervise it. My only wish from you is that you allow them in.'

Until I met Mark, laundryironingcleaning had not played a material role in my life. So, I was surprised at myself, when this wish flew out of my mouth quick as a shot. However, I really did not see any other way out, because the house was just too big for me to clean it like that, on the weekends, not only the dirt of the last decade, but also Mark's dirt of the preceding week. And I did not want to do that, anyway. It was crazy for me to pay for a cleaning lady, at home, and then to spend my weekends cleaning after Mark. But, of course, such a cleaning team would be a major intrusion into Mark's privacy. So, I decided to make it my only wish. In Zurich, he would have to get used to my cleaning lady, anyway. That would take some convincing.

Mark needed a while to muse, 'So bad?'

I just nodded and gave him a hug. I knew that every word I could say would hurt him.

'Okay. If that's how it is.'

I took this as consent. Of course, I would have loved to get this done, before Christmas, so that the children and I would feel comfortable, but I knew that Mark would need time to digest.

When buying presents, I also felt closer to Mark's children. Naturally, the situation had to be strange for them. Even without the age difference – after all, they were closer in age to me than Mark was –, it had to be weird to see their father with a new woman. I was a little worried about whether they would accept me, but Mark ensured me that they were looking forward to meeting me. And because of that, I wanted to make Christmas as good for them as possible, without acting like a substitute mother. Overall, a tricky undertaking, but with Mark's help, I would manage.

I bought Swiss knives for them, too, and had their names engraved, plus some cook books, a silk scarf from China for Anna and a tie from Thailand for Frank, that should work. And, of course, no chocolate. But cookies from Basel.

On one of my trips to *Bahnhofstrasse*, where the Christmas decorations were hanging over the street like stars raining from the sky, I had a look for a festive gown. Of course, I would not celebrate Christmas all dressed up, but just having a look would be nice. Maybe for an evening out in the *Philharmonie*. The store would close in ten minutes, but that should be enough for a peek. I had never been to the top floor with the big robes. So, I was completely taken by surprise when I found the wedding dresses, there. A wedding gown. In white! I looked around. I was all by myself. No one would notice. I could just try on a dress that would be a little bit too small. Then, it would not fit, and I would know that wedding gowns were not for me. And then, it would not hurt so much when I would give in to Mark and give up on this dream. He had started to make derogatory remarks about every white piece of clothing we saw in the streets, and he ostensibly changed to the other side of the road when we passed by the bridal store around the corner. It was extremely important to him that I would not be the white bride. But still, I wanted to feel such a dress on my skin, once. Just once. Be a bride.

I shivered when I took a dream of silk, ruffles and lace from the hanger and pulled it over my head, expecting with absolute certainty that it would not fit, and that I would be mad at myself for my stupid dream. But the dress denied me that favour. It fitted perfectly. The material was cool and cosy on my skin. The whole dress rustled when I lifted the skirt to make sure to keep it clean and white.

The shop assistant approached the changing room, 'Excuse me; we will be closing, soon. Can I help you?'

I stepped out. Just walk a few steps. Hear the rustling.

She came to the rescue, 'Just a second, I will close the bow. Yes, now, it's perfect. What a beautiful bride! Have a look; I can hold the mirror up so that you can see yourself from all sides. It's the perfect dress for you. Now, that's rare. We don't even have to change a thing.'

I closed my eyes. I did not want to see myself. Feeling

the dress was enough. Too much, actually. But I had to undress. And in the changing room, there was a mirror, too. Remorseless. She was right. No matter how hard I tried to tell myself that I looked like a ridiculous piece of cream pie: All I saw was a beautiful bride. The bride I had been dreaming of as a child.

Leave, I had to leave. Just get away from here.

When I arrived at Mark's, that Friday, I happily presented my yield for the children.

'That's really sweet of you. But you don't have to do this, they don't expect that. And don't get anything sweet for them. I don't want them to get fat.'

'Darling, I made sure not to get them any chocolate. I know how much you hate that. But your children are adults. I'm sure they have enough judgment not to overindulge. On the photos, they looked…'

'Well, actually, Frank is a bit chubby. And I feel that, as their father, I have to look after that.'

I could not help but notice the irony in the situation. Here was richly-bellied Mark, who had inhaled the Truffes du Jour and who had also found and destroyed my chocolate supplies, abhorred by any notion of his son's getting a piece of chocolate. On the other side, it was sweet of him to be so worried about them. Maybe, he just wanted to protect them from becoming as fat as he was. But still, one piece of chocolate would not let them explode.

'Mark, if they haven't learned that by now, you will not make a big difference on the few days a year that you see them. And, soon, the roles will reverse, anyway.'

'What do you mean?'

'That's the change of the time. At some point, the children give the directions. And the parents must learn to accept that.'

'Well, my children better not try that one on me!'

'Maybe, that cannot be avoided. How did that play out between you and your dad? Didn't you give him advice, every now and then?'

'That was a completely different story. I was the first in the family who had gone to university. So, it was natural that I was the patriarch.'

'See, and your daughter will be the matriarch, as far as health issues are concerned. That's the way things go. And that's no different than what happened between you and your dad.'

'Yes, it is.'

I laughed and gave him a hug, 'Because you're the pride of creation, right, my darling?'

I kissed him on the mouth, but he did not kiss back. Well, so be it. Maybe he was still hurt because of our preceding ritualized soup debate.

On Saturday, I was cleaning the house, while Mark was out and about on his bike. I wanted the children to feel comfortable, and it was just another week before Christmas. But knowing that there would be professional cleaners coming, soon, things were no longer quite as gruesome. Plus I did not want them to think that all of this was my dirt. To make things less frustrating, I had also bought a headset for the telephone, so that I could use the cleaning time to talk to my friends and Christian.

Sometimes, I also used his home trainer. He did not want me to go to a gym, 'That will be the day! Absolutely not! You with all these trained, testosterone-pumped monkeys staring at you. If you love me, you don't go there. And I don't want you to go in Zurich, either.'

I chose not to respond. Zurich was my turf. Things

were different, there, and they would stay different.

For lunch, Mark still cooked by himself and with enormous passion, all the way through his favourite dishes, including squab with liver stuffing. He had obviously forgotten our discussion about that. I praised like hell and ate around the liver. Mark ate what was left on my plate. Sometimes, a problem solves itself.

He also proudly sent me photos of his Lucullan masterpieces, during the week, and I praised. This was much easier, because one round generally sufficed, and I could copy/paste previous comments. Maybe, I should print speech balloons: 'How scrumptious!' 'The best thing I ever ate!' 'Where on Earth did you learn to cook? It's out of this world!' 'How do you do this? No one cooks like you!' 'Down with Jamie Oliver! Long live Mark Kinsey!' I assumed he would not have deemed such signs a very appropriate and funny Christmas gift, though. Well, I would have. But then, the short moment of fun was not worth the trouble that would ensue.

Back in Zurich, a totally unexpected excursion to the wonderful world of interpersonal relationships was waiting for me. Nandika called; a friend from Frankfurt was in town, and she had sprained her ankle. Now she thought if maybe, I could spare an evening?

Sure, no worries. In the old days, I would have asked whether he was single, but that was no longer an issue.

I realized that Nandika had obviously not yet received the message, when a stranger waiting at the main station thrust a rose made of marzipan into my face. I did not know what Nandika had told him, but his joyful smile did not vanish when I mentioned my fiancé. Well, so be it, I decided to have a fun evening. I showed him my Zurich and gave my best to extract something other than admiration from him, but there was nothing. My gosh, there had to be something, I mean, something – S-O-M-E-T-H-I-N-G! Admiration and smiling is all good and nice for five minutes, but this was not feature-length by any means. Yes, of course, in the movies, the arcane silent one was mysterious, interesting and strong, but that worked only because the couples-to-be were always stranded on some remote island where the choice was maximally reduced. In real life, however, you have to start dabbling somewhere, and that's difficult when the other side serves only 'yes' and 'no' and dashing eyes.

When we bid our farewells after three looooong hours, he was still smiling, 'Say, do you have time, tomorrow? It's so exciting to listen to you, I could do that for hours.'

Yes, I was afraid he could. But, too bad, so sad, the next highlight of the year was already around the corner, and scheduled for that exact day: Our company's Christmas party. Of course, it was no longer the bombastic party in an expensive restaurant like before the financial crisis. But at least, I could have a chat with colleagues who I had no time to squeeze into my busy days, otherwise.

At our department's party, Urs approached me, raving and good-looking as always. I had followed Tina's advice and not contacted him, any more. And, as she had expected, I had not heard from him, either.

'Hey, Jo! How are you? Gosh, we haven't seen each other, in ages! At least since the summer, right? What have you been up to?'

'Yes, that really seems like it was in a different life. You know, I'm good.'

'Is this an engagement ring? Are you getting married?'

'Yes, I'm engaged.'

'Really? Wow, what a coincidence! I'm engaged, as well. You know, I thought you and I, we might get together. But you never said a thing. And then, I met my fiancé, at a wedding. Anke. We really hit it off, and the next day, she proposed. We're getting married, in June.'

I was stunned, 'So, you were waiting for me to propose?'

'Well, Jo, you know how it is. Men don't marry, they get married. If it wasn't for Anke, I would stay single. But, tell me, do I know him?'

'No, I don't think so. Sorry, Urs, I have just seen Vincenz, back there, I have to talk to him about something. Work, you know.' This discussion had been going on, long enough. Or longer. I avoided Urs, the rest of the evening. And I did not care whether he noticed or not. I had a breaking point, as well.

I did not sleep well, that night. The light from the house across the backyard found its way into my sleep. I was convinced that I had to move into this brightly lit apartment, right now. The thought frightened me. I woke up from my own screaming.

Amélie Bastet

And here it was: The weekend before Christmas. I was excited to finally meet Mark's children. I had actually managed to get the time between Christmas and New Year's off, given that I now had family, sort of. This was also exciting, the longest time we had ever spent together.

Mark picked me up at the airport, 'so that you don't have to carry the suitcase all by yourself.' Of course, he could not really carry anything, with his knee and all. But it was the thought that counted.

I had hoped that he would spare me the soup debate, as an advance Christmas present, but life wasn't that good to me. Well, at least he did not say a word when I escaped to my mattress, afterwards.

On Saturday, Mark's grocery shopping appeared totally appropriate and sufficient for a two week training camp of a cooking academy. No chocolate, of course.

We came by the newspaper store. A sign announced that a 52 million Euro jackpot was at stake.

'Did you see that, Mark? 52 million! Just imagine winning that! Come on, let's play! Just for fun!'

'Well, I know I won't win. Because I won't play.'

'Mark, don't be such a Grinch! Especially not around Christmas. Just imagine! If you were to win, what would you do?'

'Maybe buy shares. But do you even know what the likelihood of winning is? Zero.'

'I know that, absolutely. But I don't expect to win; I just buy a little dream for a few days. And no one can take that away from me, even if I do not win. And if I ever did win anything, so much the better. My mom always played. And with the money she won, we went out for nice dinners, she bought new clothes, and…'

'What? She must have played quite a bit, then.'

'No, of course not. That's the point. She did not win whatever little money she won. She gained the claim to a little unreasonableness.

'So, she just threw the money down the drain, first to the lottery, and then for unnecessary crap?'

'No. She bought a little dream. And then, she lived that dream.'

'With all due respect, it's been a long time that I heard such stupid stuff.'

I did not want to give up, 'But, just for the sake of argument, imagine you had all those millions, all of a sudden. What would you do?'

'I told you, I don't know. Maybe buy shares.'

'But shares are no fun when you have enough money, anyway. And you told me that you wanted to do something for children, a foundation, or a school or something. In November, on the boat to Lucerne. The dream of your life.' The first moment when I had felt close to him seemed so far away, so suddenly.

'Yes, maybe,' he snipped.

Probably, he just had to concentrate on traffic. I understood. I waited till we were at his place and let him toy with the thought, a little more.

'And, any more ideas?'

'What ideas?'

'Ideas what you would do with the money. From the lottery.'

'Johanna, we have already discussed this.'

Maybe, he really didn't know what to do. I did, and I was happy to share this piece of information. 'Well, I know what I would do. First, I would buy a really nice house for my brother. With a sister-flat for me. And for all my friends who have children, I would also buy apartments or houses. And pay for university for their children. For Anna, too, of course. And I would go someplace to sing with my choir, a place we would otherwise not go. I would invite all my friends and family for the concert. And a tour of wherever we go. Maybe the Sydney Opera House, or the *Philharmonie.* Or the amphitheatre of Epidaurus, then we would also do something against the Greek economic crisis. You know, I once sang there, you…'

'Or Carnegie Hall, that seems more appropriate.' Mark's tone ripped the happiness I had just talked myself into to pieces.

'Mark, that was mean.'

'I am just honest. Your little choirboys and -girls in the Sydney Opera. Tell me another! And, anyway: If I win, then it is my money, and I don't see the slightest bit of a reason why I should share it with anyone. And, just so you know, the theatre in Epidaurus is not an amphitheatre. An amphitheatre forms a closed circle, but the theatre in Epidaurus is open on one side.'

Did I care, right here and right now? Was this the big, precious heart with which mine was to beat as one?

We cleared the groceries away, and Mark stated happily, 'Schatzele, I'm so looking forward to Christmas with you. We will have such a great time. We will MAKE this such a great time.'

We were almost past lunchtime, so Mark resiled to his kitchen exile, and I – well, I cleaned.

On Sunday, after Mark's bike tour, the long expected text message from Lars arrived, 'Dear friends, Amélie Bastet has finally arrived. The most perfect gift we could have asked for. Mother and child are doing well, mother and father are overjoyed and tired.'

I showed the text to Mark. He hugged me, 'Darling, I want that, too. Being pregnant, that's the biggest gift a woman can give to a man. It doesn't even have to be for Christmas. What do you think?' He kissed me.

I wiggled out of his embrace, 'When do we want to see them? Maybe on the 27th?'

'Let's wait and see. Now, it's Christmas.'

Somehow, Mark was lacking true enthusiasm when it

came to seeing my friends. We also had not discussed the wedding, any further. I did not mind. But it meant that children were not really on the agenda, for the time being.

'Well, we should try to see them, given that I am in Berlin. After all, I am not here, that often.'

'Oh, yes, thank you for mentioning it, Johanna. We should start looking for a job for you. In January, there are always loads of jobs out. The best thing would be to go for something in administration, with a nine-to-five job. That would be much better for the children, you know,' Mark beamed at me, 'I take it you will not stop working, right? I would appreciate that. I just feel safer with two incomes, and if we want to keep our standard of living with the children, then we need that. Plus the house needs some work, too.' He was still beaming.

I took a deep breath, 'Mark, that's not what we discussed. You wanted to go into early retirement and move in with me, in Zurich.'

'Oh, Schatzele, you know, I've been thinking about this. And I make more money than you, anyway.'

'Mark, that's the exact opposite of what we agreed on. And how do you want to know how much money I make? We haven't even discussed that. You had…'

'Schatzele,' he interrupted me, 'don't be mad at your Marky, Pleaseplease!'

'Mark, this is not about being mad at my Marky, this is about…'

'Pleasepleaseplease, don't be mad!'

'Mark, stop interrupting me! This is not a discussion about some nitty gritty, this is about…'

'Pleasepleaseplease, be good, again!'

'Mark, I am trying to have a communication among adults. If you are not able or willing to do that, then this makes no sense.'

Mark's mouth descended on me, small and pointed, 'This has nothing to do with being a grown-up, this is just about love. All about love. If you love me, you move here.'

I held his face with both hands, looking him straight in the eyes, hoping that he would listen to me. He did not feel comfortable. His eyes begged me silently to just leave him alone and give in. But I could not grant him any mercy. This was too important, 'Mark, I don't want to say anything that I might regret, later, certainly not shortly before Christmas. But I just need to be very clear that I won't move into this house. This is a fundamental decision for our relationship. You suggested that you would move to Zurich, we have made this decision, and now you cannot change it unilaterally.'

'Okay.' Mark pressed his lips together, turned around and left me speechless.

Our discussion had not really put me in a festive spirit. I had to use violent force and mental power to press my inner rose-coloured glasses onto my nose and convince myself that this did not confuse and hurt me as much as it did. Presumably, Mark was just stressed out, so shortly before my first encounter with his children. I did not want to make things worse for him. But I also didn't want to give up my whole life for him, and certainly not move into this house. Dang it, where were those stupid glasses?

Mark was smoking in his office. I knew how strenuous such discussions were for him and let him calm down. Shortly after, I heard him snore. I let him sleep and used the time to wrap some presents, to make some phone calls – and to clean.

At night, another one of those dreams. This time, the

house grew around me, like a huge germ, which separated over and over again. More and more rooms added themselves. And as the property did not grow, it became tighter and tighter, and the outer rooms swallowed the inner ones. And I was lying in the middle. I got up and looked for the way out, but all around me were walls. Only walls. Walls coming closer. Walls crushing me. I screamed.

Mark came running, froze and stared at me. I had told him that I sleepwalked. If so, all he should do was to say, 'Everything is fine. I will take care of this. You go back to bed.' Those were my magic words. My parents had always done it like that, and it had always helped.

Instead, Mark clasped me, dragged me to his bedroom and held me tight. I froze, sorted out my thoughts and brought my panicking heart under control, until I found the concentration to wake myself up. Now, he started whispering, 'Calm down. Calm down. I'm here. Your Mark is here. Just sleep. I'm here.' After some minutes, he fell asleep and snored. After a torturing eternity, I managed to wrest from the prison of his arms and returned to my mattress.

The next morning, I let him sleep in and made breakfast. When Mark came down, he embraced me and smiled at me, proudly, 'Do you know that you were sleepwalking, last night? I read an article about this. You must never wake sleepwalkers up. So, I just held you tight, and you calmed down, immediately. So, how did I do?'

Wrong. You did it all wrong. You sent me off whirling in panic, and if I wasn't more aware than you even when sleepwalking, I would have fought back and resolved any and all questions relating to children. With a final twist for you. No, of course I did not throw all of this at his head held up high. Instead, I responded, 'Mark, I am sure you meant well, but a newspaper article is a newspaper article. I had told you that I sometimes sleepwalk. And I had told you what to do, then.'

'Yes. You wanted me to send you back to bed.'

'And why didn't you do that, then?'

'It didn't say that in the article. And apart from that, one must not talk to sleepwalkers.'

'But this is not about the sleepwalker as a species, it is about me. And I know myself best. Better than a newspaper article, anyway. And, by the way, it is also an urban myth that sleepwalkers don't remember anything, the next day.'

Breakfast was a silent one, and so was the whole day.

Frank

I woke up knowing that this was a very special day. Excited, almost like a child. But not about Christmas Eve, the festive spirit or the presents – no, this was a REALLY important step. I would meet Mark's children.

Mark brought breakfast to my mattress – scrambled eggs. I got sick and ran off to the loo.

Mark followed me, 'Schatzele, what's wrong? Are you sick? Schatzele, does that mean... oh, that's the most wonderful Christmas gift. Darling, you make me so happy.'

I closed the door. For some things, one definitely wants to be alone. When I came out, Mark was standing there, waiting for ,me. He hugged me so hard that I became sick, again: 'My love, my great love! See, now everything will be alright.'

I suppressed my nausea and extricated myself from his

embrace. 'Mark, what do you mean?'

'Oh, don't you know, my little silly you? A woman, MY little woman, getting sick in the morning – that makes my pregnant-o-meter run berserk!'

'Mark, I'm on the pill. And I told you that eggs in the morning make me throw up. I cannot stand the smell, and I certainly cannot eat them.'

Mark's energy oozed out like the air from a pierced balloon. I could have sworn I heard a faint 'Pfffft'. I did not want to hurt him, but I could not become pregnant just to please him. In particular as Mark had started to talk more and more about my preferably quickly and repeatedly effected pregnancy, but less and less about the ensuing children.

I followed up at the breakfast table, 'Mark, you keep talking about how much you want me to become pregnant. But there's an outcome to a pregnancy, and I am not quite sure any more whether you even want children. After all, you already have two, and you could become a grandfather, soon.'

Mark looked at me, squinting slightly. I could hear him think. After what felt like an eternity, 'I don't know.'

'What do you mean, you don't know?'

'It means that I don't know if I want children, again.'

'But, Mark, you want me to stop taking the pill. And then, you don't know if you want children?'

'Well, if you stop the pill, that just means that you love me and want a child from me. But whether that works, that's a whole different story.'

I forced myself to sound loving and calm, 'Mark, I cannot stop taking the pill, just to show you that I love you.'

'Of course, you can. And then, we wait and see if something happens.'

'No, Mark. Only Peter Pan in Neverland can plan his life, this way. 'If something happens,' I am pregnant, and your adult children have a little brother or sister. And you are father of a baby, with all that comes with it. Do you want that? Being a real father, sharing equally?'

'I don't know. Well, I mean, I would be more like a granddad, I think.'

'And is that what you want, a child that views you as a grandfather?'

'My god, the way you say that, that sounds horrible. I would just have another role. Read bedtime stories, have him on my lap, and all that. And I would always be there for you and the child.'

'Can you define 'be there for me and the child', please?'

'I have always been a good father. You can ask my children about that, if you want. I would never leave you in the lurch, the child would want for nothing. I would always pay.'

After all his stories about his life with the children, I had viewed Mark not just as a pay dad. 'Of course, you would pay. And it's good that you share that notion. But that's the bare minimum. That doesn't make you a good father.'

Roller blinds of complete incomprehension gradually covered Mark's eyes. I saw that he could not follow. And I realized that we would not have children. My unfathered children deserved a father who wanted them, who would pick them up when they fell. In every sense. Like Christian picked up his Larissa, Lars his Amélie, Jon his Cordelia and Leo his Carl and his Ariane. Fortunately, I had control over that. We did not have to pursue this.

'Say, Mark, have you already wrapped your presents?'

'No, I don't do that. That's too much trouble. And apart

from that, you just rip it open, and then, it's all over after two minutes, and you sit on a pile of trash.'

'Wow, Mark, your environmentalist heart! Great! But no worries. I use the same gift bags, every year. Or calendar sheets. And apart from that, I have an idea for tonight to slow things down a bit. Then, it will not just be about the presents but also about getting to know each other.'

'What's that?'

'Well, I brought along my old Trivial Pursuit. For the right answer, you can open a present.'

'Well, if you think that that's a good idea.'

'Darling, we don't have to do this. I just thought it would be a good idea. It would give us something to do instead of just sitting in silence. What do you do for Christmas?'

'Presents, eat, read. But I like your idea. Let's do that.'

'Mark, we can discuss with the children, and then we decide together. After all, it's a family thing.'

'Thank you for being so considerate about the kids. That's how we will do it.' We kissed each other.

'Mark, do you want me to wrap your gifts for the children? I have brought enough bags and ribbons and all.'

'Well, if you're already at it. Wait a second, I will get the stuff.'

Mark brought a soft violet cashmere sweater for Anna and disappeared. After a few minutes, I heard him, 'Shit! Dang it! I don't believe this! Where is this stupid thing? I know that I ... Darling! Can you come here for a second, please?'

I found him in front of his closet. His suits were lying on the floor, mingled with sweaters, jeans and shoes, 'Darling, I cannot find the cufflinks for Frank. I had bought him the same ones that I wear. And now I cannot find them.'

The closet was empty – so, I wouldn't find them there, either, 'Okay, do you remember putting them in the closet?'

'I put all presents in the closet.'

'Do you specifically remember putting the cufflinks in there?'

'No.'

'When did you last have them, I mean, definitely?'

'At the *KadeWe*, in the Bulgari store. The shop assistant put them into a big paper bag.'

'What colour was the bag?'

'Black.'

'And where did you go from the Bulgari store?'

'To the deli food department. To the oysters.'

'And there, you still had the bag?'

'Yes, I put it on the floor, and then – dang it, I left it, there.'

'Well, good. Let's call the customer service of the *KadeWe* and ask if someone handed in the bag.'

Unfortunately, the finder had not been enlightened by the festive grace of Christian charity. No one had handed in the bag or at least the box with the cufflinks.

'Just imagine the finder could never have afforded such an expensive gift,' I tried to lift up Mark's spirits. 'Maybe this was the first time that he lucked out. He should have handed them in, but maybe it was just too much for him.'

'That's crap! He's a mean thief!'

'Yes, of course. But if you cannot change it, anyway, just build a positive story around it. It's your choice if you want to get upset. Well, things are what they are, so what do we do? Do you want to go shopping?'

'No, I really don't feel like it. And by the time we are in the city, the shops are closed.'

He had a point, 'Okay, what else have you got for

him?'

'Nothing. But I bought him the cufflinks.'

'Yes, you did. But that doesn't help him, now. After all, you do want to give him something.'

'Yes. And I bought him something. I have spent the money, and I won't get that back, after all.'

'Mark, you cannot just have nothing for Frank. If you lost them, then you have to buy something else. Or you give him your cufflinks, for the evening, and buy new ones together with him, after Christmas. This way, you do something, together, and he gets exactly what he likes. And that's also good.'

'Johanna, please keep out of that. The whole thing is annoying enough, as it is, without your good advice. I have bought something for him, that's enough. Frank will understand.'

Fortunately, our discussion was interrupted by the doorbell. Anna, a tall, blonde twen with a shy smile. She shook my hand, 'Hello, Johanna, may I say Johanna?'

'Yes, of course, you can. You are Anna, right? I am happy to meet you.'

Anna left for her room – my room. It had been obvious for weeks that I would have to sleep next to Mark, over Christmas, but that did not make the prospect any more comfortable.

A few minutes later, Frank arrived. He looked more like Mark – but he seemed to do sports, 'Dr Johanna Lenné? Wow! Happy to see you, again!'

'Hi. Frank? Have we met?'

'Well, sort of. I was at your presentation in London. And I was really impressed.'

Mark was visibly confused, 'Frank, that's nonsense. You must be mixing up something. Johanna doesn't have a PhD. Or do you? You would have told me, right?'

'Yes, I do have a title. I don't talk about it, but it's on my card, at the door, on my mailbox, my email signature – just everywhere.'

Mark disappeared into the kitchen. Anna, Frank and I made the beds. Anna was happy, 'Say, did you clean up all of this? And clean the windows? It's not been this clean and neat since mama died. Thank you! That's sweet of you. Frank, look, even the windowsills! And the butterfly from the dining room?'

'I'm sorry. It was so old and dusty, it just fell to pieces.'

By now, Frank had come to join us, 'No worries, Johanna. You know, it is so much nicer, here. I mean, I could even bring along my girl friend, now. I have never brought her, it was just too embarrassing. And I cannot blindfold her when she's here.'

They started asking me questions, told me about themselves. Getting to know them was by far less complicated than I had feared it would be. In particular, I liked Anna. An intelligent girl, confiding but shy, but most of all kind. The minute we had welcomed her at the door, I had noticed how lovingly she looked at her father. That had given me hope that, maybe, Mark was a particularly good father, after all. I was eager to see him with his children.

But first, he spent the day in the kitchen, chasing away intruders and rejecting any offer of help. So much the better. More time for us.

They told me about their childhood with their mom. Mark seemed to have played a peripheral role, which was not too uncommon, though, in dads from his generation.

So, I turned the tables on them and told them how lovingly their father had talked about them, and that I had started to fall in love with him for the way he loved them. Both looked at me happily but also incredulously, 'Really? Dad said that? Seriously?'

Obviously, they were just getting to know their father from a new angle – which was also a Christmas present.

For lunch, we had soup. And I found my masters when it came to soup praise. Both kids slurped loud and clear and took turns in their encomia, 'Dad, I was so looking forward to your soup. The whole flight, I could hardly think of anything else. And then, the flight attendant came through, offering her sticky sandwiches, and I just said that I didn't want any, because I would get something so much better, soon.'

'Dad, I told all the other students about you and your soup. And everyone is envying me for my amazing dad.'

'Oh, dad, there is nothing better than slurping your soup. When I eat out with clients, I cannot do that, of course, and then I always have to think of you and wish I was eating your soup, instead.'

They glanced at me, every now and then, but when I did not say anything, they just went on, 'Dad, the soup is really getting better with every sip I take.' 'Dad, have you tried a new spice on this? I can taste something, but I just cannot tell what it is.'

Well, I probably should say something, as well, 'It's really good, Mark. Absolutely delicious. Thank you so much for spoiling us so much.'

For me, everything had been said – and more. But the children carried on. Mark was over the moon. Until his wrath fell upon me, 'I am very happy that you like it so much. Well, Johanna does not like my soup. She usually refuses to eat it. So, taking that into account, it is probably a Christmas gift for me that she condescends to eating with us.'

I did not want to spoil the evening, so I stayed quiet.

'See, children, not even a comment.'

The children were inspecting their plates.

I fought for the softest possible tone, 'Why don't you just let go? The soup is very good, and we all have told you so. Say, you told me about that yummy raw milk cheese you bought. Wouldn't that be a good idea, now? Can I lend you a hand?'

Without a word, Mark got up and went to the kitchen.

Anna continued to stare at her plate, 'Johanna, our mom also had this soup fight with him. All the time. If you want peace, just play along.'

'Anna, your praises are absolutely over the top. I mean, it is soup, it's not the cure against malaria.'

'Yes, but if you want peace, do as we do.' Frank consented dissentingly.

'And just see how happy he is. After all, you also want him to be happy, don't you?'

I was stunned. In this family, the children were definitely the better parents.

Mark came back with a cheese platter, and even though he had not made but only bought the cheese, he visibly invited praise. This time, I joined the choir and chimed in. Mark's spirits were lifted into orbit.

When Mark disappeared into the kitchen to prepare the venison, Anna came over to me and whispered, 'Johanna, thank you for the cheese. We usually don't get such things. Dad is afraid we could become fat.'

I looked at Anna and her model figure, 'But you are really the opposite of fat. And Frank isn't remotely fat, either. That's absurd.'

I had to swallow remarks that a father should spoil his children and not bully them, that he should be proud to see that they had inherited his love for good food. And that he was certainly no example of self-restraint and weight control. But none of that would have been news to her, anyway.

'Well, without you, we would not have gotten any of the cheese. We usually meet in the kitchen at night and try, when dad is sleeping.'

I bit my tongue. His own children had to sneak into the kitchen like thieves to eat – this was really bad. On the other hand, I had also built up my chocolate stash – and lost it. Eventually, I was no better off than them. This realization hurt.

I showed them the hedgehog mansions in the basement, even though there hadn't really been anything to see, for weeks. While Frank and Anna were mooching around the house and Mark was cuisine-ing, I called Christian. Of course, it was not yet Christmas, in the U.S., even though Leanna had tried hard to convince her parents that half Germans like her had to celebrate Christmas, on December 24, already – and get presents, most importantly. Unfortunately, her parents insisted on adherence to local customs, in this respect. No, the call of a well-meaning aunt could not help her over that disappointment.

When I had hung up, the telephone rang.

It was Dr Xavier, 'Good evening, ma'am. Could you please connect me with Dr Kinsey?'

I took the telephone to Mark. What could REX want from him, on Christmas Eve? I did not want to eavesdrop, so I went out, but when I returned to get a tea, half an hour later, I became an unwillingly willing witness to their conversation, 'No, Richard, I cannot come by, tonight. It's Christmas. Don't you have anyone else? – No, you cannot demand that from her, as an employer. – Yes, I do understand that you want to send the letter out, today, but if you are honest, that's not what this is about. Richard, it's Christmas. Let her go. Susan has a child.'

Mark smiled at me. It was really sweet of him to stand up for Susan, like that. I embraced him and gave him a hug. The discussion would take a while, and I left him alone.

The night was setting in, and we prepared the gift-giving spree, with the presents on the sideboard and Trivial Pursuit on the table. Anna and Frank had immediately jumped on the idea. It was only when I saw the presents for Frank that I remembered: Mark really did not have anything for him. But I had no idea what I could do about that.

To start, everyone got to open one present without having to answer any questions. The children chose the presents they were giving to each other. Mark picked the parcel with the solar charger and ripped the box to pieces, 'Shit! What a fucking stupid box! How can anyone open that?'

Well, obviously, he had never seen a box sliding open on the side. So, brute force was his best friend. Always a good first resort.

I opened a present from Mark: An anti wrinkle cream. Whoopee!

Mark lit his pipe, accompanied by the comments from the children, 'Dad, I've been so looking forward to that! When you smoke your pipe, that's when it gets cosy. That's when Christmas starts.'

I did not say anything. Everything had its limits.

Right from the start, it became obvious that my idea to combine Trivial Pursuit and gifts had been a good one – but that I had missed an important detail: My version was 20 years old. Questions like 'Which female athlete won the most medals at the Olympic Summer Games in Los Angeles?' immediately revealed to all of us how quickly fame could fade. Even when I read the answer (Kristin Otto), Frank didn't have a clue. And neither did I, actually. The question 'Who was the first negro with a comedy show on U.S. TV?' was immediately classified as politically incorrect – but not answered, either. Mark and I had a clear advantage. In theory. In practice, I no longer remembered many of the day-to-day events, and Mark's broad knowledge overlapped scarcely with that of the people who had developed the questions. That surprised me, somewhat. What surprised me more, however, was that he demanded his presents with more and more nagging, like a spoiled little brat – while his children and I had fun on our trip back to the past.

After an hour, the yield was still meagre: the children and Mark had unpacked the pocket knives, Mark had unwrapped the tea boiler and a book from Frank, thanks to a very generous interpretation of his responses. I had unwrapped a CD from Anna, a cream for eye wrinkles and a perfume from Mark. So, we stopped the experiment and opened the remaining presents without further ado.

As I had hoped, my gifts were well received. The children had also put a lot of thought into their presents, both for Mark and me. Unfortunately, I did not get a cleaning voucher. Instead, I received Mark's dissertation, bound in leather. About Russian mining law. In communist times. Mark embraced me, 'Darling, I had it bound just for you. And when you lie in bed, at home in Zurich and read it, I will be close to you, and you will be close to me. And when you don't understand something, you just give me a quick call, and then we will be even closer.' He pranced to the stereo, put on Anna's jazz CD, and danced through the living room like a gorilla with epileptic fits and a grin on his face. Anna looked at him lovingly, like a mother watching her child dance.

Frank went to the sideboard, several times, inspecting the area, but did not find anything from his father. Anna helped him search. I felt helpless. What should I say? That his father had lost his present and now just thought that that was that? No, that was not my construction site. That was between them.

After a while, Mark came back to the table, and Frank asked, 'Say, dad, is there something missing?'

Mark had no problem, 'No, why?'

'Well, your gift for me…'

'Oh, yes. That. No, there's nothing missing. You know, I had bought cufflinks for you. Very expensive ones, by the way. The ones I'm also wearing. And I left them at the *KadeWe*. That's a pity, now, but that was not intentional. It's the thought that counts, and the thought was there.'

Frank bit his lip.

When Mark had left for the kitchen, Frank approached me, 'Johanna, don't worry about it. That's okay. At least, he did buy something for me, this year. He really must love you a lot if he so wants to impress you. And thank you so much for all your efforts. This way, I did get something. That's fine.'

It was hard for me to be loyal in this. I knew that I would not find anything positive to say, so I just took Frank into my arms.

No, I would not have children with Mark.

Mark returned, and we ate his masterpiece. I told the children about Klara's wedding and the venison – of course interrupted by Mark, every five seconds, but I did not mind that. After dinner, I asked, 'So, how do you usually spend the rest of the evening? It's only just 9 pm.'

'Well, we usually go to the midnight service at church,' Anna responded, 'and after that, we meet with friends.'

'But, of course, you won't do that, today, after all that

Johanna has done for you. We want to stay together, tonight, don't we?' Mark intervened.

'But, dad, we do this, every year. And all our friends from school are here to see their parents. We haven't seen them, for a whole year.'

'If you leave now, then don't even dream of coming back here, tonight. You will be drinking, and you will be loud and use the bathroom and wake me up. I want to sleep. So, if you leave now, then stay where you are.'

Anna burst into tears, ran to the bathroom and locked the door. I was too perplexed to say anything. Mark looked at me, 'You also want to sleep, don't you?'

'Mark, it is just for one night, and if they don't get to see their friends, otherwise, they should do that.'

'No. They will come back home and go to the loo and take a shower. They will wake me up. I don't see why I should accept that. After all, they are visiting, and visitors have to fit in.'

Mark pressed his lips together and sat down bolt upright, his arms folded, looking down at me. 'If they leave now, they can come back, tomorrow. Not tonight. I want to sleep.'

'Mark, it is not their fault that the only useable bathroom is adjacent to the bedroom. Please.'

'Stop nagging about my house, will you! I love my house. And the bathroom is always next to the bedroom. In every house.'

It would only make things worse if I told him that that was news to me.

Mark did not flinch, either, when Frank brought Anna back to the table. Anna was all puffy eyed, Frank looking on the ground, 'Dad, we have called friends. We can stay at their place.'

Mark uttered a grumpy 'Good, if this is what you

want.' Anna started crying, again. It hurt to see this. But I realized that I would not be able to accomplish anything, here, and I did not want to criticise Mark even more, in front of his children, at our first meeting. No, never children with him.

The children left, and we went to bed. Mark fell asleep, immediately. He embraced me from the back. My head was throbbing, and I did not know whether this was only due to Mark's noise emission.

What was I doing here? Was I in love with Mark, or just with the short positive moments with him? And was I even in love? Or did I just want to be in love and was just trying to convince myself?

Or was it a normal up and down in a relationship? After all, both of us had bumped through enough life to have our bumps and edges. And wasn't it normal to squabble and get together, again? Was I expecting too much? Or too little? Was it just the Christmas stress? Was all of this too much for him?

I wrestled myself from his embrace and looked at him. Lying there beside me, like a gigantic happy baby, he had something that touched my heart, and I wished I could understand him. Maybe, there was a reason for his egoistic behaviour, and maybe we would be able to master this, together. After all, I had also seen his loving and sensitive side, especially when he talked about his children. I believed him that he loved them, in his way. And they clearly loved him, so this could not be his typical behaviour with them.

Eventually, I did fall asleep. I was rowing a boat on Lake Tegel in Berlin. Around me, fishes jumped from the water, one of them directly into my boat. It grew and it grew, until finally, Mark was sitting in the boat with me, rowing too. He smiled at me and said, 'Darling, together, we can make it. I am so glad to have you. You are my big love. Big love. Big love.'

We continued to row, and Mark gave the beat, 'Big love. Big Love. Big love.'

But he was rowing in a different direction than me. I rowed faster, but he just laughed, calmly pulling the oars through the water. The boat went in his direction, no matter how desperately I was rowing. Over the fish. We left a red trace in the water. We became faster and faster, until we were too fast to jump the boat. I screamed. My screams woke me up. Mark put his arm around me heavily, pulled me to him and murmured, 'Don't be afraid, my darling, I'm here.'

Fini

Mark and I woke up in an empty house. Rather, I did. Mark was snoring. I got up and made tea. With boiling water. Like normal people make normal tea. Mark came downstairs and embraced me. 'Are you still mad at your Marky?'

'Good morning, Mark. Mark, this is not about me being mad or not, that's not the point. It's about your children. I am not mad. But I simply do not understand you.'

'But, darling, I thought you would understand. You always say that the family comes first, and I just wanted them to respect that. I did not want them to leave on Christmas Eve.'

'Mark, give me a break. You did not want to be disturbed in your sleep, that's all. It was not about the children or the family, and it was not about me. It was about you. Only about you. I am not stupid.'

Mark let go of me. 'Well, obviously you know what I want much better than I do.' He went into the bathroom.

The children came for brunch. They did not mention the evening. Neither did Mark. Nor I.

Mark served everything the kitchen had to offer, I only had to remind him of the cheese. Anna kicked me under the table and grinned at me. When Mark was in the kitchen, Frank turned to me, 'Johanna, thank you, again, for last night. That was very sweet of you. This has been the best Christmas we had, in many years. I am happy that dad has found you. He is much more relaxed with you than he was with Beate. You are okay.'

'Who is Beate?'

'Beate was his last girlfriend, until a month ago or so. But we did not like her that much. He told us that she was only after dad's money.'

So, Mark was still in a relationship when we got together? That was new. I would never have dated him had I known about Beate. Men in a relationship were taboo. And men who kept a partner in the backhand while checking out the next one were disgusting. It dawned on me, though, why he had been so astonished to find out that I was not the jealous type: He had given at least his last partner every reason to be jealous.

But maybe, he was completely innocent and had left Beate much sooner, and the children just did not know. I would have to discuss that with Mark. But not now, not on Christmas Morning. Not in front of Anna and Frank.

After Breakfast, the two left. I liked them.

Mark went into the kitchen; I sat down in his office and opened my Christmas mail. That was one of my rituals: My Christmas cards were presents for me, in many years the only ones.

In particular, I had to smile about Alex's card:

'Dear Johanna

Sometimes, life is kind. My life killed me with kindness when I had the pleasure of meeting you. You are a wonderful person, and your fiancé is a lucky man. I hope he knows and appreciates that.

I wish you a Merry, Happy Christmas and hope that we soon get to shoot some balls at each other, again. If need be snowballs.

Cordially

Alex'

I was happy. Very. I put my cards with Mark's.

I noticed the sender address on the top envelope: Beate Schmitz, Berlin. This had to be her. I did not touch the letter. I would not spy on him.

Finally, I had the time to read some of the papers I had bought for the flight. And in the literature section: An interview with Jon. With a photo. About his new book, which had already been translated into German: '*Peace and Freedom – Allies or Enemies?*' Mark would like that. Friends to discuss the big topics of life and mankind.

'Mark, look, a photo of my London friend in the newspaper. Jon's new book has just been published in German. What do you think about a trip to London for Easter?'

Mark threw a cursory glance at the photo. His reaction inundated me, faster and faster, louder and louder, finally he was yelling. 'Always you and your friends. What about me? When is it about me? And now, you want to go to London, and then you kip at his place, and then he comes over and sleeps here. And I have to cook for your cool friends, and they guzzle in my wine and then I can't do what I want any more, in my own house. I can't run around naked, any more, and cannot belch and fart any more like I want to. I have to run around in a bathrobe and cannot be me. And all that just so that you can doss for free. At this smug guy's. And then, their friends will come over, too, and then, I come home in the evening and the whole house is full of strangers. You are always nagging about my house and about me and about my life, but the truth is that you are just waiting to move in and live for free and then you invite your fucking feel-good friends and party with them. And I have to get up early in the morning, but you don't care. Just like my kids. For once, I ask them to consider my needs, and you side with them and not with me. Once, just once I ask for something. For our family. And what do I get? Criticised! Don't imagine that I don't see that you are yearning to invite your fucking friends, each and every weekend. And then, I have to host them and I have to pay for everything and I have to cook for them. And all that just so that you can crash there for free. Do you really think that I do not have friends? I have friends, too, I just don't brag about it like you do. I have friends, too. And my friends are important. Not like yours. Yours are just looking for someone who pays for them and where they can sleep. But don't try that on me. Oh no, not on me.'

Mark was facing me, panting like a sprinter after a 100m finale.

I saw my life before me, with an outwardly elderly and inwardly old, naked, belching, farting man whose physical and mental presence deprived me of the air to breathe, in a dirty house with no door, in a relationship with no room for a second person. Without friends. Without family. Only him. And whatever would survive of me.

I felt inside, searching for love and understanding. He had switched off all feelings for him. Apart from pity, maybe. Had there ever been anything else? Or had I just fooled myself into believing that there was something? I felt sick. All I wanted was to leave.

Mark gasped. 'I am tired. I go to bed.'

I embraced him and kissed him on his cheek. Like an old acquaintance. 'Sleep well.'

Mark went to the bedroom and closed the door. I packed my bags. He snored. I left. Into the open. Into the free, fresh air.

Konrad

After the past months full of doubt and searching for answers, everything was clear, now. I was calm and almost euphoric.

I called my refuge. 'Hi, Konrad. Merry Christmas! Say, Klara had said that I could come to you for Christmas. Is this offer still valid?'

'Hi, Johanna. This is a little surprising, but, yes, sure. Of course. But, tell me first: Is something wrong? Are you alright?'

I confirmed.

'Good then. That's what I wanted to know. You will tell us everything when you are here, right? Can I pick you up, somewhere? I am happy to come and pick you up, Klara is cooking, anyway, I have the time.'

I looked around. It was snowing. 'No, that's fine. I take the bus, it's coming in five minutes. So, I will be at yours, in half an hour. At around 2.'

'Okay, but give me a call, then I will at least pick you up from the bus stop.' Konrad was a good guy.

'Will do. See you later, then.'

As promised. Konrad picked me up. His beard had grown back – well, somewhat. Klara welcomed us with open arms and hands, all covered in dough. 'Sweetie, what has happened? How are you? Are you all right? Say something! Do you want Konrad to leave so that we can talk?'

Konrad agreed. 'I wanted to get some fresh air, anyway.'

'You both are really beyond precious. No, no, really not. I am fine. Really. All good. I have left Mark. But that's really no big deal. I am not all crushed on the floor or anything. I have just realized that we have different values and ideas and that I would never be happy with him. And that's that.'

'Really? That's it? Just like that? How are you?' They stood before me like worried parents whose child had just fallen off a tree and was inquiring with its inner self whether it had a reason to cry.

'Yes, really, everything's fine. And I AM fine. I don't have to cry, it doesn't hurt, it's just good the way it is.'

Klara was still not convinced. 'I don't quite buy that. Well, anyway, you stay with us as long as you want to. And now, we bake cookies and you tell us everything. I spread the dough, you cut the cookies.'

And so, I told them about all the many small and big pieces of the puzzle that had made a whole picture, today – a picture that I neither could not wanted to live with. About the old men's comments, REX, the soup, the non-present for Frank and the accommodation issue, about Beate and the desire to have a pregnant woman who would never give birth, about Berlin and Zurich, feel-good friends and strategic alliances. Klara and Konrad rarely interrupted, and when I had finished, Klara just said 'Well, that was really no loss, then. Jo, I feel downright guilty for bringing you together with him. But you must believe me that he conducted himself in a totally different manner when I met him. I really thought that you two could make a match. I had no idea that he is such an old geezer on the inside.'

'Klara, I was also misled. And it may even have been more me fooling myself than him deceiving me. Anyway, just in time.'

My mobile chirped. A message. 'Darling, you snuck off like a thief. Like a thief. Where are you? Your loving Mark'

I considered it inappropriate to break up via text message, so I responded. 'Mark, I would like to come by tomorrow. Would 10 am work? Kind regards, Johanna'

'Yes, of course. Lovingly, yours Mark'

After I had told the story once, it was no longer an issue between Klara, Konrad and myself. We chatted late into the night, had far too many cookies and went to bed tired like dogs.

The next morning, Konrad drove me to Mark and waited outside, ignoring my protests. 'Johanna, I just feel better this way. I walk up and down a little and keep an open eye and ear. And if you have not come back in half an hour, I come in. Sorry, but I have to do this. Klara would kill me if I didn't.'

Mark had made tea and we sat at the kitchen table. No birds outside.

Mark seemed sad but calm. 'I guess this was it, then.' I nodded.

Mark continued. 'You know, the mistake we made was that we did not get married fast enough. And that you took the pill. Otherwise, you would be married and pregnant, by now, and could not get out any more, and things would be fine.'

Unknowingly, he had just confirmed my decision. I did not feel like a response would serve any value. 'If that's how you feel, Mark. You know, I just wish you that you find the woman who shares your ideas of life and that you are happy together. And look after your children. They both are absolutely great. I will pack my stuff and leave.'

Mark took me to the door and shook my hand. 'Bye, Johanna. Fare well. And if you change your mind, let me know. You have a rain check. I will be here. Forever.'

'Bye, Mark. Fare well.'

Epilogue

September. The late summer sun was shining through the high windows of Kartzow castle, on the set table, reflecting in the cutlery. Desi had confirmed that she would come. I was curious.

After my separation from Mark, I had stopped the search for a partner and instead focused on the things that I enjoyed. I had gone biking or hiking, almost every weekend, and I had enjoyed talking to men just for fun, without any afterthought. At least twice a month, I invited friends, also just for fun, to talk, without any hope of a home delivery of a potential partner. I organized visits at the museum or at the movies online, and when we visited the Traffic Museum, even MomInZurich attended, with her children. She was just going through a divorce, which also shed a different light on our less pleasant previous exchange. In the choir, a new bass had joined, single and very likeable, and we had gone out a few times until we had realized that we would not hit it off. And that was fine. Alex and I played tennis, on a regular basis and had dinner afterwards. I liked him and enjoyed the time with him, regardless of whether this would grow into 'something' or not. Urs and Anke invited me to their wedding. A cheerful party with a very resolute bride and one single older than 30 in the room. But that, too, did not bother me.

Given that I had already booked so many flights to Berlin, I visited Klara and Konrad, Tina, Lars and Amélie on a very regular basis, and became Amélie's godmother, as well. Only Desi never had time.

Sinéad visited me in Zurich with her new partner, a

friendly and unobtrusive Klaus. I would probably never know whether Bernd hat been bitten by his snake. In summer, Anna and I spent a long weekend in the mountains, like friends. Mark was with a new partner. A friendly one. And that was fine, too.

All in all, my life had fallen back on track smoothly, and I did not regret my decision for a split second. I was no longer expecting frogs to transform into anything else but, well, frogs, and this had given me the equanimity required to fully enjoy single life. Life was good. It was a single life, and New Year's Eve would never be my favourite event of the year. But that was fine, too.

Actually, I had not thought of Mark in a long time, and when I thought back of the past year, it looked like a good one. I was curious to hear what had happened in Desi's life. When she entered the restaurant, the question became moot: Desi was pregnant. She looked happy.

'Desi, am I right in thinking what I think? Really? Tell me – who is the father?'

'Hello, Johanna. Is it that obvious, already? Yes, I am pregnant. And I am married, but I hope that you understand that we did not invite you. And Klara and Konrad, neither. This would have been inappropriate after all that had happened.'

I felt and Desi saw that the incomprehension was closing in on my face like a jalousie. She added, 'Johanna, of course I know that you were with Mark, and he told me that he left you because you did not want any children. I always wanted children. And now, we are about to have one. Everything happened so fast. I know that this must feel strange for you. For me, as well. But I hope that we can still stay in contact.'

'Desi, that's fine. Perfectly fine.'

Yes, indeed.

Enjoy life!